WHITESPACE

Season One

SEAN PLATT

DAVID W WRIGHT

STERLING & STONE

WHITESPACE

Episode 1

Chapter 1- Milo Anderson

In the not too distant future …
   Hamilton Island K-12
   Hamilton Island, Washington
   Friday
   Sept. 1
   7:15 a.m.

WHERE IN THE *hell is Mr. Heller?*

Milo glanced at the clock, again. It wasn't like the teacher to be late. And while the rest of Mr. Roger Heller's 11th grade English literature and composition class were clearly enjoying their few moments of unexpected free time, Milo wanted it to end immediately since Manny wouldn't shut the hell up.

"So, are you gonna do it? Are you?" Manny asked for the third time.

Milo turned to his right, where Katie and Jessica were talking a mile a minute in front of Jessica's desk two rows over, to make sure they hadn't heard, then turned back to his left, where Manny sat like a big, stupid dog who didn't know how far the sound of his barking carried.

"Shut up," Milo whispered. "I already said I don't wanna talk about it, especially not here."

"What?" Manny said, again, even louder. "They can't hear me." He leaned toward Milo but didn't lower his voice. "So, are ya gonna ask her or not?"

"I don't know," Milo whispered, wishing Manny would drop it. He never should have said anything to Manny or Alex when they were hanging out in front of the school before the first bell.

The moment Manny heard a tasty bit of gossip, he was all over it and wouldn't let it go until he'd talked over every little detail. Sometimes, Manny seemed more like a girl in that respect than the girls they hung out with.

At least Manny had the smarts to stop yammering when Jessica and Katie joined them under the flagpole. But now that they were in class Manny wouldn't, or couldn't, shut up, despite the fact Jessica, the subject of this particular piece of gossip, was just two rows away from them.

"But it's perfect timing!" Manny insisted. "It's her birthday. She can't turn you down on her birthday! That's like, socially illegal."

Milo turned again, praying the girls hadn't overheard the word "birthday." If they had, then everything would be doomed.

Tomorrow was Jessica's seventeenth birthday, and everyone was getting together at Milo's house for a surprise party. Not a huge bash, just their immediate circle of friends — himself, Manny, Jessica, Alex, and Katie.

Milo planned to finally reveal his true feelings for Jessica — feelings he'd harbored in secret for at least four years.

The only reason Milo had even asked the guys for their advice, divulging his secret, was because Alex's girlfriend, Katie, was best friends with Jessica. Surely, Katie would've said something if she knew how Jessica felt.

"I don't know," Alex had said. "Katie's never said anything

one way or another. But I say go for it. I've seen the way Jessica looks at you. And she's always asking what you're up to."

"Really? Why the hell didn't you tell me before?" Milo playfully shoved his best friend. "How long has this been going on?"

"Just recently," Alex said. "I think a better question is why didn't *you tell me* you were into Jessica until now?"

"Yeah, what the hell, man?" Manny inserted himself into the conversation. From that moment on, the big dork had focused on nothing but Milo and Jessica. Milo practically expected him to start singing, "Milo and Jessica sitting in a tree ..."

The girls had arrived a few minutes later, and the conversation had died ... until Manny started up after they got to class.

"I say go for it," Manny said. "I agree with Alex. Jessica wants you."

Milo turned, praying she hadn't heard her name mentioned.

Katie and Jessica were looking at him and whispering. Jessica giggled, and Milo looked down as if studying the carving on his desk. It said, *God can see you,* and looked like it had been there forever.

Manny laughed. "They're talking about you."

"Shut up," Milo whispered again, wondering if they were, and feeling his face burn. Maybe Alex said something to Jessica when she was walking with him to his first class.

Shit, I knew I shouldn't have said anything.

Milo grabbed his cell and texted Alex, hoping he'd left his phone on vibrate rather than ringtone.

DID *you tell Katie about me liking Jess?*

A full minute passed, then Alex texted back: *No. Why?*

No reason. Where's your dad? He's late.
Dunno. Haven't seen him. He left early. Should be there.

MR. HELLER WAS Alex's dad, and he was never this late. Usually, he was in class an hour before the school doors opened, which was why Alex usually walked to school or caught a ride with Katie on the days her mom let her drive the car they shared. At least, that's the reason Alex gave for not coming in with his dad.

Milo suspected something else, however — Alex was embarrassed by his dad. As cool and laid back as Alex was, Mr. Heller was nerdy, straight-laced, and talked like someone from one of those old TV shows with the big, happy, and thoroughly unrealistic families. The girls flirted with Mr. Heller, and the guys pretended to care about his lectures, but Mr. Heller was too oblivious to see they were messing with him. Despite the heckling, students generally seemed to like him, though. He was lenient, not prone to mood swings like many of the teachers, and you'd have to be an idiot to get anything less than a B in his class.

Mr. Heller was dorky, clueless, and wore clothes about fifteen years out of style.

But Mr. Heller was never late.

Milo hoped they didn't have a substitute. Subs always gave them busy work. One of the cool things about Mr. Heller, and the reason the kids probably liked him most, was he spent at least half the class talking. And it was the kind of talking that he never quizzed students on, so you could catch a few Z's, which made the class Milo's favorite first period since home economics in eighth grade.

The door to the classroom squeaked opened behind them, and the class fell silent, except for the sound of students rushing back to their desks and cracking open their books as if they were earnestly attempting to unlock the finer points of grammar.

Manny had his book open, but it was upside down. Milo laughed at his idiot friend and made a face, then gestured toward the book.

When he looked down, his eyes widened. Then he laughed and turned the book right side up.

Idiot.

Katie took her seat behind Manny and gave Milo a suspicious look.

He turned away quickly, feeling his face flush again.

Alex did tell her! Or maybe she heard Manny Big Mouth.

Milo looked to his right to see if Jessica was also looking at him. But her eyes were up front, as was the attention of the rest of the class.

Mr. Heller set his briefcase on the desk, then straightened his shirt, which was uncharacteristically wrinkled and half untucked, with one tail spilling down below his waist. He looked nervous, or … scared.

Milo turned to see if Manny had noticed. He had, making a face as if to say, "What's up with Mr. Heller?"

Katie wore the same expression, as did the rest of the class.

Mr. Heller stood behind his desk, hands on either side of his closed briefcase, as though exhausted, too tired even to lift his head and look his students in their eyes. His hair, usually precisely combed in the exact same, old-fashioned style, was a messed up sweaty mop atop his head.

Class with Mr. Heller began exactly the same way every day. He'd wait for the students to settle down, giving them a full minute after the final bell before he stood up, turned to the whiteboard, and then neatly wrote the topic of the day's conversation. Once the topic was recorded in neat black lines on the whiteboard, he'd turn to the class, and say something like, "Good morning, class. Today we're going to discuss foreshadowing," or whatever subject he'd written. Most days, he'd also throw in a terrible pun to kick things off.

Mr. Heller was such a stickler for routine that Milo could easily imagine the man starting his weekend mornings the same way at home, in front of a whiteboard with the words *bacon and eggs* written on it. "Good morning, family. Today we're going to have bacon and eggs. Here's a little joke I heard. This one will *crack* you up."

Seeing Mr. Heller just standing there, staring down at his desk, was unsettling enough to send a shiver down Milo's spine.

"Are you okay?" Stephanie Blankencamp asked from her front-row desk.

Mr. Heller said nothing.

Instead, he turned around, grabbed a black dry erase marker, and started to scribble on the whiteboard. His handwriting, normally block-perfect and in a straight line, was wild and erratic like he was writing in an angry rush. He scribbled one word.

Eleven

ELEVEN? *What the hell? Is that how many beers he drank before class?*

Milo turned to Manny and Katie, the three of them exchanging quiet confusion. Then he looked over to Jessica, who was staring back with the same bewildered and nervous expression.

Mr. Heller turned from the whiteboard, finally making eye contact with his students. His face was clammy, his eyes bloodshot. His hands shook as he turned his head back and forth as if he were counting students ... or searching for someone.

Looking down at his desk again, he opened his briefcase with a loud snapping sound. He stared into it for what seemed an eternity, as Milo, and probably the entire class, wondered what he was focused on. Had the class done so poorly on their reports the previous week that he couldn't bring himself to pick up the stack of graded papers?

Mr. Heller reached into the briefcase and pulled out a pistol.

Time stopped for Milo, even as a million things seemed to happen around him at once.

First, Manny laughed, like Mr. Heller was going to show them a cool trick or joke or something using the gun as a prop. Or perhaps it was the nervous laugh of a brain which hadn't quite registered the threat. But someone else, Amber Riley, screamed. Several students gasped.

Mr. Heller aimed the gun and fired, shooting Tommy Hopkins, the school's star rower, right in the face. The gunfire was thunder in the enclosed classroom, like an explosion in Milo's ears as Tommy fell to the ground.

Chaos erupted. Mr. Heller turned, as calm as a man choosing his doughnuts from behind the glass, and fired another shot, then another, barely audible over the high-pitched ringing between Milo's temples. One shot missed one of the students and sailed through the wall into the next class-room. Milo heard muffled screams from next door. Had the bullet hit someone, or were they screaming in response to the sound of gunshots?

Students scrambled in every direction but with one goal — escaping the classroom. Milo remained rooted to his desk, unable to think straight, much less move. And then something caught his attention. Jessica was running toward him, eyes and mouth wide open. He had to get up and protect her.

But he was too late. Milo's attention shifted from Jessica to just over her left shoulder, where Mr. Heller's blurred figure came into crystal-clear focus, gun aimed directly at Jessica.

No!

Milo opened his mouth to warn her, but his speech was cut

short by the thunder of another gunshot that sent her forward, straight into him. Milo, Jessica, and his desk tumbled in a painful collision of flesh, wood, metal, and carpet.

And blood, spreading across the front of Jessica's powder-blue sweater.

Jessica stared up at him, scared and searching for a reason. She said something, but her voice was muffled as if he were hearing it through a wall of cotton. He pulled her to him, as though he could protect her from more bullets.

The gunshots stopped, and the only sound was the whistling in Milo's ears.

Milo turned his head and saw another victim of Mr. Heller's gun — Manny, lying in a river of blood. He appeared to have been shot in the stomach. His eyes were glassy, but he wasn't dead. Yet. He was staring back at Milo, eyes pleading for help.

Just as Milo wondered where Mr. Heller had gone in all the madness, the teacher appeared, walking toward them, gun drawn in his shaky hand.

Milo wanted to get up, knock the gun away, or do something. But he was still paralyzed, afraid he'd do the wrong thing and get himself or his friends killed. He looked down to see Jessica's blood seeping into his shirt and jeans. Her eyes were closing, and he prayed Mr. Heller would keep walking out of the class and past them, so he could save his friends, even if he had no idea how he intended to do so.

Mr. Heller paused, looking at Manny with hollow eyes, and his expression drifted from nervous to one of bottomless sorrow. He kneeled beside the boy, face almost apologetic. Manny began to tremble, unable to move as Mr. Heller leaned down and said something to him.

Milo couldn't hear what Mr. Heller said, or read his lips. But whatever he said seemed to remove the fear in Manny's eyes.

Milo's mind was suddenly focused on the acrid scent of

piss, though he wasn't sure if it was Manny, Jessica, Mr. Heller, or himself who had lost control.

Mr. Heller turned to Milo and held his gaze.

Milo winced, preparing for death.

Why is he doing this? Why is he going to shoot me? What did I ever do to him?

Oh God, I don't want to die.

"Please, don't kill me," Milo cried, tears streaming down his face. "I'm friends with Alex. You know me!"

Hearing his son's name seemed to waken something in Mr. Heller's eyes. He stared at Milo as tears dripped down his face. He looked back at the whiteboard and pointed at the word *Eleven* with the gun.

What does that mean? What the hell is Eleven?

Mr. Heller then raised the pistol, but not at Milo.

Instead, Mr. Heller parted his lips and shoved the gun into his open mouth.

Oh, God, no!

Mr. Heller pulled the trigger, and Milo screamed.

Chapter 2 - Alex Heller

Wednesday …
  Sept. 6
  Noon

JUST LIKE THAT. In a flash. Everything was gone.

Before Alex's father killed himself, he shot and killed five students, including Jessica. He shot Manny and put him in a coma. And seemingly by accident, shot and killed a teacher, Sarah Hughes, in the next classroom.

And all Alex had were questions and a bottomless well of grief.

No matter how many different ways he tried to pull sense from the senseless, Alex could not make sense of the tragedy. This was the kind of thing you saw on TV, that happened to other people, not to his friends — not to his family.

Everything felt like a bad dream. He hoped to wake up any minute and find things normal again. Except he wasn't waking up. Nobody was. This nightmare was real and had shaken the entire island to its core.

Neither Milo nor Katie would return his calls.

He wasn't sure if it was because they didn't want to talk to him, or if their parents had forbidden them to talk to the son of the madman.

Alex sat in his bedroom, staring blankly at the television as it broadcast collages of the funerals from earlier, photos of the victims, photos of his father, reporters standing outside the school, a flock outside the funeral home, and even the island's most famous celeb, Jon Conway, though Alex wasn't sure what the hell he had to do with this. The only thing Alex was grateful for was the reporters were finally gone from the front of his house.

The TV cut to a reporter in front of the island's police station, where Alex's mom stood, fielding yet more questions she didn't have answers to. Probably variations of the same questions they'd asked him.

"DO *you know why your father did this?"*
"Were you aware that your father had a gun?"
"Did he ever talk about any of his victims?"
"Has he ever hit you?"
"Has he ever hit your mother or sister?"

ALEX'S ANSWER was the same for all the questions. "No."

He was as shocked as anyone, if not more so.

Since he didn't have answers, the police ransacked their house, seizing every computer, flash drive, and journal his father had kept over the years. Alex wondered if they'd found some answer in the "evidence" they took, and maybe that was why his mom was down at the police station.

He watched as the TV showed a blonde reporter talking. He didn't bother turning the volume up. Not like they'd said anything new since Friday, just speculation heaped on top of sensationalism. After the reporter said her piece, the TV flashed to a familiar video that Alex had almost forgotten about, an interview with Alex's dad after he'd won a Washington State Teacher of the Year award three years ago, a prestigious honor for the island and the school, in particular.

Alex turned the volume up to hear his father discussing the importance of connecting with students and how he used stories to teach. As his voice came through the TV, Alex felt a sudden hollow in his stomach, realizing that confiscated computers meant confiscated photos of his father. This video on the news might be the only chance he'd get to hear his voice again. Alex grabbed his TV remote and hit record on the DVR.

Dad looked so happy in the video.

So normal.

So unlike the man who opened fire in his classroom, who killed his own students. It made no sense. He was a devoted man, who often spent his own time and money to help teach his students, above and beyond the job. He loved teaching, loved his students. Dad was practically a genius. Surely, he could have struck it rich had he done anything other than teach.

For him to do something like this, there had to be something wrong.

If that were the case, the next question was, for how long had something been wrong? The sting of guilt for not noticing was sharp. While their family was relatively close, especially compared to other families Alex knew, it wasn't like they had real conversations, at least not many that went more than a few inches below the surface. Alex was wrapped up in his own world, with his own problems, and rarely allowed his parents a glimpse inside, or looked beyond his to see into their worlds.

If things were different, would he have seen the signs?

Could he have prevented the massacre?

The TV returned to a scene outside one of the funerals.

Alex lowered the volume, stared at his cell phone, then dialed Milo again.

Still no answer.

He left a voicemail. His fourth.

"Please, Milo. Call me. I need to talk to someone," he said, trying not to cry.

He hung up, feeling stupid for talking about *his needs*, when Jessica, the girl Milo had a big crush on, was dead, and their closest friend, Manny, was in the hospital in a coma and on life support.

As long as he'd been friends with Milo, Alex had been the more popular of the two. Milo had always been his nerdy sidekick. But he loved the guy like a brother. Milo was hysterical, and into the same games, movies, and stuff Alex liked. He was the perfect hangout buddy, never too serious, never depressing, despite his family problems, and almost always around. Perhaps the coolest thing about Milo was that he was an awesome writing partner. The two had written several scripts together, TV shows and movies they hoped to someday pitch to Hollywood. But suddenly, none of that mattered.

Whatever friendship they had was severed by the inexplicable actions of Alex's dad.

Alex considered calling Jesus, Manny's brother, to get an update on Manny's situation beyond the TV reports. But Alex figured he was the last person in the world that Jesus, or his family, wanted to hear from.

He set the phone on his bed and crawled under his covers, listening to the soft white noise bleeding through the baby monitor. His six-month-old sister murmured in her sleep, and he hoped she wasn't gonna wake up soon. Aubrey was too young to understand that "Daddy is in heaven," and kept looking for their father, waiting for him to come back home. It broke Alex's heart, and he wasn't very good at comforting her. At least if his mom were there, she could cuddle with Aubrey and distract her.

Alex felt a flash of anger at his father.

How could he do this? To his students? To his family?

But as soon as the flash came, Alex felt more guilt.

His father *wouldn't* do this. Something must've been wrong with him. There was no other explanation.

Alex closed his eyes, exhausted.

He needed a nap.

He rested his head on a pillow, but only for a minute before the itch at the back of his head worked its way forward and forced him to his feet.

Alex opened the door to his father's office and flicked on the overhead light. He stepped inside, picturing his dad sitting behind his desk, facing the doorway, looking up from his work and smiling. He hadn't always smiled when interrupted — most times, he was too busy to even look up. But Alex chose to remember the times he had looked up, happy to see him.

The office was a disaster. The cops had tossed books from shelves, dumped boxes unceremoniously onto the ground, and pulled all the drawers out of his desk, leaving them sitting in a pile. Wires and cables were tangled atop his desk where his father had his computer set up so neatly just a few days ago.

The office looked like it had been robbed. And in a way, it had been, of everything his father had created.

Alex felt a sudden rage at the cops for leaving this mess for him and his mother to clean.

He grabbed one of the empty cardboard boxes that had been in the closet loaded with files and school paperwork, then sat on the ground and started putting stuff away. He didn't know what he could do to help his mom through this, but there was no reason she should have to clean the cops' mess. And maybe, if the cops hadn't taken everything important, Alex might find some answer to why his father snapped.

He got through the bulk of the mess in about twenty minutes, putting papers into boxes and books back on the bookcase. He wasn't sure what they would do with all of his dad's stuff.

There was something so alien about a person's possessions once that person was gone. It was almost as if they took on new properties, transformed by the absence of their owner — ordinary made special, mundane made magic, and junk turned to treasure imbibed with memories.

It gave Alex an idea for a short story about a dead man's possessions mourning their owner. He filed the idea away to mention to Milo, and then wondered if he and Milo would ever write together again.

Or was their friendship as dead as the bodies being buried this week?

Alex picked up an old baseball off the ground and placed it back on a wooden stand on the bookcase. Alex wondered what the ball meant to his dad. It wasn't signed by anyone, nor did it appear to be from a professional baseball game, at least as far as Alex could tell. Alex had seen it a hundred times, yet never thought to ask his dad what made the ball so special.

Alex was surprised to find so many books by authors he liked, such as Stephen King, Clive Barker, George R.R. Martin, Ray Bradbury, Neil Gaiman, and Phillip K. Dick, among the tomes of classic literature.

Alex felt the same hollow thud that had been thrumming through his body all morning. He had never known his dad was into so many of the same authors as he was. A few minutes here and there would have clued him in to that and so much more. It might have made all of the difference in the world.

It wasn't as though they'd never discussed fiction.

They'd talked about writing a lot, in fact. His dad had always wanted to be a novelist and had started a few books over the years, but he'd never let Alex read them — said he wanted to wait until he'd written something he could be proud to show his son.

Though a harsh critic of his own work, Dad had always been supportive of Alex's efforts. He seemed to genuinely enjoy many of Alex's stories, though he didn't shy away from offering constructive criticism. Alex regretted not showing his dad the scripts he and Milo had been working on. He had wanted to wait until they were polished, more mature. Something he and Milo could feel proud of.

But now . . .

Alex closed his eyes, wanting to cry, to let it all out.

But he couldn't.

He hadn't cried since the shooting, even though he was sad, devastated, and all the things that *should* make a guy cry. But the tears hadn't come.

Why?

Did that mean he didn't really love his dad?

He picked up a photo from the box, one of him and his dad at the shore on the north side of the island before it was fenced off. They'd spent the weekend, just the two of them, camping and fishing. Alex was eight and holding the tiniest fish you could probably catch with a hook. It was his first fish, and the bobber almost dwarfed the thing, but to Alex, at the time, it had been the size of a whale. His dad had held the camera outstretched to squeeze them both into the frame, and though the picture was slightly out of focus, it managed to capture the magic of the moment. The photo was in a thick, brown frame, placed prominently on his father's desk. Dad had said he put it there to remind him why he worked so hard, and so he'd remember the things that were truly important.

A man like that doesn't shoot up his classroom.

Not my dad.

The sound of the doorbell repeatedly ringing broke the silence and sent a fresh panic flooding through Alex.

Someone pressed the doorbell over and over, as if the house were on fire.

"What the hell?" Alex raced downstairs before the noise woke his sister.

He threw the door open to find a short, beefy man in a dark-blue T-shirt and jeans. Bruce Henderson, father of Teddy Henderson, one of the victims of the shooting. He was holding an aluminum baseball bat in his hands. Before Alex could even gasp, Mr. Henderson started swinging and screaming.

Alex ducked, but just barely in time, and the bat caught him in the back, sending him sprawling to the porch, crying out in pain.

"You're gonna pay!" Mr. Henderson screamed, his face an angry red, eyes wild.

"Please, Mr. Henderson," Alex cried, "Don't hurt me."

The man froze, bat over his head, poised and ready to strike. Then something shifted in his face, as the rage turned to confusion, as if he were shaking off cobwebs from the thick of a dream. He looked down at Alex, as if he was surprised to see him there, and then up to the bat, seemingly surprised again to find the weapon in his hands. He lowered the bat, looking around, as if lost.

Alex breathed a sigh of relief and started to stand. But then, just as Alex thought he was safe, Mr. Henderson's eyebrows arched in anger, and he raised the bat again.

A gunshot exploded behind Mr. Henderson, then a man in a black Paladin Security uniform appeared seemingly from nowhere. He aimed a pistol at Mr. Henderson and screamed, "Drop the bat!"

Mr. Henderson turned to the security guard, and then, again, looked like he'd just been woken up and realized what he'd been doing.

"Put the bat down," the guard repeated.

Mr. Henderson looked up, then at Alex guiltily, and placed the bat on the porch — gently, as if it might explode if he wasn't careful.

"I'm so sorry." He broke into tears as the guard grabbed one of his arms and twisted it behind him, then the other, handcuffing him. Once Mr. Henderson was restrained, the guard used his radio to call dispatch.

"This is Sanders. We've got a situation over at Mr. Heller's house."

As Sanders started to inform dispatch what had happened, Alex heard the sound of his little sister screaming from inside the house.

Oh, shit.

He pointed at the house. "My baby sister! I'll be right back." Alex motioned to Sanders, who nodded okay as he continued speaking into his radio.

Alex went inside and closed the door, even though he wasn't sure what he was supposed to do. He sure as hell wasn't going to leave it open with Mr. Henderson on the verge of violence, restrained or not. Alex bounded up the stairs and into Aubrey's room to see her red-faced, screaming, crying her eyes out.

He picked her up and pulled her to his chest. "It's okay," he whispered repeatedly, holding her tight, rocking her in his arms as he'd seen his mom do a hundred times before.

To his surprise, Aubrey calmed down, snuggling her tiny face against his chest.

Oh, my God, she's letting me comfort her!

Alex finally cried.

He held Aubrey for a long minute, inhaling her scent and feeling the glow of being a big brother that he'd never felt before.

Aubrey was asleep in minutes, also to his surprise. He lay her back in her crib, covered her with her baby blanket, then went back downstairs in case Sanders had any questions or needed to take his statement or anything.

He opened the front door just as a black Paladin SUV rolled up into their driveway. Sanders led Mr. Henderson to the SUV and placed him in the back. The man kept crying, "I'm sorry, I'm sorry" to the guards, too distraught to see Alex in the doorway.

Probably a good thing. Alex feared the man might see him, go off again, and get himself shot.

Sanders took out a notepad and pen as he approached Alex. "Can you tell me what happened?"

Alex stepped onto the porch, keeping the door partially open so he could hear if Aubrey cried again. The black van was still in his driveway, probably waiting for Sanders to finish. He gave his statement and said Sanders didn't miss anything, as he showed up pretty quickly right after Mr. Henderson got there. "Thank you. You saved me."

"No problem, kid," Sanders said, even though he was thirty, tops, hardly an old man, with a baby face and brown hair, cut military style, like all the guards who worked for Paladin. "Now, did Mr. Henderson say anything to you?"

"No, he just said 'You're gonna pay.'"

"Because your dad killed his son?" Sanders asked, matter-of-factly, as if he were used to asking kids about their crazy dads who had just shot up the school.

"*I guess.* I don't know what else he could've been mad at. I mean, I didn't know Teddy all that well."

"And you're sure he didn't say *anything else?*"

The way Sanders asked 'anything else' struck Alex as odd. As if there were something, in particular, he thought that Mr. Henderson might have said. Alex was about to ask what he meant when his mom's silver Passat pulled into the driveway.

She was out of the car in seconds, her eyes wide and scared as she dashed to the porch. "What's wrong?"

"Nothing, ma'am," Sanders said. "There was just a little . . . *incident.*"

"What kind of *incident?*" She looked at Alex and then back at Sanders.

"One of the fathers, um . . . one of the fathers who lost his son in the shooting. He came to your house. He was pretty upset. Had a baseball bat."

"A bat?!" Her voice rose five octaves. She turned to Alex and grasped his shoulders. "Oh, my God, are you okay?"

Alex hugged her. "Yeah, Mom, everything's okay. Officer Sanders arrested Mr. Henderson before he could do anything."

She turned and glared at the SUV still in the driveway.

He'd rarely seen his mom get angry, and this was the most furious he'd ever seen her. He was certain she was seconds from running to the SUV, pulling Mr. Henderson out, then pounding on him, despite being a small woman who'd never hurt a fly.

"Everything's okay, Mom." Alex put a hand on her shoulder and met her gaze. "He's just upset about Teddy. I could tell he was just confused and angry. He said he's sorry."

He wasn't sure why he felt a need to downplay the incident and protect Mr. Henderson, who'd just tried to kill him. But there was something in the man's eyes, sadness, or something along with the confusion in the moments between his bursts of anger. And that something called to Alex, asked him to show compassion.

Mom wasn't feeling compassionate, however.

"I want him in jail. I don't want him anywhere near my family!"

"We're going to take him to the police station now," Sanders said. "They'll have to decide what to do with him and will probably ask if you want to press charges."

"Damned right I do," she spat.

Alex put his arm on her, trying to calm her. Her overreaction embarrassed him, especially given what his dad had done. People had a right to be angry. She couldn't get too worked up.

"Okay, ma'am. We'll have someone get in touch with you. Might I make a suggestion?"

"What's that?" Her tone was slightly calmer but suspicious.

"Would you mind if we posted someone outside your house to keep watch? You know, just until things calm down a bit?"

She turned to Alex, her expression growing more concerned. Then she turned to Sanders. "Do you think that's necessary?"

"I don't know, but it's better to be safe than sorry. Your son is lucky I happened to be in the neighborhood when I was and got here before Mr. Henderson could really hurt him."

"What do you mean *really hurt him?* Did he hit you, Alex?"

"Just a little, on the back." Alex didn't wanting to whine about the throbbing pain.

"Let me see." She yanked up his shirt, embarrassing him further. "Oh, my God! Your whole back is bruised!"

"It's not that bad, I swear. I've been hit harder in soccer. This'll be gone in a couple of days."

"Yes." Mom turned to Sanders. "I want someone here to watch over us."

Alex closed his eyes and sighed. The last thing he wanted was for people to see that they — the family of the man who shot their sons and daughters — had security stationed at their house. It would be seen as a big "fuck you" to the victims' families.

"Yes, ma'am. We'll send a truck by in twenty minutes to keep an eye out for you all."

"Thank you," she said. "I don't know what we would've done if you hadn't been here. We're so lucky you happened to be in the neighborhood."

"Right time, right place." Sanders handed her a card, wished them well, then headed toward the SUV.

As it rolled away, Alex found his mind turning over the phrase Sanders had said.

"Right time. Right place."

That's when Alex realized he hadn't seen Sanders arrive in a car. Had he *just happened* to be walking by on foot at the exact moment Mr. Henderson decided to go apeshit? Something wasn't right.

Aubrey started crying, pulling Alex and his mother into the house. But he continued considering the odd coincidence of Sanders saving the day.

Chapter 3 - Jon Conway

Seattle, Washington
  Tuesday
  Sept. 5
  7:20 p.m.

JON CONWAY STARED out the window, counting the minutes before the 747 descended into Sea-Tac. Butterflies flittered through his stomach, just like they always did when he had to deal with his family in person. Although he was lost in thought, he felt someone staring at him.

He turned to his left and saw the teenage Goth girl, across the aisle in the window seat, was no longer hiding the fact that she'd recognized him despite the shades, black baseball cap, and bulky black coat he'd tried to hide in.

"Are you … Jon Conway?" she asked.

The man beside her, likely her father, muttered an embarrassed, "I'm sorry."

"It's okay," Jon said. "And yeah, it's me."

"Oh, my God! I told you, Dad. I'm such a fan! I love all your movies. Even the ones the critics shit all over."

The man shook his head. "Amber!"

"Sorry, Dad," she said to her father. "Can I get a picture?"

Jon tried not to let his annoyance show. He hadn't done a movie in four years, but that only seemed to intensify fan reactions when he ran into them in public. He was especially popular with young girls, and even their moms, for his portrayal of the moody vampire in the *'Darkness Everlasting'* series, the flicks that launched him from critical darling to box-office juggernaut, even though he found the two sequels creatively bankrupt.

"Sure." He posed with the girl as her dad fumbled with her iPhone to snap a pic.

He put his arm around her, resting it on her shoulder, and she melted into a series of giggles which belied her "I don't give a fuck" look of disaffected teen.

After her dad snapped a couple of pics, the girl reached up and hugged Jon, as he awkwardly exchanged glances with the girl's dad. Jon imagined the dad was thinking one of two things — *talentless douche bag* or *get your hands off my daughter, you pervert.* Probably both, and particularly the latter, given Jon's reputation as someone who slept with half of Hollywood's A-list.

After the girl thanked Jon and headed back to her seat, her dad surprised him.

"Can I get a picture, too?"

Jon was caught off guard, enough to accidentally laugh.

"I loved your work in *This Ends Now,*" the man said.

The indie film, *This Ends Now,* was a scathing satire of the consumerist culture Jon had written, directed, and starred in. While some critics loved it, others dismissed it as another pampered star, from a billionaire family no less, whining and biting the hand that feeds him. The movie also tanked at the box office, causing some to wonder if Jon's days as an A-lister were over. He'd been so disgusted by the bullshit following the movie that he'd turned down every script since.

"I loved that movie, too," the girl said as she took their photo. And then after a long pause, she added, "Are you going to do another *Darkness Everlasting?*"

The author of the series had originally planned the series as a trilogy. But apparently, she'd been unable to turn down a huge advance to bring the characters back for another book. Jon hadn't read the fourth book but had heard it was little more than a blatant money grab, and he had no interest in making another shit film. "I don't know. Maybe with the right script and director. You never know."

A bell dinged, and one of the flight attendants made the announcement asking everyone to take their seats and return their trays and seats to their upright positions.

"Thank you." The girl's dad reached out to shake Jon's hand.

"You're welcome."

The girl thanked him as well.

"Take care." Then, Jon returned to his seat.

Jon strapped in and tried to avoid looking back over in their direction and getting trapped in a conversation, or worse, having a conversation extend beyond the airplane. He'd have to pretend he got a call or something to break away and hope he didn't look like a giant prick. Even after all these years, meeting fans still made him apprehensive, so he tried to avoid it whenever possible.

As the plane landed, Jon thought again about his family and felt that old, familiar dread creeping through him.

Jon had returned to Hamilton Island as few times as possible in the decade since he left the island for good at twenty-one — the year he was finally certain he wanted little to do with his father, Blake Conway, and nothing to do with Conway Industries, the biotech company that had nudged their bloodline into the top one percent and built Hamilton Island into one of Puget Sound's most ideal getaways and homes. Conway Industries not only had its headquarters and several research laboratories on the island, it also owned and operated a small hospital that employed many and contributed reduced or free health care to the service industry workers who lived in the island's subsidized housing.

On Hamilton Island, the Conways were revered by residents and politicians alike for their generosity. In reality, however, the Conway kingdom was built on hubris and treachery, which Jon wanted nothing to do with.

He had squirmed free from nearly every obligation that would have pulled him back to Hamilton Island. But Sarah was dead, an accidental victim in a school shooting, and he never would've forgiven himself if he didn't go to her funeral.

She was, after all, the one who got away.

Well, he got away. She stayed put. But now that she was gone, it felt as if some future he imagined someday having with her was now dead, too.

THE PLANE LANDED. Jon drove a rented Toyota Avalon to the ferry, then watched the island grow larger against the darkening sky as the ferry inched him closer to the countless memories he'd love to forget.

Forty-five minutes later, he parked his car at the Sands of Time hotel.

Jon walked directly to the counter, dropped his bag at his feet, then glanced at the name on the hotel clerk's badge. "Hi there, Lydia, I believe my assistant reserved the top floor for me? Under the name John Kafka."

Lydia looked him up and down, as she tried and failed to keep her mouth jaw from dropping lower. She stuttered before finding her voice, then looked Jon in the eye. "Of course, Mr. Conway. Er, I mean, Mr. Kafka."

Jon smiled, then shook his head and softly said, "Thank you."

Lydia smiled, typing on her keyboard.

"How many keys will you be needing, Mr. Conway?" Then after a moment added, "There are ten rooms, total."

"Can I get two cards, all keyed to all the rooms?"

"Sure." She smiled, then giggled and twirled a finger through her long, dark hair. "At least, I think so. I've never done this before."

After a few minutes, she handed Jon two cards, and smiled. She was cute, likely in her mid-twenties, too cute to be working behind the desk of a hotel on Hamilton Island. But he kept such thoughts to himself. This wasn't a pleasure trip. And while a night with Lydia could be fun and relaxing, the days after would be problematic and not worth the trouble.

After another minute spent finding out if there were any new restaurants on the island, Jon was waiting for the elevator to ding then open to his private floor. He was exhausted but wasn't sure if he should get to bed early and wait to see everyone at the memorial in the morning, or catch up with Sarah's twin sister, Cassidy, first.

Last he'd heard, Cassidy was still working at The Shipwreck, an appropriately-named bar in the south end of the island. Of course, the last time he'd run into Cassidy, she'd been rude, probably holding a grudge for how things went bad between him and Sarah.

The elevator dinged, and Jon decided that he was too exhausted to subject himself to Cassidy's anger, which would likely even be worse following the death of her sister. Though the twins fought as often as he did with his own family, Cassidy and Sarah actually had something the Conways didn't — love that bonded them together despite their differences.

Jon crossed the hall, slipped his keycard into the door, dropped his bag by the door, then collapsed onto the king-sized bed, fully clothed. He was sound asleep two minutes later.

~

WEDNESDAY

Sept. 6
Afternoon

JON SAT two rows from the rear pew, in the back of Great Endeavor Church, a nondenominational church that was also the island's biggest. It had that classic New England church architecture he admired, though he'd never been particularly religious. This had also been his church, though only from age eight to twelve or so, during the time his parents enrolled him in Sunday school. Of course, they rarely went to church themselves. Their driver usually dropped him off.

He flashed back decades to the many Sundays he sat next to Sarah, and sometimes Cassidy, trying not to giggle as Pastor Avery preached. They'd never been able to go a whole service without getting a stern look from the pastor.

Jon's trip down memory lane was cut short when he realized Pastor Avery was looking at him as he addressed the congregation. Jon wondered what the old man must've thought of him — *the godless heathen given to a life of excess and sin, come home to reap what he's sown.*

But the pastor wasn't that kind of man. He was serious, but kind, not someone who'd remind you of your sins when tragedy struck. The only voice in that guilty choir was Jon's conscience.

This was the fourth service today, with the church holding a private friends and family service for each of the six victims of the school shooting. Later in the evening, the church was holding a mass joint service for the public. There were two dozen people in the church besides himself and Cassidy, their mom, and Sarah's daughter. Jon sat in the back, wearing dark shades and a black hat, which he'd used to avoid the press outside. The last thing he wanted was to have the press spinning this story and putting him into it, detracting from the tragedy and the memories of the victims. The memory of Sarah.

His agent, Marty, had already informed him they were getting calls seeking his comment on the tragedy, simply because he'd lived there for so many years. The press had spotted him on the island already, so it was only a matter of time before the circus began. Marty suggested using Paladin Security to keep people away from him. "You might wanna consider it. Especially once they find out you and Sarah have a history."

Jon hoped to be off the island before those dots were connected. His family owned Paladin, and he hated asking them for anything.

He turned his attention back to the service. Every word from Pastor Avery's mouth was a cold blade in Jon's stomach.

"Sarah Hughes was funny and warm." The pastor's hands were in the air. And though his gaze traveled over each person in the room, Jon felt as if they lingered particularly longer on him. "She was easy to talk to — a great listener — and so incredibly easy to like. Sarah loved teaching, cooking for her friends, talking on the phone, and growing her roses." He smiled, as though remembering their scent. "The Abraham Lincoln was her favorite. Sarah loved foot rubs, the beach, and swimming. And she loved great food, especially Italian — the good stuff from the North — along with midnight snacks." He patted his tummy. "Mostly ice cream."

Pastor Avery found Jon's eyes and held them. Jon was certain he wasn't imagining it.

"Sarah loved staring at the stars, pondering our place in God's universe, and believing the impossible kept itself just one good idea away. She loved the laughter of children, especially her daughter, Emma, and every kid at Hamilton Island

K-12." He raised his hands in the air again but locked his eyes on Jon. "Sarah Hughes loved everyone in this room."

The pastor held the moment, then lowered his arms and surrendered his gaze. Jon felt his own tears welling as the pastor began to pace the pulpit. "Sarah would never have called herself an intellectual, but I would have disagreed. She was whip-smart, understood things in seconds when they should've taken minutes, and minutes if hours. She may not have known everything, but she knew all there was to know about being a good person, a great mom, and about leading a wonderful life. Sarah Hughes is gone before her time and will be forever missed."

Tears painted the sides of the faces of Sarah's family at the front of the churchy ha.

Pastor Avery continued. "Sarah pointed her life toward everything that was most important to her, and everyone in this room would have to agree her aim was true. A mother to Emma and a daughter to Vivian, a confidant to her friends and a guiding light to her students, a true blessing to Cassidy."

Jon was grateful for an excuse to stare at Cassidy, capitalizing on the opportunity. Though she was Sarah's identical twin, the years had not been nearly as kind to her. While she didn't look old, she was starting to look weary and jaded. She was still almost as beautiful as her sister, though, with long, chestnut hair, green eyes, and Sarah's porcelain, flawless skin. Jon felt as if he were looking at Sarah's ghost, and a chill ran through him.

Emma buried her face in Cassidy's chest. Cassidy pulled her closer and held her tighter, as if proximity would keep herself from surrendering to tears.

Pastor Avery smiled at Cassidy, waited for her to smile back, then continued.

"Sarah will always be remembered by her students as one of the best teachers they ever had, by her friends as truly loyal and wonderfully funny, and by her family as remarkably strong. It has been a joy to know Sarah, from the time she was a tiny child through last Easter when, as an adult, she sat with her hands folded in the pew, just three rows behind where the three remaining Hughes girls are sitting now."

Pastor Avery gestured again toward the Hughes girls.

Cassidy managed to keep her torrent inside, but Vivian, never one to shy away from theatrics, erupted into a fountain of tears while Emma bawled between them. Seeing their grief, particularly the young girl's, cut deep into Jon's heart. He sniffed back tears as the pastor went on about how we can't know God's will, but should find comfort that He has welcomed Sarah to the kingdom of heaven.

Though Jon would normally roll his eyes at such a thought, he found an odd sense of comfort in the old man's words.

Pastor Avery then invited mourners to approach the front of the church one by one to give their farewells. Jon sat silently, heart racing, as Sarah's co-workers, friends, and family spoke of her in loving memory. Hearing their words made Jon sad that he'd missed out on so much of Sarah's life. It also made him wonder who would speak at his funeral. He had few people he could call friends. And the closest thing he'd ever had to love was now in a casket.

He wondered if he should step forward to give a few words. Given their history, he feared that to *not* say anything would be an insult. At the same time, he didn't want this to become about him. If he went up to speak, someone in the audience might shoot video on their iPhone and it would be on YouTube or TMZ within the hour. That was the last thing Sarah's family needed. The last thing any of the mourning families needed.

Jon stayed put, though he wasn't sure if his gesture was kindness or cowardice. When it came right to it, he couldn't bear to go anywhere near the urn holding Sarah's remains. It was all he could do to look at the silver jar from the back of the church, where it was merely a shape.

~

THE MEMORIAL ENDED, and Jon did his best to blend in with the herd, which was nearly impossible with the dozens of eyes pretending not to stare. He shuffled behind the mourners, slowly drifting toward the hors d'oeuvres, waiting for the crowd to finish consoling Cassidy, as his heart filled, then broke, with every fleeting glimpse of the small girl trembling by her side.

Emma looked lost, waiting for a mother who would never return.

Jon ate his cold cucumber sandwich and sipped the cheap coffee, hating his family for not donating something better, and watching the Hughes family from the corner of his eye.

Cassidy was bookended between Russ Haskell and Mitch Kilborn, two jocks he'd gone to school with. Time had been less kind to them, each of them looking at least a decade older than they were, especially with the premature silver flocking the tips of Mitch's bangs and sideburns.

Emma ducked from under Cassidy's arm, then slipped away from her aunt and grandmother. She made a beeline for the dessert table and stuffed an assortment of cookies into her purse, starting at the far side of the dessert table and gradually making her way to the right, focusing only on the smaller cookies, apparently going with quantity over quality.

Emma looked almost exactly the same as her mother at age nine. Another ghost who tore at Jon's heart.

She looked so sad, and almost angelic in her innocence. He laughed as Emma stuffed cookies into her tiny, purple purse, and thought of the way he often couldn't help but shove matchbooks, mints, or toothpicks into his own pocket, whenever he was leaving a restaurant, whether he'd ever use them or not. Jon wondered where the girl's father was, or if she even knew *who* her father was.

Sarah had gotten pregnant after she broke up with Jon, the result of a fling she had to supposedly "get over him."

It had been almost ten years ago when he'd made the biggest mistake of his life. He was on the set of his first movie when he got drunk and slept with a model. It was the first time he'd ever been unfaithful to Sarah, who had, to that point, been the only girl he'd even gone out with. He confessed what he did. At first, he thought they'd get past it. She said she'd forgiven him. Then a week later, she called him, while he was back on the set, and said she couldn't do it anymore. She couldn't stop thinking of his betrayal. It was over.

He tried to make things right, but she refused to take his calls, refused to see him, and even ignored his e-mails and letters. About five weeks after they broke up, Cassidy called Jon and said he was making Sarah miserable and needed to stop calling.

And that was that. He went on with his life. And she went on with hers, apparently getting knocked up along the way.

An old friend had told him Sarah was pregnant. He'd heard rumors about different men who might be the father, including a waiter, a visitor to the island during tourist season, and even another teacher. Whoever it was didn't stick around and left her high and dry.

Jon had considered reaching out to offer help if Sarah needed it. But by then, it had been so long, and she seemed to be getting along fine on her own with help from her sister and mother. He didn't want to cause her any more stress by popping back into her life.

Now, as he watched Emma, his heart broke. The child had no mother or father. She was an orphan, all alone in the world, save for a drunk grandma and a pill-popping aunt.

When Emma was just a few feet away, Jon couldn't take it any longer. He took one long, final sip of his coffee, set it on the large tray with the rest of the empties, then went to the edge of the dessert table, picked up the largest, fattest cookie he could find, and kneeled next to Emma.

"I think you're missing out on these." He held up a slightly larger cookie. "They look just big enough to be truly delicious."

The girl looked up at him, then narrowed her eyes as she studied the cookie. She shook her head. "Nope, that one has peanut butter in it. I don't like peanut butter. Especially in my cookies."

Jon looked at the cookie, noting the telltale ridges of peanut butter rippling across the surface, then back at Emma. "Hmmm, you know, I think you're right. I didn't even notice." He wrinkled his nose and shook his head. "I don't like peanut butter, either."

Still kneeling, Jon gestured toward the table. "Which of these would you suggest?"

Emma smiled, tiny but there, then pulled a wee cookie from her little purse and handed it to Jon.

Jon took the tiny, white cookie, about the size of a quarter and the color of the island's sand under a summer sun, freckled in white. "What is it?"

"It's called a Hamilton Island Biscuit. Mrs. Rasmussen makes them, but only on New Year's, the first day of summer, and on special occasions. It was Mommy's favorite cookie."

Jon smiled and blinked, his eyes getting wet. "Oh, wow. I remember these." He turned the cookie over in his hand. Then, mostly to himself, he added, "How old is Mrs. Rasmussen now? She was like seventy when I was a kid."

"I don't know," Emma shook her head. "I asked her one time if she was a hundred, and she laughed and said no, but she didn't tell me how old she was."

Emma looked closer at Jon, as if seeing him for the first time. "Did you live on the island when you were little?"

"I did."

Emma glanced at her shuffling feet, then back up at Jon. "Did you know my mom?"

Jon nodded. "I did."

"Do you think I look just like her?"

Of course, Jon did, but the oddness of the question put a crack in what little voice he had to answer. "Yes … yes, you do."

"That's what everybody says, but I think we look different."

Jon said, "That's only because you didn't know her when she was your age." He smiled. "But your mom and I were great friends when we were young, and I do think you look just like her."

"Maybe." She made a face, a sideways sort of smile, which sent a chill through Jon.

It was the exact same kind of face he made, a face he used to make Sarah laugh.

As Jon looked into her eyes, a growing realization crept over him. Yes, she looked a lot like her mother as a child, but she also looked like someone else … him.

He began to pick through the dates in his mind, trying to figure out if he might actually be Emma's father. Had Sarah lied to him? And then another horrible realization.

Is that why she broke up with me?

Jon felt as if someone had pulled the world out from under him.

"What's your name?" The girl looked at him sideways.

"Jon." He barely found the word.

She reached out to shake his hand, smiling her best despite her sadness. "I'm Emma, it's nice to meet you."

He shook her hand, so tiny and frail in his, and felt a growing certainty that his suspicions were right.

And then Vivian appeared from nowhere, with her arm suddenly around her granddaughter. She looked at Emma. "We've got to go. Please tell Mr. Conway to have a nice day."

Emma's eyes went wide, then she turned to Jon. "Wait, are you the guy in the movies?"

He laughed, still kneeling. "Yes."

"Oh, my God! You knew my mom?"

Vivian sliced the exchange to nothing, shot Jon a sour look, then led Emma past the dessert table and to the bright light outside.

Jon stood boiling, his hands twitching. He turned to leave, then crashed into Cassidy, who was standing behind him.

"Sorry about my mom," she said. "You know, old wounds and all."

Jon shook his head and held her gaze. "I understand. I'm sorry about Sarah, Cassidy." He held his arms open, and Cassidy accepted, allowing him to pull her into an embrace. She cried softly against his chest for a minute, then pulled away.

"Thanks for coming," she said. "I didn't know if you would."

He shook his head. "I wouldn't have missed it."

After an awkward silence, Cassidy said, "Thank you. She would have wanted you here."

Jon swallowed, trying to work up the courage to ask the question on his mind.

Cassidy looked back where her mother and niece had gone. "I should probably get going."

"Okay." He said goodbye with an awkward hug.

He felt as if he were hugging a ghost.

Chapter 4 - Milo Anderson

Wednesday
  Sept. 6
  1:17 p.m.

MILO SAT IN HIS BEDROOM, hating everything on the other side of the door.

His dad was gone, like always. Beatrice, or "Other Mother," as Milo called her, sometimes to her face and always when she wasn't around, was left in charge of the house.

Milo's dad worked as an analyst for Conway Industries. While most people who worked for the company lived on the island, or on the mainland, Milo's dad was out of the state more often than not. Milo figured his dad was good at his job, given the money he made. Beatrice was good at hers, too, though her job was much easier since her main duties apparently were to spend his money and be a bitch.

According to Beatrice, Milo just didn't appreciate her or see things from her perspective. She said that as far as hard jobs went, being a stepmother was right up there with being an air traffic controller. Milo thought that was bullshit, particularly since he was seventeen and practically an adult. He wasn't sure what she did on any given day that could be deemed a parental responsibility, save for the occasional dinner she made.

He'd given her plenty of chances, but she'd blown every one, starting with the day his dad announced they were getting married. She stood beside him, smiling like she was standing in an open vault, and said, "You can call me Mom!"

Thanks, Beatrice, you evil bitch.

She wasn't his mother and never would be.

It was hard enough that his mom vanished without a trace when Milo was twelve. Even harder when everyone thought she was one of many victims to jump from Tanner's Pass, and his father had her declared dead.

Perhaps his father could replace her, but that didn't mean Milo had to accept Beatrice.

He hated how she always tried to insert herself into his life and get him to call her "Mom." The worst was when she started her sentences with, "Your father and I always …" as though she had to constantly prove their union by broadcasting the great times they were having when Milo wasn't around, making it all too easy to imagine doing everything from spending money Milo's father actually had to work for to doing things in the bedroom Milo didn't even want to think about.

Milo still remembered the minute he went from merely wishing she wasn't in his life to actually hating her. He had been caught getting drunk with Manny, and the next day had come home to a "family meeting."

He sat on one couch while his "parents" sat on the other. Beatrice said, "Did your mother bring you up to do that?" while his dad sat beside her, either wondering the same thing or acting like too much of a coward to say otherwise.

Milo had hated her ever since. His mother wasn't an alcoholic. And she wasn't a drug addict, despite the rumors. She was clinically depressed and on several medications, any of which might explain her disappearance.

Beatrice called from the other side of the door. "Milo, honey, I'm making lasagna. Would you like it with sausage or without?"

Milo ignored her, like he had for the last hour she'd been trying to get his attention and draw him from his room. He almost felt bad, since she seemed uncharacteristically genuine at a time when he expected to see her at her worst.

Beatrice didn't like it when things didn't go according to plan, especially when her plans included leaving the island for yet another weekend getaway. She and his father were scheduled for a weekend at The Fairmont Sonoma Mission Inn & Spa in California Wine Country. They were booked and ready to leave Friday afternoon as soon as his dad came home early from work. But they had to cancel everything when they heard about the shooting at school.

The quiet house had heard maybe five hundred words the entire weekend. His dad, the only one who even tried to make conversation, had to fly to New York for another conference on Tuesday.

Beatrice's plastic personality made it pretty easy to see through her shallow attempts to mimic emotions. She couldn't give a shit about Milo and was probably marking red X's on a calendar somewhere, waiting for him to graduate and leave the house.

She'd been trying to get him to go to Jessica's funeral service all weekend, but Milo didn't want to talk about it. Now she was trying to lure him out of his room with lasagna, which he loved. Hers was admittedly good, and Milo could smell the scent of sauce she'd been cooking all day traveling up the stairs and into his bedroom.

Milo was tempted to leave the room, just long enough to get some lasagna, when his cell phone rang. He hoped it wasn't Alex again. He'd been ignoring Alex's messages, not even bothering to listen to them. He couldn't hear Alex's voice right now. It was too soon, the horror still raw. How could he possibly remain friends with the son of the man who murdered his friends and classmates?

It was bad enough that he saw Jessica's dying eyes every time he went to sleep.

He grabbed the phone off his nightstand and saw that it wasn't Alex. It was Jesus, Manny's older brother, who'd come back from Stanford University to be with his family. They'd talked briefly Saturday when he learned Manny was in a coma.

"Hey, Milosauraus," Jesus said, "How's it hanging over at Casa de la Anderson? Other Mother still being a bitch?"

Milo felt a slight flush of shame as the scent of lasagna bled beneath the door. "Nah, she's being all right. For the moment, anyway. How's Manny?"

"Wish I knew," Jesus said. "The doctors aren't saying shit. He's still in a coma. Might make it, might not. Changes every hour. Dad's stopped asking, Mom can't keep from crying. We're taking turns hanging out at the hospital, just in case he wakes. Right now is my shift."

"I'm sorry, man," Milo said.

Jesus sighed. "Yeah."

There was a long, awkward silence. Milo wasn't sure what to say, but Jesus didn't seem like he was in a hurry to hang up. After a while, Milo gathered enough courage to say what he had wanted to say on Saturday. "Hey, Jesus, can you call me as soon Manny wakes up?"

"Of course, man."

"I mean immediately, I want to be there as soon as I can see him." After a pause, Milo added, "Before other people start talking to him."

An edge of concern crept into Jesus' throat. "What's going on? What aren't you saying?"

"It's probably nothing," Milo said. "But I can't stop

wondering something. Right before Mr. Heller blew his brains out, he knelt down next to Manny. He looked like he was sorry he shot him. Like he didn't know what he was doing, or perhaps hadn't meant to hit Manny, I'm not sure. But the weird thing was that he said something to Manny."

"Said something? What did he say?"

"I dunno, that's what I want to ask him."

"You and me both," Jesus said. "You and me both."

Chapter 5 - Jon Conway

Wednesday
   Sept. 6
   6:50 p.m.

THE SKY WAS UNSEASONABLY clear for a summer on Hamilton Island, with not a single cloud in sight. In fact, the only thing spoiling the bruised-orange, pre-twilight sky was a pair of long, white contrails, stretching from the other side of the tree-lined hills on the west side of the island to the snow-capped Mount Rainier on the eastern horizon.

Jon drove his rented Avalon past the Chamber of Commerce and the Visitors' Bureau buildings, past the outer limits of the tourist trap downtown, then finally along the freedom of the winding coast to Greenwood, where the rich people lived, then up into Cedar Park, where the houses got larger, acres went to triple digits, and money poured like rain in Washington.

Cedar Park had the largest estates on the island, but even the most massive was dwarfed by Conway Gardens, which sat at the crest, like an idol looking down from the peak of a mountain.

While Jon had made it his mission to leave Cedar Park behind as soon as he could, his older brother, Warren, was still sucking on the family teat, living with his wife, Melinda, and their daughter, Anastasia, at the Gardens.

Warren had invited Jon to dinner, and of course, Jon had to accept. Though he could avoid the family when he was home, he couldn't do so when returning to the island without offending everyone. Their father, Blake Conway, had a way of bringing the Conway men together, whether they wanted a union or not. But he wasn't responsible for this particular visit, nor would he be present. He was out of town. And Anastasia was in her freshman year at Columbia, so it would be just Jon, Warren, and Melinda, plus the usual staff.

Jon swung a left and felt the Avalon struggle. Only slightly, but for the first time since he was handed the key, Jon missed his own car — a BMW Z8, which cornered like it was on rails. The Avalon was a golf cart by comparison.

He idled by the gate and pushed the buzzer but didn't have to identify himself since he was looking into a closed-circuit video camera.

A crisp voice crackled through the speakers. "Welcome home, Mr. Conway."

"Thanks, Xavier," Jon said, smiling. "It's good to be back."

The gates opened, and Jon pulled the car around the long, circular drive, parking behind what had to be his brother's brand-new Bentley. Warren was such a dick. Their smallest garage was big enough to house a family, which meant the Bentley was out for him to see. Jon couldn't fathom why his brother always felt such a need to compete. Well, he had a few ideas, but diving into Warren's psyche wasn't something Jon cared to do at the moment. His brother was a lost cause, not worth the time or effort. Once an asshole, always an asshole was Jon's belief in general, and iron law when it came to Warren.

Jon killed the engine then went to the front door, which swung open before he could knock. The Conways' oldest living employee, Madge Rasmussen, smiled at Jon, asking him if he had a coat, even though it was a perfectly crisp seventy-four degrees outside.

"Hi, Madge," Jon said to the woman who had first introduced him to her sister's cookies twenty-five years earlier. "How are things?"

Madge gave him a sly smile. "The usual, Mr. Conway."

"I really hate it when you call me that. You can tell Xavier the same thing."

Madge held his gaze but said nothing.

"Jon, or hell, even Jonny, if you like."

"As you wish …" She started to say "sir" but mercifully didn't.

"So, is the family circus waiting?"

"Yes. Mr. and Mrs. Conway are waiting for you in the dining hall."

"You mean Warren and Melinda?" He smiled. She smiled back, but he wanted to see it go wider, so he added, "Or Humpty and Dumpty as I like to call them."

Madge surrendered to a hearty laugh, "You're so bad … Jonny." She then told Jon to follow her, as if they'd moved the location of the dining hall.

"Jon!" Warren set his iPad on the end table beside an over-stuffed chair. He stood and crossed the carpet to greet Jon like he was some beloved hero returning from war.

Melinda was reading on her own iPad several feet away. She set hers down as well, then followed Warren's lead.

"How are you?" Warren wrapped his arms around his brother. Melinda stood to the side, like her usual cold fish self, but Warren was uncharacteristically warm.

Jon surrendered to his brother's embrace then pulled away.

"Better than most, not as good as some, I suppose. How are you?"

Warren smiled. "Good, not great. Same as you, I guess. Dad's driving me crazy, but nothing new there. You know how that goes."

"I try not to," Jon said.

Warren met his smile with a thinner version. "Hungry?"

Jon realized he was starving. "Yes. I guess I haven't really eaten today, except for a couple of cookies and a half-gallon of coffee. What's on the menu?"

Warren laughed. "Carmen figured you would want a steak. So, we're having Kobe and lobster. Ready when you are."

Jon smiled as his stomach growled. A steak sounded great. Carmen didn't make the best steak in the world, that honor belonged to Queue de Cheval Steak House in Montreal if you wanted fancy, and Peter Luger's in Brooklyn if you didn't. But she did come in third, and third was his favorite, since it was the only one that could make Jon remember everything from being eleven years old and building his own treehouse in the backyard, to being seventeen and losing his virginity with Sarah inside it.

The steak and pasta were on the table just minutes after they sat, and the 2006 Chevalier-Montrachet before that. Jon cut his meat, imagining the taste as he looked down at the gorgeous, red flesh, then put it in his mouth and let his mind wander to Sarah's girlish grin and his final words before that long-ago evening had taken him from boy to man.

"Are you sure you're ready?" he had asked.

"I'm always ready for you, Jon," she had said. "Thank you for waiting." She lay on the sleeping bag, curled her finger, and beckoned him forward.

It was a beautiful memory, one of his favorites. He hoped it wouldn't make him cry.

More than he wanted to keep his tears inside, Jon hoped

Warren would soon steer the conversation away from business and toward golf. It wasn't that Jon liked to talk golf. It just happened to be the only topic Warren could go on forever about, which kept his tongue too busy from saying something stupid like he usually did, ending dinner with drama.

Warren went on and on about the latest in augmentation technology. To hear Warren put it, Conway Industries was on the verge of something big, but he couldn't really say anything yet. At least, not to an outsider such as Jon.

It was just one more of Warren's subtle jabs at his brother, trying to puff up the importance of whatever project they were working on. Usually, when he pulled a stunt like this in front of their father, the old man would call his son out.

"It's an artificial eye, Warren. Don't be so damned cloak and dagger," Blake would say, putting Warren in his place and bringing a subtle smile to Jon's face.

But Blake wasn't there during this dinner, so Jon just let it slide. It wasn't as though he really cared. The biotech business may have made the family rich, and Conway Industries was revolutionizing limb and artificial organ replacement, but it all bored Jon to tears. He wasn't a scientist, nor a businessman. He was just an actor, a kid who never grew up and made lots of money playing pretend. It was the best job in the world, and no matter how much Warren tried to belittle acting as a profession, Jon wouldn't let it get to him.

After Jon failed to grovel and beg to hear more, his brother stared at him, his eyes redder than his glass of wine. Warren poured himself a third, then changed the subject, moving immediately into golf.

Jon laughed.

"Am I amusing you?" Warren said.

"No, not at all." Jon smiled and shook his head.

Melinda placed a dime-sized piece of steak into her mouth, chewed, then swallowed. "So, what brings you to town, Jon?"

Was she really that oblivious to the rest of the world? He cleared his throat, then said, "The memorial, Melinda," adding her name to the end in a quiet *fuck you.*

"Oh." She put another mini piece of meat into her tiny mouth. "That. Yes, that was so tragic, all those poor kids."

Warren took another large swallow of wine, then said, "Jon used to date Sarah Hughes, the teacher who was shot. They grew up, best of friends. Used to do everything together. You know the bunch of wood out back Dad had cleared out four years ago? That was Jon's 'Clubhouse.' He used to spend a million years out there with Sarah, the two of them making out all the time and Jon acting like no one knew what they were doing."

Jon chewed his steak, growing more annoyed by the second.

"Oh, I'm so sorry." Melinda's eyes grew soft and kind. "I didn't know."

"It's okay." Jon put another piece of steak in his mouth.

"Did you see her sister?" Warren asked. The way he said the first syllable of "sister" made Jon want to walk to Warren's side of the table and punch him in the ear.

"Yes," Jon said, no emotion. "Sarah's sister was at the memorial."

"She kick the drugs yet?" Warren took another long sip of wine.

Jon almost laughed at the irony, but held his laugh, and the nasty response he wanted to give, firmly in place.

"I don't get daily updates on the Hughes family," Jon said, "but Cassidy looked good."

Jon was pretty sure Warren was about to say something that might get him out of his seat and over to his brother's side of the table, but before Warren could open his mouth, Melinda set her fork down and opened hers.

"How long are you going to be in town?" she asked.

Warren answered for him. "I'm sure Jon has pressing business back home."

Jon could feel his blood boil, like it always did within an hour of stepping foot inside Conway Gardens. He caught the glint in Warren's eyes — interest, anxiety, maybe concern. Whatever it was, the hairs on Jon's neck didn't like it a bit. So, he lied. "Actually, I'm between projects, reading some scripts. Since I'm back at Hamilton Island, I figured I might as well stay awhile, catch up with some old friends." He swallowed, then added, "I'll be here at least a week." Jon turned from Melinda to Warren, then asked, "When's Dad coming back?"

"He'll be back next week," Melinda said.

Warren shot her a look.

Jon smiled ear to ear, his eyes fixed on Warren's. "Excellent," he said. "I'll stay until then, at least."

Jon continued to smile as his brother twisted under the thumb of discomfort. The rest of the meal had talk small enough to be mostly invisible. Jon finished his meal, muscled his way through polite goodbyes, then went to the garage where the family kept the classic cars and a motorcycle, and traded his Avalon for his silver Porsche 356, built in 1963, and still looking showroom shiny. He was glad he'd asked Xavier to have someone maintain the car in his absence.

Jon climbed into the driver's seat, thrilled to find the keys in the glove box where he'd left them a year ago. His face lit with a smile as he fished beneath the seat, hoping his treasure was still buried there, too.

It was.

Jon pulled out the small, wooden box, smiled, then flicked the latch and opened the lid to a vacuum-sealed baggie and seven perfectly rolled joints. He wondered how long weed stayed fresh but figured anything was better than nothing.

He turned the engine, pulled the car from the garage, then left Conway Gardens, waving to a smiling Xavier on his way past the gates. When he hit the coast, he gunned the engine and sped toward the island's north end.

The entire north side of the island belonged to the Conways, originally as his grandfather's retreat where he wined and dined politicians and the powerful, then later as home to several Conway Industries laboratories, where they worked on the more sensitive research and, he suspected, government projects.

Jon followed the winding road through acres of unspoiled woodlands, which were beautiful during the day but nothing more than blots of darkness against the night sky as he headed toward Jensen's Cove, his favorite chill-out spot on the island.

He needed time to think about Emma and the possibility that she might be his daughter. If she were, why hadn't anyone yet told him? Had Sarah kept the secret even from her family?

As Jon drove through the darkness, he felt more alone than ever, wishing he had a friend he could dig into the deep shit with. Odd, he thought, how the closest people to him these days were his agent, Marty, and his assistant, Alicia. But neither relationship was one which Jon would consider intimate.

It wasn't that he didn't trust them. He did, implicitly. But they weren't friends with long, shared histories. They weren't the kind of people he talked to about the stuff that kept him up at night. Truth was, he hadn't had anyone like that since Sarah. Perhaps the closest thing to a friend he had these days was his private detective buddy, Brock Houser. But he wasn't sure if this was something he'd feel comfortable talking to Brock about.

A mile from the cove, Jon was surprised to find a gate that wasn't there before, blocking the narrow road with a large, red *No Trespassing* sign set snug between two others, warning trespassers that they *WILL BE PROSECUTED.*

Jon stepped from the 356 to get a closer look at the fence,

and to see if he could maybe pick the lock. Houser had showed him how plenty of times before, and the last couple of times it had even started to stick. He was searching the trunk of his car for something he could either pick or break the lock with.

The bright beam of a flashlight suddenly blinded him. Jon felt exposed as the light drew closer, and whoever held it remained obscured. Jon's hand gripped the tire iron, just in case.

And then, as the light grew closer, he could see who was holding it — a Paladin guard.

"Can I help you?" Jon said, noticing the guard was on foot, without a vehicle in sight.

The guard replied, "I was about to ask you the same question. What in the hell do you think you're doing out here?"

"I'm trying to get to the cove, but someone put up a damned fence." Jon let go of the crowbar. "You got keys? Maybe you can unlock it for me?"

The guard looked Jon up and down, no recognition in his eyes, surprising given the Conways paid for the security force. "I'm going to need to see your license and registration," he said, unnecessarily rude.

Jon shook his head. "No, you don't. My name is Jon Conway. Of *The* Conways. You know, the people who pay your salary. The people who own this land. So, I need you to step off right now like you never saw me."

The rent-a-cop pulled a gun, then aimed it at Jon. "I'm serious as a stroke, mister. I need to see your license and registration, now."

Despite the gun aimed directly at his chest, Jon took a step closer. No way was this clown going to shoot him.

"Is there something about 'I own this land' that you didn't understand?" Jon shoved his finger in the rent-a-cop's chest.

The guard lowered his gun, but grabbed Jon's finger, giving Jon the excuse he'd been looking for. He slapped the guard's hand, then punched him in the face, hard. A spray of blood flew from his nose and coated Jon's knuckles.

The rent-a-cop fell to the ground, just as a second guard appeared from nowhere. Jon saw the gun a second before its trigger was pulled.

The dart slapped him in the shoulder. He swayed on his feet for a second before falling on his face. The second rent-a-cop cuffed him as the first stood from the dirt.

"You're under arrest," he said.

Chapter 6 - Cassidy Hughes

Wednesday
  Sept. 6
  8:42 p.m.

CASSIDY FLIPPED THROUGH channels as Emma curled up beside her on the couch.

"Are we going to watch something, or are you gonna keep going too fast to see what's on?" Emma asked.

"I'm gonna keep going too fast to see," Cassidy said. "What do you want to watch?"

Emma said nothing. But then again, what else was there to say? They'd both exhausted themselves, talking and crying then talking some more. Cassidy had done everything she could to comfort her niece, swearing that everything would be okay and giving her hope and comfort in the way her sister would have wanted.

As opposed to the angry death rattle from Vivian.

Fortunately, Vivian was in the other room, sleeping off her countless glasses of wine.

It must've been especially confusing for Emma, losing her

mother, then staying with someone who looked so much like her. Genetics made them identical, though life and their ages made it easy to tell them apart. Sarah had softened edges, while Cassidy's years of hard living were clear from the lines under her eyes to the matching, faded-pink scars lining both her wrists.

Cassidy found an episode of *SpongeBob SquarePants* and left it on. She wasn't sure if Emma even liked the show, but at least she could be certain Nickelodeon wouldn't break into programming with pictures of Sarah and news footage of bodies in black bags outside of the school.

"Are we going to stay at Gram's forever?" Emma nudged herself closer.

Cassidy wished she knew, for herself and for Emma. But it wasn't as though Sarah's death had been marked on the calendar. There was no contingency plan, just a drunken promise two years earlier when Sarah made Cassidy swear on her life that she would take Emma if anything happened to her, since their mother was too "batshit crazy" and unreliable to be trusted for the job.

And sure, their mom may have been crazy, but that didn't mean Cassidy was any better suited for the job. At least their mom had raised children before. Two of them, in fact. And she'd done a good job with at least one.

What in the fuck did Cassidy know about raising a child?

She shouldn't have to deal with raising a child, but then again, what choice did she have? Sarah was right about their mom, and Cassidy sure as shit wasn't going to give Emma over to her father.

The way Jon had looked at Emma at the service made Cassidy wonder if he'd figured things out, or if perhaps Warren had told him the truth after all these years. And if so, what then? Would he sweep in with his high-priced attorneys and take Emma away?

While Cassidy didn't know the first thing about raising a

kid, Emma was family, and she'd be damned if she'd give her up to Jon Conway. His family had done too much, hurt too many people, to ever be entrusted with a sweet child like Emma. And while Jon was perhaps the best of the lot, it wasn't saying much. He might not be an evil prick, but she'd seen him on TV getting drunk, fighting with paparazzi, sleeping with models, actresses, and singers. He was just as much of an addict as she was.

No. No way she could turn Emma over.

Cassidy stroked Emma's hair as she pulled the girl into a tight hug. Tears streamed down Cassidy's face as she wondered what in the hell she would do next. She was sick and goddamned tired of being at the mercy of others, particularly the Conways. She should have left Hamilton Island years ago when she had a chance. Now she had obligations — a mother who, despite what she said, needed her, and now a child to take care of.

Why did you have to die, Sarah?

Fuck.

Cassidy felt a flash of guilt. Sarah had been dead since Friday, but Cassidy had barely had time to miss or mourn her twin sister before she was thrust into the role of caregiver. She had to arrange the funeral, call people, and talk with lawyers and insurance people. Someone had already screwed up, cremating Sarah instead of burying her properly, for which Cassidy was being blamed by her mom. "Just another Cassidy Fuck-Up."

Cassidy wasn't sure if burying ashes was better for Emma than seeing her mom's dead body, but she thought maybe it was. Perhaps she should thank God for the mistake that spared Emma one more horrible memory.

The past few days had been filled with too much to do, and Cassidy hadn't even had time to sort through her own feelings of loss. Sarah was not only her twin, but her best friend.

Perhaps the worst part in all of this was that Cassidy had known Sarah would die.

Three weeks ago, Cassidy had fallen asleep in front of the TV and woke up thinking someone was in her apartment. There wasn't anyone there, but as she woke she remembered a dream she'd had, vivid as daylight. Someone at the school had started shooting kids. A bullet went through the wall between the classrooms and struck Sarah, killing her instantly.

The dream on its own might not have meant much. However, she had the dream again every night for the next two weeks. Every night.

She wanted to tell Sarah about the dream, warn her.

But what could she say that wouldn't make her sister think she was using again?

When Cassidy had been using, she'd had several instances where she dreamed something that was going to happen. They were little things, usually, but accurate enough to make shit weird. So she told Sarah. But she'd been so manic when she told Sarah that her sister came down hard on her, knowing that she was using.

There was no way Cassidy could tell Sarah about these dreams without her sister thinking she was using again. And besides, she hadn't had any of her weird, prophetic dreams since she'd stopped using. In all likelihood, she figured these were just regular dreams, fueled by a preoccupation of Cassidy's fears of responsibility for others.

So, she kept her mouth shut, not wanting to see that familiar look of disappointment in her twin's eyes.

She could take that look from her mom, her friends, her lovers, and co-workers, but not from Sarah. She didn't care if everyone in her life thought she was the black sheep of the family, the "bad sister" and the "fuck-up." But letting Sarah down was the last thing in the world she wanted to do. She owed her sister too much.

And yet, in not telling her sister of the dreams, she had done just that. She let her down. And now Sarah was dead.

Cassidy began to cry harder.

Emma saw and felt Cassidy's tears. She put a hand on Cassidy's face, wiping a tear away, saying in a soft voice, "It'll be okay, Aunt Cassidy."

Cassidy squeezed her eyes, and Emma, tighter, wishing she could believe the child.

❧

EMMA FELL asleep in Cassidy's arms, and Cassidy found her eyes glazing over from the soft glow of the TV cartoons, her mind returning to a familiar place.

She couldn't take much more. The familiar itch began to gnaw at her brain, telling her how to make everything okay.

The pills.

Once an addict, always an addict.

For the first time in who knew how long, Cassidy needed the drugs. Not *wanted* the drugs — she always *wanted* the drugs. She was a fucking addict, always would be. And life for an addict was one day at a time. But now, she *needed* them. Again.

The addict lived in the back of her brain, nested like a parasite crouching in the dark, waiting for its host to grow less vigilant, more complacent, no longer willing to do the hard work of digging the well and dipping the bucket into the pure water.

Cassidy had a friend, Gina, who had been her Narcotics Anonymous sponsor. She'd been hooked on the hardcore shit, heroin, and was sober for four years. But sure as shit, three months ago she went back out and started to use. One month ago, she died.

Once an addict, always an addict.

There is no starting over. The addict in the back of your brain can nudge its way to the front whenever the fuck it wants. It drives the bus when it decides to get behind the goddamned wheel, or when life makes it an offer it can't refuse.

Cassidy would never be cured, could never afford to walk away from the things that got her sober and kept her clean.

Like Sarah.

And Emma.

And the three of them together.

Once an addict, always an addict.

Cassidy could picture the look in her new sponsor's eyes when she called in the morning to tell Roberta she'd relapsed. She could hear Roberta's voice saying she'd already buried too many friends and didn't want to bury another.

No, she didn't *have* to relapse.

Except she did.

Once an addict, always an addict.

The addict inside her was working hard, hungry for its first pill in three years, seven months, and sixteen days. Each of those days filled with emotions that threatened to steal her sobriety at any moment.

Pain. Fear. Fury.

Guilt. Rage. Grief.

Panic. Dread. Anger.

Agony. Blame. Terror.

Misery. Sorrow. Despair.

Torture. Sadness. Suffering.

Bitterness. Resentment. Indignation.

And now those feelings were returning in full force, and all at once, ready to take her at her weakest moment.

One pill. Instant gratification. Immediate relief from every unpleasant emotion.

Relief and relapse were both a phone call away. Her addict was doing a Snoopy dance inside her, knowing Cassidy was minutes from crossing to the darker side of her inner fissure. The little girl who had lost her mother might be months away from losing her aunt. Hell, maybe Emma *was* better off with Jon Conway. Who was she to think she could ever take care of another when she could barely take care of herself?

Once an addict, always an addict.

She rose and carried Emma to her bedroom at Gram's house. Surprisingly, Emma barely stirred as Cassidy slipped her into her bed and covered her in the same strawberry-colored blanket she'd had since she was four.

Cassidy then passed her mother's room, the door ajar, the blue light of the TV illuminating the woman in bed, sleeping away her half bottle of Pinot, which was on the nightstand.

Cassidy left the house, dialing Craig's number before she even had her car in reverse.

She had to call Craig instead of Lewis, since Lewis worked at The Shipwreck and had a big mouth. Craig was more expensive, but he knew how to shut the fuck up. Besides, Lewis was sometimes dry. Craig never was.

The addict inside her didn't want her clean side to get a chance to fight back.

Craig was happy to hear her voice, and ready at the door when she traded several twenties for a barely rattling bottle.

Once an addict, always an addict.

Cassidy was going to go back to her apartment to zone out, but decided she'd get less friction if she went back to her mom's place and slept in one of the two guest rooms as she'd done for the past two nights.

She went to the guest room set up for her and crawled into bed. She pulled the covers over herself, clicked on the TV, and found an old episode of *Curb Your Enthusiasm.*

Cassidy slipped two pills out of the bottle, downed them with a bottle of Diet Coke, and closed her eyes, waiting for sweet oblivion to claim her.

Chapter 7 - Jon Conway

Wednesday
  Sept. 6
  11:57 p.m.

JON WOKE to find himself in a jail cell, one of four in the tiny Hamilton Island Police Station. This was the first time he had woken in a jail cell sober, though the pain in his head felt like a hangover. Then he remembered the dart he'd been shot with by the rent-a-cops.

The other cells were empty. He wasn't awake long when the red door leading into the jail opened and a young police officer with jug ears and a big, toothy grin entered. Jon was pissed that he'd been detained but was glad that Paladin had at least brought him to the police station instead of to Paladin Security Headquarters, a pristine, high-tech palace that hid the heavy-handed, thug-like behavior of many of the Paladin guards.

The cop with *Henry* on his badge said, "Chief Brady says you're free to go."

Officer Henry slid a key into the cell and opened the

squeaky cell door. He lowered his head as Jon walked by. "Sorry about all the trouble."

"No problem." Jon turned his head toward the cop. "Not your fault. Besides, I needed a nap, and nothing says comfort like the Hamilton Island Police Station, though I was disappointed not to find a mint on my pillow."

Officer Henry laughed, though it was a delayed laugh, as if he wasn't sure Jon was joking or not. Obviously, the Hamilton Island Police Department attracted a different caliber of cop than Paladin.

They walked through the red door that led from the tiny prison and down a hall with three open doors, along with a fourth closed one. Jon looked at a giant, old clock on the wall over the door that led to the front of the station and its lobby. Before they reached the exit, the only closed door in the hall opened, and the familiar face of Jon's old friend Kevin Brady came into view. Though they were the same age, Brady looked pudgy and tired, his dark, curly hair graying above the ears. Jon wondered if he looked so ragged because of stress from the job or from having a wife and twin six-year-olds.

Brady thanked Officer Henry, then went through the door to the front of the station and met Jon, slapping him on his shoulder with his left hand as he offered him his right. "Sorry about the trouble, Jon."

Jon shook his hand, noting the clammy palm. "Thanks for letting me go with a warning."

"Of course." He gestured toward his office, stepped inside, waited for Jon to enter, then closed the door behind them.

Brady sat behind his cluttered desk and waved a hand for Jon to take a seat opposite him.

The small, messy office looked about thirty years past due for a makeover. As did Brady's ancient desktop computer. Yellow smoke stains pocked the ceiling tiles above the desk.

"So," Jon said. "You made police chief, eh? Damn, you're the youngest chief by two decades."

"Well, I don't know how impressive it really is. Nobody else wanted the job, if I'm being honest. The real money is with Paladin."

"Yeah, don't get me started on those assholes."

"You mean the assholes on your family's payroll?" Brady said, then looked like he wished he'd kept his mouth shut.

"Yeah, well obviously they've forgotten who butters their bread. So, what's the deal with the fence? And all the security? How many damned officers do they have?"

"Officially, they've got forty guards. Unofficially, I'd say triple that."

"What the fuck?" Jon said, shocked. "They starting an army?"

Brady smiled nervously, and then answered the other part of Jon's question. "The fence went up two years ago. This your first time seeing it, I guess?"

Jon nodded.

"Yeah, they fenced off the whole northeastern part of the island. They had some lab break-ins, but it was mostly to cut down on the deaths."

"Deaths?"

"You know that bridge that runs across Tanner's Pass? Well, kids have been crossing the girders along the bottom of the bridge on dares and stuff. And a lot of them have fallen into the water and hit the rocks. We had ten kids die two years ago, and another fifteen kids and adults who'd gone missing, believed to be suicides who either washed out to sea or into some of the caves along the pass.

"Jesus."

"Yeah, and since your family owns the land, they're looking to cut down their liability, though I'm not sure who in their right mind would sue the Conways."

Jon nodded. He knew all too well how vicious his family was when it came to the courtroom.

"So, they put up a fence and set up guards around the perimeter."

"A lot of work to keep people from killing themselves on an old bridge, don't you think?"

"I dunno." Brady clearly wanted to change the subject. "So, what brings you to town? The funeral? Sarah?"

"Yeah." Jon considered asking Brady if he knew anything about Emma's paternity, but decided to keep that question close to his vest for now. Though Brady had been a close friend, that was many years ago.

"I'm sorry," Brady said. "I know how close you two were."

Jon sighed, "Yeah, it's a tragedy. You know what happened? Why the teacher snapped?"

"No, not a thing. Hell, five minutes into the shooting, the feds swooped in and took over the investigation."

"The feds?"

"Yeah, and get this … they're coordinating efforts with Paladin."

"Is that even legal?" Jon asked.

"Well, the township made Paladin the same as us, really. Though given the size of Paladin, I'd say we're nothing more than figureheads at this point."

"Shit. They're keeping you in the dark, even though you're the chief?"

"Pretty much. They took all the evidence we collected and acted like they were doing us a favor. To be honest, they probably are. We don't really have a staff to handle something like this. And the way people are pissed off, let Paladin and the feds deal with this shit."

"You sound burned out," Jon said.

"You don't even know, brother. Used to be that being the chief meant something, you know? But now, I'm just the hired help. But I figure if I keep my head down, just handle the shit I've gotta handle, I can provide for my family, ya know?"

They talked a bit more, catching up as much as Brady's

reticence would allow. It was around one in the morning when Brady walked Jon to his car. He looked around, making sure Officer Henry wasn't within sight, then reached into his jacket and handed Jon his stash of weed.

Jon's face flushed. Even though Brady had been a friend a long time ago, he was still a chief, and to see his stash in the hands of the law sent a chill through Jon, fearful Brady was about to come down on him.

"I think someone accidentally left this in your car."

"Yeah, I'll see if I can return it to its rightful owner. Probably an old guy with really bad glaucoma."

"Yeah, glaucoma." Brady grinned.

The smile faded as Brady looked around again, however, and then met Jon's eyes. "You need to leave the island, Jon."

Jon stepped back, confused. "Huh?"

"You need to get out of here. Something bad is going to happen."

"What do you mean?" Jon said, noticing the fear in Brady's eyes.

"I can't say anything more. Not here. They're probably watching."

"You sure you didn't smoke any of this?" Jon patted his pants pocket where he'd put the weed.

Brady didn't laugh. "I'm serious, Jon. Get out while you still can."

With that, Brady turned and headed back inside the station.

"Hey!" Jon tried to get his attention so he could ask a few follow-up questions.

But Brady kept walking.

Jon got into his car, shut the door, and glanced in the rearview and side mirrors, looking to see if anyone was watching.

There was only darkness.

Chapter 8 - Liz Heller

Wednesday
   Sept. 6
   10:14 p.m.

LIZ WAS CUDDLED on her bed, the comforter and blankets pulled tight around her as she stared at the TV, watching a rerun of *Everybody Loves Raymond*. She wasn't in the mood to laugh and wasn't really paying attention. She just wanted something familiar, something to make her feel a little less alone in the bed she'd shared for so long with Roger. Something other than the constant barrage of news coverage of her husband's shooting "rampage," as the talking heads on the TV news were calling Friday's tragedy. Rampage, like Roger was some sort of monster instead of the sweet, sensitive, sometimes goofy man she married twenty years ago.

Five days had passed, and though reality had forced itself upon her, it all still felt unreal.

Five days of going through the motions of life, trying to pretend they would ever have anything close to a normal family again.

Five days of wondering if she could be strong enough for Alex and Aubrey.

Five days of kicking herself for missing the signs that the "experts" said "someone" should have picked up on.

Five days of having her husband's life dissected and invaded by specialists, authors, and news anchors, who were all suddenly experts on the subject of Roger Heller.

But there had been no sign. Not that she'd seen, anyway.

Liz wasn't even sure if she would have recognized a sign if it had been there. Though Roger was sweet, he was often in his own world — distant and holed up in his office for hours on end on nights and weekends. But he'd always been that way.

He needed his personal space to write. He'd had a few stories published in literary magazines, and a few articles in writing magazines, but he'd never been able to finish a novel, not one that he liked, anyway. And after he turned forty last year, he began to spend even more time than ever writing, convinced he was running out of time to create the "Great American Novel."

Though Roger's distance had bothered her at times, it wasn't as if she didn't have her own life going on. Until Aubrey was born in May, Liz was a ninth-grade English teacher at the school, which had kept her busy day and night. She had decided to take an extended maternity leave so she could be with Aubrey until her daughter turned one. During her leave, Liz managed to get a few freelance illustration gigs for magazines and a few websites. She'd always loved cartooning and was thrilled to have a chance to get back into it. And make money in the process. She had hoped to get enough work that she might never have to go back to teaching. The way things were going, she could work from home and not have to put Aubrey in daycare. They could've gotten by on Roger's salary and her freelance work.

Now everything was in limbo.

While trying to get her husband's body from the medical examiner's office so she could arrange a funeral, she'd not even had time to figure out whether Roger's insurance policy would pay out, or whether she or the children could collect his pension or Social Security. She was pretty certain the insurance wouldn't pay anything since he shot himself.

As for everything else, Liz had no idea.

Then there were the families of the victims. She wasn't sure what they might do and didn't know if they could sue his estate or her for civil damages. She needed to talk to a lawyer, and soon. But at the moment, she was overwhelmed, and all she wanted to do was crawl into bed and wake up when everything was over.

But now she was a single mother, raising two kids on her own. Well, raising Aubrey on her own. Alex was self-sufficient, though that could change now that his father was gone. Though Alex hadn't shown much emotion in the past few days, it had to be tearing him up.

Liz closed her eyes, the sound of the TV barely audible over the sound of the baby monitor on the nightstand beside her bed. The monitor that had kept her up so many nights, braced for the sound of Aubrey waking to another nightmare or a stuffy nose. But at that moment, the sound of Aubrey's fan coming through the monitor was giving Liz comfort, a white noise to drown the thoughts racing through her head.

Liz was drifting off when her daughter murmuring caught her attention.

Aubrey did that a lot at night as she shifted between phases of sleep. She'd make sounds for a few minutes and would either wake up crying or drift back to silent sleep. Some nights, Liz was lucky to get four hours of shuteye between Aubrey on the verge of waking or actually waking and needing to be comforted back to sleep. Liz didn't remember Alex being such a finicky sleeper, but perhaps that was just a rose-tinted memory.

Liz waited anxiously, and then her daughter grew quiet again. Only then did she allow herself to drift into sleep, praying for a night without visions of "rampages."

~

1:11 *a.m.*

LIZ WOKE to the sound of Aubrey giggling over the baby monitor.

Though she was tired, she wasn't too exhausted to find some joy in the sound of Aubrey laughing in her sleep. She smiled, found the remote, turned off the TV, and cast the room into darkness.

Liz's eyelids were heavy. She closed them again, listening to the soft white noise, waiting for it to lull her back to sleep. She wasn't sure how long she'd been asleep when another sound came through the monitor.

More laughter, followed by a sound she couldn't possibly have heard — a whispered "shhhh."

Liz's eyes shot open, as she reached out and turned the monitor up, to make sure she wasn't just hearing things.

Nothing but the white noise, albeit louder, of the monitor.

Then, more giggling, followed by Aubrey saying, "Da-da."

A voice whispered, "Don't wake your mommy."

Liz shot from her bed and out through her bedroom door in seconds, bursting into Aubrey's room, fists balled and ready to attack whatever intruder dared come into her house.

But there was nobody in the room, except Aubrey, staring out the window, through the open curtains that Liz was pretty certain she'd closed.

"Da-da," Aubrey said again, looking at the window.

Liz went to the window, checked to make sure it was

locked, and saw nothing but darkness outside and the black security van parked across the street.

"Da-da," Aubrey said from her crib.

A chill ran through Liz's body.

~

2 A.M.

LIZ COULDN'T CALM herself after rocking Aubrey back to sleep.

No matter how many times she'd gone over what she thought she heard, it failed to make sense. *Just like Roger shooting people doesn't make sense, eh?* There was nobody in her daughter's room. The window was locked tight. And even though Aubrey was saying, "Da-da," there was no way in hell Liz was going to start believing in ghostly visitations from her dead husband.

The only answer that made sense was that she'd imagined the voice. She was stressed out, tired, and had been running on empty for five days running. She needed sleep before she lost her mind completely.

Liz headed downstairs and into the kitchen where she made some hot cocoa. She pulled the large, green mug from the microwave, added a splash of milk, then scooped a handful of marshmallows from a glass canister on the counter. From the first sip, she savored the creamy, sugary, chocolate concoction.

Hot cocoa made her feel like a kid again. Maybe it would also help her sleep. She glanced at the clock on the microwave. It was blinking *12:00*.

When did the power go out?

She went into the living room and looked at the clock on the cable box that read 2:04 a.m. She might get four or five hours of sleep if she crashed right away. Aubrey usually woke up somewhere between six and seven in the morning, which made some days tougher than others to get through. Tomorrow looked like it would be a long one. Especially if she didn't get to sleep soon.

But something was bothering her. An itch in her brain — something she felt like she was supposed to remember, but couldn't.

She walked from room to room with the mug of cocoa in her hand, hoping she'd see something to jog her memory.

Is it something I'm supposed to do tomorrow? A bill I need to pay?

She found herself in Roger's office, clicked on the light, and smiled when she saw that Alex had straightened it up so it no longer looked like a burglar had torn through the room.

Poor Alex.

Roger's death had rocked them all, but Alex seemed to be taking it the hardest, even if he hid it the best. Liz knew he was hurting. She'd tried to reach out to him, but she didn't know what to do. Part of her felt like she needed to give him his space to deal with this and come to terms with what happened. But another part of her felt that no matter how old Alex was, he still needed his mother.

She'd tried a combination of both approaches, but nothing seemed to be working particularly well. Which was why the cleaned office made her smile. It was the first thing he'd done since Friday and seemed to suggest progress.

Liz fought a fresh batch of tears, and just as she was about to turn the light off, that itch returned to her brain, demanding she give it attention.

She turned around, wondering what she was supposed to see in Roger's office.

"What is it?" she asked the room.

She sat at Roger's desk, set the mug down in front of her, then ran her hands across the surface, remembering him sitting behind it on so many nights, working on his papers, or writing his books. She hoped the police would return the books and journals he'd been writing. She hated to think she'd never get to read the things he'd spent so many hours on. Hated to think that Alex might never get to read what his father had written. Though Roger didn't share his work with them, she knew that in this situation, he'd want them to read what he'd devoted so much of his life to.

Liz wiped away the threatening tears, then leaned her head back and closed her eyes, feeling tired enough to sleep right there.

A full minute passed, and as it did, the idea of sleeping at the desk seemed all the more attractive.

But the baby monitor wasn't in here. She opened her eyes and was about to get up when she noticed the light in the fire alarm wasn't lit green. It wasn't lit at all.

That's weird. Did the battery come loose?

She got up from the desk and dragged Roger's chair over to a spot beneath the fire alarm so she could reach up and twist the bottom cap. Two objects, hidden in the fire alarm where the battery should have been, fell to the carpeted floor before she could catch them.

Why the alarm hadn't beeped to indicate the battery wasn't working? Maybe Roger cut the wires.

But why? What was he hiding in there?

She checked the inside of the cap to make sure there was nothing else squirreled away inside the alarm, then screwed it back into place. After hopping off the chair, she knelt and picked up the fallen objects.

A flash drive and a folded piece of paper.

What the …?

She set the flash drive on the desk, not having a computer to access it, and began to unfold the paper.

As she flattened the note, she saw it was written in her husband's precise block-like handwriting.

A list of five names.

The paper began to shake in her hands. Her stomach flopped as significance dawned.

It was a list of the students her husband had shot.

Four of them, anyway.

Manny wasn't on the list.

But Alex's girlfriend, Katie, was.

Chapter 9 - Cassidy Hughes

Thursday
Sept. 7
1:11 a.m.

CASSIDY WOKE to the sound of voices whispering, coming from somewhere in the room. When she opened her eyes, the light from the TV was strobing on, off, on, off, casting the room from bright to pitch black over and over, in unequal measures. The picture on the screen was nothing but snow.

On, off, on, off, like a power surge, in an oddly-syncopated pattern.

The effect on her head was disorienting. Cassidy rose from her bed, and the room spun.

On, off, on, off, and then . . . nothing.

The TV stayed off, and the room was utter blackness.

She put her hands out in front of her, trying to feel her way to the bedroom door. If she could make it to the kitchen, she could find a flashlight in the junk drawer. She moved slowly, unfamiliar with her surroundings, hoping she wouldn't stub her toe or knock something over and wake everybody up.

As her hand touched the doorknob, the room went bright again and the TV blared back to life. She whirled around to see the snowy screen, something she hadn't seen since cable went ubiquitous. Beneath the sound of the TV's white noise, she heard whispering, like the sound of a man saying something.

She walked toward the television then lowered her face toward the speaker to listen closer to the whispering.

The man was saying the same thing over and over, as if a recorded loop.

"ELEVEN. ELEVEN. ELEVEN. ELEVEN ..."

SUDDENLY, a shape appeared, overlapping the snow, like a ghosted image from a 1950's broadcast or something. A man's face, barely visible, speaking the same word over and over. A chill went through her, as if she were somehow seeing a ghost or message from the distant past.

"ELEVEN. ELEVEN. ELEVEN. ELEVEN ..."

THE TV WENT DARK, returning the room to pitch-black and dead silence.

Cassidy reached her hand out again, finding her way to the bedroom door. Her hand lowered, found the knob, then opened it. The moment she did, a bright light in the hallway blinded her, as if someone had placed giant spotlights at either end, then flicked them on the moment she stepped over the threshold.

She shielded her eyes.

The light was so bright, so pervasive and stinging, that

even closing her eyes couldn't keep the brightness at bay.

Cassidy heard the TV click back on in her room. It played the sound of white noise, with the whispering man saying "Eleven" over and over. But he was soon drowned out by another sound — a scream from Emma's room.

"Emma!" Cassidy stumbled blindly into the hall, one hand covering her eyes, the other feeling the wall, tracing it to Emma's door.

"Help!" the girl screamed. "Mommy!"

Cassidy moved faster, found the door, and burst in.

A loud popping sound echoed through the entire house, then everything went black.

CASSIDY WOKE to an infomercial on the TV and saw that the time on the clock beside her bed was blinking *12:00* in its soft-blue LED display.

What the hell was in that pill?

Her head was pounding, and her body ached. Usually, the pills made her slightly nauseous at worst. Nothing like this. She vaguely remembered having a dream — a nightmare — but it was all a blur behind the headache.

She was pretty sure this was the worst headache she'd ever had. Was it a reaction to the pills, or an accumulation of all the stress? As a child, she used to get horrible migraines, pretty close to this. Maybe she was getting them again.

Fuck.

She found the pill bottle beneath her pillow, took another two pills — for pain this time, not recreation — and swallowed some water.

She lay down on the pillow, watching as the clock's blue digits blinked on and off, on and off, on and ...

When she woke again in the morning, Emma was gone.

Episode 2

Prologue - Cassidy Hughes (Age 10)

Hamilton Island, Washington
   20 years ago

CASSIDY LOVED THE TWILIGHT, the last vestiges of freedom before darkness swallowed the world and she and her sister had to go home.

The sky was that beautiful shade of blue that wasn't quite blue, almost on its way to purple, giving them just enough light to play chase in the woods surrounding their neighborhood, even though their mom never wanted them in the woods so close to dark.

"Ready or not, here I come!" Jonny Conway called from home-base after counting to forty.

Cassidy crouched behind a large tree about twenty yards away, probably closer than the other three kids hiding. While the others sprinted off as far as they could go in forty seconds, Cassidy thought it better to hide closer, figuring Jonny wouldn't think to look so close.

She perked her ears above the howling wind and leaves scraping along the forest floor, a wind that only added to the spookiness of playing in the woods at night, straining to hear the sound of Jonny's footsteps. Cassidy wanted to peek around the tree but didn't dare. Jonny was eleven, the oldest of the group, and the biggest and fastest, so she was as good as caught if he spotted her.

The silence stretched, and Cassidy became more convinced that Jonny was sneaking up on her. The anticipation made her feel like her bladder might burst at any second.

Cassidy crossed her legs, wishing she hadn't drunk so much grape Kool-Aid with dinner.

A twig snapped nearby, and a chill shot up Cassidy's back as she looked back and prepared to run for home base. There was nobody behind her. Yet. But she had to get moving soon before the others made a run for home base.

Chase was like hide 'n' seek, but better. Whoever was it had to find *and* catch the hiders before they reached home base. If all the hiders made it back to home base before they were caught, the person had to be it again. However, if the seeker caught you, you were it next.

Cassidy's strategy was to stay close enough to home base to easily sneak back once Jonny went off searching for the others.

Suddenly, she heard laughter from the north, along with running. A chase was on. Jonny was running after Tommy or Eric. Somewhere in the woods, her sister, Sarah, was also hiding, and likely eying home base. Sarah, despite being Cassidy's identical twin, was faster, though Cassidy always played a smarter game.

"Safe!" the boy shouted. Cassidy peeked to see it was Eric.

Jonny turned his attention to the surrounding area to see if any of the other hiders had moved closer to home base during the chase. If he headed south, she was as good as busted. As Jonny moved closer, Cassidy was pretty sure she'd start peeing the minute she tried to run.

Crap.

She stepped out from her hiding spot. "I surrender."

Jonny ran up to her as if he thought she might run away at the last second, a strategy she had used to catch him off guard twice before, and nearly tackled her.

"Sheesh!" she shouted. "I surrendered. You didn't need to jump on me!"

"Okay." Jonny laughed. "Cassidy is it!"

"All right," Cassidy said, "I need to take a time-out to pee."

Sarah and Tommy emerged from the woods now that it was safe to do so. Sarah looked up at the darkening sky. "We should get home, Cass, it's getting late."

"No way! She's it," Jonny said. "You're not bailing now. It's her turn."

"I'm not bailing," Cassidy said. "I just have to pee. Then we'll play one more round."

"Mom's not gonna let us back out if you go home to pee now," Sarah said.

"I'm not going home to pee. I'm gonna go over there," Cassidy said, stepping deeper into the woods, looking for a spot out of sight.

One of the boys laughed, but she wasn't sure which. They all sounded sorta the same when they laughed their stupid laughs. Cassidy found a spot, made sure nobody could see her, then pulled her pants down and squatted to pee. She finished, pulled up her pants, and went back to the group.

"You took forever. You sure you weren't pooping?" Tommy was eight, the youngest of the group and chubby and slow, which made him fun to chase. He was sometimes it three or four rounds in a row, usually until someone felt sorry for him — often Sarah — and let themselves get caught.

"Ha-ha." Cassidy headed to home base. "You're so funny."

"I think we should go, Cass." Sarah's voice grew whiney as

it always did as nighttime approached. "If we're late, Mom's not gonna let us out tomorrow."

"One more game," Cassidy said. "Don't be such a goody-goody."

"I'm *not* a goody-goody."

Tommy and Eric laughed, and Cassidy cringed. She hated having to bring Sarah along when they played with the boys, especially since Jonny and Eric were two of the coolest kids on the island. Sarah always embarrassed her. Times like these, Cassidy wished she was an only child.

Cassidy leaned against the tree, buried her head into the nook of her arm, then started counting loudly. "One ... Two ... You all better run!"

She heard the others take off in every direction.

Cassidy finished counting, then scanned the darkness. The purple sky that wasn't purple had given way to black, and if it weren't for the light from the full moon above, she wouldn't be able to see anything.

"Ready or not, here I come!" she shouted, hoping she'd see Tommy somewhere and end the game quickly. She wasn't really in a rush to get home. It wasn't as if their mom would even notice if they were late. She was probably good and drunk by now, asleep in front of the TV. But she didn't want to hear Sarah whine anymore, either. So it was best to get the game over as fast as possible.

Footsteps slapped the ground behind her, and Cassidy spun around, shocked to see fat Tommy touch the tree and shout "Safe!" wearing a giant grin.

He must've been hiding, like, right behind me or something!

She growled at him, then scanned the trees for any sign of the others. Now that Tommy was safe, her next best bet was Eric, or maybe Sarah.

A shadow rushed past her about ten yards north. It was Jonny making a break for home base.

Crap, crap!

She had an angle on him and might be able to catch him if she could move fast enough. It would be pretty awesome to end the night catching the fastest player. She ran, pushing her legs as fast as she could, fire burning through her thighs and calves as she drew closer, three yards away.

Jonny's eyes widened as he looked back, his tongue sticking out playfully. He sped up, about ten yards from home base and quickly closing in, laughing.

Now I have to catch him!

Cassidy forced herself to speed up, grunting as she pumped her legs faster, quickly pulling even with Jonny, now just three feet away.

He was almost at home base.

One extra push and she launched forward, reached out, grabbed Jonny by the shoulders, and yanked him down. She was moving too fast to slow down, and rolled over, on top of him, the two of them tumbling through the leaves in a tangled knot.

They rolled to a stop just inches from home base, Cassidy straddling Jonny, who was lying there with his eyes closed. After a few seconds passed, she was certain she'd hurt him. Then his eyes opened and his gaze met hers. He opened his mouth with a giant laugh. "Good God, girl! You playing football?!" he said.

Cassidy breathed a sigh of relief and then stood and offered her hands to help him up. He took them, and she pulled him up with a big grunt.

"You're it!" she shouted, beaming proudly, secretly relieved she hadn't hurt him. She also felt herself blushing a bit, because she was pretty sure that as he stared into her eyes, he saw she had a crush on him. Of course, he was eleven and she was ten, and he was Jonny Conway and she was just a middle-class girl with an alcoholic mother, so there was no way he was gonna actually *like* her.

Jonny dusted himself off and reached toward Cassidy,

pulling a twig and leaf from her hair. He smiled tenderly. "You okay?"

"Yeah," she said, suddenly shy.

As Eric emerged from the woods, Tommy shouted, "Man, you missed it! Cassidy tackled Jonny big-time!"

"No way!" Eric said. "You got tackled by a girl?!"

"Shut up," Jonny said, "I bet she'll knock you down even faster."

"Yeah, right." Eric looked Cassidy up and down, as if insulted, though she was pretty sure she saw a bit of fear in his eyes. He glanced at the sky. "We should probably get home."

"Oh, you don't wanna get tackled by a girl?" Jonny winked at Cassidy.

She laughed.

"No," Eric said defensively. "It's just getting dark is all, and I don't want the girls to get in trouble."

"Yeah, I need to get home, too," Tommy said, coughing as he reached into his pants to pull out a pack of Marlboros. Cassidy thought he tried a bit too hard to prove himself cool because he was the youngest kid, but she wasn't about to put him on the spot if nobody else was.

Cassidy waited to hear what Jonny would say. If he wanted to stay out another hour, she would, too. Even if Sarah didn't want to.

"Yeah, we should probably head back," Jonny said. "Same time tomorrow?"

"Yeah." She agreed more eagerly than she'd intended, but covered by turning to Eric. "So I can show you up, boy."

Jonny laughed.

"Hey, where's Sarah?" Tommy took a puff off his cigarette and coughed again.

Cassidy looked around, surprised. She'd been so caught up in talking with the guys, she'd not realized that Sarah hadn't come forward, even after it was safe.

"Sarah? It's safe to come out. I got Jonny!" she yelled.

Nothing but silence.

She better not have gone home without me!

"Sarah?!" Cassidy called out into the darkness.

HER VOICE WAS MET with a crash of thunder, louder than any thunder Cassidy had ever heard. The sound was so loud, she jumped, bumped into Jonny, and held onto him. As she clung to him, the forest was suddenly ablaze with an explosion of lightning, bright and repeating like strobe lights, so bright that she had to throw her hands over her eyes.

Then all was dark and silent again. She felt awkward clinging to Jonny but didn't let go.

"What was that?" she asked.

Sarah's sudden scream shattered the silence.

"Sarah?!" Cassidy called, pulling away from Jonny, racing toward the scream.

Jonny joined her, right by her side, then in front of her, calling, "Sarah!"

Behind them, Eric and Tommy followed, and all of them yelled, "Sarah!"

Still no answer.

Cassidy raced as fast as she could to keep up with Jonny, hoping someone wasn't hurting her sister. She lost sight of Jonny for a moment, then nearly ran into him when he'd stopped dead in his tracks, staring at the ground.

Cassidy's heart froze as dread flooded her guts. She swallowed hard, then moved closer to see what Jonny was looking at.

Sarah's clothes were in a heap on the ground, but her sister was nowhere to be found.

Chapter 1 - Jon Conway

Hamilton Island, Washington
Thursday
Sept. 7
7:07 a.m.

JON SPLASHED cold water on his face in attempt to shake off his exhaustion and cool a raging erection left over from the dream he'd woken from. The last thing Jon needed was to start having sex dreams about Cassidy.

Sex dreams about Sarah were normal, regular even. Less frequent than they used to be, but even after a decade removed, she still haunted his dream world. And it was the mornings after those dreams that he woke up missing her most. He still dreamed of everything from slow kisses along Sarah's long neck, to the rhythm of their personal pushes and grunts. Mostly, he dreamed of their conversations — whispers and laughter, yelling and promises, every regretted word, and syllable left unsaid.

Despite the twins looking identical to most, there were always subtle differences that you picked up on when you got to know them. Those differences became more pronounced as Cassidy and Sarah's lives had taken divergent paths and time had exacted its toll. The pink lines on Cassidy's wrists. The look of defeat in her eyes. The sarcastic curl in her lips.

So, when Cassidy played host to Jon's sexual desires in last night's dream, he was shocked to see her. It didn't seem right to think such thoughts about Sarah's sister, as if it would offend the memory of Sarah. Nor did it seem right to Cassidy, to project his unresolved feelings for Sarah onto her.

Jon woke up hard, guilty, and unwilling to relieve himself.

He turned off the faucet and stared in the mirror, more exhausted than he should be, and wondered what it was about the island that made it feel like both home and prison. Perhaps there were too many bad memories here. Every familiar sight, sound, and person served as constant reminders, giving the memories so much more weight on native soil.

He left the bathroom and turned on the TV, shuddering at the thought of what he might see, with half his attention aimed at the screen and the other half cast on the room service menu, trying to decide what he wanted for breakfast.

Fortunately, there was nothing on the news linking him to Sarah, at least not yet. Just more about the school shooting and the memorial from the day before.

Jon tossed the menu on the table, ran his hand through his hair, and sighed, feeling like an asshole for thinking everything on the menu sounded like tired, beach town crap. He didn't want cereal or oatmeal or yogurt or smoothies, nor did he want an omelet nor pancakes nor waffles. He wanted almond-crusted French toast made with brioche or challah bread, and strawberries. Sure, they'd probably make it for him, but he'd rather just order from the menu than feel like a jerk for the rest of the day for being too demanding.

Just order what you want, man. Don't always worry about what everyone thinks.

Jon picked up the phone and asked if room service made

French toast even though it wasn't on the menu. The man on the other line said, yes, of course. Jon was glad the man didn't add, "Anything for you, Mr. Conway." Jon also asked if he could have some strawberries and a small cup of almonds. The man said, of course.

Good enough.

Jon thanked the man, hung up the phone, and waited for his breakfast, trying hard to remember the dreams he'd had before the sex ones. Whatever the dreams had been, they must've been awful. He vaguely recalled waking up screaming and seeing his covers clear across the room.

Growing up on the island, Jon often had nightmares, though he rarely remembered them. The nightmares were usually coupled with exhaustion and headaches. Just like he was feeling now.

He slept like a baby everywhere else, except, it seemed, on Hamilton Island.

Jon laughed out loud. *Sleeping like a baby* fit the description of his island sleep more than the sleep he usually got. Babies didn't sleep through the night. They woke up every few hours, often screaming. Jon laughed again, but mid-chuckle thought of the baby who was now nine, and probably his.

The dull ache inside him felt like a scream against the silence of the hotel. His fault for wanting a private floor. That was how it had to be. Jon didn't want people tiptoeing around him. That was even worse than public fawning.

This was the life he chose, and he wasn't bitching, not even to himself. Jon couldn't count the number of times he'd been out, wanting nothing more than a moment alone, when a fan started freaking out and screaming, drawing attention like bees to a hive. Sometimes, people played it cool, coming up to him and starting a regular conversation about everyday stuff, but nearly every exchange was either about his work or Hollywood gossip, and Jon didn't care to talk much about either.

Even that was better than the gazes met on the island, where he wasn't just Jon Conway of *Darkness Everlasting*, but he was also Jon Conway of *The Conways*.

There was a light knock on the door, and then a polite exchange with the attendant as he made a small show of setting the food in the middle of Jon's room. Jon tipped him $20, feeling the usual discomfort, amplified by the island. Jon had never been able to find the *just right* in his tip. Too little felt wrong, and too much felt arrogant.

The French toast looked great. Jon took a look, salivated, and got ready to sit. As he did, the hotel phone rang.

"Hello?"

A slight pause, then, "Good morning, Mr. Conway. This is Lydia, from downstairs at the front desk. I have a Cassidy Hughes on the line. I tried telling her you weren't here, but she said she knew you were. She sounds rather upset and insists you must speak to her. She said it's either on the phone now or a few minutes from now in person."

Jon sighed. "Of course, Lydia," he said. "And thank you."

Jon used the pregnant silence to shove a piece of French toast in his mouth, quickly chew, then swallow, just as Cassidy tore onto the line.

"What the fuck, asshole?"

"Good morning to you, too, Cass." Jon sank into the chair and stared off the balcony, out at the sea. He was already exhausted, four accusatory words into the conversation.

"Don't bullshit me, dickface. What the fuck did you do with Emma?"

Jon sat straight up in his chair, then launched to his feet. "What the hell are you talking about?"

Maybe thirty seconds of silence, then, "Emma's missing."

Jon said, "Are you *sh* ... *sh* ... sure?" Not knowing what to say turned his words to a stutter.

"Of course, I'm sure. You think I *wanted* to call you?" A

pause, then, "I saw the way you were looking at Emma. You know, don't you?"

Jon felt suddenly wobbly, as though the hard concrete of his world was getting wet beneath his feet. He choked, then said, "She's mine, isn't she? Why didn't anyone tell me?"

Cassidy sounded surprised. "Wow, you really didn't know?"

Jon said, "I thought Sarah left me because I slept with that model."

Cassidy snorted. "She was madder than a fucking hatter about that, but that's not why she left."

"Then, why?" Through gritted teeth he asked, "Did my family have something to do with her leaving me?"

"Don't ask questions you don't want to know the answers to," Cassidy said. "Do you think they took Emma?"

"So, they *do* know?"

"Like I said, don't ask questions," Cassidy said. Then she added, "I can't talk about it, Jon. But yes, they knew."

Jon wanted to scream. Wanted to punch something. Wanted to drive to the house and beat Warren to within an inch of his life until he spilled everything he knew, everything he had to do with this being kept from him.

"Jesus," Jon said.

"Do you think they'd take her?" Cassidy asked again.

"The Conways might do a lot of evil shit, but no, they wouldn't do that. They wouldn't have any reason. Would they?"

"I don't fucking know!" Cassidy whined. "I don't know why they do half the shit they do. All I know is Emma is missing. You're back. And I sure as hell don't believe in coincidences."

"I swear to God, I had nothing to do with this," Jon said. "I wasn't even sure Emma was mine until about two minutes ago."

"You swear?" Cassidy asked, now sobbing on the other end.

"I swear," Jon said calmly. "Have you called the police yet?"

"No, Vivian told me to call you first."

Jon shook his head at the stupidity of that advice. "Listen, Cassidy, call the police right now. I'll call Warren and see if he knows anything. Then I'll make some more calls. We will find her, Sarah."

A long pause, and then Cassidy said, "You called me Sarah."

"Sorry," Jon said.

"It's okay," Cassidy said. "I can't stop thinking about her, either. I'm gonna call the police now."

"I'll get back to you in ten minutes, one way or another. And I swear, I'm not leaving this island until we find her."

After a long pause, Cassidy said, "Okay." Then with audible pain, as though having a tooth pulled, she added, "Thank you," before hanging up.

Jon scrolled through his contacts for his brother's number, and for the first time in his life didn't smile as he pressed the name marked *Asshole*.

The phone rang twice, then Warren said, "Oh wow, a celebrity calling me before eight o'clock in the morning. To what do I owe the honor?"

"I'm not in the mood, Warren," Jon said. "Where is my daughter?"

"Your daughter?" Warren said. He couldn't even make his disbelief sound believable.

Asshole.

"Don't you dare pretend not to know," Jon growled. "You lie to me right now, I will spend a fucking lifetime making sure you regret it."

Jon could have mentioned any bits of the Conway's dirty

laundry, but went with the light touch, instead, allowing Warren's fears do most of the intimidation.

Warren pissed off Jon further by laughing again. "You get a scriptwriter to write that for you? And this early? Great delivery, Jon. Should've put that kind of emotion in your last movie. Now, you want to tell me what the hell you're accusing me of, *Brother?*"

"Emma's missing. Where is she?"

Warren laughed. "I don't know anything about the kid, but Lord knows that dumb, white trash, junkie whore can't take care of her. Call the cops. I'm sure it's so open and shut even Barney Fife and his Beachside Goons will be able to solve it in less than ten seconds. Hell, Cassidy probably sold her for drug money. If you want, I'll give you the number of the captain of Paladin. I understand you already made quite an impression on them."

"Fuck you." Jon hung up.

He stared out the window at the sea, trying to slow his rising anger and breath, before calling the one contact in his phone he knew he could turn to at a time like this — Brock Houser.

Chapter 2 - Brock Houser

Las Orillas, California
Thursday
Sept. 7
Morning …

BROCK HOUSER SAT in his car with his eyes on Bill Benedict's house.

Benedict was a slip-and-fall case seeking a payday from the insurance company of the store where he fell. Given Benedict was forty-six, an Army vet, a loving father of a six-year-old child with autism, and a husband whose wife battled breast cancer the year before, he would likely clean up in front of a jury. So, the adjuster was looking for anything they could get on the guy.

Which was why Houser was now working his nineteenth day tailing the guy, despite never seeing him do anything remotely incriminating. The man never even left his house, and the most damning evidence Houser had gathered so far was video of Benedict stepping from the front porch to collect his mail one afternoon. Other than that, he was a recluse.

Houser had exactly dick on the guy, and if he didn't get something soon, the insurance company would have flushed $600 a day right down the drain, which was fine by Houser. He didn't care for the adjuster assigned to the case at all. The guy, Victor Reynolds, had a hard-on for Benedict for no good reason, and Houser didn't want to be part of screwing over a guy who hadn't done anything wrong. So, as Houser wound down his time watching Benedict, he almost found himself hoping *not to* catch the guy doing anything.

Most insurance frauds were stupidly easy to catch. People usually got busted in one of three ways — in the act of doing things a disabled person couldn't do, posting pictures and video to their social media accounts of themselves doing things they claimed they couldn't, or getting greedy taking a second job.

Benedict wasn't doing any of these things. He used his Facebook wall to complain about the pain, depression, and not being able to work. The guy was either the real deal or the most committed faker Houser had ever seen. Houser had a good sense for these kinds of things, and he'd bet his last dollar that the guy was legit.

The other thing about insurance fraud cases, however, was that you could spin evidence any way you wanted. The adjuster didn't need airtight evidence on Benedict, just enough to sway a jury to side with the poor, embattled insurance company against the evil scammer looking for a payday on the backs of rates that the hardworking people like the ladies and gentlemen of the jury had to pay.

Houser was bored shitless. He had one eye on his iPad, flinging angry birds at green pigs and passing time, while the other stayed on the house.

Suddenly, he spotted movement in his rearview mirror.

Houser had his hand at his shoulder holster and fingers on the butt of his gun in an instant, prepared as always for someone seeking vengeance.

The figure wore a black shirt, black jeans, and a black ski mask pulled over his face. He also had black gloves and was carrying a crowbar. After slipping between the cars parked along the street behind Houser, he headed to the front door of the house next door to Benedict's.

Is this fucker actually wearing a ski mask in broad daylight? Doesn't he even see me sitting here?

Houser let go of his gun, grabbed his cell with one hand and dialed 911, then waited for dispatch to answer. With his free hand, he grabbed his video camera, popped out the video he'd been using to surveil Benedict (the client insisted on videotape, not digital) then fumbled through his center console and grabbed another tape. He slid it in, pressed play to make sure he wasn't taping over anything important, then hit record and raised the camera to catch video of the burglar.

A dispatch operator picked up, and Houser filled her in on what was going down. His time as a cop led him straight to the point.

The dispatch operator, a friendly sounding woman, asked, "What's he doing now?"

"Just broke into the house." Houser trained his camera on the front door. "You got someone coming?"

"Officers are on the way, sir."

The burglar popped out of the house a few minutes later, a black duffel bag bulging at the seams and slung over his shoulder.

"He's out." Houser turned the camera, following the guy as he sprinted across the yard to a car parked three behind Houser. The guy got inside then pulled away. "He's in a red Camry, heading east on 17th, just north of Gardenia Drive."

Houser looked at Benedict's house and figured the guy wasn't going to come outside doing gymnastics in his yard anytime soon, so he pulled from the curb and followed the burglar. Moments later, he updated the dispatcher, "He just turned south onto Greenview."

"Are you following him?"

"Yes, ma'am," Houser said. "Uh-oh, I think he spotted me, he's speeding up. But don't worry, he's not gonna lose me."

"Sir, do not chase him," the dispatcher said.

"You don't want to catch him?" Houser asked. "I'll back off when I see some cops. Until then, I'm following."

The dispatcher was silent. She must be new.

He sped up, pulling closer to the Camry. Houser hit sixty in a forty-five to keep pace. The community was on the quiet side, without much traffic, but that could change in a heartbeat if the Camry pulled onto an artery road headed toward the city.

"He's going about sixty-five, just passed Franklin," Houser updated the dispatcher.

"Sir, I must advise you not to speed."

Houser laughed. "Yeah, okay."

The dispatcher repeated her warning, but Houser ignored her, lowering his right foot. The Camry turned sharply, trying to turn onto a crossroad, but instead, slid out of control, and hit a parked Audi.

"He just crashed into a parked Audi." Houser pulled up behind the guy. "He's stalled. Should I sit here with my thumb up my ass or you got someone coming?"

"Officers are on the way," she said.

Houser looked around, "Unless you've got some new invisible cops I don't know about, I don't see, or hear, anything close by. Uh-oh. He's out and on foot. I'm gonna go get 'em."

"Sir, please let the officers handle this," the dispatcher said.

"Sure thing . . . when they get here." Houser put the camera down, then hopped from his car.

Ski Mask turned around, eyes wide as he saw Houser giving chase. Houser was six foot five, two hundred sixty pounds of muscle, an intimidating fucker standing still but hell personified when charging. A white mom and black dad made Houser the perfect shade of mocha, just dark enough to intimidate most white guys when he wanted, but not so dark he had trouble getting into places where the only non-whites welcome were on the payroll.

Ski Mask dropped his duffel and reached behind his back.

Oh, shit!

Ski Mask didn't have a gun, but he did have a blade. Houser smiled. From ten feet, the blade was a kernel of corn in a pile of shit, unless Ski Mask was a ninja. Houser pulled his gun. "Drop the knife."

The dispatcher spoke, "Sir, do you still have a visual on the suspect?"

"You could say that," Houser said, "he's waving a knife around, but I'm pretty sure I can squeeze off six shots before he reaches me. What do you think?"

Houser said this for Ski mask's benefit, not the dispatcher's, who only answered with an uncertain sigh. Houser was pretty sure she was starting to take a shine to him. Ski Mask's eyes were wide and terrified. He dropped the knife, then the bag.

"Good boy." Houser advanced, gun still drawn, ready to drop the phone in a moment's notice to either chase or fight. He didn't have to do either. A siren blurted behind him, followed by a woman's voice over the speaker. "Put the gun down, sir."

"I've gotta go now," Houser said to the dispatcher, then set the phone on the ground beside his gun, nice and slow. As two uniformed officers approached, guns drawn on him and Ski Mask, Houser turned to explain the situation, then smiled at the familiar face of Detective Stephen Chan.

"Oh, Jesus." Chan grinned. "I heard some crazy asshole was chasing a suspect around the city. Should've known it was you. What the hell are you doing here?"

"Nice to see you, too." Houser pointed toward his gun and phone. "May I?"

"Yeah." Chan nodded.

Chan and Houser came up through the academy together, working for the Ocean County Sheriff's Office. Chan was one of the few guys Houser didn't piss off during his tenure. Last he and Chan talked was about a year back, when Chan contacted Houser about a cheating spouse case Houser had been working that turned ugly.

The other cop, a short woman with auburn hair in a short ponytail and thick horn-rimmed glasses, cuffed Ski Mask as Chan grinned and shook Houser's hand. "So what, you were bored and figured you'd swing by and help us out?"

"Something like that." Houser holstered his gun and clicked "end" on the phone, now that he didn't need a recording in case shit went south and he got shot. "I was working a slip-and-fall case and saw this dumbass sneaking around in broad fucking daylight with a ski mask and crowbar, breaking into a house."

Chan's partner pulled the ski mask off, revealing a pale, teenage kid with a lip ring and a bad case of acne. His hair was bleached white, making his fuzzy, dark eyebrows look like angry caterpillars.

"Wow, he is one ugly motherfucker," Houser said.

"That asshole chased me down! I didn't do shit." Ski Mask's face twisted and reddened.

"Yeah, yeah, tell the judge." Chan's partner yanked Ski Mask off his knees and led him past them to the back of the squad car.

"That's Sgt. Vickers," Chan said. "You two would get along great. She's a charmer."

"Yeah, I can tell." Houser grinned. "I wish *I* had a partner that cool back in the day. Anyway, I've got video if you wanna see."

"Wow, you must be *really* bored. I'm surprised you didn't apprehend him, too." Chan followed Houser back to his car.

"Well, I was trying. But then you all roll up like the heroes, after I did all the work."

"You ever think about coming back? It's a lot different here than OC."

"Yeah?" Houser asked, "You guys making money now?"

"What do *you* think?"

"Then I think you know my answer," Houser said. "Besides, you know I don't play well with others. Can't stand the politics. You call me when you make chief, maybe we'll talk."

"I didn't say *I* wanna be your boss. I don't need the headache," Chan joked.

Houser opened his car, pulled out the video camera, then hit rewind. He let the tape go back a bit farther than he meant, and the video screen showed a cop in a dark alley with a prostitute blowing him.

"Whoa!" Chan said, "What the hell is that? Your home movies?"

"Whoops, didn't realize I still had that in there."

"Who is that?" Chan asked.

"Some asshole traffic cop in New Mexico who made it his mission to pull me over every goddamned day I was there during the summer."

"New Mexico? What you doing over there?"

"I go all over, man. One of the perks of working for myself. Anyway, dude kept pulling me over, saying I was going way faster than I was, giving me tickets and shit. I had enough tickets to line a litter box. Not sure why he had such a hard-on for me, so after I wrapped up business, I decided to dig into his life."

"Ah," Chan said, smiling wide. "Obviously he hadn't heard about your infamous exploits with OCSO."

"Yeah, right? Anyway, fucker was up to all kinds of fun

stuff. First, I was just looking to prove he wasn't even using the radar correctly, *which he wasn't*. Then ding-ding bonus, I caught him doing a whole heap of unsavory shit. I decided to fight the tickets and sent a copy of this video to the local news anchor the day before. Needless to say, he didn't show in court."

Houser fast-forwarded the tape to show the burglar.

"Remind me not to piss you off." Chan shook his head, still smiling.

"Like I said, I don't play well with others." Then Houser returned to his car.

~

HOUSER RETURNED to Benedict's house to find; big fat surprise, the guy was still home.

After another two hours of sitting in front of the house, Houser found himself reliving the rush of the earlier chase, then surprising himself by pondering Chan's offer. He wasn't sure if Chan was being polite or if they really needed cops, but Las Orillas seemed like a decent enough place, idiot burglars aside. A quiet, seaside town, artsy community, people with money, but without all the bullshit you'd find in Ocean County. Most of all, though, Houser missed having someone to hang out with on duty while killing the tedious boredom. Chan was one of his closest friends back in the day. Now, he spent much of his time waiting for people to do stupid shit while he stared at his iPad.

Houser had been working for himself for seven years, building his agency with three other investigators, and was now taking only the jobs he wanted to take. He was in the best position of his life, making good money — a ridiculous amount, sometimes —and providing two other investigators with regular work. But there were times when he missed his work having any real meaning beyond catching a cheating spouse or someone for insurance fraud. He rarely had the chance to help real people in need.

Sure, he helped people protect their assets and insurance companies reclaim their money, but he wasn't nailing violent criminals, solving murders, or any of the other things Chan did on a daily basis.

Of course, if you asked Chan how he felt about his job most days, he'd probably say he was frustrated they couldn't do more to help people. Annoyed that more often than not, the bad guys walked or the cops got there too late or there wasn't anything they could do to protect abused kids or spouses.

Then there was the Cecilia Ramirez case. The one that crushed him. That one that still plagued his nightmares.

No, can't go back to that.

He put his pointer on his iPad, flicked another bird at the pigs, and decided he was just fine doing this for the next decade, if need be.

After ten more minutes of bird flinging, Houser's phone rang. It was Jon Conway.

"Whatup, Jonny Hollywood?" Houser said.

"I'm never in the mood for that. And never less than now." Jon sounded pissed.

Houser laughed. There probably wasn't a rich fucker in the world he liked more than Jon. Jon was richer than all of them. He had manners, overpaid, and was always happy to take Houser exactly as he came. "Okay, *Jon*, how may I help you today?"

"You busy?"

Houser looked over at the house, then shook his head to himself. "Well, I guess it depends on your definition of busy. I've got cases coming out of my ass, but every one of them's boring as shit. You call to bring some excitement into my life?"

"Can you come to Hamilton Island?"

"Hamilton Island? I said I want excitement, not retirement. What the hell you doing back home? The old man die or something? I didn't see shit on the news about it."

"No, but there's a missing girl." After a pause, Jon added. "My daughter. How soon can you get here?"

Houser kept his questions to himself since he could tell by Jon's voice he didn't want to talk about it, at least not over the phone. "Gonna fly me first class?"

"Have I ever not?"

"No, but I like busting your balls, Jon." Houser laughed again. "I'll be on the next flight, even if it's coach, and swim across the channel if I have to. You can count on me."

"I know. That's why I'm calling," he said. "I'm staying at the Sands of Time Hotel."

"Anything else I should know? Maybe look into while flying?"

"No," he said. "See you in a few hours. Just keep the daughter thing to yourself, of course."

"Of course," Houser said.

"Thank you."

"You're welcome. See you soon." Houser hung up, then turned to the teddy bear in the cop uniform riding shotgun. "Well, buddy, we said we were bored. Shit's about to get interesting again."

Chapter 3 - Milo Anderson

Hamilton Island, Washington
  Thursday
  Sept. 7
  10:24 a.m.

HELLER TURNED FROM THE WHITEBOARD, *toward the classroom — face clammy and eyes bloodshot, hands shaking as he turned his head back and forth.*

He looked down at his desk again, hands on either side of his brief-case, then pulled out a pistol.

Amber Riley screamed as students gasped around her.

Heller aimed the gun and fired, shooting Tommy Hopkins in the face.

Jessica ran toward him, eyes wide like her mouth.

Milo wanted to protect her, but Heller was faster.

Milo tried to speak, but the gunshot murdered his voice and Jessica. Blood pooled across her powder-blue sweater.

Manny was shot in the stomach, lying on the carpet, twitching, eyes glassy.

Heller came toward Manny, gun shaking in his hand. He paused, stared at Manny with hollow eyes, kneeled and whispered something to him.

Then he turned to the whiteboard, pointing at the word "Eleven" with the barrel of his gun.

He parted his lips and shoved the gun inside his mouth.

Heller pulled the trigger, and Milo screamed.

MILO SHOT FORWARD from his mattress, screaming, wondering if he would ever be able to dream anything else ever again. It was hard enough to have witnessed the horror of what happened, but he wasn't sure how much longer he could go on seeing the visions played out over and over every time he fell asleep.

He swung his legs from bed and threw the covers toward the footboard, shaking his head. This couldn't be real. Alex's goofy dad couldn't have gone Columbine. It didn't make any sense.

Milo went to the bathroom, took a piss, and wondered if today's misery would be any dimmer than the day before. He sure as hell hoped so because the school was reopening its doors tomorrow, and Milo was damned sure he was gonna have a bad day.

He scratched his arms, annoyed that his stupid allergies were coming early. They seemed to itch even more than they had the day before.

Milo had thought skipping the funeral would make him feel better, would keep him from staring icy reality in the eyes. He couldn't bear the thought of seeing Jessica, or the others, frozen forever. But it wasn't just that. Milo could have forced himself to look inside the coffin. It was everyone else who would tear him apart. Despair he could deal with, as long as no one spoke to him. Once they did, Milo would break.

Milo perked his ears but didn't hear Other Mother at all. He could always tell when she was in the house, even when she was quiet. The house had a different feel and sound when others were in it. For the moment, Milo was alone.

He crossed his room, opened the door, and spied the pink Post-it stuck on it. He peeled it off and read her note:

IN SEATTLE *with Janet and Teena. There's $50 downstairs on the kitchen counter. Go out and do something fun or order a pizza. Whatever you want. I won't be home any later than 4:00 or so. Take care of your-self. Maybe order a movie from PayPerView? Whatever you want, it's okay. xoxo*

MILO HATED the X's and O's, and hated Beatrice for writing them. She could be gone a whole month with Janet and Teena for all he cared. That would save him from having to play nice and pretend like they were some kinda happy family.

Was it even worth leaving his room? He sat at his desk and opened the lid to his Mac, then logged on to his LiveLyfe page, the social media site many of the kids flocked to once Facebook became their parents' number one hangout.

He updated his status:

GOING THROUGH HELL.

MILO SCROLLED through his news feed, looking through his friends' posts and videos and pics, pausing at an entry from Leslie Sissom, another junior at Hamilton Island K-12.

THIS IS AMERICA, *where you can find a gun easier than mental health services.*

. . .

MILO GAVE it a High-Five by clicking on the icon of the open palm, then continued to scroll, wiping his tears as he reached the bottom and waited for LiveLyfe to load older posts to the feed. He moved his cursor to the LiveLyfe search box and typed, "Hamilton shooting," then stared at the list that swallowed the page, scrolling until he hit the fourth choice — Hamilton K-12 Shooting Survivors Group.

Milo clicked on the link, then started reading through the posts from the kids at his school, a mix of names he recognized, screen names he didn't, and names involving clever plays or words involving either 420, genitals, some racist term, or often a combination of all three.

ONE DAY *I'll leave the island, but every time I hear a firecracker snap or a balloon pop, I'll see blood and probably jump.*

WHAT A PSYCHO, *shooting up a school like that. Good thing Heller's dead.*

I HEARD THE GUNSHOT, *then saw the empty expression on Mr. Heller's face, just before he pulled the trigger.*

MR. HELLER KILLED MY BFF. *I HOPE HE ROTS IN HELL!!!!*

ALL THE ASSHOLES *on the news are asking, why did this happen on Hamilton Island? They blame us for not taking more precautions, but how can you prevent crazy?*

. . .

IF SCHOOLS *around the country can do metal detectors on kids, they ought to do it on the teachers, too!*

I KNEW *Heller was a bit too 'nice' and 'squeaky clean.' Makes you wonder what else he was up to?*

MILO KEPT SCROLLING, getting angrier as he read – his rage at war with his swelling sadness. There were a few legitimate fears and thoughts about the students who died. In a school as relatively small as Hamilton, everyone pretty much knew everyone else. The grief may have been real, but that didn't give anyone the right to act as if they were there or stand on the shoulders of the victims so they could gaze out at the rest of the world. Christopher Swart, the guy who said he'd always have nightmares, was the only one on the page who was even in the room. Roland Wilder, the asshole who commented on Heller's empty expression, wasn't even in the same grade. And then some of the names he didn't even recognize. Probably trolls just looking to hit the hornet's nest to see what comes out.

One troll in particular stuck out, a name that despite seeming like a real name, struck him as made up — Cody Brandt. He'd posted:

MR. HELLER WAS SCREAMING *at everyone, telling them to kiss the floor as he waved the gun in the air. His eyes were crazy, and he was drooling like a dog.*

THE POST MADE Milo so mad he felt like punching his laptop.

Milo typed:

UNLIKE YOU, *I was there. I was the only one who was there, other than Manny, who saw Heller shoot himself.*

THERE WAS A DING, just seconds later. A private message.

CODY BRANDT: *You were there?*

MILO A.: *Yes, who are you? You shouldn't be making stuff up.*

CODY BRANDT: *Someone who thinks there's more to this story.*

MILO A.: *What do you mean?*

CODY BRANDT: *Did anyone talk to you yet about what happened?*

MILO TOOK A SECOND TO THINK, mentally scrolling through the long list of reporters, police department and Paladin officers, all asking a similar series of questions, with varying degrees of compassion. He wrote:

MILO A.: *Of course. Reporters, cops, everyone. What do you think?*

CODY BRANDT: *What did you tell them?*

. . .

MILO A.: *The truth, unlike you.*

THERE WAS A LONG PAUSE. Milo was ready to log off and leave the asshole behind, when there was another ding.

CODY BRANDT: *Did Mr. Heller say anything to you before he killed himself?*

MILO A.: *No, but he said something to my friend, Manny.*

CODY BRANDT: *Then your friend is in danger.*

MILO A.: *WTF do you mean?*

THERE WAS NO RESPONSE, not then, or for the five minutes Milo spent waiting, scratching his arm and cursing his goddamned allergies. Cody Brandt had crept under his skin, along with the pollen.

A loud knock on the door downstairs made Milo jump from his chair.

He went to the window, slipped his fingers into the slats of the blinds, then pulled them open enough to see outside. Alex.

Milo turned from the window, then collapsed onto his bed.

Fuck him and his father.

He could stand out there all damned day for all Milo cared.

He hoped it rained.

Milo closed his eyes and decided he wasn't ready to wake up today.

Chapter 4 - Alex Heller

Alex knocked on Milo's door, feeling exposed and alone standing on Milo's doorstep, as if behind every closed window on the street, prying eyes peered from barely opened curtains and blinds.

There he is, the son of the murderer.

Come on, Milo. Open the door. I know you're in there.

He didn't know if Milo was home, but figured he was since his stepmom's SUV wasn't in the driveway. Milo's dad usually kept the sedan in the garage, but Alex doubted his father was home, either. Never was. And if he were, Alex wasn't horribly concerned that Milo's dad would freak out nearly as much as his Other Mother. Milo's dad was laid back, and a nice guy. Why he'd married Beatrice was beyond Alex. Sure, she was hot. But there were tons of hot women who weren't blue ribbon bitches.

Alex knocked again, listening at the door to see if he could hear music or the TV. Nothing but silence.

Alex grabbed his cell and called Milo.

It went to voicemail.

"Come on, man. I know you're home. Please, come to the

door. I want to talk. I want to tell you how sorry I am about my dad. I'm just as freaked as anyone. Please, Milo."

Alex hung up and waited a few minutes at the door to give Milo time to listen to the voicemail, maybe change his mind and come to the door. He waited nearly five minutes before turning from the door and heading back to his bike.

He rode, uncertain where to go. Maybe to Katie's? But her mom might not react well. Almost losing your daughter to her boyfriend's father had to be the kind of thing that would make Alex an unwelcome guest for the foreseeable future.

Maybe he'd go to the ferry, get on, and never come back. He could go somewhere and start over in a place where he wasn't known as the son of Roger Heller, *murderer!* But he couldn't just up and leave his mother and sister. They needed him more than ever. They were alone, left to pick up the pieces and start over, attempting to rebuild their lives.

How do you start over when the world is pulled out from under you?

Having nowhere else to go, and not daring to reach out to any of his friends, Alex decided to go home. As he passed the Paladin security truck parked in front of his house, he saw Katie's car in the driveway, pushing his heart to a rapid thud in his chest. Finally, someone to talk to. Not just someone, but his girlfriend – assuming she was still allowed to see him.

Or wanted to.

He hopped off his bike before he even hit the brakes, then kicked the stand and ran inside his house. Katie was sitting in the living room with his mom and Aubrey, talking. Her eyes were red and so was her nose. She held a fat cluster of used tissues in the palm of her right hand.

Katie stood up, then came to Alex. She met his gaze for a long moment, then hugged him.

At first, the embrace seemed obligatory, as though part of her was afraid to fully commit. Was this a sign of new distance between them? Maybe she was getting ready to break up with him. He squeezed her tighter, closing his eyes, trying his best not to cry. His hands found her thick, long, brown hair, and he stroked her mane through their embrace. He whispered, "God, I missed you."

The warmth of her embrace was a blanket after the icy nothing that had swallowed his life since Friday. She smelled so good, too, like that raspberry soap she got from The Body Shop.

Alex parted before he allowed himself to cry, then met her eyes. This time she didn't look away as she wiped her tears away. "Your mom wanted me to tell her exactly what happened on the day of the shooting," she said.

Alex felt his stomach drop. "Oh."

"Do you want me to tell you?"

Alex didn't know what to say. He'd heard the unbelievable details on the news from police statements based on witness accounts. He'd watched the constant replays on TV of the security camera footage of students running through the halls, screaming. Would he learn anything new? Would hearing the details from Katie somehow make things make sense? Alex looked at his mom.

She nodded and patted the couch beside her. "I think you need to hear this."

Alex sat next to his mom while Katie sat on the connecting love seat to their right and told them what happened, starting with how he was late to class and finally arrived looking disheveled, then how he wrote the number "Eleven" on the whiteboard.

As Katie spoke, Alex stared at his little sister, lying in her playpen, playing with her stuffed Eeyore doll, biting its tail, oblivious to the three people discussing her father and his horrible acts that would change the island, and their lives, forever.

"He looked so … different. He wasn't himself. Like he'd been up all night, or … drinking or something."

"Dad, drink? No way." Alex shook his head. "The hardest thing he ever drank was iced tea."

"It's all so weird. This is the kind of thing you see on the news, not something that happens to people you know. Not to your friends." Katie stared at Alex, though her gaze looked like it was somewhere in Seattle. "I shouldn't have run. Maybe Jessica would be alive, or maybe Manny would be here, instead of a hospital bed, if I'd stayed put. Maybe I could've talked your dad out of …" Katie's voice started to crack.

Alex got up and moved beside Katie, hugging her, as her voice finally broke and she surrendered to sobbing.

His mom stood, tears streaming her cheeks. "I'll be back." Then she headed up the stairs.

As Alex held Katie, he felt torn, as if he should be upstairs comforting his mother. Truth was, he didn't know how to comfort her, or if it were even his place. She was his mom, after all. She'd always been a strong woman, independent, and part of Alex felt she needed to feel strong now more than ever before. If she knew he'd seen her weaknesses, it might make her feel even worse.

He stayed on the couch, holding Katie.

She pulled away, wiped her eyes, then asked for more tissues.

Alex grabbed the box his mom had been using and handed it to Katie.

She blew her nose then met his gaze. "Does 'Eleven' mean anything to you? Do you know why he wrote that?"

Alex racked his brain, trying to think of any significance the number held for his dad, or maybe their family. Other his dad's birthday was in November, the eleventh month, Alex couldn't think of anything that stood out, much less rose to the importance of being the last thing he communicated to the world before opening fire on his students.

"I have no idea," Alex said. "They didn't mention that on the news. It's weird."

"I know. Usually, he'd write something on the board before class, and then he'd talk about the subject. Sometimes, he'd even do it creatively, starting with a word or phrase that didn't seem to have anything to do with the story he was going to tell, and then in the end, he'd come back to it, and you'd be sitting there thinking what a genius he was."

"Yeah, he was."

Aubrey giggled at something apparently only she could see, momentarily distracting Alex and Katie. In that moment, conversation stalled and an awkward silence sank between them. Alex had no idea what to say. Finally, he cleared his throat and managed, "So, does your mom hate me?"

"No, not at all." Katie shook her head. "She told me to give you her love. She feels horrible about what happened."

"What about you?"

"I could never hate you." Her gaze locked onto his. "I just … I just feel awful, like I want to somehow take all this away, make it not happen. It's so tragic. For everyone."

"Yeah." Alex watched his sister play and wondered what his mother was doing upstairs. Was she crying? Was she just freshening up? He wanted to find out but didn't want to move from Katie.

"Milo hates me," Alex said. "He had a huge crush on Jessica. We were planning a surprise party for her at Milo's house for her birthday, and he was gonna tell her then."

"Oh, God," Katie said, fresh tears flooding her eyes. "He must be devastated. Have you talked to him … you know, since?"

"I called. I even went to his house; that's where I just was. But he's avoiding me."

"You want *me* to talk to him?"

Alex hadn't even considered that, but the idea of sending his girlfriend to smooth things over didn't seem too great an idea. "I dunno. You just might remind him of Jessica."

"Yeah, maybe."

"Did you go to any of the funeral services?" Alex asked.

"I didn't go to the big one. I went to the private ones for Jessica and Miss Hughes. I can't believe that Miss Hughes got shot, too. She had the most adorable little girl. I feel so awful."

They'd both had Miss Hughes for English the year before, and she was one of Alex's favorite teachers of all time. Not only was she beautiful, she was the nicest teacher he'd ever had. She truly cared about her students. Alex had only met her daughter once, on Take Your Child to Work Day, but he remembered how sweet she was, and how much she looked like her mom.

"What's gonna happen to her daughter?" Alex asked.

"I dunno. I saw the girl with Miss Hughes' twin sister at the funeral. Maybe she's gonna take care of them. I also saw Jon Conway with them."

"Really? How does he know them?"

"Everyone knows everyone on the island, I figure," Katie said. "I think they're the same age, so they probably grew up together. What's going on with, um ... your dad's funeral?"

"I dunno," Alex said. "Mom's not saying much. I think she's still waiting for the medical examiner's office to release his body."

"They *still* haven't released it? How long do these things take?"

"I dunno, but I know she's upset about it. But I figure the longer it takes the better. God only knows what kind of media circus there will be when we bury him. *If* we bury him. Hell, mom might not even want to; who knows? I think people might lose it if we bury dad in the island's only cemetery, where his victims are buried."

"Oh, yeah." Katie sighed. "They're gonna be all over it, along with the media, and harassing you all."

Alex's mom appeared behind them, her hair pulled back in a ponytail, and her face fresher, like she'd splashed some water on it.

"I need to get out of the house for a bit. Would you mind looking after Aubrey?"

"Sure, no problem." Alex stood and followed his mother to the door.

Katie followed. "How about I make you two dinner when you come back, Mrs. Heller?"

Alex's mom smiled, though there was something off about it that sent a creeping concern through Alex. She looked somewhere between anger and something else Alex couldn't quite place.

"Is everything okay?" Alex asked.

"Yeah, I just need to take a drive and calm my nerves."

She kissed Alex on the cheek, said goodbye, and left in a big enough rush that she forgot to kiss Aubrey goodbye.

Aubrey, seeing her mom race out the front door, started crying.

Alex ran to his sister, picked her up from the playpen, then went outside to try to catch up with his mom before she left. He was too late. His mom's car was already halfway down the street, as Aubrey wailed for her mommy.

Chapter 5 - Cassidy Hughes

Hamilton Island, Washington
   Thursday
   Sept. 7
   Morning ...

CASSIDY SAT ALONE in Chief Brady's office, hating the fucker for leaving her alone when she needed help the most. It was like he was doing it just to make her sweat.

Not like that had never happened before. Asshole cops were always the same. At least every other time she'd been made to beg for water or sit for far too long under harsh fluorescents. Today, she had walked in voluntarily, though. This was bullshit.

She hadn't done anything wrong. They were making her feel like a criminal. Like always. Meanwhile, she needed help. Fucking Brady. At least he was better than the former chief, Walter GODDAMN Benson, who had made her life miserable for nearly ten years before Brady finally took over.

Cassidy tried to count the number of times Chief Benson had dragged her ass into the station, both legitimate and horse shit, but was embarrassed to realize she had no idea. Might've been fifteen, but it could have easily been thirty. There was a stretch, about nine years back, not too long after her short stint at Promises Kept Rehabilitation Center, when it seemed like Cassidy was getting dragged down to the station every other week.

She stared out the window at the nasty gloom hovering over the island. Why in the hell she had ever returned? The island was miserable, always had been. Hamilton Island wasn't just filled with the haves and have-nots, it was haves and never-gonna-gets, no matter what.

If only she'd stayed in Seattle after she got out of rehab. She'd even been offered a catering gig that would've paid the bills. But she'd come back to the island for Sarah. Then stayed for Emma.

Cassidy sucked on her tongue, trying not to cry, knowing she'd be pissed enough to punch walls if Brady came in the room to see her red-faced and swollen.

She sniffed and swallowed hard. At least it wasn't Benson. Most of the island had hated the previous chief, but that was only because he was a hard-ass. Unfair to Cassidy or not, hauling her in was a part of his job. She was a junkie, and he knew it. Junkies did whatever they needed to do to find their next fix and weren't exactly model citizens. That was bad enough on the mainland, but it was a fucking cancer on an island, and Cassidy was always smart enough to get it, even if she wasn't smart enough to steer herself from the wrong side of the road.

Brady was a kiss-ass, though, which was exactly why most of the island loved him. It was easy enough for Benson to get replaced when the new chief had the Conways' shit on his nose. Brady had always been soft on the Conways and had even been a part of Jon's merry crew of dickheads ever since seventh grade or so. An old memory wrinkled the corner of Cassidy's mouth – Brady and Jon getting caught making fruit bombs in seventh grade, maybe eighth. Jon got off with a slap. Brady swallowed a three-day suspension.

Cassidy hadn't been to the police station a single time since she'd gotten sober again, and it was an Eiffel Fucking Tower of irony she'd be in again just one day after she fell off the wagon. All Cassidy wanted was to help Emma, but part of her thought, or feared, the exchange would turn into a sour lesson on recent island history. After all, she had a missing child. And Brady had barely been able to say hello before leaving her alone in the office.

She wiped her brow, then turned toward the door as she heard it open behind her.

Brady entered his office with a half-smile, dropped a fat manila folder on the top of his desk, plopped into his seat, then turned toward her. "Hi, Cassidy." His smile seemed genuine enough. "I'm sorry to keep you waiting. Tons of stuff happening on the island, all of it sudden. Paladin's helping, but with just the three of us on day shift, we're all chicken, no head."

Cassidy was surprised by Brady's gentle voice. She hadn't had an actual conversation with him in maybe five years, and hadn't seen much of him, save for a few times in passing, and once when he happened into The Shipwreck about six months ago.

Brady pulled a notepad from the corner of his desk, scattered with scribbles, and turned it to a clean sheet. He moved his gaze from the fresh page to Cassidy. "How long has Emma been missing?"

"I dunno. I woke up this morning, and she was gone. Last time I saw her was last night when I put her to bed."

He looked down, moved his pen across the page, then turned his attention back to Cassidy. "What time was that?"

"I dunno, maybe nine p.m. I'm not sure."

"So, she could have disappeared last night?"

Cassidy swallowed. "I suppose that's possible."

Writing, not looking at her, he asked, "Where were you last night, after you put her to bed?"

"Home, with Emma and my mom."

"All night?"

"Yes, all night."

Brady scribbled for another few seconds, then looked up. "You sure?"

She hated the way his right eye seemed to home in on her, matching his rising brow.

"Yes, I'm sure. My mom was sleeping her wine off to *Seinfeld*. I fell asleep not too long after that. When I woke in the morning, Emma was gone." Cassidy wasn't sure if she was sweating through the lie or not and wasn't brave enough to check the dew on her brow. She held Brady's stare without a quiver and found herself distractedly tracing the scar on her left wrist with her right thumb, both obscured from Brady by his desk.

"Emma ever done anything like this before?"

"What, disappear? No, Kevin, she hasn't! What kind of question is that? Emma didn't just get up and run away. I wouldn't be here if she did. I'd be out looking."

Brady shook his head. "It's possible. The girl just lost her mother, after all. You don't know the power of grief. She could've done anything. Did you check Sarah's house?"

"Yes, I went over there right before I came here," she said.

"I'm sorry," he said. "I didn't mean it like that."

"It's fine. No, Emma's never done anything like this before. And yes, she's hollow as a ghost. But being sad would keep that girl inside *with us*, not out of the house, wandering the island." She could feel the tears leaving her eyes and hated allowing Brady to see her vulnerable and in need of his help. "I think she's in trouble. I don't know what else to say, except that I can feel it. And I need your help."

"Okay." Then he did something Cassidy never pictured him doing. Brady opened both his palms, extended them across his desk, and invited Cassidy to lay hers inside the cradle.

She didn't want to, but surrendered anyway, her hands shaking as she set her pink scars face-down just above his fingers.

"Everything will be okay," Brady promised. "We'll do everything we can to help."

Brady then went over all the details with her, asked her what Emma was wearing last, and if she had a picture of the girl. She hadn't thought to bring a photo and felt like an idiot. But then she remembered that she had a photo of Emma, taken just last week, on her cell phone. She pulled it up on her screen. "Here. Will this work?"

"Great," Brady said. "Can I take this to our tech guy and get him to upload it to our system?"

"Sure."

Brady was out the door before she thought about her phone history and calling the dealer last night.

Shit.

She waited patiently for Brady to come back, hoping like hell he wouldn't be digging through her phone without permission.

He'd have to ask for something like that, right?

No, you're a suspect now. They can search anything they want, sister. Plus, you handed it to him, so he can use anything he finds.

Shit. Shit.

She kept her eyes on the nasty, gray outside while collecting her breath, trying to calm the inner fear and the voice of the addict in her brain.

Her addict had been on its best behavior while Brady had sat on the other side of his desk, but it came out to play the second he left for a moment.

When are you going to feed me?

Cassidy ignored its cry.

Like always, it got louder, pulling her into the usual argument.

Come on, it's not like you're hurting anyone.

Ah, starting with the biggest pile of bullshit first.

Cassidy had done enough damage to herself, and everyone around her in one form or another, during her repeated trips down addiction's road. Yes, she'd slipped last night, but she had to be strong enough to get past that. Once she found Emma, she would call her sponsor, get to a meeting, dump the pills, and get right. If last night taught her anything, it was that she couldn't slip. Not now, when people truly needed her.

One slip, and Emma was gone.

She couldn't help but feel responsible, that perhaps if she were sober and awake, or sober enough to wake up if she heard Emma being taken or walking out, Emma would be safe now.

But, no. She'd caved to the addict. Now, she was paying with a headache that wouldn't go away, and her niece was missing.

What the hell have I done?

If they had your problems, they'd do it, too.

Okay, maybe the addict hadn't started with the biggest pile.

Everyone had problems, not just her. But some people managed to take care of their problems without resorting to pills. Pills were lighter fluid on problems: a blazing inferno of sabotage. Cassidy had made that excuse — that other people did pills to cope — a million times during the depths of her addiction. Yet, once she'd been clean a week, some of life's biggest problems started fading on their way to nothing.

Playing victim could give anyone a convenient excuse to self-medicate. Cassidy's mom had been doing it for years with alcohol.

You've already kicked it, Cassidy. You proved you can stop any time you want. One more pill won't kill anyone. Might even help you think more clearly. Help you find Emma.

Ah, there it was. Her addict's best friend and closest compatriot. Denial.

Cassidy told her addict to fuck off, and it did, but not without leaving the craving behind. It hadn't been there so much when she woke, but now it was growing. The irritability swelled inside her. Then came the shakes, the sweats, the stewing sickness in her stomach. She wasn't sure what parts were anxiety and what parts were craving. In either case, she knew of a fix, just waiting for her at home.

Not now.

She had to help Emma first.

Cassidy turned from the window and caught her reflection in the glass door of Brady's bookcase, and hoped she didn't look half as ghostly, or a quarter as sweaty, as she appeared.

The door opened behind her, and Brady entered the office. He sat in his desk and widened his eyes. "You okay? You look worse than when I left." He pulled three tissues from a pastel-colored box, then handed them across the desk to Cassidy, along with her phone.

"Thank you." She slipped her phone back into her purse. "I'm fine. Just upset, and worried."

"I understand," Brady said. "We got the picture uploaded to our website, sent out to the local news and the state's missing child system."

"Oh, God, we're gonna be all over TV?"

"Maybe. But you want to find Emma, right?"

"Yeah," Cassidy rubbed her wrist again and imagined the media spotlight shining brightly on her.

DRUG ADDICT TWIN *sister of slain teacher loses child!*

. . .

SHIT, *shit, shit.*

Brady had been looking at Cassidy with kinder eyes than usual, but after he returned with her phone, he had a different look to him. A suspicious look reminding her a little of Benson.

"I promise we'll make this our top priority, and I'll call you immediately if anything comes up." He handed her his card. "That's my cell phone, Cassidy. Don't be afraid to call for anything, okay? What number can I reach you at?" He handed her a pen and pad of paper. "Will you be home?"

"I'm going to meet up with Jon Conway." She wrote her number down and passed the tablet back to Brady. "He's going to help me look around the neighborhood and make some calls and stuff."

"Good. The Conways are very resourceful," Brady said. "Like I said, we have limited resources, but I've got two officers on it. I also reached out to Paladin to pull CCTV footage from your street to see if we can find anything. Additionally, Paladin has harbor guards out searching the Sound. They've also set up a task force at the port, searching the cars of anyone leaving. If someone has taken her, they're not going to get off the island."

"What if someone already took her off the island last night? Do you think we'll find her?" Cassidy asked, afraid like hell that Brady would say no. Cops never promised things they couldn't deliver, right? And yet, here she was, asking him to do just that.

"We'll find her." Brady met and held her gaze. "I promise."

Cassidy left his office, hoping that this would be the one time she could count on the police. And then a new fear rose to the surface. Would the CCTV footage catch her in the lie that she'd stayed home?

Chapter 6 - Liz Heller

Hamilton Island, Washington
  Thursday
  Sept. 7
  Afternoon …

LIZ HAD to leave the house.

She couldn't stand looking at Katie and feeling the overwhelming guilt, knowing her husband had planned to shoot the girl.

Before finding his list, which she hid in the bottom of her bathroom cabinet, she'd tried to tell herself the shooting was some kind of freak accident. That something must've happened to Roger to cause him to snap and shoot his students. Maybe he'd been given drugs by someone or something. None of it made sense otherwise.

He didn't even own a gun, so far as she knew. As much as she tried to think her husband was incapable of murdering anyone, much less the children he taught — he loved teaching, for Christ's sake! — there was no denying what the list implied. A list that was in his handwriting. A list including the students he murdered. It was deliberate and, even more frightening, planned.

Since all the computers in her house had been confiscated, Liz had to find somewhere else to discover what was on Roger's flash drive. And this wasn't the kind of thing she could take to a friend's house, if she even had any friends since Friday. Nobody had reached out to her. The only phone calls she got were from the media. She had to find somewhere else to use a computer. Somewhere that wouldn't attract attention.

Liz drove to the library, hoping she could use their computers to see, praying there wouldn't be anything on the flash drive that might raise the suspicions of anyone walking behind her.

She wasn't yet sure what she'd do with the list, or with the flash drive. She knew she should turn it over to the investigators, but some part of her, most of her, couldn't. At least not until she knew what was on it.

Would it be evidence to clear Roger's name or something to indict him?

Liz parked the car in front of the Hamilton Island Public Library and scanned the parking lot. There were maybe twenty cars, meaning there was a good chance she'd be seen by someone she knew inside. That was the last thing she wanted. She couldn't handle seeing anyone now, whether they offered condemnation or sympathy. She just wanted to get to a computer station and see what was on the flash drive.

She stepped from the car, slipping the drive into her purse, and headed inside the library. As she walked toward the front doors, she took notice of the many Paladin closed-circuit television cameras in the parking lot, and no doubt the library. She'd never really given much thought to the way the security firm had turned the island all Big Brother several years ago, until now, when she had something to hide.

Nancy Altaire, an older woman who used to volunteer at the school, sat behind the desk where Liz would "rent" a computer by showing her library card. Though they'd never worked directly together, there was no way Nancy wouldn't recognize her immediately. And if she didn't, the name on the card would give her away.

Liz squared her shoulders as she approached. "Hi."

Nancy looked like she'd just been caught saying a filthy word. Then she plastered a big fake smile on her face, as though she didn't know exactly who Liz was or what her husband had done. "Hi. How can I help you?"

"I'd like to use a computer." Liz passed her library card across the counter.

"Okay." She directed Liz to a table with eight computers, four per side. The computer station was smack in the middle of the library, with a clear view of the front desk and of the rear of the library where some people were sitting at long tables, studying or doing work.

Liz was surprised to see only one person on a computer, an older man who seemed focused on his work. She looked around, didn't see anyone in the immediate area, and took a seat on the opposite side of the table. Thank God for the privacy screens on the monitors. She'd be able to work in relative anonymity, assuming someone didn't come right up behind her or sit too close. The security camera above her was at such an angle that it couldn't see what was on the computer. At least, she didn't think so.

She looked around the library again, seeing familiar faces, but so far, no one had seen her … yet. But every second she wasted made her presence more noticeable. She reached into her purse, retrieved the flash drive, then slid it into the USB port on the front of the PC. After a moment, a folder icon popped up. She opened it.

Inside the folder she found more than one hundred other folders, all with names and dates stretching back at least three years. A chill ran through her when considering that Roger had been up to something so secretive for three years.

What the hell? Three years?

She clicked on the first folder in the series, the earliest created and almost three years to the day. The folder prompted a password.

Shit.

She didn't have time to guess at passwords, nor did she want to enter the wrong password and trigger any sort of auto delete procedure, though she wasn't even sure if that was possible or just something from the movies.

Liz closed the password prompt and clicked on another folder, then another, each one asking for a password.

She kept going down the list, and started jumping around, skipping folders, clicking at random and hoping one would be unprotected.

Someone sat down two computers to the left of Liz, an older woman she didn't recognize.

Liz edged herself closer to the computer screen, leaning a bit to her side to block the woman's view without being too obvious, also trying to hide her face, considering it was all over the news. But as Liz leaned one way, Nancy passed by to her right, carrying a book toward the back of the library while glancing over suspiciously. God, she hoped Nancy wouldn't come over.

She didn't, but as she walked, she kept turning and staring.

Liz turned her attention back to the computer. Did the library have a way of recording what she was doing on the computer or the contents of the flash drive? Her heart thundered at the thought.

Nancy put the book on a shelf and then walked back to her station.

Liz kept searching for an unprotected folder. Not having any luck, she decided to just click on the final folder, with a date of last Tuesday. She was surprised when it opened.

Inside the folder was a video file named "c-7913.mp4."

She looked around to make sure nobody was paying attention, then pressed play.

The screen was black at first, and for a moment, Liz wondered if the video wasn't working. She heard a loud shuffling sound, then reached out and turned the volume down on the speakers, looking around again. The woman to her left looked at her, then back at her computer.

As Liz turned back to the screen, she saw the reason the screen was dark, the video was being recorded in the woods.

What the …?

Then Roger said, "Just inside this cave."

Cave?

The only caves she knew of on the island were on the north end, fenced off.

She kept watching, wondering what Roger was doing on the north side, and even more so, what he was doing in caves.

The screen went pitch-black again for a moment, and a camera flash or flashlight illuminated the inside of the cave.

"Just ahead," Roger whispered, as he navigated his way through a tunnel until he reached an opening.

"There they are." He aimed the camera into the darkness, and the screen went black again. But he must've realized he was too far away for the camera to capture the light because the picture brightened again and showed two nude bodies face down in the dirt. They looked like men, though one might have been a woman.

Corpses.

Her heart sped up as she looked around, praying no one had seen the screen.

Nancy spoke to a Paladin security guard then pointed at Liz.

The guard looked her way.

Oh, shit.

Liz started to panic as the guard approached her. He was about thirty yards away.

Oh, shit. Oh, shit. Oh, shit.

Her hand hovered next to the flash drive, ready to yank it out the moment the guard drew closer, but she wanted to see what was on the screen. Had to see what the hell Roger was filming in secret.

Roger's face appeared in the video, "As I said in the last video, here's the proof."

Proof? Of what?

Roger reached down to turn one of the bodies over.

The guard was now ten yards away and getting closer.

What is he trying to show?

The Paladin guard was now just a few seconds away.

The video footage bounced and shook as Roger fumbled with the camera and started to bring it back up to reveal whatever it was he was trying to show.

"Mrs. Heller?" The guard was now just on the other side of the table and about to walk around to her side.

Liz yanked the flash drive from the computer and palmed it, clicking the browser window to restore as the guard rounded the table.

"Yes?" Liz smiled, her heart making a new home in her throat.

The guard, a thin and serious-looking young man with cold, blue eyes, looked down at the computer and then at her. "Ma'am, I need you to come with me."

Liz tried to bury her rising panic, telling herself that everything was okay. There was no way Paladin knew she had a flash drive, much less what was on it. But she'd never been very good at lying to herself. "What's wrong?"

"Please, come outside. There's something you need to see."

Her fear suddenly switched from being busted with the flash drive to something having happened to Alex or Aubrey. A knot formed in her throat at the thought of more tragedy.

She stood, grabbed her purse, and as the guard led the

way, slipped the flash drive into her front pants pocket. As they approached the library exit, Liz could feel the stares boring into her. Her anonymity was gone, taken by the guard at her side. There was no way she could return to the library today, or maybe even tomorrow, without attracting unwanted scrutiny.

As they reached the doorway, Nancy glared from her station, as if she'd somehow defended the library's sanctity against the wife of a murderer. Liz swallowed as they passed through the doors and went out into the parking lot, where she saw why the guard asked her to follow him.

The front window of her blue Honda Odyssey had been spray-painted with red lettering. One single, large, damning word.

MURDERER!!

Chapter 7 - Jon Conway

Thursday afternoon …

THERE WERE parts of Hamilton Island and Washington State that were as beautiful as anywhere else on the planet — and having spanned more than his share of the globe, Jon would know — but most times the weather was cold and windy. Though the Northwest had a reputation for constant rain, that was *a bit* of an exaggeration. Mostly, it just seemed as if it was always *about to rain*. Hamilton Island existed in a perpetual state of gray gloom.

During his time away from the island, Jon had been spoiled by the clear blue skies and crisp, dry yearlong weather of California.

Not so on Hamilton Island.

Occasionally, the sun would sit in the sky just right, showing the nonbelievers just how gorgeous the island could be, with glistening forests of hemlocks, spruces, maples, firs, cedars, and every other tree that made the area look like a Christmas card. As much as Jon hated the weather, and his family, the island still held a nostalgic beauty of a slice of his youth when he was still happy.

At least it's not raining now, he thought to himself as they walked the streets of Vivian's neighborhood.

Jon was walking with Cassidy and her neighbor, Mrs. Lindley, Vivian's best friend and fellow soldier in the Infantry of the Slightly Insane. She was batty as Bruce Wayne's basement, but unlike Vivian, Mrs. Lindley didn't pour her crazy from a bottle. She made it all upstairs in the wacky whatever that seemed to hold court in her head.

Vivian was staying home in case Emma returned or someone came with news of finding the girl. Just as well, so far as Jon was concerned. He'd never much liked the woman, and she sure as hell hated him and his family, with a venom unlike any he'd ever encountered.

"I really like the headband she's wearing in this picture." Mrs. Lindley gestured toward the photo of Emma. "Makes her look like *Punky Brewster* with all the colors. Do you remember *Punky Brewster*?"

Cassidy said no. She also didn't point out that the poster was black and white, or even turn to face Mrs. Lindley as she stapled the MISSING poster onto the weather-beaten telephone pole.

"I liked that show," she said. "I thought Henry was so handsome, though he was a bit old for me then." She suddenly lit up like New Year's. "He's perfect for me now, though!" Then she frowned. "Unless, of course, he's dead."

Mrs. Lindley had lived next door to Vivian forever, ever since she moved to the island from Aberdeen after her husband passed in a logging accident. She took the life insurance and decided to live on an island like she'd always wanted to do. Island living turned out nothing at all like she expected, she often said. Jon had found her amusing more often than not when he was a kid, but the odd bird had definitely grown odder since he'd left.

Mrs. Lindley's company wouldn't have bothered Jon so much, except he needed to get Cassidy alone so he could find out more about his family's involvement in keeping Emma secret and breaking him and Sarah up. Cassidy had said he wouldn't want to know, and that she couldn't tell him. Little did she know that he wouldn't leave the island without getting to the truth.

As they searched and knocked on doors, asking questions, Jon kept flashing back to talking to Emma at the funeral as she stuffed cookies into her tiny purse. She was so adorable. So much like her mother. That was, of course, when he got the first hint that she was his daughter.

Why had Sarah kept her a secret?

What could his family have done to prevent her from telling him?

And who in his family had done the deed?

He suspected Warren, but he couldn't rule out his father. The old man had become a recluse of late, but that wasn't the case a decade ago when he had a firmer hand on the company ... and the family. His father had often scolded Jon for associating with the Hughes girls, saying they were nothing but trouble. "That whole family is bad news," his father had once said, suggesting there must have been some bad blood between him and Vivian, perhaps.

Jon wasn't sure how, but he was determined to make whoever was responsible for the deception pay.

Looking at Cassidy, Jon wondered how much he'd be able to get out of her today even if Mrs. Lindley wasn't there. She seemed distracted, far off. Probably because her niece had gone missing, that was certainly understandable, but it seemed like there was something else, too. Something beneath the surface.

He wondered if she was using again.

From everything he'd heard, Cassidy had gone clean, and she looked fine at the memorial, albeit beat to hell. If you were anywhere near the edge of the wagon, though, losing your twin could give you a helluva nudge off it. Especially if your twin was someone like Sarah.

Jon had known stronger people than Cassidy relapse over far less than that, though it did seem as though she had kicked it the hard way rather than checking into some bullshit facility like Crossroads, Betty Ford, Promises Kept, or any of the other posh thousand-dollar-a-day or more revolving door "treatment" centers most of the people he knew had gone to, where they focused more on meditation and yoga than shoving a pillow on the face of addiction.

Mrs. Lindley said, "Did you know I had a dog once? His name was Bobby, and everyone said he was half giraffe."

Neither Jon nor Cassidy responded. He couldn't see her face, but Jon wondered if Cassidy ever answered Mrs. Lindley's more obvious crazy with a smile. He would have liked to see, just to satisfy his curiosity, but he was mostly happy to stare at her back.

No matter how different Cassidy and Sarah were on the outside, and inside to those who knew them best, Cassidy was still close enough in appearance to Sarah to make him feel as if he were walking with a ghost. It wasn't just the way she looked, it was the way she moved, too, as though the shadow of impossible was given every shade of reality.

Good thing they sounded nothing alike. While there were similarities in their tone, Sarah's voice was sweet – French to Cassidy's German. Cassidy's language was gruffer, far more profane, though maybe it was just because she hated him. There had been a time, years ago when they were all kids, that he actually liked playing with Cassidy more. She was the fun sister, one of the guys, who wasn't afraid of anyone or anything. Sarah was the more reserved, cautious, shy sister. The one who won Jon's heart.

Mrs. Lindley drew her shawl tighter around her shoulders.

"It's gonna rain." She looked up at the sky. "Are we gonna be out here much longer, ya think?"

Cassidy said, "Just 'til we get to the center of town. I'd like to put the rest of the posters up at the post office."

"Where's Vivian?" Mrs. Lindley held her hand out for another stack of posters. "Shouldn't she be out here with us?"

Cassidy shook her head. "She had another one of her headaches. She wanted to come but would've been miserable, and we would've, too. Plus we needed someone to stay behind in case Emma came home."

"The migraines?" Mrs. Lindley shook her head. "Seems like she's getting them even more than she used to."

Cassidy looked far off, barely whispered, "Yeah, a lot more."

Mrs. Lindley said, "Blue marbles aren't any sort of gumdrops."

Cassidy looked back at Jon, almost smiling. He smiled back. The two of them quietly laughed as they followed her toward the intersection of Lighthouse and Main.

Ten minutes later, the two of them were standing in the center of town. Mrs. Lindley went to the small laundry over on Grover to see if anyone had left any quarters in the change machine, while Cassidy went to drop off a few fliers at the Stop and Shop, then the rest at the post office. Jon said he'd hang his final few posters on the two light posts, then on the bulletin board in front of the community center.

When Cassidy returned, Jon was staring at the bulletin board with his mouth open wide. There were fourteen pictures on the board, five in color and nine in black and white. Eleven adults and three children – all missing.

Jon turned to Cassidy, shaking his head. "Hamilton Island isn't that big. Missing people shouldn't be too hard to find."

Cassidy looked up at the board like it was graffiti in her own ghetto, then back at Jon. "You can't find people if they don't want to be found. Or if they're dead. Most of 'em probably ran away, and a bunch of them are probably suicides, or falls, off Tanner's Pass."

Jon just kept shaking his head. "That can't be."

Cassidy laughed, but there wasn't any happy in the music. "You've been gone a long time, Jonny Conway. Wearing your rose-colored Armani, Bono-looking glasses. You don't remember how depressing this place can be, or maybe you never had a clue to begin with, living up in the Gardens and all."

Jon ignored her. "If these are suicides, or even runaways, the numbers are still big enough to make the news. In Seattle, at least."

He looked around at all the CCTV cameras hanging from light posts, off the corners of buildings, and pretty much anywhere you could put a camera. There were enough cameras on the island to shoot the most invasive reality show ever. Cameras installed by Paladin, via his family, to keep the Conways safe during a time that crime was starting to rise on the island ten years ago.

"All these damned cameras, and they can't keep people safe?"

Another cracked laugh from Cassidy. "Ha! No one gives a shit about the dirt on the island."

Words stuck in Jon's throat as a thick, sickly mucus made its way into his mouth. He didn't know what to say, wasn't even sure *what* to think, but a creeping horror had wormed its way in his head and was now slithering through his body.

Jon held Cassidy's gaze as the wind tousled his hair. He stared into the bottomless depths of her eyes with a sudden craving to know everything she knew.

"I found fifty cents!" Mrs. Lindley yelled, running toward them.

"We need to talk," he said.

"We need to find Emma."

The gray in the sky turned black and rain poured down on them.

Jon wiped the rain from his face, then followed Cassidy and Mrs. Lindley back toward the house. As they walked, Jon couldn't help but feel like they were being watched.

Chapter 8 - Milo Anderson

4:00 p.m.

MILO WOKE UP PISSED.

He was angry at Alex for coming over. They would talk someday, probably, but not for a while – not before the sun had set on the horrors of what happened. When every thought of Alex made Milo think of Jessica, even the daylight was dark.

Alex's dad murdered the light.

He was also pissed about the Cody guy who was winding him up online, talking like he knew something, saying Manny was in danger. And then, when pressed for questions, the fucker stopped talking. Just another online troll just looking to mess with people. It was one thing to fuck with people who deserved it, but why would you mess with grieving people? People who had lost friends, loves, family?

Asshole.

More than anything, though, Milo was pissed at himself for missing Jessica's funeral, just like Other Mother said he would be. He supposed he knew he would be, too, somewhere deep in his heart. But the pain of seeing Jessica's lifeless body was something he couldn't bear.

Perhaps today he could find some closure and pay his respects at her grave.

He looked outside his window. It looked like rain, so Milo put on a sweater, grabbed a chocolate-colored hoodie from the closet, then went downstairs and opened the garage, figuring he'd work up the courage to visit Jessica's grave along the way.

Milo rode his mountain bike up the long and winding trail leading toward Oxley Cemetery, pumping his legs at the top of the mountain, feeling his heart gain a hundred pounds or so with every few hundred feet he pedaled closer to Jessica's grave.

Knowing he'd turn coward about five hundred yards before he did, Milo made a long circle around Oxley, then stopped pedaling as his bike careened dangerously fast down the hill toward the bottom, where Hamilton K-12 had sat without incident for forty-two years. He pedaled past the front lawn, hating himself for being so weak.

Seeing the school was like hearing fresh gunshots. A hundred thoughts pushed him to keep moving.

Milo was surprised to see so many cars in the parking lot and wondered what was happening inside. Maybe there were people inside still cleaning up for tomorrow's opening. Was it even possible to get all the blood out of the classroom so quickly? And Mr. Heller's class? Would it be closed off and the students shipped off to different rooms for the remainder of the year?

As he rode past the parking lot, he saw his guess was wrong. A large, blue signboard was set up at the entrance.

Missing & Survivor's Group Meeting 4:30 - 6:30 p.m. Thursday.

He thought about going inside, but only for a moment, knowing the crowd would only make him sadder.

Besides, he couldn't stand the thought of running into

Jessica's mom. Ever since her dad had passed three years earlier, the two of them were best friends. They did everything together, from binging on old *Gilmore Girls* DVDs to the dates they had to get their nails done together after school every other Tuesday.

Milo couldn't begin to imagine what Mrs. Ruiz was going through, and if he went inside, he would have to look her in the eyes. He rode the rest of the way home, hoping it wouldn't rain and promising himself he would finally say goodbye to Jessica tomorrow. He owed it to her, and to himself.

He was three blocks from home when the first splatter of rain hit the back of his head. Without stopping, or even slowing, Milo reached back with his right hand and lifted the hoodie over his head.

When he pulled up to his house, he felt a slight chill, possibly because of the cool wind that came as the freezing rain started to splatter his back, but probably because of Beatrice's white BMW X7 idling in the driveway, engine running, door open and lights on.

It didn't make sense for her SUV to be there at all. She was supposed to be in Seattle with Janet and Teena. Hamilton Island was reasonably small, and not exactly the sort of place where you had to worry about getting your vehicle stolen, Beatrice was usually neurotic enough to lock her car tighter than the vault at Chase Manhattan, even if she was just going inside to "tinkle," as she liked to say. Probably to annoy him.

Milo leaned his bike against the closed garage door, then peered into the BMW's cabin. Nothing seemed out of place. Her Maroon 5 CD was spinning like always, barely loud enough to hear outside the SUV, since Other Mother seemed allergic to listening to anything at a volume which might be mistaken for being enjoyable.

He looked toward the house. The front door was slightly ajar. He was probably being silly, and there was almost certainly nothing to worry about, but his heart started racing anyway.

Milo stepped inside the house and then into the living room but saw no one inside.

Same for the kitchen.

He stepped into the hallway and broke the silence.

"Beatrice?" Milo swallowed, then only half aware of what he was doing, yelled, "Mom!"

Still nothing.

He ambled the rest of the way down the hallway, then into his parents' bedroom. Beatrice was standing statue-still in front of the TV, staring blankly at a screen with snow as a constant whoosh of white noise filled the room.

"Mom?" he repeated, slowly approaching.

Still nothing.

Other Mother stood, as if in a trance, not seeming to realize Milo was in the room.

Great, she's started using drugs. More shit dad can't afford.

Milo turned to leave but only got halfway to the door before circling back. He couldn't step into the hallway when every fiber inside him was screaming that something was wrong.

He tiptoed back toward Beatrice, suddenly terrified that maybe she'd had a stroke.

Is it possible to suffer a stroke standing on your feet?

Milo inched closer until he was standing directly in front of Beatrice.

Her pupils were large and black and ... *empty.*

He stepped back, mostly nervous, though slightly terrified.

Milo turned around and looked back at the TV. Maybe there was some connection between the snow on the screen and the lost look in her eyes. If there was, he couldn't see what was holding her attention, assuming she was actually aware of anything.

He turned back to Beatrice and again saw the vacant look in her eyes, then terror swallowed his anxiety.

"Beatrice?" His upper lip trembled.

She turned, just slightly, from the TV toward Milo. He wasn't sure if she was moving in slow motion or if it was merely a trick of his imagination and the surreality of the moment.

Other Mother closed her eyes tight, shook her head, then opened them again, the dilated pupils now normal-sized. She flashed her plastic smile. "Oh, hi, Milo. I didn't see you come in. How was your day?"

"F … fine, I guess."

Beatrice headed toward the kitchen, opened the fridge, then started shoving sliced meat into her purse. She looked up from the fridge's glow as though caught in a puzzle. Then her face brightened with memory.

She thrust her face back in the fridge, wrapped her hand around a large tub of whipped butter, then dropped it into her purse and smiled at Milo on her way out the door.

"Okay, see you later, honey." Then she walked out the door.

Milo stared at the door in disbelief.

What the fuck?

Chapter 9 - Cassidy Hughes

Hamilton Island, Washington
Thursday
Sept. 7
10:20 p.m.

CASSIDY AND JON had knocked on every door in their neighborhood and searched a chunk of the woods in the area, but they'd come up blank.

They stood on her doorstep, exhausted.

"See you in the morning?" he asked.

"Yes. And thank you. I appreciate your help."

So far, they'd avoided talking about why Emma had been kept secret and why Sarah had broken up with Jon. Cassidy hoped to keep it that way, at least until Emma was found. Once Jon knew the truth, there was a good chance he'd go ballistic, hating his family and hating her. And right now, she needed his help, not his hate.

They'd also avoided talking about what would happen once they found Emma. Would Jon seek custody? Was there any way he'd trust her to care for his child? The odds slimmed along with the hours. That was assuming, of course, they even found Emma.

What if Emma was gone for good? What if she had wandered off and drowned in a lake or the sea? What if someone had kidnapped her and was holding her in some kinda dungeon? What if someone had taken her off the island before Paladin sent guards down to the ferry? Kids went missing every day. And many just vanished with no explanation or trace.

Just gone.

Forever.

She began to cry again.

Jon took her into his arms and hugged her tight. "We're gonna find her."

The same promise as Chief Brady. She wished she could believe them.

Fate had never really worked in Cassidy's favor. If something could go wrong, it inevitably did. Perhaps Jon's involvement would neutralize her negative karma. Bad things didn't happen to Jon or any of the Conways. They were blessed. Bad things don't happen to the children of the blessed.

Even as she thought it, she knew that was a lie.

At the moment, Cassidy would take any lie she could find, though, if it meant holding out hope.

"I'm going to meet a buddy of mine tonight," Jon said, "and we'll get started fresh in the morning. He's a private eye and damned good at finding people."

"Really?" She pulled from the hug and looking into Jon's eyes.

He seemed so much kinder than usual. Gentler, even. Cassidy had always wondered why Sarah had fallen for him. Jon had always seemed more Cassidy's type — bold, brutally honest, brash, and prone to troublemaking and bouts of excess. Perhaps Sarah had seen a layer of Jon that Cassidy had overlooked — a kind, gentle side which mirrored Sarah's own.

Cassidy felt another wave of guilt for her role in their breakup.

Had she been clean, none of this would have happened. Jon and Sarah would still be together. Sarah would be alive. And they'd be with Emma, one big, happy family.

Now, because of Cassidy's weakness, her sister was dead, her niece missing, and Jon was alone.

"I'll see you in the morning." Cassidy turned quickly before Jon could see her break down. Before she spilled her guts and told him everything.

"Goodnight." Despite his puzzled tone, he retreated to his car without argument. "Call me if you hear anything."

"Okay." Cassidy went inside her dark house and closed the door. Once inside, she slumped to the floor, crying her eyes out in the darkness. Wanting to just close her eyes, wake up, and have the past week not happen.

The pills in her guest room called loudly.

Welcome home, Cass. We've been waiting for you.

She scrambled to her feet and went upstairs, not strong enough to fight anymore.

On the way toward the bathroom to wash up, she passed her mother's room. The door was open, and Mom was sitting in her bed, the glow of *Seinfeld* on the TV lighting the darkness. The way the shadows fell on her face, Cassidy couldn't tell if her mom's eyes were open. "Mom, you awake?"

"Oh. Hi, Sarah." Her voice slurred with drink.

See, everyone needs a little something to cope. Your mom drinks. You have pills.

"It's me, Mom. Cassidy."

"Oh, *you.*" The word dripped with disappointment. As always.

"Cassidy ignored her mom's drunken insult. "Any word about Emma?"

"Emma?" Vivian asked, as if she didn't know the child was even missing.

"Yes, your granddaughter. She's missing. Jesus, Mom."

"Ah, yeah, Emma. Yeah, yeah, don't worry. They'll bring her back."

Cassidy's heart nearly froze. She wanted to flick on the light and ask her mom "Who?" but resisted the urge to shake her up, in case it caused her to get distracted and forget what she was saying. "Who, Mom?" she asked as shadows danced across her mother's face, hiding most of her features. "*Who* will bring her back?"

"The people in the sky. They always brought you back, Sarah. They'll bring her back, too."

Episode 3

Chapter 1 - Brock Houser

Ocean County, California
10 years ago ...

DETECTIVE HOUSER KNEW he was staring into a set of guilty eyes the second the sleaze-ball peered from his side of the flimsy security chain that would pop off in an instant if Houser kicked the door in.

There is an undeniable look in the eyes of the guilty — a look you got to know as a cop. A look Houser had become aware of, and well-tuned to, as a child. For Houser, instinct was as accurate as any of his senses. His eyesight had failed him a few times, his instincts, at least in this area, not even once.

This was his man, sure as shit. The twisted fucker who had kidnapped six-year-old Cecilia Ramirez.

"Can I help you?" the man said from the shadows of his dark apartment.

"Hi, my name is Detective Houser. We're talking to people in the neighborhood about a missing girl. I'd like to ask if you've seen her."

Houser raised the photo for the man to see, fixed on his eyes the entire time.

Recognition? Yes.

Guilt? Yes. Without a doubt.

Richard Jurgen was his man.

"Nope, haven't seen a thing." Richard shook his head.

"Are you sure?"

The man took a second, longer glance at the photo, studying the gloss for a half-minute or so before raising his nervous eyes to meet Houser's. "Nope, ain't seen her."

The monster started to close the door.

Houser slipped his boot against the bottom of the door, keeping it ajar. "I'm sure you won't mind if I ask you about something one of your neighbors said."

"Sure." Jurgen eased up on the door.

Houser kept his boot in place but didn't push on the wood. "Someone said they saw you last Tuesday, with your hatchback backed up to the garage, late at night. They said it seemed like you were carrying something pretty heavy."

Houser kept his eyes fixed on the monster, waiting for him to drown himself in a lie.

"I don't remember." He dove into the deep. "I often go out on my rounds late at night, picking up junk, looking for the furniture and stuff people leave out for the trash. That's not a crime all of a sudden, is it?"

"No, Mr. Jurgen, not at all." Houser shook his head, then looked down at his notes, flipping back a page for effect, then looked back up at the monster. "Odd thing was, your neighbor said the garage light was out, just like the light in your car."

"So, what of it?" The fear in his voice started to smother the calm. "I can see well enough with the street lights. I can see you just fine, right?"

Bet both balls in the sack, this is our asshole.

"Okay. Well, then, Mr. Jurgen, you won't mind if we take a quick look around." He nodded to his silent partner,

Chan, who was standing to Houser's left. "Just to save us some time, so we can get on with the search and rule you out."

"You have a search warrant?"

Fucker.

"No, but based on what I do have, a warrant's exactly one short phone call away. I was hoping, since you've nothing to hide, you wouldn't mind if we took a quick look around so we can get out of your hair. We have to follow up on leads, if only to rule you out. I'm sure you understand."

"I know my rights," the monster said, his voice still even. "And I'm not letting you do anything without a warrant."

"Okay." Houser pulled his boot from the doorway, then turned around and walked back to their car. Once he and Chan were inside the cruiser, he said, "Motherfucker. She's in there. I can fucking feel it."

Chan put in a call to Judge Cleary, seeking a warrant while Houser waited as patiently as he could, listening to Chan's side of the conversation.

Come on, judge, don't fuck this one up.

The tricky part of getting a warrant with this particular case was that the neighbor who alerted them to the suspicious activity, an old busybody named Earl Moody, had a long history of calling the cops on Jurgen for the sort of routine bullshit most neighbors handled themselves. In short, the two had bad blood, giving the judge enough cause to deny the warrant.

Chan's voice went up an octave, letting Houser know where the conversation was headed.

Houser wanted to snatch the phone from his partner and rip Cleary a new one, but he was already on thin ice with Cleary — likely the reason the judge was giving Chan a hard time in the first place.

"Yes, your honor. Thank you," Chan said, hanging up. He shook his head. "No dice."

"Fuck!" Houser screamed, slammed his fists into the steering wheel, then turned back to scowl at Jurgen's house.

The fucker was in his living room, peeking through his blinds at the cruiser.

Houser turned back to Chan. "You like this guy, right? It's not just me."

"Yeah, he's hiding something, all right."

"Okay, we need to talk to more neighbors. See if we can find something from someone who isn't the neighborhood douche bag, then ring Cleary back."

Chan agreed, then suggested one of them hit the courthouse when it opened in the morning to see if they could find anything on the guy that wasn't yet in the database. The courthouse was currently in the process — which seemed to be taking years — of moving their old records to online archives, so most of the crimes older than ten years were still in their giant file vault.

Houser hated combing through old files slightly less than he hated sitting on his hands while Jurgen was inside his house with time to do God knows what, flushing evidence, arming himself to the teeth, raping the hell out of the girl, or whatever it was the condemned might do before the jaws of justice clamped on their ass.

Chan said, "Is that your way of saying you want me to go?"

Houser turned, with his biggest smile, "Pretty please?"

"You know I hate you, right?"

Houser laughed. "As if anyone could hate me. But one of us has to sit on this fucker in case he decides to bolt, and to be honest, I wanna be the first one through the door to knock the fucking smile from his face. And let's face it, I'm a helluva lot faster than you if it comes to a foot chase."

"Yeah, yeah, whatever. But you owe me."

"Whatever you want, man. Just name it. I got dinner for the next week. Okay?"

"Week? How about two?"

"Two? Do I look rich?"

"Richer than me. You don't have a wife, kids, daycare bills, or any of that shit."

"Wah, wah, I'm so jealous of your sexy, single life, Houser," Houser said, mocking Chan playfully. "All right, two fucking weeks. But you better find something we can take to Cleary!"

∼

CHAN DID.

At 8:15 a.m., fifteen minutes after the courthouse opened, Houser's cell rang.

Chan was practically yelling into the phone. "Seems our guy got busted peeping in some windows eleven years ago. One of the windows was of a little girl. Somehow he got off with a slap on the wrist."

"Fuck! Okay, I'll call Cleary."

"Too late," Chan said. "I already did. Warrant has been issued."

"I love you, man. Three weeks! On me. Okay, I'm going in. I've got another unit here, and we're going in."

"Okay, I'll be over in five."

"All right," Houser called into the radio, alerting the officers camped behind Jurgen's house, and to the side, just out of the man's line of sight. "Let's get this fucker!"

∼

HOUSER BURST through the freshly kicked-in door, stunned to see Jurgen standing right in the living room, naked, and aiming a .45 at Houser.

Houser fired, but not before Jurgen.

Jurgen's shot slammed into Houser's Kevlar vest, knocking him to the filthy carpet, and clearing the air from his body.

Houser's shot hit the man between the eyes, killing him instantly.

Sgt. Combs kneeled next to Houser. "You okay?"

Houser sucked in air, and took a moment to check beneath his vest, making sure there was no blood, before nodding. He would be bruised as hell, but he'd live.

Four cops, in addition to Houser, began to scour the man's place, searching for any sign of the child. Upstairs, in an unused bedroom, Houser picked up the scent of paint, and noticed the fresh color on the wall behind a large bookcase — the same color of yellow, but brighter than the rest of the room. Drywall dusted the carpet. Houser put a finger behind the bookcase and pulled it away, yellow.

"Get up here!" he shouted, pulling the bookcase to the floor and sending volumes pouring from the shelf and into a pile.

A large, wet paint spot barely concealed a bad plastering job, covering a wide hole in the wall. Houser knocked on the wall twice

"Hello?"

Houser heard a muffled cry.

Oh, God.

His heart sped in his chest as the remaining officers poured into the room. Houser punched high where the wet spot started, straight through the quickly crumbling drywall, and began to tear at it, throwing chunks of drywall to the ground.

Inside the wall, he found Cecilia, hands and feet bound, mouth gagged. Dark eyes stared up at him as she barely clung to life.

He reached into the wall and pulled her out, holding her closely. She was so tiny. And dirty, wearing the same pink — but now filthy — pajamas she'd been reported missing in.

"It's okay, you're safe now." He lay her on the floor.

"Get the paramedics in here!" one of the other officers shouted. Paramedics were on standby downstairs.

Houser pulled the gag from the girl.

"Thank you." Her voice was so tiny as her eyes rolled to the back of her head.

"No, no, no!" Houser shook his head and hoped to God she wasn't gonna die. Not now, just seconds after they found her.

Two paramedics rushed into the room and began to give the girl CPR.

Houser watched from behind, helpless as they attempted to revive her.

But they couldn't, despite an eternity of trying.

Cecilia Ramirez was dead.

Her dying eyes and whisper of a voice were immediately and forever etched into Houser's memory.

As the officers began collecting evidence and the paramedics rolled the girl's body from the house, Houser stood, went downstairs, then into the back yard for a moment alone.

He wanted to cry.

He wanted to scream.

He wanted to fucking shoot something.

But eyes were on him, cops and neighbors, and soon the media's.

Houser had to stand quietly, holding his rage, swallowing regret, and making silent vows that he would never, ever let anything like this happen again. A late search warrant and an overcautious judge had murdered Cecilia Ramirez just as much as Richard Jurgen.

Chapter 2 - Liz Heller

Hamilton Island, Washington
  Thursday
  Sept. 7
  Afternoon …

LIZ PULLED INTO HER DRIVEWAY, hopped from the car, slammed the door, then raced to the side of the house. She twisted the spigot like it was the face of her enemy, yanking the hose by the nozzle and scattering the spool into a slithering snake as she returned to the car and pulled the trigger, spraying at the *Murderer* scrawled in hate across her windshield.

The paint, unlike the pain, had dried. But like the pain, it was impossible to wash away.

"Damn it!" she cried, rubbing her left palm against the windshield.

She seemed to remember reading about ways to take paint off, somewhere. Maybe with gasoline?

Liz was about to run inside the house to look on the Internet, then remembered her house had been stripped of computers. And she never did figure out how to get her phone's Internet browser to work worth a damn.

She stared at the word *Murderer*, rage building inside her.

Why would someone do this to her car? Had they mistaken it for Roger's, which was still at the impound? Had they targeted her because she was the only vessel into which they could pour their rage? If so, was her family safe? How long before someone came after Alex? Part of her felt like she should leave, but where could she go? Roger's family had all passed away, and she hadn't spoken to her brother in years, nor could she turn to him for help. Her few friends were on the island. How many would be willing to step up now?

It was only then, staring at the accusation in red, that Liz realized how truly alone she was on Hamilton Island.

The hose fell to the ground. Liz wanted to fall down beside it and let her harbored anguish bleed to the puddle of water spreading beneath her.

The front door opened, and Alex came running outside with Katie. His eyes locked onto the windshield, then found his mother. For a moment, it seemed as if time had frozen, an unspoken truth finally screaming between them.

Alex dashed to her side and hugged her. Pain shook through her sob. Alex cried, too. Katie moved back to the front door, giving them space and privacy.

When he pulled away, his eyes were red, his jaw was clenched. "Who did this?"

"I don't know. I was at the library, and when I came out, someone had painted the window."

Alex turned to the black SUV parked in the road outside their house, and the Paladin guard assigned to them sitting inside. He stormed over.

"Wait!" Liz called, but Alex kept walking.

"Why didn't you follow her?" Alex shouted, though the guard's tinted window was still closed.

The window rolled down, and the guard, the same man

who had saved Alex from getting beaten with a baseball bat, said, "We were watching the house, sir. Your mother didn't ask us to follow her."

Liz apologized for Alex's outburst. "It's okay, I'd rather you watch my son and daughter. I don't need an escort, thank you." She pulled Alex away from the guard and back toward the house.

"It'll be okay." Odd that she almost believed her verbal Band-Aid.

"This is bullshit!" Alex pointed to the car. "We didn't do anything! It's not our fault what Dad did!"

Liz was surprised that Alex was now admitting what Roger had done. He'd seemed to be in denial for so long. She wondered what her son would say if he saw the list or flash drive. But no, she couldn't show him. Couldn't destroy the love Alex had for his father. Not when she was no longer certain whether something bigger was at play, or what Roger had stumbled onto.

Alex picked up the hose and began spraying the windshield.

After a few minutes and having no success with the water, he tore off his shirt, wadded it in his fist, then started scrubbing the windshield.

"Fuck!" he screamed as the paint remained on the window.

Alex threw the hose aside, stormed to the garden, picked up a large, gray stone and heaved it with two hands above his head.

Liz screamed, "Put that down!"

But it was too late.

The rock flew from his hands and through the windshield, safety glass raining beneath the weight of the stone as the entire window collapsed inward.

"All gone. I'll call the insurance company." Then he disappeared into the house.

~

DINNER WAS A QUIET AFFAIR, with both Alex and Katie seemingly lost in their own thoughts, perhaps thinking about the fact that school was starting tomorrow. Liz was no longer certain that she wanted Alex to go back so soon. Particularly after what happened to her car.

Katie made spaghetti and meatballs, and while Liz didn't think she'd be hungry, her appetite surprised her. The past few days had been a diet of microwave meals and stuff poured from bags. Pasta was a welcome and delicious change. As they ate, Liz kept staring at Katie, wondering why Roger placed a bull's eye on the girl and the other kids. She couldn't imagine the aftermath if Roger *had killed* Katie. Alex would have been devastated even more than he already was.

And while Sarah Hughes, someone Liz had been close to for years, wasn't a target, but rather an accidental victim of Roger's shootings, a small part of Liz hated him for having killed her. For taking away little Emma's mother. If Roger had killed Katie, she imagined her son would also feel that hate — if he didn't already.

Even as Liz stewed in guilt for her husband's plans and actions, some small part of her kept returning to the video on the flash drive.

What had he seen in the caves?

What was it about the bodies that prompted the madness to follow?

And what in the hell could Katie, or any of the other students, have had to do with it?

Liz felt another twinge of guilt as she saw Katie smile at Alex. This guilt was new, tinged with suspicion.

Was there something about Katie Liz should be worried about?

Liz had to stop her thoughts before they plunged down the same rabbit hole of crazy Roger had fallen into. She looked over at Aubrey, sucking on one hand while playing with the mess of sweet potato, painting her highchair tray.

"I'm going to school tomorrow," Alex said, as if he'd been waiting forever to make the declaration and was waiting for her objection.

"Let's talk about it later." Liz and Alex were both on edge. It wasn't a good time for a heated argument, especially in front of Katie.

"There's nothing to talk about," Alex said. "I didn't do anything wrong. I have no reason to hide my face or take any bullshit."

"Alex! Not in front of Aubrey," Liz said. "I *said* we'll talk about this later."

"And *I* said there's nothing to talk about. It's not your choice to make. It's mine. I'm not gonna hide in my house like I'm guilty while some security guard stands outside. It's like *we're* the ones being arrested for what Dad did!"

Liz didn't know what to say. She looked at Katie, who looked down before Alex took her hand and held it, rubbing his thumb across her palm. Then he raised his gaze to meet Liz's. "I'm not afraid of these people. Let me go back and prove we're not the monsters they think we are."

There was no point in arguing. The more Liz resisted, the more Alex would push back. And now, more than ever, she needed him to communicate, to come to her with his thoughts. Something he wouldn't do if she took a stand here.

"Fine," she said. "Tomorrow, you'll go back."

Chapter 3 - Cassidy Hughes

Friday
Sept. 8
Morning

CASSIDY WATCHED her mom dip a spoon into her soggy oatmeal, fish for Craisins from the bottom, then skim off the top, leaving semi-solid lumps down below.

She could tell her mom's ears were ringing from the usual migraine. The headaches had grown alarmingly regular. Like the alcohol in her pores, the blood in Vivian's eyes was impossible to hide. She would've been wearing the deep bags anyway — a bottle of Yellowtail usually made sure of that — but her eyes always looked worse with the migraines.

And the migraines were always worse after the Yellowtail.

Fucking drunk.

Not like the apple fell too far from the tree.

Cassidy smiled good morning at her mom, opened the fridge, then pulled a full carton of Donald Duck Orange Juice from the cold. She went to the cabinet, took down a tall glass, filled it to the rim, then started sipping, keeping her mouth busy until she figured out what to say.

She wanted to ask her mom about the night before, wanted to know what in the hell she meant by "They'll bring her back," and "The people in the sky." Cassidy didn't even care that she'd been mistaken for Sarah — she was used to that shit — but her mom had been so definitive, it was more than unsettling. It was an open cut in her mind she wanted to close.

Not like Cassidy put much — if any — stock in the crap her mom spewed from her mouth. She wasn't half as cracky as Mrs. Lindley, but she was cracky enough. Last night's rambling was more than cracky, though; it seemed almost … candid, like she was telling Cassidy there was something black between her teeth.

Vivian was snoring a few seconds after she said it, so she went to sleep, wondering what in the hell her mom meant. She'd woken up wondering the same thing. Cassidy would've blurted her question immediately, but the lingering weirdness she was feeling from her nightmares held her back.

The last few nights had haunted Cassidy with dreams she couldn't remember, no matter how hard she tried. As soon as sunlight streamed through the blinds, her mind went blank, even though chaos from the evening's dreaming was still buzzing.

Last night's seemed especially important. Cassidy wanted to remember, hungered to know, somehow convinced it had something to do with Emma.

Like the dream about Sarah.

Or all the dreams from before.

Cassidy had even gone to bed with a small, spiral notebook on the nightstand, so she could scribble the first thing she remembered once she opened her eyes. She had the ball of her pen on the flat of her paper, just seconds after she opened her eyes, but five minutes of staring had left just two blue smears to mar the white of the page.

Cassidy set her half-empty glass of orange juice beside her mom's bowl of oatmeal then sat next to her. "So, what were you trying to say last night?"

Her mom looked up from her breakfast, curling four fingers around the handle of her spoon. She peered at Cassidy, trying to focus on her, the red of her hangover swimming through the whites of her eyes. Vivian's nose twitched, and her gaze narrowed on her daughter. Her face brightened, then dimmed, and for a few seconds she seemed to skate along the lip of memory. Finally, the look faded, leaving her with an expression of someone who had lost their keys. "What? Was I talking in my sleep again?"

"Not exactly. At least it didn't seem like it. It wasn't like when your eyes shoot open in the middle of a snore and you're yelling at me or Sarah to take out the garbage." Cassidy took another sip of orange juice and swallowed quickly. "Even though you were snoring by the end of the sentence, you were wide awake when you started talking about Emma. Since I seem to be the only one in the house worrying about our nine-year-old girl gone missing, you were trying to convince me I was crazy for caring."

Cassidy looked at Vivian, holding her gaze to make sure she was listening. "You said the 'people in the sky' took her, and I didn't have to worry since they would bring her back, like they always brought me back. Except you thought I was Sarah."

Vivian stared at Cassidy, the blank look back on her face, her nose twitching and stare narrowing in an echo from a moment before, again skating at the edge of memory. Finally, she laughed with enough of a cackle to qualify as a bark. "You're fucking with me, right?" She lifted a Craisin-heavy spoonful of oatmeal into her mouth. "I believe I called you

Sarah." She laughed. "But the rest, I don't think so. I mean, really, Cassidy."

"No, Mom, I'm not kidding." Cassidy shook her head. "And not only did you say it, you seemed pretty goddamned sure about what you were saying." She took another small sip of orange juice.

"Well, hell, Cass, I'm *always* certain around midnight with a belly full of two-buck chuck." She cackled again. "Must've been dreaming. What was on last night?" Vivian dropped her spoon long enough to scratch her head, then turned to Cassidy, "Must've been watching *The X-Files* or something if I was talking about people in the sky." She patted the table, coming nowhere near Cassidy's hand. "Don't worry. I'm sure it was nothing."

Vivian ate the last Craisin and ended the conversation. She filled her mouth with nothing but oatmeal, then turned her gaze toward the window, settling the pair into several minutes of silence. Just as Cassidy was about to excuse herself for a quick shower before leaving to look for Emma, Vivian said, "Hey, Cass, would you mind getting me my pain meds from the bathroom? My back feels like there's a buffalo trying to mount me."

Before Cassidy could argue that she didn't really feel like playing house servant, she saw the visible pain etching lines onto her mom's face in misery.

"Sure, Mom." Cassidy rose from the table, dumped the rest of her orange juice into the sink, then set the glass in the dishwasher. She went to the bathroom, opened the medicine cabinet, and scanning the four rows of the chest, seeing nothing.

Cassidy called, "I don't see anything, Ma!"

Vivian yelled back, "They're in the third drawer of the wicker cabinet."

Cassidy snarled.

Fuck her.

There was only one reason for Vivian to stuff her pills inside the wicker cabinet, and that was to keep them from Cassidy, like she couldn't be trusted. Just like Cassidy imagined, the small bottle was wrapped inside a scarf, and pushed to the back of the drawer.

Cassidy pulled the bottle from the drawer and looked at the label, shocked to see it was Ourocettes.

Fucking A, why'd I pay for the shit when I coulda just scored some from Mom?

Her addict piped up.

The bottle is full, Cassidy. Filled six months ago. Obviously, your mom doesn't use them, or even need them. At least, not that often. Not like you do. One at a time will take all of your pain away, Cassidy.

Just.

One.

Pill.

The addict's whisper was warm in her ear. The bottle was warm in her hand.

Her addict's voice echoed in her head.

What are you waiting for, Cassidy? Don't be stupid. Craig is an idiot. And dealing with him will get you busted. This bottle means you don't have to.

This bottle will make everything go away.

Cassidy opened the bottle, hating herself, then spilled six pills into her palm and dropped them inside the front right pocket of her jeans. She tapped the bottle once more, dropping one more pill into her hand, which she brought to her mom with a tall glass of water.

"Thanks, Sweetie." Vivian swallowed the pill. After a gulp, she turned to Cassidy. "I'd advise you not to think you're the only one concerned about Emma. I've been looking after that girl one way or another since she was born, while you were off doing who knows what, who knows where." Her gaze sharpened. "And with who knows who. I've been feeling so wrecked the last few days, I could barely move. And right now, I barely have the strength to stand. I'm sorry I've not been able to help more, but that doesn't mean I don't care."

"Sorry, Mom," Cassidy cut her mom mid-sentence, but her apology was severed by the doorbell.

Vivian said, "That has to be good news, right?"

Cassidy swallowed and shrugged, then ignored her chills and went to the door.

Jon stood on the porch, awkwardly smiling. "Morning, Cass. I just checked in with Brady. I'm sure you have, too. Since there's no news, I was wondering if you'd like more help looking this morning."

She did and was surprised by how happy she was to see Jon Conway standing on her mom's porch for the first time in ten years, at least.

"What in the hell is *he* doing here?" Vivian's face soured as if she were sucking on a lemon.

Cassidy looked at Jon apologetically, then turned to her mom. "He's here to help us look for Emma."

"Hmph, I'll bet," Vivian growled. "Like he doesn't know anything about it."

Cassidy was impressed at the way Jon managed to hold in the smile that flickered across his face. "Give me a second," she said, then closed the door.

Cassidy went to her room, grabbed a sweater, then turned to leave. Halfway into the hall, she returned to her room, emptied the pills from her pocket, and dumped them into the bottle from Craig. Reconsidering, she dropped one back into her pocket, just in case.

Smart girl, her addict said.

Cassidy left her room and joined Jon on the porch. She turned to her mom and said, "We'll be back," then hooked her arm through Jon's and closed the door behind her.

Chapter 4 - Jon Conway

Jon held a stack of full-color glossy photos — Emma smiling in front of the monkey cage at the small zoo the Conways had sponsored and installed four years earlier. Jon found them online the night before, then had them printed, risking ridicule. It would have been typical for Cassidy to call him an asshole or a showoff or some other horrible name, simply because he had the audacity to use his money and resources to make their job easier. Fortunately, she didn't. Instead, she smiled like she meant it, and held out her open palm for her half of the glossies.

Jon felt like he had to apologize anyway, "People are visual, and color matters. If it gives us even a degree of a chance of finding her faster, I figure it was worth it."

"I get it, Popcorn." She pulled her sweater tighter around her body as they crossed the street, doubling back to where they'd gone the day before.

He let the "popcorn" nickname slide, an obvious snipe at his stardom. Funny how home was the one place he was made to feel almost apologetic for his celebrity.

They were planning to cover another section of the island but figured they should hit every house where residents hadn't been home the previous evening, just to be certain. Before leaving their block, Cassidy suggested they bang on Mrs. Lindley's door and see if she wanted to help.

Jon shook his head. "Not sure that's gonna help much."

"I wouldn't be asking if it was just Mrs. Lindley," Cassidy said. "But Mrs. Carlson knows everyone on the island, and everyone loves her. She only leaves her house for groceries, or to fill her shift at Conway Medical Center. When she's not at the hospital, she shuts herself in tight and won't leave except for maybe three people. Mrs. Lindley happens to be one of them."

"Why?" Jon asked.

"Probably because Mrs. Lindley makes her laugh." Cassidy pointed across the street to a tidy cottage with a fat hedge of pink and purple hydrangeas bunched beneath the window. "She lives over there. She was working Conway Medical Center yesterday, but she's home now."

Sure enough, Mrs. Lindley loved the idea, and so did Mrs. Carlson. They agreed to cover Aspen Park together, while Cassidy and Jon hit the shore.

"Chief Brady said the Paladin officers would help with the search, too," Jon said, stepping from the porch of their sixth, *"No, sorry, haven't seen her,"* on their way to the seventh.

Cassidy was silent.

Jon added, "Paladin said they could spare six officers."

"Wow," Cassidy said, "A whole six officers? That's amazing. Who's going to be left to guard Daddy's miles of chain link fence?"

"That's in addition to the guards they already agreed to yesterday, including some who are working the Sound."

Cassidy looked sorry as soon as she said it, but he'd never know whether she would have apologized since his phone started ringing before she finished the word "fence."

He looked at the screen: *Houser.*

"What's up?"

"Hey, Jonny H.," Houser got right to the point. "You ever heard of some dipshit named Larry Whistler? Lives three streets over from the girl's grandma and has a bit of a history."

"What sort of history?" Jon looked over at Cassidy, who was suddenly fascinated by his phone call.

"Seems Whistler had a bit of trouble at a day care a few years back while living in Rochester, New York."

"Go on."

"He was accused of touching a mentally disabled girl, but the case fell to shit when they couldn't find any evidence outside an upset mom and dad willing to swear on a high stack of Bibles. So anyway, Whistler left town with the stink of kiddy diddler on him, and moved cross country. Got a job working a church on Hamilton Island, serving as a youth pastor, no less." Houser paused, then added, "I looked up the church website. Seems to be run by Pastor Avery. You familiar with him?"

"Yes, I know him." Jon was careful not to repeat Avery's name, not wanting to upset Cassidy until after he was off the line.

"Well, Whistler's not on any watch lists or anything, but he's sure as shit worth a man-to-man."

"All right," Jon said, "I'll call Chief Brady as soon as we hang up. He promised he'd stay on standby, said Emma was his top priority. I'm sure he'll be able to swing over to Whistler's immediately."

"Fuck that noise," Houser said. "If I wanted red tape, I'd drive down to the goddamned hardware store and buy myself a jumbo roll, maybe two. I want answers and happened to wake up this morning with all the shit needed to get 'em."

"You sure about this?" Jon asked.

"Sure as my big, swinging sack, and both balls in it."

Jon was silent, trying to figure whether he even wanted to talk Houser out of whatever he had in mind.

Houser interrupted the thought. "I'm in front of his house already. Asshole left for work about forty minutes ago. I'm going inside to see what's up."

The line went dead, and so did Jon's choice in the matter.

He dropped the phone in his pocket.

"Who was that?" Cassidy said.

"My friend, Brock."

"And?" Cassidy stared. "Spill it, Jonny. I read between the lines already, now tell me the shit I don't know."

"Know a guy named Larry Whistler?"

Cassidy thought for a moment then shook her head no.

"He lives about three blocks from you. Before Hamilton was home, he lived in Rochester, New York. And, allegedly," Jon measured his words, "he had some trouble keeping his hands to himself there."

Cassidy gritted her teeth and began to breathe heavily through her nostrils.

Jon continued. "A mentally disabled girl's parents swore he was guilty, but there wasn't any evidence, so the powers that be had to drop the case. Whistler packed up and headed here." He finished the sentence he didn't want to say. "And now he's a youth pastor working under Avery."

Cassidy's eyes went wide. "I know him! At least I've seen him. I thought he seemed a little too damned happy to be teaching kids. So, what's your friend gonna do?"

"Whatever will get him the answers we're looking for."

"How do you know he can get them?"

Jon swallowed, hoping Houser made the right move. "Because once Houser gets scent of something, he doesn't stop until he gets what he wants."

Chapter 5 - Brock Houser

Houser pushed the front door open, gun drawn in his ungloved hand, as he made his way into Larry Whistler's home.

The house was two stories, common from what he'd seen on the island so far, with a well-manicured lawn, plenty of trees, and a tall, brown privacy fence surrounding the back yard. The inside of the house was another story, though, something from a hoarder's wet dream, with boxes, newspapers, garbage bags stuffed with all sorts of something, open boxes of food, and empty pizza boxes filling nearly every inch of the bottom story. The house reeked strongly of cat urine. At least Houser hoped it was cat urine.

"Jesus," he whispered, searching the bottom floor, room by room, wading his way through more of the same. Evidence collection in this house would be a bitch and a litter. He hoped, for the investigating officers' sake, this pig wasn't guilty of anything more than filth in his sty.

"Jon's paying me double for this bullshit," he said, navigating his way through the pyramids of laundry littering the stairway.

The second floor was more shit decorating shit, crowned

on piles and mountains of crap. Shockingly, the man's bedroom was nearly immaculate, especially compared to the rest of the dump.

A large TV sat on the dresser beside an ancient-looking PS4. On the nightstand lay a plate with half a muffin and a cup half-filled with water. Beside the plate was a bottle of lotion, and next to that, an iPad.

Houser holstered his gun and picked up the iPad with his gloved hand to see what sort of shit the man was into and maybe sort through his e-mail for anything that could tie him to the missing child.

He didn't have to search long.

There were several photos of children playing on a playground, which all seemed to be taken from far away with a telephoto lens. Houser's stomach turned as he swiped with his ungloved hand through the images. All the photos were of young girls, with the occasional boy in the background. A high percentage of shots aimed up the girls' skirts.

Jesus! Fucking scumbag.

Houser kept swiping until he saw Emma in a photo.

A chill ran through his body. He swiped forward, five, ten, twelve photos of Emma in a row, suggesting the perv had a thing specifically for Emma — all the proof he needed to make this asshole as his prime fucking suspect. Houser flipped through more photos. No nudes or child porn, but the pics were enough to get him a room with a mirror down at the station.

Not finding anything else of note, and not wanting to tamper with what might wind up as evidence, Houser set the iPad back on the nightstand, then searched the rest of the room, stomach sinking as he opened the nightstand drawer on the other side of the bed and found several pairs of girls' underwear, many stained and all small.

Houser's blood began to boil, more certain than ever that he'd found the fucker who took Emma. He prayed to God the man hadn't already killed her and dumped her somewhere. On an island like this, filled with tons of woods? The odds of finding the poor girl alive weren't looking good.

Houser searched the rest of the top floor, then the remainder of the house, looking for anything else that might tie the guy to taking Emma, or even to Emma herself. Many of these old houses had crawl spaces, basements, and attics, plenty of places to hold a kidnapping victim. Hell, the man could have five kids downstairs under the mountains of bullshit.

Finding nothing inside, Houser hit the backyard. There was a blue shed in the rear of the property, which might house yard equipment, but could easily pull duty as a prison. He walked through the back yard, glancing up at the window of the house next door where an old, white-haired woman was watching him — the same house that hadn't answered the door when he knocked earlier. Houser waved, pretty sure she was calling the cops. He had to act quickly, so he hurried to the shed.

Wasn't surprised at all to find a padlock on the doors.

He pictured Emma on the other side. At first, he imagined her alive. Then he remembered finding Cecilia as the life was fading from her eyes.

Please don't be dead. Please don't be dead. Please don't be dead.

He knocked on the shed, the tin door bouncing in its track from the weight of his blows.

No response.

"Hello? Anyone in there? I'm here to help you."

Nothing.

Houser looked around for something he could use to pick the lock or smash it if he had to, but saw nothing. He could shoot it but didn't want to attract any more of an audience than he already had. Nor did he want to take the chance of hitting someone inside.

So, he stepped back a bit and kicked the door off its tracks with a loud crash.

If the old lady hadn't already called the cops, the kick had to dial the three digits.

There was nothing in the shed, except for a motley assortment of gardening tools. A shovel leaned in the corner, with dark, fresh soil staining the business end. The sick in his gut said it was more future evidence.

Houser looked behind him, glancing around the yard, but saw no indication of any recent burials.

He glanced back up and saw the old lady duck from the window.

Time to go.

He ran back inside the house, closing the back door, then raced out the front, locking the bottom lock on his way out.

Once in his car, he put the car in motion and called Jon.

"Hey, just left his house. No sign of Emma, but fucker has an ass ton of pics on his iPad — little girls on a playground. Particular interest in Emma, a dozen or more shots, right in a row."

"Jesus," Jon breathed. "Now what? Do we call the police?"

"Not yet," Houser said. "I'm on my way to the church right now."

"The church?" Jon swallowed.

"Yeah, I'm not waiting around all day for him to get home. Say, do they have a playground at the church? Emma ever go there?"

Jon took a moment to fill Cassidy in on the details, then asked if Emma ever went to the church or the playground. Then he was back on the phone. "She's not sure if she went to Sunday school there, but yeah, they went to church services sometimes. And to the playground."

"Okay. Right now, this guy is our suspect, and I'm gonna go pay him a visit."

"Don't do anything stupid," Jon said.

"Don't *you* do anything stupid," Houser said. "Like calling the cops. Let me do what I do well so this guy doesn't lawyer up before I get a chance to let him smell the sweetness of my breath on his ears."

"Okay. I'll wait to hear from you. Actually, no, we're gonna meet you at the church."

"It's up to you. But I've gotta warn you, I think the old lady next door may have called the cops already, or maybe even called him at church. So if he's on the move, I'm not waitin' for you."

"Please," Jon said, "find her."

"Call Chief Brady. Call Paladin. Tell them to get search teams in the woods around Whistler's house. Just don't say anything about Whistler, yet, unless you have to."

"Do you think she's ... dead?"

"I'm not gonna lie to you, Jon. We're running out of time."

~

THE CHURCH GROUNDS had five buildings and a playground. The largest building was the church, a massive, traditional-looking, wood-and-stone structure with high arches, several stained glass windows beneath winding spires, and a giant cross on the steeple you could see from the sea. Beside the church, there were four squat one-story buildings forming an X in all four directions. The two buildings in the front were set up in rows, probably classrooms for daycare. The buildings in the back looked administrative or like they maybe doubled as meeting spaces. In the back of the property, nudged up against the woods, was a large playground — the one from the photos.

There were about twenty preschool-aged kids playing there, with two female teachers watching. No sign of the pervert, yet.

Houser parked his car and threw on his black sports jacket to conceal his gun. He bypassed the church, approached the rear buildings, toward the administrative offices, then opened a door marked OFFICE.

A chubby red-headed woman in her mid-thirties sat at a desk tapping at a keyboard, her gaze fixed on a paper-thin screen. She looked up, surprised to see a tall stranger standing in front of her.

"Hello, my name is Brock Houser." He showed her his badge. "I'm a private attorney working for the Hughes family, searching for their missing daughter, Emma. You've seen this on the news, I assume?"

"Yeah," the woman said, concern creeping across her face. The nameplate on her desk read, *Mrs. Mallory.*

"Good. Her grandmother is worried sick, and I believe someone who works here may have some information that could help us in the case."

Mallory's eyes widened and she gasped. "Someone here?"

"Yes." Houser lowered his voice to a whisper, gaining her confidence through the revelation of a 'secret.' "I'm trying to keep things hush-hush so as not to have people thinking this guy is dangerous or anything. His name is Larry Whistler. His neighbors said he worked here and might be able to help us find her."

"Mr. Larry?" Mallory said, alarmed. "Yeah, he works here. He's a youth pastor on the weekends but teaches music class during the week. Did he do something wrong?"

"Oh, no. I just need to talk to him because he might be able to help out. And I don't want to see his name all over the news for no good reason. You know how ugly the media can get and how rumors can spread. Pretty soon everyone's talkin' how Mr. Whistler works here, and he'll look after the kids *real good*, if you catch my drift."

Mallory nodded. "Oh, yes. We wouldn't want that. Mr. Larry is so great with the kids."

Yeah, I'll bet. "Can you tell me where I can find him?"

Mrs. Mallory paused, and for a moment Houser was afraid she was going to call her boss for permission — permission he'd never get. People had a habit of protecting their own, even when giving solace to monsters.

Then Mrs. Mallory picked up the phone, pressed two digits, and said, "Mr. Larry, can you come to the office, please?"

"Yes, Mrs. Mallory," he said over the speakerphone.

He suppressed a sigh of relief that he hadn't read her wrong.

While he waited, Mallory made small talk with him about Emma and how tragic it was that she'd go missing right after her mother was killed. She talked about seeing Emma the day of the funeral, how sweet the girl was, and how much she looked like her mother.

The door behind Houser opened, and Whistler entered the room. The moment he saw Houser standing there, something clicked in his eyes. Asshole knew trouble when he saw it.

"This is Mr. Houser, an investigator," Mallory said.

Before she even finished her sentence, the scumbag turned and ran out the door.

Shit!

Houser tore after him through the churchyard, yelling, "I just want to talk!"

Whistler was surprisingly fast for a guy in his late forties, but not fast enough. Houser caught him at the edge of the parking lot and slammed him to the ground.

"I didn't do anything!" the man screamed, kicking Houser, just barely missing his crotch.

"You *did not* just kick me!" Houser grabbed the man's leg, then twisted his ankle back, taking his time while he considered how loud he wanted the asshole to scream.

Houser decided to bend him into a roar.

Whistler shrieked with what sounded like two parts pain

and three parts terror, then flipped to his stomach as he tried squirming away.

Houser was on him in seconds, wrenching his wrist back and slapping cuffs on him as the pervert tried to wiggle away like a worm through the dirt.

Now that he had him down, Houser punched him hard in the back of his ribs.

Whistler screamed again.

"Where is she?"

"Where's who?"

Houser punched him again, harder. "Don't make me fucking ask again. Tell me now. Or else I'm gonna cut your balls off and hang them from my rearview."

"I swear I don't know what you're talking about!"

Houser spun the man, stomach to the sun, then grabbed him hard by the cheeks and squeezed them together hard enough to turn them purple. He violently shook Whistler's head back and forth.

"I know what you are. You might be able to hide your sick little fetishes from your friends, these good people at the church, and maybe even God above. But you can't hide it from me. I know what you are." Houser leaned in close enough for Whistler to smell the sweetness of his breath as he growled. "Don't make me ask again. Where is she?"

Whistler cried, "I swear, I don't —"

Houser smacked him hard in the face, then grabbed him by the cheeks again, splaying his fingers over Whistler's flesh then squeezing even harder.

"Where is Emma Hughes?"

Whistler's eyes widened, recognizing the name, maybe even thinking of the photos he'd snapped of the girl or where he was holding her.

"Ah. See. You *do* know who I'm talking about." Houser's smile spread. "Now, tell me."

"I don't know." Whistler's lips quivered in fear as he sobbed.

Houser shook his head, "Oh, man. That's too bad. I was really hoping you wouldn't make me get Betty."

"Betty?" Looks of fear and confusion crossed his face. "Who's Betty?"

Houser pulled the gun from his holster, and displayed it for Whistler, enjoying the terror in the man's eyes. "Oh, you don't know Betty? That's a shame, because she's just itching to know you." He set the barrel of the pistol against Whistler's forehead.

Whistler cried out.

Houser could sense eyes on him, from the church, from the playground, and the surrounding buildings. He paid them no attention. While he didn't want to do this in front of kids, possibly scarring them for life, the alternative was to waste time he might not have bringing Whistler somewhere where they could talk.

Time for conversation had run out.

Now was time for truth-telling.

"You ever see a gunshot wound to the head up close?" Houser asked. "I do love Betty, but she's a messy bitch. Guess you don't need to care about that. It's not like *you'll* have to clean up the mess."

"Please," Whistler whimpered.

"I'm gonna count to five, Larry. And then I'm gonna stop counting, and I'm gonna let Betty get her way."

"No!" Whistler cried louder, trying again to squirm free.

Houser pushed the gun harder against his head, pressing his weight even more onto the man's chest.

"Five!"

"No, no! Please, I don't know anything."

"Four!"

"Please. I never touched her. All I did was look."

"Three!"

Whistler let out a long wail, running out of excuses.

"Two."

"I swear!"

"Now or never, Larry!" Houser yelled.

And then Houser heard the yell behind him.

"Put the gun down!"

Houser turned to see a police officer and two Paladin guards, weapons drawn and every gun aimed at him.

Fuck.

Chapter 6 - Cassidy Hughes

11:30 a.m.

JON AND CASSIDY were standing beneath the fluttering flag at the police station, the cold wind biting the both of them as a dark cloud loomed on the horizon. She was thankful for his presence, and grateful she was too tired and too worried about Emma to properly hate him.

They were waiting for Sgt. Sam Johnson to finish questioning Whistler and for Chief Brady to let Houser go from the holding cell. She was anxious, but Jon had a surprisingly calming effect on her. And so far, she'd been able to avoid the craving for the pill in her pocket.

Cassidy lit her Marlboro Light, took a drag, then offered the pack to Jon.

He shook his head.

"What, you're too good to smoke now?"

"Not too good to smoke. Just don't want to. I quit a few years back."

"You were chain-smoking in *Bullocks*."

Jon laughed. "That's a movie, Cass. I'll smoke for a movie,

especially because it pisses the MPAA off, and a bunch of the whinier bitches in Hollywood, which always makes me happy." He looked at Cassidy, realization lighting his face. "You saw *Bullocks*?"

She looked down, embarrassed, then laughed, "Yeah. It was good. At least better than that *Everlasting* bullshit."

"Ha," Jon said. "No argument there." Another six seconds of silence, then he held out his hand. "Okay, give me one."

Cassidy gave him a cigarette and offered him a light. "Still smoke weed?"

Jon took a big drag, then blew the smoke toward the sea. "Every chance I get."

She laughed. "Don't suppose you brought any with you? Private jet and all?"

He shook his head. "I fly commercial. Besides, aren't you sober?"

"Weed doesn't count. It's the pills I've gotta be careful with." She took another drag, happy to have a break from hating Jon, however temporary it might be.

"Think Johnson's getting anything?"

Cassidy narrowed her eyes and shook her head. "I don't know, but if Whistler hurt Emma, I'll ruin his fucking life." She pulled on her cigarette hard. "That fucker has no idea how small this island can get."

The first drop of rain spattered the concrete. Jon gestured up at the sky, then toward the overhang sloping over the front door of the station. He waved Cassidy forward, then hopped up the six steps of the porch just behind her. Chief Brady opened the door just as she hit the top step.

"Sorry." He lowered his head with a silent confession of defeat. "We've got nothing. I'm waiting to hear back from the officers on the scene, to see what they find in his house."

"I wanna see Houser," Jon said. "I'll pay his bail."

Brady shook his head. "Not necessary, Jon. No bail needed. I'm happy to let Mr. Houser go, but just so you know,

Mr. Whistler can press charges." He sighed. "And he probably will."

Jon looked like he could've torn the head from a chicken. It was hard for Cassidy to hear him clearly through his gritted teeth, but she would've bet the pill in her pocket he said, "I'd love to see him try."

She flicked her cigarette over the ledge into dirt already well on its way to mud, then took a step toward the chief.

"What the fuck, Brady? There's a missing nine-year-old girl on the island. What in the hell are you going to do about it? Emma could already be dead or dying or worse." Cassidy wasn't even sure what was worse than dead or dying, but her lip was quivering and her body was suddenly shaking with something more than what she'd expect from the sea's chill or the pills' itch.

Brady's eyes softened. "We're doing our best, Cassidy. And there's nothing I'm focused on more than Emma right now. I promise. We're doing, and will continue to do, everything we can to find her."

"Why don't you let Paladin handle this? They're obviously more suited to the search, with more cars, officers, weapons, and balls."

Brady kept his cool. "There are more than a dozen Paladin officers helping us right now. That's generous enough."

"Bullshit!" Cassidy yelled. "That's bullshit, and you goddamn know it! They could send in a force. You know there'd be at least two dozen of 'em if there had been another break-in at one of their precious labs."

Cassidy waited for an answer, but if Brady had one, he was keeping it to himself.

"Why don't you demand it, Brady, right now? Call Conway Industries and tell them there's a missing nine-year-old girl on the island, and if she isn't found pretty goddamn quick, her crazy aunt is just loony enough to call *The Times* and see what they say about the bazillionaire family who won't let the local law share their pet police force to find her."

Though Cassidy's entire body was shaking, it wasn't vibrating too fast for her to miss the look of terror that tore through Brady's eyes.

"That won't be necessary, Cassidy. Just calm down, and we'll figure this out."

Brady's phone rang. He reached inside his pocket, fished for his the phone, then glanced at the screen. "Excuse me."

Jon nodded.

Cassidy stood rooted to concrete as Brady stepped inside the station.

Jon looked at her, like he was smart enough to say nothing, then proved himself an idiot by opening his mouth anyway. "You okay, Cassidy?"

Cassidy nodded, and Jon got stupider.

"You know, you're gonna have to settle down. Brady's doing the best he can to find Emma. Everyone is."

Cassidy thought, *bullshit,* but ignored Jon.

"And Houser will help. He's the best, I promise, maybe even better than the best."

Jon gave Cassidy a thin smile, but she continued to ignore him and kept ignoring him until the front door of the station swung open and Brady's boots were back on the porch.

He seemed both taller and sadder as he walked up to Cassidy and looked her in the eye. "You wanna tell me again where you were the night Emma went missing?"

"I told you," Cassidy said, her voice steady. "I was home. I fell asleep, and when I woke the next morning, Emma was gone."

"So, you didn't go anywhere?"

Cassidy could feel Brady's doubt rising like heat waves over the asphalt but lied anyway. "No, I was home with my mom. You can ask her."

She sensed Jon's eyes burning with the same heat as Brady's.

The chief said, "Really, Cassidy? Because one of my guys is over at Paladin reviewing the security footage taken from your street the night Emma went missing, and he says you left for a bit. You wanna tell me where you went?"

Cassidy said nothing, just shoved her hands inside her pockets and stared at Brady.

"Wait," Jon said. "You guys have the surveillance video? Did you see Emma leave?"

"No. There was some static on the camera around three in the morning or so, which lasted about two minutes. Other than that, nothing."

Cassidy didn't answer the chief's question, but instead asked her own. "And did you get footage from Whistler's house? Huh?"

"I've asked for the footage, yes. Now, you wanna tell me where you went?"

Cassidy felt Jon's eyes on her. Judging her. Accusing her. It was only a matter of time before they found the truth if they pieced all the island's CCTV footage together. But it seemed unlikely that they'd spend that much time on doing so unless Emma wasn't found. Or was found dead. So, she'd lie her ass off until then.

"I went for a drive. My mom was driving me nuts. I was stressed out, and missing Sarah." She began to cry. The tears were fake, at first, but quickly became real.

Jon surprised her by opening his arms and hugging her.

She accepted his embrace until Chief Brady excused himself, saying he was going inside to see if he could get something out of Whistler.

The lie had worked. But for how long?

As the door closed, she let the tears flow, and was surprised at how much better she felt hugging Jon than hating him.

Chapter 7 - Alex Heller

The first half of Alex's return to Hamilton K-12 was relatively quiet, even if supremely uncomfortable. Teachers seemed afraid to look him in the eye. Students eyed him suspiciously, accusation in their faces. Conversations and jokes once passed with friends had twisted into awkward glances and, at best, quiet nods. Alex wasn't sure if people hated or feared him, or maybe they just didn't know how to talk to him. He felt like a tourist in a world where he'd always been a citizen.

He understood the suspicion, but Alex had yet to bury his father and was mourning, the same as they.

But he doubted he'd get a single "I'm sorry" from his schoolmates, and if he was being honest, couldn't imagine feeling much like giving one if he'd been on the other side of the violence.

Not a single student had spoken to him between first period and lunch, except for Katie, who added a few awkward words to her smile on the few occasions when he passed her in the hallways. Before fourth period Alex met her in front of her locker and admitted he'd made a mistake by coming back to school so soon. "I'm getting out of here at lunch. Interested?"

Katie looked nervous. "I'm not sure."

"It's fine with me either way," Alex said. "But if you wanna bail, meet me behind the racquetball courts." He added, "See ya when I see ya," then took off down the hall.

~

SECURITY WAS TIGHTER in the school than it had been, with four Paladin guards instead of one, patrolling the campus. But none was watching when Alex made a break for the racquetball courts and the hole in the fence Alex and his onetime crew had used to escape into the surrounding woods a few times before.

Normally, getting caught skipping school meant an automatic suspension, which always seemed ironic to Alex. Skip school and get punished by being sent home for one to three additional days. *Hey, I'll take that punishment!* But Alex wasn't too concerned about getting busted on his first day back. The dean was sure to go easy on him, considering the circumstance.

Alex didn't head straight to the hole in the fence, however. He sat far back in the corner of the racquetball court on the right, where the walls met. It had rained earlier, but the sun was out now, and the court had dried. He set his backpack on the ground, then pulled his Moleskine notebook and Pilot pen from the bag. He wanted to explore the story idea he had the other day in his father's office, about inanimate objects mourning their lost owner. It was a unique idea, and writing about it might give him a chance to work through some of his feelings about his father.

He was one line in when footsteps paused his pen. Alex looked up, expecting to see Katie. But it wasn't her. It was Jake Brewster, whose best friend, Eddie Tarroza, had been one of the victims. He was with Ray Wilson, another of Eddie's friends. All three had belonged to the row team and were pretty much the Unholy Trinity of royal assholes.

Eddie was the one death Alex hadn't missed a lot of sleep over.

"How's it going, Heller?" Jake said as the pair closed in on Alex, cornering, and hanging over him.

"Okay." Alex kept his attention on the book, pretending to write, knowing shit was seconds from going bad, which was the very thing his mother had warned him might happen.

Eddie and Ray were two of the only kids Alex ever had problems with back in middle school. They had bullied him for a few weeks until Alex's dad said something to Eddie's, and they finally backed off. Though they'd stopped outright fucking with him, they never passed Alex again without snickering. Jake was all too quick to join in the snickering, of course.

Jake and Ray towered over him, taunting him in their silence. Alex stopped writing, wondering who would open their mouth first, or if they were just going to start hitting him. He wanted to look up but didn't dare tempt them. There were two of them and only one of him. Even if it had just been Jake, Alex would have had a tough fight on his hands. And there was also an excellent chance Katie would be coming around the corner at any moment. The last thing Alex wanted was for her to see him getting his ass kicked. Or worse, have her get caught up in the fight.

That was assuming they only wanted a fight. Maybe they intended to spill blood for blood.

Jake kicked Alex in the chin. It wasn't hard. He seemed more interested in provoking him than actually hurting him.

Alex looked up. He said nothing as he met Jake's dark, beady-eyed stare.

Ray kicked next, without holding back. His foot landed on Alex's arm, hard, knocking his moleskin and pen to the court.

"Get up, pussy!" Jake said.

"I don't want to fight." Alex tried to blink away the pain while bracing for another blow.

"Too bad," Ray said. "You're gonna pay for what your father did."

"He killed Eddie!" Jake swung a balled fist at Alex's ear.

"Fuck!" Alex screamed and trying to rise.

Ray kicked him in the right ribcage, sending Alex reeling back into the wall. Hard. Pain tore through his right shoulder.

Ray and Jake blocked his escape. Jake reached into his pocket and pulled out a knife, pushing a button which popped a blade from the black handle. The knife wasn't large, though big and sharp enough to kill.

Alex's eyes darted between the thugs, weighing his options through the thin slivers of seconds. He didn't want to fight, but the knife stripped him of the choice.

Fighting might not be enough. Alex might have to kill.

"Leave him alone!" a girl's voice shouted, bouncing off the court walls – Katie.

"Get outta here, bitch," Jake said, turning to Katie. Ray turned toward her, too. This was Alex's only chance.

He ran at Jake, grabbing his right wrist to keep him from using the knife, then reached up and hit Jake's head, shoving it backward into the concrete wall with a loud thud.

Jake dropped the knife and slumped to the ground.

Oh, shit, I killed him!

As Alex stared in shock at Jake's motionless body, Ray grabbed him from behind and knocked Alex to the ground, falling on top of him with a fury of punches.

Alex squirmed, trying to break free, putting his arms out in front of his face, as his arms were mercilessly battered.

"Get off of him!" Katie screamed.

As Katie ran toward them, fear coursed through Alex's veins, terrified that Ray might turn and hurt her, or worse.

But Ray never had a chance.

Katie grabbed him from behind, lifted him from Alex, then threw him from where they were beside the left wall, all the way to the right one, where Ray slapped the wall and fell to the ground, screaming.

Alex stared at Katie in disbelief.

Did she just pick him up and throw him?

That's impossible!

Katie grabbed Alex's book and pen and dropped them in his backpack. Then she tossed him his bag.

"Let's go." She spoke like some kind of military commando, quick, to the point, and ready for action.

Alex stared at Jake, still motionless on the ground, then turned to Ray, who was starting to get up, in obvious agony.

"Run!" Katie said, pulling Alex from his state.

He ran, following her into the woods, wondering two things.

Had he murdered Jake?

And did Katie really do what he thought she did?

Chapter 8 - Milo Anderson

Milo sat in economics, his final class of the day, hating life in general and himself specifically. Normally, his last class was with Alex, but Alex's seat was empty.

It didn't help that Milo was bored out of his mind, which he probably wouldn't be if he could keep his mind on anything, and everything wasn't a constant reminder of Jessica, Manny, or Alex.

Milo's phone buzzed in his pocket. He looked around the room, though he didn't care nearly as much as he usually would whether or not he was caught or not.

No, he wasn't supposed to have his phone outside of his backpack, and yes, checking texts in class was grounds for detention, but Milo cared about whether or not he got a pink slip for detention approximately not at all.

He palmed the cell from his pocket, turning his thumb on the outside so he could see the caller ID.

The text from Jesus sent a hard lump into Milo's soggy throat.

Manny is dead. Died in his sleep fifteen minutes ago. Thought you should know.

Milo had to chew his bottom lip to keep from crying but

was seconds from springing a leak, anyway. He looked around the classroom at the mostly vacant faces, then up at Mrs. Mellakar, wondering if he should make an announcement to the rest of the students.

Would his classmates want to know that Manny was dead? Or would that only add to their misery? They would all find out eventually, so did he have to be the bearer of bad news?

What would Manny have wanted?

Jesus must have had something else to say, because Milo's cell started buzzing inside his pocket a second after he slipped it inside. Or maybe Jesus just wanted to make sure Milo had seen the first message since he hadn't responded.

It was easy enough to check a text, texting back might be pushing his luck.

His cell went quiet, then buzzed again a few seconds later.

Milo pulled the phone from his pocket and looked at the new text that wasn't from Jesus. It was from Cody, the weird guy he'd seen on the LiveLyfe message board. The text said: *Need to talk. Now.*

Milo felt a horrible chill wondering how Cody had his number in the first place. Somehow, Milo felt his text had something to do with Manny.

"I have to go to the bathroom, Mrs. Mellakar." Milo raised his hand with one arm while clutching his stomach with the other, not bothering to wait to get called on.

Milo wasn't sure if it was the arm on the stomach, the look on his face, or the fact that his best friend's dad gave two of the most important people in his life a matching set of bullets, but Mrs. Mellakar simply nodded.

Milo slowly rose from his seat, then walked to the door and closed it behind him. Once in the hall, he tore off toward the bathroom, locked himself inside a stall, then waited for Cody to text or call. Two minutes later, a chill shot through his body as the phone buzzed in his hand.

"Hello?"

"It's Cody." Definitely not a kid. Maybe in his thirties, though it was hard to tell since he was obviously trying to disguise it.

Milo said nothing.

Cody said, "Manny is dead."

How did he know that?

Curiosity had Milo swallowing his tongue. It took him a half minute to find it before he said, "Yeah, I heard. From his brother. How about you?"

"I have my sources." After a long pause, he said, "*They* got him."

Cody said *They* like it was a curse word.

"Who are *they*?"

Cody ignored him. "Who else knows you saw Heller say something to Manny? Did you tell the police? Do they know you saw?"

Milo nodded even though Cody couldn't see him. "Yeah, but why does that matter? Are you saying they had Manny killed? Because "they" didn't. Manny died naturally. His brother was there when it happened, and he's the one who told me."

Jesus had actually texted Milo, not told him, and Milo had no idea if Jesus was actually in the room when Manny passed, but that didn't change the truth. No one killed Manny, and whoever Cody was, he was probably just trying to scare him.

"They have their ways," Cody said.

It wasn't what Cody said, but how he said it that felt like a cool blade of ice slipping beneath the heat of Milo's skin. He gulped.

Cody said, "I didn't think they'd strike now. In fact, I was sure they wouldn't. But they did, and that means they're more worried about what Manny was going to say than I realized." He paused, then dropped a ton of bricks on top of Milo. "That means you're probably next."

"What?" Milo cried, curling his knees to his chest and

pushing his back against the cold tile of the bathroom stall. "What do you mean?"

"They might think you know more than you're saying, Milo. You need to get out of town. Now."

"That's crazy. *You're* crazy. This whole thing is crazy. I can't leave the island. I don't have anywhere to go."

As though Milo hadn't protested at all, Cody said, "I'll be in touch later tonight. We'll work this out."

Horror flashed through Milo's mind.

Mr. Heller paused, looking at Manny with hollow eyes, his expression drifting from nervous and glassy to haunted. He kneeled toward Manny, lying in a pool of blood and screamed, or whispered, hard to tell which through the chaos. He stood, pointed his gun at the word Eleven, then placed the pistol in his mouth and pulled the trigger.

Sudden terror turned his voice to a whisper. "How do I know I can trust you?"

"You don't," Cody said. "But if you want to live, you don't have a choice."

The line went dead.

Milo sat on the top of the porcelain until he could calm his breathing into a steady beat. Then he lowered his feet to the tile, opened the stall, walked to the mirror and stared.

Milo looked worse than he had expected, and exactly like what he was — a hollow shell of the boy he had been a week and one lifetime before.

Chapter 9 - Brock Houser

Houser was driving back to Whistler's to check the woods surrounding his house while Jon and Cassidy hung out at the police station, waiting to see if Whistler spilled his guts.

If Brady had let Houser interrogate him as requested, guts would have been spilled already. But Brady was a stickler for "rules" and wanted to be sure whatever happened at the station didn't help the fucker avoid prosecution. Houser couldn't complain too much. Brady did let him walk, which he didn't have to do. Still, Houser would have loved to have had a few minutes alone with the sick fucker. At least he could've gotten a feel for whether Emma was still alive.

Houser drove in silence, glancing down at Ted E. Bear, riding shotgun as always, and found his mind meandering down memory lane.

No.

Can't think about her now.

Need to keep my head in the game.

As Houser neared Whistler's house, his cell phone rang. Caller ID indicated it was Jon.

"Yeah, boss?"

"Can you meet us back where we met this morning? Vivian's house?"

"Yeah, why? What's up?"

"Cassidy remembered something. It's weird, but it's better than the nothing we've got."

"So, Whistler didn't talk?"

"Not yet. He asked for a lawyer."

"Shit," Houser said. "Okay. See ya in a few."

~

THEY MET in front of Vivian's house, where Jon was sitting in a white Toyota Avalon beside Cassidy.

"Hop in," Jon said. "We're gonna take a ride."

"Okay." Houser ran back to his car, grabbed his gear bag and Ted E. Bear, then hopped into the back seat of Jon's car.

Cassidy turned from the front passenger seat. "What's with the teddy bear?"

"Don't ask." Jon smiled.

"An old friend. I don't leave home without him. So, what do we have?"

"Last night, my mom said something really weird when I got home," Cassidy said. "She was drunk as hell, even drunker than usual, and said something about Sarah being taken by 'people in the sky.' When I woke up this morning, she denied it, saying she was drunk, but when I brought it up to Jon, he said he had a dream once about something happening to Sarah when we were kids. She'd been taken while we were playing hide 'n' seek. And the weirdest thing is, I vaguely had a dream just like that. And the really weird part is I didn't even remember ever having the dream until Jon mentioned it. Like déjà vu."

"Okay, so you're saying Emma was taken by ... um, an alien or something?" Houser tried not to laugh.

"I don't know what I'm saying, but when Jon mentioned

the dream, and where we'd been playing in the dream — the woods by Mom's house — I thought maybe we should try looking there."

"It's not near Whistler's house, though, is it?" Houser asked.

"Well, the island isn't that big. Everything is relatively close to everything else," Jon said.

Houser was going to ask why they were going on a hunch, but there was something in Cassidy's eyes, that look of guilt, that made him wonder if maybe she had something to do with the missing girl after all. Was she leading them to the girl's body now that they had someone to pin the crime on? He'd seen that story play out a dozen times or more on the news and hoped to Christ it wasn't the case this time. He had no tolerance for monsters, especially those who killed their own kids.

She didn't feel like a murderer to him, though. But there were definitely fireworks behind her eyes — something bad she was hiding. Perhaps it was an accident and she panicked and hid the poor girl's body in the woods. It wouldn't be the first time something like that happened, either, and certainly not the last. Cassidy looked back at Houser, and their gazes met.

Yes, she's guilty of something. What did you do, Cassidy Hughes?

If she were friends with anyone other than Jon, he would have her in a room next to Whistler and hedge his bets. But since she was Jon's friend, and this was Jon's daughter, Houser would keep his suspicions to himself — for now.

"So, you gonna tell me more about the bear?" she asked.

Houser looked up and caught Jon's face in the rearview, about to open his mouth and spare Houser from retelling a story Jon knew by heart, every version.

"It's okay," Houser said. "I don't mind."

Maybe the story might move Cassidy to come clean about whatever she was hiding.

"It was ten years back. Me and my partner, Chan, were searching for a missing girl. Cecilia Ramirez. She was six years old. You hear of her? It made the national news."

"No." Cassidy shook her head.

Houser told her the story, and how they'd failed to get a search warrant in time. When they finally got to her, the girl was dying. It was the case that more or less closed the coffin on Houser's career.

"About two weeks after she died, I was on desk duty when this little Spanish guy came in. He was wearing a mechanic's uniform, dirty as hell, and I barely recognized him at first. But then, as he approached my desk, I remembered. It was Juan Ramirez, the girl's father. He and his wife had been devastated. They heard on the news before I was able to tell them in person. Goddamned fucking media. Anyway, the minute I saw him, I felt like shit. Because I'd done something I'd never done before."

Cassidy's eyes were starting to well up. Houser went on.

"I promised him we'd find his girl. Alive. I don't even know why the fuck I made the promise, except maybe I wanted it to come true so bad. When I came to their house to tell them, he and his wife were furious with me. His wife punched me on the chest. Juan told me to please leave and never come back."

"Oh, shit," Cassidy said.

"Yeah, so here he was in the station, and I'm dreading it. He's holding a brown paper bag, and part of me is thinking he might have come in with a gun to either shoot me or himself. But instead, he pulled out this teddy bear here. He said it had been Cecilia's. He handed me a picture of her and the bear together. She was smiling so brightly, and it was so unlike every other image of her that I had in my head. She was so sweet and happy. He said he wanted me to have the picture and the bear, so I'd have a good memory of Cecilia."

"Oh, God." Cassidy wept openly.

"I about broke down right there. Then he hugged me. And that's when I lost it."

"I'll bet," Cassidy said.

"So, yeah, that's how I came to partner up with Ted E. Bear. He's quiet, but on the plus side, he doesn't eat all my snacks on stakeouts. I wish I could say that for some of my human partners."

Cassidy smiled and wiped the streaks from her cheeks.

As she did, he looked into her eyes, trying to read what was there and dig to whatever she hid in the depths of her sadness.

THEY SPLIT INTO THREE, walking through the thick forest and calling for Emma. Houser could hear Jon and Cassidy, calling her name every thirty seconds or so, coming close to alternating turns.

"Emma!" Houser called, as he looked in the sky at the darkening clouds up above.

A cold wind started to tear through the trees, causing his companions' words to fade into a fogged mumble. Houser kept moving, searching for any sign of Emma.

Houser happened upon foot traffic, three pairs of feet, and followed it until the trail stopped dead at a set of tire tracks.

He wondered if the footprints belonged to the kidnapper, or just some people out hiking in the woods. Maybe some kids fucking around out here.

The wind began to howl louder as clouds overheard gathered mass and speed, nearly blotting out the sun even though it was just past two p.m.

Houser flashed back to his search for Cecilia, and begged God not to make history repeat.

Please, God, I don't ask for shit. Er, I mean much. Sorry, God.

Please, please, help us find Emma safe and sound, so she can be with her family again.

Please, God. If you do this I swear I'll believe in you again.

Houser doubted God would come through, but went on anyway, hoping it wouldn't start raining again. It was bad enough the weather had turned the woods wintry and black. Say what you wanted about California being a cesspool, at least the weather was always nice.

"Emma!" he shouted again.

Houser heard something weird above the wind.

What the …?

He stopped walking, listening instead, and heard the crackle of static.

Static out here?

He reached down and checked his phone to see if maybe it was making the noise, but it wasn't. His phone was blinking, the screen flickering on, off, on, off, over and over.

The sky poured icy rain down in a torrent.

Houser continued, despite not hearing his partners, deeper into the darkened woods.

"Emma!" he screamed.

In the distance, the howling wind was murdered by a high-pitched scream, almost digital sounding, like the screech of an ancient Internet dialup connection. Thunder crashed. Sounded as though the forest was exploding around him.

"What the hell?" he said to nobody as chaos erupted. The wind was so strong, he fell back. For a moment, he was certain he was about to be sucked away like Dorothy to Oz.

But then, as sudden as the freak storm came, it left. Or more accurately, *stopped.*

A hush draped the woods in quiet and black. Houser looked overhead and saw only swirling dark clouds.

A blinding white light bled then burst through the darkness in a rattling thicket of trees just beyond Houser.

"Emma!" he screamed, running like a rocket toward the light.

Houser was nothing if not agile, particularly for a guy the size of a linebacker.

"Emma!"

As he reached the top of a rise and the last of the trees between himself and the brightness, the light flickered then faded, casting the world into an even deeper black as his eyes struggled to recover from the light.

"Help!" called a small girl's voice.

Houser shot through the black and into a clearing where someone was standing, barely visible in the shadows — a naked girl, drenched and shivering, and crying for her mother.

Chapter 10 - Milo Anderson

Beatrice was in her BMW, sitting in the parking lot of Hamilton K-12, waiting for Milo. Weird, since she picked him up once upon a never. He saw her white SUV sitting two rows from the entrance, the engine running and Other Mother staring.

Though Milo had been looking forward to the walk to clear his mind from the chatter of students and pointless lectures from Mrs. Mellakar, he was happy to have a ride and get him home sooner so he could log on to LiveLyfe and see if he could find Cody. He didn't believe Cody's threats at all, but he was curious to find out just who the hell this guy thought he was and why he was fucking with Milo.

Milo opened the cabin and climbed inside, nodding at Beatrice as he tossed his backpack onto the passenger floor. *Thanks* would have required more kindness from him than he felt. Instead, Milo said, "Why are you here?"

Beatrice said nothing. Probably pissed because he wasn't falling all over himself to worship Her Royal Highness for taking time from her busy day of stuffing shopping bags and signing her name to pick him up from school.

Beatrice put the BMW in reverse then backed out, not looking behind her and making Russ Harvey dart out of the way as she exited space. Harvey dropped his bag on the asphalt and scowled at Beatrice, turning his palms to the sky in a *what in the hell?*

"Whoa, Bea," Milo said. "This is school, not the speedway. Kids everywhere. You wanna watch out?"

Beatrice said nothing, just stared straight with her eyes on the road.

Great. Now she's gonna be a bitch all afternoon.

Milo figured he'd get the silent treatment for correcting her, like always. Beatrice hated to be corrected, especially in public, which he'd not done. The few times he had come with a high cost later.

One time, Other Mother and Dad had thrown a dinner party with a few contenders for the crown of Island's Most Boring. Beatrice told Milo he had to play nice during the meal, even though he'd rather have been playing Grand Theft Auto 6 in his room. He said fine, and was genuinely trying, until midway through the lobster manicotti when Beatrice started mouthing off about the time Milo went on the Timberhawk at Wild Waves and pissed on himself.

Beatrice loved the story since she had told him to use the bathroom right before they'd started standing in line and Milo refused, not realizing how badly he had to go until the metal bar was locking him in place. The coaster was on its way downhill when the dam burst. The girl beside him screamed and turned to Milo in horror. He asked her what her problem was, even though the problem was soaking his side of the seat, too. She called him a pervert and told him he should ask his mommy to buy him some diapers.

Milo took the story like a sport, mouth full of enough sauce and cheese to hide his scowl. He even let Beatrice make it through all the way to the end. But once she did, he lost it, reading her the riot act across the table, yelling that the story wasn't appropriate dinner discussion and that she had no right to embarrass him in front of strangers.

Beatrice smiled, dabbed linen at the corners of her mouth, then laughed her half-cyborg cackle and told Milo he was right. But once company was gone, she started screaming while his father pretended to scroll through the headlines on his tablet, too preoccupied to notice.

"I don't mind being spanked, Milo," she growled, like a female dog. "But if you ever spank me in public again, I will find new ways to make you sorry."

Beatrice didn't talk to him for two days, not once responding to anything he needed. Like that was supposed to discourage him? He could make his own damned lunch, fuck you very much.

But even ignoring him was better than this. Milo didn't understand the silence beside him, which was creepy more than anything else. Beatrice didn't seem angry so much as not quite there. Kind of like yesterday, when he'd come home and she was just staring at the TV and then went to the fridge and put food in her purse. Perhaps it was time to adjust one of the many medications she was on.

Just as well, Milo told himself. If she was being her regular non-bitch mode self, he'd either be listening to crap from the stereo or crap from her mouth. And without some Maroon 5's greatest hits grating his nerves through the speakers, he could sort through the confusion that came with the call from Cody.

Could Milo trust a guy he didn't know, saying stuff he wasn't sure he believed? According to Cody, Milo had no choice. According to Milo, the whole thing was ridiculous, conspiracy theory-sounding bullshit. What Milo needed was outside perspective.

He considered calling Alex but wasn't sure he was ready to rip the bandage from that particular wound. Every time he thought about Alex, the lump in his throat came back. What could he possibly say?

Milo started to sweat, trying to keep his mind from Heller's hand reaching inside the briefcase.

Heller looked down at his desk, then opened his briefcase with a loud snap and stared for what felt like eternity. He finally pulled out a pistol. Manny laughed. Amber Riley, then everyone else, screamed. Heller shot Tommy in the face, and chaos erupted, Heller firing one shot after the other, with students scrambling in every direction. Jessica ran toward him, eyes and mouth hanging open. Heller's blurred figure came into focus, aiming at Jessica.

No!

Milo swallowed, staring out the window as Beatrice made a left onto Beechmont instead of a right. They must be stopping at Jordy's Foods for groceries. Would've been cool if she had asked if he minded.

"We stopping for groceries?"

Beatrice said nothing.

Bitch.

"Mind if we pick up some stuff to make nachos?" he asked. "Fridge is a bit bare."

Beatrice kept staring at the road, ignoring Milo, so he decided to be an asshole. "Fridge went a little empty last night after you decided to start filling your purse with meat. Anything else you manage to get in there? I noticed the aged Romano went missing."

Still nothing.

"That was pretty weird, Bea."

Silence.

"I'm not spanking you in public. Hell, I'm not even spanking you. Just thought it was batshit to load up on cold cuts inside the Gucci. Dad probably wouldn't like that, considering how much the handbag probably cost."

Milo figured *that* would piss her insides out, but Beatrice was still letting the cat run around with her tongue.

Bitch and a half.

Milo wished he could see her eyes, and wondered if they

looked as crazy gone as they had the night before when she'd been staring at the TV, just before she decided to dump the deli in her handbag. But Milo couldn't see anything. Her eyes were with the rest of her face, pointed straight ahead out the window.

They were drawing closer to Jordy's, and Milo was suddenly impatient. Why in the hell had she come to pick him up if she didn't want to? It wasn't like they were trimming minutes from the trip. By the time they left the grocery store, Milo could have already been home, and without the Chilly Willy from Beatrice.

Without moving her eyes from the road, Beatrice reached over to the console and flipped on the stereo. Adam Levine started singing, but only for a moment. Other Mother flipped from iTunes to Sirius, then twisted the dial to the right, finally settling on a station broadcasting nothing but static.

Milo could swear the corner of her mouth twitched in a smile, though her eyes never left the road. She pressed down on the gas, taking the car from forty-five miles an hour to more than sixty-five in seconds.

What the hell?

Milo shifted in his seat, his foot-stomping on an imaginary brake.

He thought of Beatrice as a waxy, plastic bitch to begin with, but she suddenly looked like she was made of plastic, like when she came home from Seattle after getting her Botox. Except when Beatrice got Botox, it looked like she was trying to smile but couldn't. Now it looked like she wasn't even trying.

She swung a left, two blocks from Jordy's, barely slowing enough to navigate the turn.

"Beatrice." He tried to keep his voice steady as his right hand gripped the strap above his window. "Are you going to say anything?"

Blood pooled across the front of Jessica's powder-blue sweater.

Eleven. Jessica stared up at him, scared and searching for any explanation. She said something, eleven, but the screaming whistle in his ears swallowed her words.

"Beatrice!"

Nothing.

"Beatrice!" Milo's voice was laced with hysteria. "Say something. Anything. I just need to know you can hear me!"

Still nothing. Thankfully, she slowed down to a normal pace as she pulled into the parking lot of Jordy's.

Two dozen cars were scattered across the rain-spattered parking lot. A few people shuffled in and out of the front of the store's sliding glass double doors — a mom holding hands with her toddler girl; a fat man, Mr. Hollis, with one arm full of groceries and the other shoving a honeybun into his mouth on his way to his beat-to-shit Silverado; and a young couple in matching jeans and black leather jackets holding hands as they went through the doors.

Other Mother should have been slowing even more but wasn't.

She reached over and turned the static louder, then did the unthinkable by lowering her foot on the gas.

Beatrice was silent.

Milo screamed, the rest of his body paralyzed by fear as they rocketed forward.

His screech, along with the radio's static and the roar of the engine, was a symphony coalescing to a crescendo as Beatrice's BMW crashed through the front of Jordy's, parting glass and aluminum in a curtain of splinters and shards, cries of terror, and fleeing shoppers.

Milo's world went black.

Episode 4

Chapter 1 - Milo Anderson (Age 12)

Hamilton Island, Washington
Five years ago...

MILO WOKE to the sound of his father screaming at someone downstairs.

He glanced at the clock on his nightstand. Midnight.

Who's here?

A chill iced through his insides, wondering if someone had broken into their house and was hurting his father. His mother had left in the middle of the night four months ago, and Milo often wondered, especially at night, if something would happen to his father next.

He opened his door quietly, then slipped through the crack and sneaked to the end of the hall at the edge of the staircase, where he realized they were alone in the house. Dad was on the phone. "No, and that's my final answer. Don't call here again." He sighed as he flipped his cell onto the coffee table and plopped on the couch.

Milo sat crouched at the top of the landing, peering down. Even staring at his back, he could tell his father was furious.

And dad rarely showed emotion, fury least of all. To see him in an unguarded moment made him feel uncomfortable, and like he should just go back to bed. He inched back, the stair beneath his foot creaked.

His father turned, startled by Milo's presence.

"What are you doing?"

"Nothing," Milo squeaked, "I thought I heard something."

"It's nothing. Go back to sleep." Dad sounded exhausted.

Milo was already at the foot of the stairs, slowly approaching the couch. He circled his father, thinking how odd he looked, how … *distraught*. His hair was a mess, and his eyes were red, as if he'd been crying.

"I said go back to bed," Dad snapped, staring at the floor instead of Milo.

Milo sat beside his dad on the couch, cautiously. Nervously.

"Was that call about Mom?" His voice was barely above a whisper.

His father looked up, eyes wide. He didn't just look worried, he seemed almost scared.

"How much of that did you hear?"

Milo's voice split with creeping fear. "What do you mean?"

"Answer the question!" He grabbed Milo's arms tight.

Milo tried to pull back, shocked by his father's sudden violence.

But Dad's grip was too strong to shatter. "How much did you hear?"

"Nothing! Let go!"

"It's not polite to spy on people, Milo." His eyelids drooped, his grip loosened.

"I didn't hear anything!" Milo jumped to his feet. "I'm not spying!"

His father shook his head and then ran his hands through his hair. "I'm sorry. I'm just having a tough time at work right now. I didn't mean to snap at you. Sorry." He patted the cushion next to him.

Milo sat, then fell into his father's hug.

"I'm sorry, buddy."

"It's okay." Tears fell from his eyes. He pulled out of the embrace and wiped his pajama sleeve quickly across his face, hoping his dad wouldn't say anything. Of course, he did.

"What's wrong?"

"Nothing." It didn't make sense to bring it up again. Whenever he tried talking about his mom, or the possibility that she might come home, his father always changed the conversation.

"Not now."

"I don't want to talk about it."

"Maybe some other time, Milo. Okay?"

His father never wanted to talk about it, always pushing it off for "later." But maybe later never came.

Milo decided to spill his guts. "I miss her."

For a long while his father said nothing. Silence stretched, then after what seemed like forever, he wrapped his long arm around Milo's skinny back. "I miss her, too."

"Then why don't you ever talk about her? Why do you pretend she never even existed?" Milo's tears choked half his words.

Dad handed him a box of tissues from the end table, and Milo blew his nose.

"It's hard to think about her," his dad said. "Without wondering what I could've done differently. That maybe she'd be here today if I'd just done something differently."

"It's not your fault she left," Milo said, even though he secretly thought it might be.

His father worked long hours as an analyst for Conway Industries. Milo wasn't sure what his dad did, exactly. The few times Milo wondered out loud, his father said it was complicated, and that it was mostly paperwork and "managing too many people and moving parts." Whatever his job was, it kept him away from home sometimes for weeks at a time.

"Do you think she's going to ever come back?" Milo asked.

His father met his gaze. "I don't think so."

Fresh tears stung Milo's eyes. "Why? Doesn't she love us enough?"

"Oh, no, buddy. It's not that." His dad hugged him even tighter. The same sort of hug that used to make everything okay, back when his dad was still Superman. Back when he could do anything, and his answers never came with "not now," "I don't want to talk about it," or "maybe some other time, Milo."

His mother's disappearance was Kryptonite, however, turning Milo's father into a mere mortal.

After Milo cried some more, Dad pulled away and looked deep into his eyes. His father swallowed, then forced words through the frown on his face. "Your mother was sick, Milo."

Milo was confused. "Sick? What do you mean?"

"She never wanted you to worry, so she never told you, but she wasn't well. She was clinically depressed."

"Depressed? No. Mom was always so happy!"

"She was, Milo, and she was taking medication to help her. For a long time, it seemed like she was better. Earlier this year, the depression started coming back again. The doctors prescribed her something else. And I thought it was working."

Milo sniffled, then wiped his nose. "What do you mean, *thought?*"

"After your mother left, I found out she hadn't picked up her meds in over a month."

"Maybe she didn't need them anymore?"

"When you have clinical depression, you can't always tell when you need your medication. And sometimes, when people go off it, they can get real bad."

Dad stared at him for a moment, as if waiting for Milo to

finally understand what he was saying. But Milo couldn't figure out what his father was trying to tell him.

"Sometimes, when people go off their meds, they get suicidal."

Milo stared at his dad, unable to believe what his dad was suggesting. "No! She didn't kill herself!" Milo shook his head violently back and forth, suddenly sobbing.

"I don't know if she did," his father said, looking down. "But we have to consider the possibility, Milo."

"No!" Milo screamed, launching himself from the couch. He ran up the staircase, taking the stairs two at a time, then went into his room and slammed the door so loud that his lamp, which was turned off, fell from his dresser and onto the ground.

Dad's feet pounded on the stairs. "Milo!"

He locked his dad out, then fell into his bed and pulled the covers over his head.

"Milo, please. Open the door."

"She didn't kill herself!!" Milo screamed.

"I was just saying that —"

"She's alive!!" Milo screamed louder.

A deafening silence thundered on the other end of the door.

As Milo continued to weep, his father dropped his voice to a gravelly whisper. "I'm so sorry, Milo." Then heavy footsteps as he trudged down the stairs and left his son to grieve alone.

Chapter 2 - Alex Heller

Hamilton Island, Washington
   Friday afternoon

"WE SHOULD GET BACK," Alex said about five minutes after running from the racquetball courts. They were in the woods just east of school, which rose steeply with the island as you headed north, until you hit the center of the island and Cedar Park. If they went east, they'd reach his neighborhood in about twenty minutes.

Alex wanted to head south instead. Hit the ferry and never come back.

"He might be dead." Alex turned back and peered through the woods for any sign of someone following them.

There was nothing but the thickness of a million branches, clawing at the angry clouds moving in above.

"Well, there's nothing you can do about it now," Katie said. "Besides, I'm pretty sure I saw him move."

"You did?"

Katie met his gaze, then looked down for a moment,

biting her lip like she always did when lying. "I think so. I mean, I'm pretty sure."

Alex grabbed two fistfuls of his hair, then paced back and forth, screaming.

"Dammit! Why the hell did he have to come at me like that?"

"He's an asshole," Katie said, standing away from Alex, eyes wide and worried and blinking, looking as though she was frightened by his sudden outburst. "So what if he's dead? He deserves it."

Alex stared at her. "Don't you get it? If he's dead, and *I* killed him, I'm going to jail. They couldn't get my dad, so there's no way on Earth they're gonna let me go. Hell, the jurors might kill me before the trial takes its first recess."

"Don't be ridiculous," Katie said. "You didn't do anything wrong. You were protecting yourself! I was there. I'll be your witness!"

"Who the hell is gonna believe that? You saw what they spray-painted on my mom's car! Everyone hates us."

Alex didn't want to cry. Not like this. Not in front of Katie.

The tears came, anyway.

He turned away, closing his eyes as tight as he could as if that would force the tears back into their ducts.

"It's not fair." He figured if he forced words from his mouth, he could keep Katie from thinking he was crying. "Everything was going normal. We were one big, happy family. Most of the time, anyway, until *bam*, out of nowhere, my dad goes nuts! What the hell?"

His words turned into sobs anyway, and he felt like the world's biggest pussy.

Katie's hands closed around his chest as she hugged him from behind, leaning into his body.

"I'm so sorry, Alex."

He turned around and hugged her back, releasing his tears like flow from a faucet.

Katie was crying, too.

"We're gonna get through this," she said. "I swear. Everything will work out."

Alex wanted to believe her. But how could he lay all his faith at the feet of hope, now of all times? Everything was fucked. And now, he might have blood on his hands. His stomach soured as the sound of Jake's head hitting the concrete wall reverberated in his mind — a sickening thud that sounded like it came with major, if not fatal, damage.

"I've gotta run."

"Are you insane?" Katie said, pulling away. "You can't go! You'll look guilty."

"They're gonna think I'm guilty, anyway."

"We don't even know if Jake's dead. Maybe he's just knocked unconscious. I definitely saw Ray getting up. I say we go to the police and tell them what happened."

As Alex was replaying the sequence in his mind, trying to figure out how guilty he would appear to the police, he remembered what Katie had done to Ray. "How did you do that?"

"Do what?" Katie looked to the side again, though she no longer bit her lip.

"Throw Ray off of me." Alex held her eyes. "You pulled him off of me and threw him at least ten feet."

"What?" She laughed. "No way. I just grabbed him and pushed him. He went stumbling back."

Why would she lie about this?

"No, you threw him. I saw it, Katie."

"How the hell am I gonna *throw someone* ten feet? Hell, I asked you to open the jar of Ragu last night, remember?"

"I dunno." Alex shook his head, feeling as if he were accusing his girlfriend when he should be thanking her for saving him from getting beat down or worse. "Maybe it was

one of those weird situations like you hear on the news —
moms lifting cars off their children and stuff. I dunno."

Maybe I didn't see what I thought I saw?

"Like adrenaline overload or something?" she said. "I'm
not sure, Alex. It all happened so fast, I didn't even think
about what I was doing. I saw him on top of you, then
grabbed him as fast as I could and pulled him off."

Alex laughed, though he wasn't sure if it was from discomfort or the thought of his girlfriend having superpowers. Or
perhaps at the tail of a miserable week, marinating in grief, it
felt good to finally laugh. "Remind me never to piss you off."

"You're a guy, it's in your nature." A hint of a smirk played
at the corner of her lips.

"So, you think we should go back to school or head to the
police?"

"I think the police," Katie said. "If you go to school,
they're just gonna call the cops. Plus, who knows how many of
Jake and Ray's friends will be there waiting, ready to form a
lynch mob or worse."

Alex sighed. "You're right. How the hell am I ever gonna
go back to school? We're gonna have to move for sure."

The duo fell into silence. The implications of his family
moving and leaving Katie behind were too heavy to hold in
the moment. He couldn't imagine being without her. He and
Katie had been friends since preschool, and boyfriend and
girlfriend since the seventh grade. He couldn't imagine not
being near her.

But things were changing at the speed of disaster. Right
now, their relationship was a luxury compared to his family's
safety.

"I think we should go home first and tell my mom everything," Alex said.

"Okay, let's do that." Katie braided her fingers into his
hand and they started walking together, heading east.

They had been walking for five minutes when the scent of

ozone gusted toward them on the tail of a cold heavy wind, shaking the surrounding trees and sending torrents of leaves raining to the forest floor. A long, dark shadow fell over them, so suddenly that Alex turned his eyes to the sky to see if there was something above them.

Alex saw nothing but black, quickly-drifting storm clouds rolling in waves over the island. Thunder boomed above them. They picked up their pace without discussion, both knowing there was no way they'd avoid the coming deluge.

They made it another hundred feet before the rain began to fall in buckets. Katie broke out in a laugh as she ran ahead of Alex. "Come on!"

He followed her. Hail began to assault them like hundreds of rocks being cast by God himself at the murderer and his girl.

"Shit!" Alex pushed himself to run faster.

Ahead, Katie found cover in a small cave.

A tree cracked and fell somewhere behind Alex, crashing to the forest floor as the wind cried chaos and the hail thickened the world around him to a gray wall of pain peppering his body.

He could barely make out the rise of the cave ahead, could barely see the maw of its dark mouth.

"Come on!" Katie cried, her voice barely rising above the angry howl.

Alex raced in as lightning ignited the sky in a celestial fireworks show.

Inside the cave, Alex collapsed against a wall, bent over and sucked in a gallon of air to recover his breath, then stared out at the wall of gray. "Holy shit, where did that come from?" He set his backpack on the ground, then turned toward Katie. She was peering into the depths of the cave, which seemed to go deeper and farther back than he'd have ever guessed from the outside. "And where did this cave come from?"

Alex and Katie had lived on the island forever and had explored most, if not all, of the parts of it they'd been allowed to traverse. But he had never seen this cave before. Maybe the sudden, blinding rain had pushed them off their familiar path. The woods on the island were like that — deceptively complex and always showing you new sights, if you were the type to open your eyes to exploration.

"I dunno." Katie shook her answer through a shivering body and chattering teeth.

The squall outside intensified as the howling wind raced through the cave, turning the inner quiet into an eerie reverb. Yet, standing in the safety of the cave, it felt as if they'd found their own little hideaway on the island, a place only they knew. Safe from the world and all its ugliness.

Alex moved to her and hugged her tight, to provide warmth. The moment they drew close, he felt movement in his pants, and was awkwardly aware of his erection. Despite having dated for so long, Katie had never let them go further than heavy petting — outside of clothing, at that.

Katies looked up at him. She bit her lip again.

Only this time, she wasn't lying.

She threw her arms around his neck and pulled herself up. Their open mouths found one another, in a passionate, hungry kiss. Alex closed his eyes as his hands skimmed over her wet shirt and down her back.

Her hands left his neck, trailed down to his chest. She lifted his shirt and peeled it from his body.

He flinched as her hand brushed one of the purpled splotches on his ribs.

"Sorry." She threw his shirt aside, then bent to get a closer look at the bruises. Her fingers danced around the bruises, and she kissed them while saying, "I'm so sorry."

The dark welts looked as painful as they felt, but the pain did nothing to dampen his piling desire.

As Katie looked back up to Alex, their gazes locked.

He put his hands on her shoulders, then moved down the front of her shirt, slowly unbuttoning it.

She looked up at him with a shy smile, but also something else. *Hunger.*

Alex removed her shirt, then reached around her to find her bra clasp. He felt like an idiot when he couldn't unhook it.

Katie smiled, reached behind her, and unhooked the bra. She shimmied out of it, spilling her breasts into the cool air of the cave. Her nipples were light-pink and a bit larger than he'd imagined, but no less beautiful.

Oh, God.

He gently cupped her breasts, then circled his fingertips over her nipples. They hardened beneath his touch.

"You are so beautiful." He like an idiot, as if he were saying it not to *her*, but to her breasts.

She reached toward his belt, unfastened it, then pulled his jeans down, leaving him in just his boxers, which stuck out like he was pitching a tent.

After staring at his erection, she looked up at him. "Do you want to?"

Couldn't she tell? "Oh, God, yes."

Katie giggled.

"Hold on a sec." Alex opened his backpack and pulled out his black hoodie. He found a soft spot on the ground and laid it down, then draped his shirt over it to make an impromptu bed, and pulled out his wallet for the condom inside it.

AFTER ALEX and Katie made love, they stayed entwined on the ground, feeling the cool air blow over their nude bodies. All the pain, angst, and horror in his clouded mind seemed to melt away with the rise and fall of Katie's head on his chest.

As they drifted to sleep, Alex could do nothing about the big, goofy grin that split his face.

Chapter 3 - Cassidy Hughes

Friday afternoon

CASSIDY WATCHED THE GIRL, wondering what things she was seeing behind her eyelids as she dreamed in her hospital bed. Wondering what hell she'd been through while she was missing.

If Whistler had touched the girl, Cassidy would move heaven and Earth to make sure the fucker never touched another living thing.

Jon and Cassidy sat in chairs on either side of the bed, neither of them saying much as they waited for an update. It had been more than two hours since Dr. Don Close had checked her over then said he'd be right back.

Houser sat in the waiting room down the hall, since the hospital wouldn't let all three of them stay in the room with Emma.

"Maybe he forgot about us," Cassidy whispered. "What the hell is taking so long?"

"I dunno." Jon sighed.

The door pushed open, and Dr. Close appeared. He was a

tall, dark-haired man in his late forties who reminded Cassidy of that actor, Jon Hamm. He invited them out to the hallway to talk out of earshot of Emma, who was still sleeping. As they stood outside the doorway, Houser joined their circle.

"Emma's going to be just fine," Dr. Close said, "I didn't find any signs of injury or sexual assault."

Cassidy brightened, but it was only a moment before the doctor cast a dark shadow on her happiness.

"However," he cleared his throat. "Emma has no memory of anything after going to bed. She has no idea how she left the house, or what happened to her until she was found. No clue how she wound up in the woods. Nothing."

"What does that mean?" she said.

"We don't know, at least not yet," the doctor shook his head. "We're running several tests on her blood right now. We'll let you know if and when we find anything." He looked down at his clipboard, then up at Cassidy. "Besides her acute memory loss, Emma is also severely dehydrated, so we're keeping her on the IV. She needs to spend at least one night for observation."

Cassidy felt like she was one sentence from cracking.

The doctor placed a hand on her shoulder. "Everything will be fine. She's been found. That means the worst is over. We've put in a call to Dr. Kinkaid, and he'll be arriving first thing tomorrow morning to give Emma a full checkup. We should have all of our test results by then, as well."

"Can I stay the night with her? Sleep in the chair?" Cassidy asked.

"Certainly," Dr. Close said. "Actually, I'll see if someone can bring in another bed if you'd like."

"That would be great," Cassidy said. "Thank you."

"You okay?" Jon asked as Dr. Close left them.

"Yeah, much better. Good to know Emma's gonna be okay. But what do you think that means? About her memory? Is that something permanent?"

Jon opened his mouth, but Houser's mouth moved faster.

"Don't worry about it," he said. "Sometimes, the brain has a way of blocking shit it can't, or isn't ready, to deal with. She'll come around, maybe slowly, but I'd be surprised if she couldn't remember anything at all. And I promise, Cassidy." Houser leaned closer. "I'll find the fucker who took her, whether Whistler or someone else, and make the SOB pay."

"Not if I see him first. There won't be anything left once I'm through with him — whoever it is."

Houser smiled at Cassidy. "You're a bag of nails, Cassidy Hughes. I like you."

She smiled back, then surprised herself by lightly laughing. "So, what now?"

"I think we wait," Jon said. "Get some rest and see what Dr. Kinkaid says tomorrow morning. In the meantime, I think you should go be with her. I can't think of too many things worse than waking up alone in a hospital room."

"Thanks, Jon," she said, the words like medicine in her mouth. "And you, too, Brock." Cassidy turned and went back into Emma's room, leaving the two men in quiet discussion behind her.

As Cassidy entered the room, Emma looked up and said, or rather squealed, "Aunt Cass!"

Cassidy knelt by the bedside and threw her arms around Emma, pulling her close and holding her tight, carefully avoiding the IV drip and the other wires that were monitoring Emma's vitals.

"How're you doing, kiddo?" Cassidy asked.

Emma thrust out her bottom lip. "I hate the smell of hospitals."

"Yeah." Cassidy nodded. "Me, too." She shivered, trying hard not to remember the torment of detox. "But at least you're safe." She punched Emma lightly on the shoulder. "You have no idea how worried you had me."

Emma wrinkled her nose. "I can't remember anything.

I've never forgotten stuff before, at least not like that." She shook her head. "I don't like it at all."

"I can't expect that you would." Cassidy scooped Emma's hands inside her own, sandwiching it between her palms. "The doctor was telling me all about it just a few minutes ago, but I don't think you have anything to worry about. Know why?"

"Why?" Emma widened her eyes and waited for an answer.

"Because I think you'll remember everything."

"When?"

"Soon enough. Maybe by this time tomorrow. But you probably have to stop trying. That's how these things sometimes work. Of course, it might be totally impossible to remember if you were sleepwalking."

"Is that what happened? Do you think I was *sleepwalking?*"

"That's what makes the most sense to me." Cassidy didn't feel bad for lying, since sometimes the white of a lie proved enough to lighten the darkest of truths.

"What if I sleepwalk again?"

Cassidy pursed her lips, trying to determine the best way to answer. "Well, we should probably prepare for the possibility."

Emma cocked her head to the side. "What do you mean?"

"Well, you'll probably start sleepwalking a lot now. I've heard once you start, it's hard to stop. But you won't have to worry because we have a team of specialists coming over to the house." Cassidy leaned into Emma and whispered. "We've signed you up for sleepwalking lessons."

Emma narrowed her eyes, uncertainty plain on her face. "What are sleepwalking lessons?"

"Well," Cassidy kidded, "we figure we're not going to be able to get you to stop sleepwalking, so we're going to teach you to do your chores instead. Starting with washing the dishes and cleaning your room. Once you're trained, you'll never leave the house again. You'll be too busy doing housework."

Emma laughed. "That's not true."

"Tell that to Sgt. Sleepwalker," Cassidy said, straight-faced. "He'll be over to the house seven sharp on Monday morning."

"Not true," Emma repeated.

"Sorry," Cassidy shook her head. "But he's already booked and paid for. Too late to back out now. Unless you want to pay for his time out of your allowance."

Emma laughed again, then let the joke die. "Where's Nana?"

"She had one of her headaches." Cassidy resisted the urge to use air quotes while saying "headache" like she would have with an adult.

"Oh," Emma said, scratching her arms. "One of the bad ones?"

"Yeah," Cassidy nodded. "Super-duper bad. Otherwise, there's no way she would've missed coming to see you. She said she can't wait for you to come home."

When the word "home" fell from Cassidy's mouth, it unleashed the worries that Cassidy had been trying not to think about. But now that Emma was safe and would soon be home, Cassidy had to acknowledge the concerns. What was Jon going to do about Emma? Would he demand custody of his daughter? Would she be able to do anything to stop him? Anxiety began to eat away at her momentary happiness, and she felt the old, familiar tug of the pills calling to her.

She closed her eyes as if doing so would keep the seeds of addiction from setting camp in her thoughts.

Though her hate for Jon had deteriorated significantly in the past twenty-four hours, he was still a Conway. And her loathing for them would not die so easily. There was too much history to ignore. As nice as he might be, Jon was still a

Conway, and there was no way in hell Cassidy could sit by while that family poisoned sweet, innocent Emma.

Sending Emma into that family would be like dropping a baby in a basket, then sending it downstream on the river to hell.

Yet, Emma was Jon's daughter. If he wanted her, there would be little, if anything, Cassidy could do to stop it. Jon had the lawyers, power, and bloodline to prove she was his in less than a day, and the resources to take Emma away for eternity.

Cassidy reached toward Emma and pulled her niece into another, longer embrace. "I love you, Kitty Cat Bubbles." She called her by the nickname she'd earned when she was three years old and wore pajamas printed with Hello Kitty blowing bubbles.

"I love you, too, Aunt Cass." Emma settled into her aunt's deep embrace.

The door swung open, and Cassidy could feel Jon standing behind her. His words, harmless as they were, flooded her with fear.

"How are my girls?"

Chapter 4 - Milo Anderson

Sunlight hit Milo in the face, forcing his eyes open to blurred, unfamiliar surroundings. His vision slowly adjusted to bright light above him, illuminating the mostly white room. A punctuated blip from somewhere behind him beeped.

He rubbed his throbbing temples and saw the first of the tubes, sticking from the middle of his arm and trailing into the IV bag dangling above him on a metal pole.

Why am I in a hospital?

He shook his head, trying to clear the cobwebs from his memory and draw clarity to his present. He looked around the room, hoping to see someone, *anyone*, but he was alone.

Milo looked for a mirror but found nothing. Just as well, since he could feel the tubes in his nose and throat, and clearly see the horrid layers of bandages snaking around both of his arms. Though it took Milo a minute to place the unfamiliar pinch, he realized with a quickly rising fear that the sharp pain in his groin was from a catheter sticking into his penis.

How did I get here?

Milo remembered getting the call from Cody in the middle of class, then Beatrice in the parking lot, nearly mowing down Russ Harvey while she zoned out like a zombie just as she had done in front of the snow-filled TV screen. Then she was riding the crazy train, right off the tracks and into the glass wall of the grocery store. Milo squeezed his eyes shut, replaying everything that happened from the moment Beatrice picked him up from school until the minute his world lost every drop of color.

Nothing made sense, and unless Milo was remembering things wrong, which he was sure he wasn't. Beatrice hadn't said a single word from the time he climbed inside the BMW all the way until he was begging for her to stop or slow or at least say something. It was if something else had taken over her.

Milo felt a sense of growing dread as he remembered Cody's warning.

I didn't think they'd strike now. In fact, I was sure they wouldn't. But they did, and that means they're more worried about what Manny was going to say than I realized. That means you're probably next.

Was Cody's message and Beatrice's behavior related, or had Milo seen too many movies and written one too many Twilight Zone-inspired short stories with Alex?

They might think you know more than you're saying, Milo.

You need to get out of town. Now.

A flutter of panic filled Milo as the room around him felt as if it were somehow shrinking and *caging him.*

Was Beatrice okay? Was she lying in a bed nearby? Or was she dead?

Milo looked to his side and saw a button on his bed rail labeled HELP.

He pressed it.

A painfully eerie silence drifted through the room, absent even the usual sounds of a hospital. While he hadn't ever been admitted to the hospital, his doctor's office was there, as was the case with everyone's on the island. The hospital provided steeply discounted medical services in exchange for huge tax breaks for Conway Industries, which owned the hospital.

"Hello!" Milo tried to murmur over the tube in his throat.

There was a sudden shuffling in the hall, and Milo saw a shadow beneath the door of someone just standing there and not entering the room.

What the hell? Come in!

The door opened so slow it seemed as if an infant were trying to push it, rather than an adult.

But it wasn't an infant.

Mr. Heller stepped inside his room.

His eyes were gone, replaced by black pits of dried blood. The entire lower half of his face was bloody, much of his bottom jaw missing, and what was there was barely hanging by shreds of muscle. Small chunks of teeth had migrated from his mouth and speckled the outside of his chin, held in place by blood.

"Eleven," Heller groaned like a brain-dead zombie as he moved closer to Milo.

Milo screamed, shuffling back in the hospital bed and shoving his back hard against the pillows. He grabbed the tube and began to pull it out so he could call for help.

"Hello, Milo." Heller approached Milo's bed.

Milo froze, tube still in his throat. He stabbed the help button repeatedly.

But no help was coming.

Heller looked up and down the length of Milo for several seconds — despite having no actual eyes — then he sighed deeply. He turned toward the corner of the room, retrieved a briefcase sitting on a chair, brought it over, and laid it on Milo's lap.

"I've very sorry." His words weren't at all inhibited by the lack of a functioning mouth. "But it seems in all the madness, I almost forgot to kill you." Heller opened the briefcase, pulled out a gun, and casually aimed it at Milo.

Milo pressed the button again and again, desperately.

Heller pulled the trigger.

Milo screamed into a symphony of static and roaring engine as Beatrice's BMW crashed through the front of the grocery store.

Milo's world went black.

When he woke up, his entire frame was furiously thrashing against the bed, his fingers yanking wires and tubes from his body as the steady beeping from the machines beside him rose in pitch and raced in frequency.

Milo tried pulling the catheter from his penis, but it felt like he was pouring fire inside an open wound. He wanted to scream but couldn't.

Three seconds later, a nurse rushed into Milo's room. She placed a calming hand on top of Milo while her other hand fiddled with the monitors and machinery. "You're okay. It's okay."

She continued to pat him until she finished tweaking the machines. Then she checking him over. "You're safe, Mr. Anderson. You're in the hospital."

No one called Milo "Mr. Anderson," except Mr. Heller.

"How did I get here?" he asked, wondering if the crash was a dream but knowing it wasn't.

The nurse was young and pretty, with short, red hair. Milo had never seen her before. That wasn't unheard of on the island, but it was slightly unusual. Even if you didn't know everyone, on an island the size of Hamilton it was reasonably easy to spot the locals. The nurse's name tag said, *Betty*, and her voice was almost as pretty as she was.

"What happened?" Milo said.

"You were in an accident," Betty frowned. "It was bad."

Hardly an accident when your Other Mother's foot is bricking the accelerator.

"How did I get here?"

"An ambulance, of course."

"How about Beatrice?" Milo asked, hating himself for the seven or so seconds he wished his stepmother dead.

Betty said nothing.

Milo repeated, "Beatrice, my stepmother. Is she okay?"

"The doctor will want to speak to you." Betty smiled then left the room without another word.

Chapter 5 - Jon Conway

"How did they find me?" Emma asked the same question in a new way, for the third time in less than five minutes from her spot on the hospital bed.

"Well," Jon said, "when we *couldn't* find you at first, Cass suggested we follow the trail of cookies."

"What cookies?" Emma asked suspiciously.

"The cookies you stashed in your purse at the dessert table the other day."

Emma looked at her blanket, then back up at Cassidy, laughing.

Jon continued, "When all the cookies were gone, we found you, standing all alone, with crumbs covering your face. It was terribly messy, awful, really." Jon shook his head. "We had to scrub you down. You were still asleep, but you kept flapping around like a fish. We think that's what finally woke you."

Emma was in hysterics, Cassidy smiling beside her. Jon wasn't sure if she was laughing at the words themselves, or the animation behind them, but he was thrilled when she burst through the laughter with the compliment he'd been fishing for.

"You're funny," Emma cackled. "You should do funny stuff instead of all the grown-up movies."

"Just because they're grown-up movies doesn't mean they're not funny." He leaned into Emma with a giant smile. "How do you know I'm not HI-larious?"

"Because my mom used to cry when she watched them. She only cries at sad movies, except for the time she cried at *Snoopy Come Home*."

Jon pulled his head back, almost in recoil, a rock in his throat before he managed to find his line. "How did you know they were my movies?"

"Because your face is always all over the movie covers on Netflix. I could hear my mom crying at night. In the morning, I could always see why when I turned on the TV. Your picture was usually the first picture under 'recently played.'"

Jon cleared his throat, then mopped his brow and exchanged awkward glances with Cassidy.

Jon *had* loved, but it had been a long time since anyone had seen the real side of it. Nine years or so. Emma's smile made Jon realize there was nothing in the world he wouldn't do for her.

Except maybe be her dad. Because he couldn't do that.

Jon wasn't a father. He was a Hollywood asshole — a nice guy sure, but a selfish one. He did what he wanted, when he wanted, and had since the forever ago when he first learned he could. While fans had often applauded his "humanitarian" efforts and his donations to various organizations, those were things he could sign a check and do some good with. They weren't long-term commitments requiring he actually sacrifice the thing most precious to him: his time. Headline some freedom rallies or concerts, yeah. But raise a child? Every single day?

That had never been something within the realm of a life he imagined for himself. Not since Emma's mother had left him, anyway.

But as he stared at the girl's sweet smile and into eyes that reminded him so much of Sarah, he wondered if he could be a good father, after all.

While he was self-centered, he wasn't without thought for others. He did lots of kind things. He often went out of his way to help new actors on the set, try to make them feel comfortable. It wasn't just the hot up-and-coming actresses he extended the kindness to, either.

And he'd never been one to shirk responsibility.

Emma is my responsibility.

Jon pictured Emma wearing a pretty, pink dress, escorting him down the red carpet at a movie premiere.

He caught Cassidy looking at him, and the smile slipped her face as if she were reading his mind, seeing his plans to take Emma as they took shape. Jon looked down, and then back at Emma as she and Cassidy started talking about milkshakes and how Emma couldn't wait to have one.

While Cassidy wasn't Emma's mother, she was still the closest thing the girl had to one. She'd gotten by fine without a father forever. Why inject himself into her life now? Was it to help her? Or fill some hole in his own life?

Who the hell was he to come in and take that away now?

No, he couldn't do that. Not to her, nor to Cassidy. Looking at Emma, Jon knew it was wrong.

It was easy enough for Jon to imagine the two of them together. Just a week before, Cassidy snuck candy to Emma with a finger on her lips and a twinkle in her eye.

"Hello!"

"What?" Jon blinked his eyes at a staring Emma.

"I said, have you ever made a kid's movie?"

"No," Jon shook his head. "I haven't."

"How come?"

He shrugged, "I guess I never got a script that interested me."

"What's a script?"

"The lines in a movie. They're written by writers. And as an actor, I get a lot of bad scripts for really bad movies. So, I try and do only good ones, or don't do any at all."

"And nobody's given you a good script for a kid's movie?"

"Not yet. Maybe Hollywood thinks I'll scare kids."

"Yeah," Cassidy said with a smile, "I can see that. He *is* pretty scary."

"I think he's nice!" Emma smiled big at Jon.

"Well, my audience has spoken. So, there!" Jon stuck his tongue out at Cassidy. "So, there!" Then he laughed. "Tell you what, Emma. I promise I'll make a kid's movie someday if you promise to make Cassidy watch it." He winked at Cassidy.

Cassidy rolled her eyes, "Sheesh, thanks."

Jon looked at Emma. "What kind of movie do *you* think I should make?"

"Something in the future, definitely."

"Like with robots?"

"No, there doesn't have to be robots. It doesn't even have to be that far in the future. Just not now. And it can't be stupid. No flying cars or anything like that."

"Can't be stupid. Cars don't fly. Got it," Jon said.

As Emma's voice grew louder, Jon's heart had to grow larger to fit more of her inside. She must have been as dehydrated as the doctor had said, because she talked herself right into exhaustion, practically falling asleep mid-sentence.

"Not often someone can do that," Cassidy said.

Jon looked at Cassidy. "Do what?"

"Verbally beat the girl into sleep."

Jon smiled.

Cassidy grabbed the TV remote from the bedside table with her left hand, while her right twitched like it was missing a cigarette. She clicked on the TV, then flipped past Dr. Phil's son to Chief Brady holding a press conference outside of the police station.

"We'd like to thank private investigator Brock Houser for

his help on this case. Mr. Houser, of Houser Investigations in California, was instrumental in this happy ending. Thank you also to Mr. Jon Conway for bringing Mr. Houser here and footing the bill. And I would like to thank Paladin Security for working in conjunction with the Hamilton Island Police Department to locate the missing child."

Someone in the crowd shouted, "Why did Jon Conway hire the detective? What's his connection to this case?"

Brady said, "I don't know of any prior connection between Mr. Conway and Mr. Houser, but Jon once called Hamilton home, and he's a good man. A child went missing, and he wanted to use his means to help, however he could."

Someone else called out, "Is it true the suspect you had in custody killed himself?"

Brady nodded. "That appears to be the case."

Cassidy looked at Jon, her eyes wide. "Whistler killed himself?"

Jon stared at the TV in disbelief. "Wow."

"He must've been guilty!" Cassidy balled her fists as her face turned red. "What the hell did he do to her?"

She looked at Emma, and her eyes started to well up again. Then she caressed the girl's hair. Lip trembling, Cassidy said, "I'm so sorry."

Why had she felt so guilty? Did she feel like she'd let her sister down? Or had she really been out that night, partying, and using drugs? He hoped she wasn't using. While he didn't want to break up Emma's family if things were working, he'd change his mind if he discovered that Cassidy was still using. He made a note to have Houser look into the matter and hoped not to find anything damning.

"We don't know Whistler did anything," Jon said. "The doc said there were no signs of trauma, right? Maybe he was just disgraced by whatever all the police found in his home. The man worked at a church, and he was recording little girls on the church playground! Even if he never touched a one, even if he had nothing to do with Emma's disappearance, there's no way his life isn't over. If he killed himself, I'm not surprised. And if he *did* do anything to anyone, let's just say it's best that he went out like this rather than force the victims and their families to live through a trial, right?"

Cassidy nodded, wiping the tears from her eyes, hands shakier than before. "I guess so. But if he's guilty, he ought to suffer, not take the easy way out."

Jon found himself looking at the scars on Cassidy's wrists again and wanting for the millionth time to ask her how they got there. But he couldn't bring it up now. One more thing for Houser to look into, perhaps.

After Brady talked a bit more about the suicide, parsing out as few details as possible, the reporters were again asking about Jon and his connection — digging for any dirt they could find.

As cameras flashed, Cassidy killed the image. "Fucking vultures."

"You have no idea." Jon looked from the black screen to Cassidy. "That was nothing."

Chapter 6 - Liz Heller

Hamilton Island, Washington
1:25 p.m.

THE MORNING HAD BEEN HELL.

Liz tiptoed away from Aubrey's room, thanking God she had finally fallen asleep for her nap. Hopefully, she'd stay down for the next couple of hours.

Aubrey had cried for nearly thirty minutes straight, refusing to sleep. She wanted her daddy, and it broke Liz's heart to see her little girl's head turn in search of Roger every time someone came into a room.

Liz didn't know how to explain the situation to her daughter. Aubrey was only six months old, and while she seemed to understand far more than Alex had at that age, Liz didn't have a way to explain a concept like death. She didn't want to lie and say, "Daddy will be back soon." So, she simply hugged her, or in most cases, distracted the child with something else.

And every time she successfully made Aubrey momentarily forget her daddy, it broke Liz's heart just a little bit more.

Today was particularly rough for them both.

Between waiting on the window guy to replace her windshield, dealing with several more unanswered calls to the medical examiner's office to find out when in the hell she'd be allowed to get Roger's body, and wondering what on God's green Earth could be on the flash drive, she barely had time to glance at Aubrey, let alone give her undivided attention.

This made Alex's return to school all the more noticeable, magnifying the emptiness of the house. Now Aubrey was missing both her daddy and her brother, and constantly looking for them, likely wondering why everyone was leaving her. And probably also wondering when mommy would leave.

Liz needed a nap and decided to sleep in the spare bed in Aubrey's room.

She headed downstairs to make sure the door was locked, for probably the hundredth time in the past few hours. As she approached the door, she saw movement outside the front window. A chill shot through her body. She went to the window and saw a police officer heading up her sidewalk.

Her stomach flopped in fear of more bad news.

Relax, he's just here to follow up on the car thing or maybe discuss something related to Roger. Maybe he's gonna tell you when you can get Roger's body and finally bury him.

She ran to the front door, hoping she could get there before the officer had a chance to ring the bell and wake Aubrey.

Liz threw the door open and saw it wasn't *just* a cop at her door, but Chief Brady. Something was wrong. She could feel it deep in her marrow. She stepped onto the porch.

"Hello, ma'am." He tipped his hat.

"Hello, Chief Brady. How can I help you?" Liz positioned herself between the chief and the slightly ajar door at her back. She would invite him in under normal circumstances but didn't want his voice to wake Aubrey. Waking to the sound of a stranger in the house would scare her even more than waking not to find Mommy next to her.

"Is Alex here?" he asked.

"No, he's at school. Why? What's wrong?" Liz said, her voice rising in pitch.

"There was an incident at the school," the chief said.

Liz felt her stomach churn. *An incident? Oh, God.*

"What happened?" She clasped her hands over her chest.

"Well, we're not sure exactly. He seems to have gotten into a fight with two kids. He and his girlfriend, Katie, were involved, and they both took off into the woods. One of the boys is in the hospital in serious condition. The other is banged up, but he'll live."

"Oh, God," Liz said. "When did this happen?"

"About a half-hour ago or so. We're looking for them and thought maybe they came here."

"I haven't seen or heard from them." She tried not to hyperventilate. "Did you check with Katie's mom?"

"I've got an officer trying to track her down now. She wasn't home."

"I think she works at the hospital in the accounting department."

"Yeah," Brady said. "He's on his way there as we speak."

"Is Alex in trouble?" Liz asked.

"Well, I'd like to talk to them both," Brady said, "to get their side of the story."

"Alex is a good kid, Chief. He would never start a fight. Those kids must've started it. Who was involved?"

"Jake Brewster and Ray Wilson."

"Oh, God. I had both of them in my class, and I can assure you they were both nothing but trouble, *always* getting into fights."

Brady looked down, as if he shouldn't be discussing their histories with her, then nodded. "Yes, ma'am, I'm rather *familiar* with them. But I still need to hear both sides."

"What are they saying?"

"Well, Jake is in a coma, so he's not saying much."

"A coma?" The reality slapped Liz in the face. The boy could die, and her son could be charged. A murderer, just like her husband.

Brady continued, "Ray says some words were exchanged, and your son just went ballistic. Says he even pulled a knife on them."

"Bullshit!" Liz didn't give a damn whether the chief was offended or not. This was her son, for Christ's sake. She wasn't gonna sit by while some punk-ass kids maligned him. "Alex doesn't even have a knife! And he would never, *ever*, 'go ballistic,' Chief. They must have provoked him! Hell, maybe they were the ones who messed up my car yesterday!"

"What do you mean?" Brady asked.

"I was at the library yesterday and a Paladin guard came in to tell me someone had spray painted the word 'murderer' on my windshield. I just had the window guy out this morning to replace the window."

"Did you fill out a police report?" Brady asked.

"No." Liz now felt stupid for not documenting the event. "With everything going on, I didn't want to call attention to it, or wind up on the news, again, or anything."

Her gaze met Brady's, as if conveying the unspoken part of that sentence ... *You know, what with my husband having gone on a shooting spree.*

"My family is being targeted!" she cried. "They must have attacked him. Alex would never hurt anyone unless he was fighting back. He's a sweet boy, and he's never been in trouble."

"I'm not judging what did or didn't happen, Mrs. Heller. That's why I need to talk to Alex, so I can get his side of the story and start sorting the facts." Brady's radio beeped. He gave Liz an apology with his eyes, then took the call, "Brady."

"It's Johnson. Katie's mother hasn't heard from her, either. Any luck on your end?"

"No," Brady said. "Did she give you any other info?"

"No, sir."

"Okay. Head back to the girl's house and see if they're there." Brady said.

"Roger that."

Brady looked at Liz. "Katie's mom hasn't seen them, either. Do you have any idea where they might have gone? Is there any special place they liked to go to get away from the world, maybe some romantic spot?"

"I have no idea," she said.

"Has he been upset or anything, lately?"

Liz stared at Brady. "His father just shot his classmates, what do you think?"

Brady looked at Liz's *WELCOME* mat. "Sorry. Of course, he's been upset." Then he looked at her. "But do you think he'd run off? Or do you know anywhere he might go if he was afraid to come home? Any friends or relatives on the island? Or off the island, nearby?"

"Nobody's talking to him except Katie. His best friend blames him for what happened, and his other friend is in a coma, and I'm pretty sure nobody else is returning his calls. And no, we don't have any other family."

"Okay, Mrs. Heller. I'm heading back to the station now. If Alex calls you or comes home, I need you to get him to come see me. Or call me, and I'll get over here immediately."

"Are you going to arrest him?"

"No, Mrs. Heller." Brady shook his head. "I just want to talk to him, and I want to get out ahead of this before anything else happens."

"What do you mean?"

"I don't know what happened today, but I think it's a safe bet that people on the island are angry, and I want to make sure nothing else happens to you or your family."

"Do you think we're in danger, Chief Brady?"

Brady turned his head toward the Paladin guard sitting in the parked SUV, then looked back at Liz. "Let's just say it's a good thing you have security outside. Here." He reached into his shirt pocket, retrieved a couple of cards, then handed them to her. "Call me the minute you hear from Alex or Katie. Or if anything else happens."

Liz looked down at the cards, then back up into Brady's kind eyes. She'd always liked the chief when he'd come into her class to talk with the kids about bullying and drug use and all the other stuff they barely paid attention to. He was always soft-spoken, kind, and had a decent rapport with the kids that didn't have him sounding like a horribly out-of-touch old fogey like the former chief. In all the confusion and chaos, Brady broadcast a calm, cool sense of security. Liz thought him nice, but more importantly, she found him easy to trust and believed he had a chance to gain control of the tensest situation the island had ever seen

Liz opened her mouth, about to tell him everything — the list she found, the flash drive, and what she'd seen on the video.

But Brady's radio beeped to life again.

"Chief, I need you to get back to the station. Whistler just hanged himself."

"Jesus Christ!" Brady said. "Is he ...?"

"Yeah," the officer said. "He's dead."

Brady closed his eyes as if this was the absolute last thing he needed to hear.

"Larry Whistler? At the church?" Liz asked. "What's he doing in jail?"

"You didn't see the news?" The chief looked shocked. "About the missing girl? Emma Hughes? Daughter of Sarah?"

"Oh, my God," Liz said. "No! What happened?"

"Emma was staying with her grandmother and aunt after Sarah died. Last night, she went missing. We arrested a suspect, Larry Whistler, and detained him, but still no word on where the girl is."

"Oh, God," Sarah had brought her daughter to work several times over the years, and Liz always loved talking with her. The girl was so sweet. To think she was missing, and that Roger might be indirectly responsible, felt like another bullet to her conscience.

"I need to get back." Brady didn't even wait for Liz to respond.

She went back inside and picked up her phone to call Alex, praying he'd answer.

~

8:16 *p.m.*

LIZ WORE out the carpet in front of the television, pacing back and forth, as the TV replayed the press conference from earlier, where Chief Brady discussed finding Emma Hughes. While Liz was relieved the girl was found safe, she wondered when in the hell Alex would come home.

She wanted to go out looking for him, but couldn't leave Aubrey, who was upstairs sleeping, alone. Nor did she have anyone to babysit. She was a prisoner in her home, forced to wait for Alex or Katie to return one of her calls or finally return. If she didn't hear from him soon, she might have to wake Aubrey up and head out to look. But what hope would she have in finding her son if the police couldn't? And what if she ran into some of the angry island residents who wished her harm?

She had to protect her daughter at all costs.

Maybe she'd ask the Paladin guard to drive them around. But the last thing she wanted to do was bring attention to the family and have Alex just be out sneaking around with his girl-friend. It would only make things worse, if that were even possible.

Katie's mom, Terri, had called Liz two hours ago, asking if she'd heard from the kids. Terri had already called Katie's cell phone and left several messages, and she was worried sick. As they spoke, Liz couldn't help but feel the layer of ice between them. While Terri hadn't mentioned the shooting, it laced each sentence and lingered through every silence. Terri then said she was going so she could drive to a few spots where the kids had been known to hang out and promised Liz she'd call back later.

As darkness draped itself overhead, Liz grew increasingly convinced Alex was no longer on Hamilton Island.

He'd left. Either alive or dead.

She couldn't explain it, but she'd always felt a connection to Alex. She could feel when he was in the house, even if she'd not left her bedroom. She often sensed when he was coming home, just moments before he opened the door, coming in all sweaty from a night playing with his friends. As long as he'd been alive, she felt this connection with him, like some kind of parental supernatural bond or something.

But now, she wasn't feeling it. And it scared the hell out of her.

She tried to put the fear to rest and deal only in the things she knew. Alex and Katie had gotten into a fight at school with two of the worst kids in school. They ran off into the woods after Alex hurt one of them. Beyond that, there was no reason for her to think them harmed.

He's safe. They're safe.

Oh, yeah? Then why isn't he home yet?

The poor kid must be worried sick that he killed Jake. He's scared.

He doesn't know what to do.

She tried to think what he might do and was stunned to

find she had no idea. As close as she'd felt to him, she didn't really know what he would do in a situation like this. This only served as a reminder of the distance growing among the family members during the past year or so. She didn't *really* know Roger.

And perhaps she didn't *really* know Alex.

She watched the replay of Brady's press conference again and noticed the two Paladin officials stood behind him the entire time, as though they were running the show rather than him. Liz wasn't sure why, but she didn't trust Paladin at all. From their ever-increasing heavy-handedness, to their closed-circuit cameras everywhere, to the way they tore through her house, as if looking for something in particular — like perhaps a flash drive — she was becoming increasingly wary of them. And also of the man outside her house.

If Brady is in their pocket, maybe it's a good thing I didn't tell him about the flash drive.

She couldn't trust Paladin or Brady. Not until she knew what was on the disk.

Brady spoke again, "We'd like to thank private investigator Brock Houser for his help on this case. Mr. Houser, of Houser Investigations in California, was instrumental in this happy ending. And thank you, Mr. Jon Conway, for bringing Mr. Houser here and footing the bill. And I would like to thank Paladin Security for working in conjunction with the Hamilton Island Police Department to locate the missing child."

Jon Conway?

Why would he pay for a private investigator, especially when his family had untold billions and an entire armed security force to scour the island for the girl?

Liz watched as Mr. Houser took the mic and thanked the police, Paladin, and the public for their help, then handed the mic back. Humble, not seeking the spotlight, like so many of these investigators Liz had seen on the news in recent years, trying to insert themselves — and their company logos — into news coverage of every tragedy they could.

There was something about Houser that Liz implicitly trusted.

Liz turned from the TV, the shadow of a smile twitching on her lips, then left the room with an idea.

Chapter 7 - Alex Heller

Nighttime …

ALEX WOKE to the sound of whispers around him, as if others had found Katie and him in the cave as they slept. He felt vulnerable and naked, with God knows what standing above him.

He tried to open his eyes so he could see who was in the cave with them, but he couldn't. Nor could he move.

Alex was paralyzed.

Panic and fear coursed through his body, as he struggled to regain control of his movement.

What's happening? Why can't I wake up?

Am I dead? Am I in a coma?

Who else is in here? Where is Katie?

The whispers grew louder without getting louder at all, as though they weren't raising their voices, but rather their number.

Yet Alex couldn't make out a single syllable of what they were saying. The whispers sounded almost like a swarm, though Alex had no idea how large the swarm might be.

Was it the police? Or perhaps Paladin guards? And why couldn't he wake up?

Perhaps he'd been stung by something poisonous, maybe a dangerous insect living in the cave?

Then Alex realized he wasn't just immobilized, he was also entirely numb. He couldn't feel a thing. Not the cool of the cave, the wind breathing through the entrance, or the sand and rock-covered ground below.

Oh, God. I'm paralyzed. Or poisoned.

Why can't I understand what they're saying?

I hope they don't think I'm dead.

Hey! Help me! I'm alive!

There was no help.

The whispers grew louder, as if multiplying in tens by the second, until the entire cave was echoing in a cacophony of whispers.

I must be dreaming. I must be dreaming.

Wake up, Alex. Wake up!

He felt a warm glow over his ribs where he'd been repeatedly kicked.

What the fuck is that?

The warmth spread like liquid fire, or ... internal bleeding.

Oh, God, what the hell is happening?

Whispers turned to a hum. Not one, but countless coalescing into a single tone, growing louder, a few decibels from deafening until they faded into silence, save for the low howl of the wind.

Alex opened his eyes to the darkness, totally alone and naked on the floor of the cave. The white glow of the moon illuminated just enough of his surroundings to see that he was alone.

"Katie?"

But there was no sound other than the night.

"Katie!"

His desperation echoed off the cave walls, mocking him.

Chapter 8 - Jon Conway

Friday evening

JON LEFT the Sands of Time to meet Houser, who had given an adios to the island hotel an hour earlier so he could drive Hamilton Island and "see what he could see."

The pair met up at Coconuts, a place that was every bit as ridiculous as Jon remembered, still decorated like a tropical island paradise even though Hamilton was a world and a half from Hawaii. The jukebox — made to look like it was manufactured in the '50s, even though it played audio files and every one of its records was fake — wore the same scars it always had. The only difference Jon could see in the entire joint was they'd changed the marquee outside from *Free Beer, Topless Waitresses, and False Advertising* to the far less charming *Beer: Because Your Friends Just Aren't That Interesting.*

They were on their second basket of onion rings, and Jon on his fifth round of Heineken, when he said, "Jesus, man. Don't you ever gain any weight?"

Houser grinned then shoved another matching set of

onion rings into his mouth. "What sorta bitch question is that?"

"All I ever see you eat is garbage. And that garbage is usually deep-fried."

"So?"

"So, you're built like an action figure!"

Houser laughed, shrugged, then shoved another bite into his still semi-full mouth. "I'll pretend you're not asking bitch questions, and you can pretend I didn't just say, 'You look just fine, Jonny Hollywood.' And don't act like you don't eat the same shit I do. I've seen the shit you eat when you're *really* hungry, when you're not ordering bean sprouts or whatever the hell it is you Hollywood types like to eat."

"Yeah. Difference is if I ate like this as often as you do, I'd never get another role ever." Jon nibbled from the edge of another onion ring.

Houser popped a whole one in his mouth. "Don't let my carefree attitude fool you. I spent years getting in shape so I could eat like shit. And I still wake up three hours earlier than I want to be in the gym while you're still banging some eighteen-year-old supermodel you met the night before. You wanna look this good, you've gotta become a monk when it comes to self-discipline."

"Well, ain't that ironic?" Jon said, laughing. "Spend so much time getting in shape, you're unable to go out and enjoy the fruits of your labor. And in case you didn't pick up on it before now, self-discipline has never really been my thing."

Houser laughed.

Jon let Houser spend a few more minutes making fun of him and his weight concerns, real and imagined, before circling back to the personal history lesson he'd been giving him.

"I want to know what happened. But I don't want to ask Cassidy." Jon took another gulp of beer. He was throwing them down faster than he had in a helluva while. "Way I see it, I've got two choices."

Houser finished Jon's thought. "You could go directly to Warren and demand the truth, or you could ask me to dip my bucket in the well and see how deep the fucker drops, right?"

Jon swallowed, finished his bottle, then slammed it on the table harder than he meant to and slurred, "Yeah, something like that. What do *you* think I should do?"

Houser took a smaller sip of his own beer, then motioned for the waitress with his eyes half on Jon. "Any harm in doing both?"

The cute waitress with the pigtails Jon had been eyeing since he first sat down spoke to the private dick while stealing sideways glances at the movie star. "How can I help you? Another bottle?"

Jon shook his head and gave Pigtails an excuse to give him her undivided. "You have any whiskey?"

"Sure," she said. "What kind?"

"I don't care. Surprise me." Jon laughed, and Pigtails laughed along with him, stealing another few seconds before slipping off toward the bar.

"You are the only asshole I would ever drink with who hogs all the attention from the ladies. That makes you less fun to hang with, just so you know."

"Bullshit," Jon said. "Makes me more interesting. And you say the word, and we can party back at the hotel with two or three more just like her."

"Ha," Houser took another swallow. "As enticing as that offer is, I'll have to decline. Something tells me you'll just wind up regretting it once the ladies see what I'm packing, and leave you sitting in the corner pulling your own pud while I rock all their worlds."

"Remind me to fire you tomorrow." Jon laughed as he took another drink. "Oh wait, you just found my daughter.

Guess I have to keep you on a bit, right? By the way, thank you for that, man. I owe you."

Jon was getting to that emotional drunk stage where he started telling people how much he loved them.

Maybe I should slow it down.

"I'm just glad we found her," Houser said. "But back to your question — I think you *should* ask your brother. No one's gonna know his vibe better than you. Stare him in the eye and don't let him look away. You'll be able to grab the lie if it's there. I'll ask around, too, see what I can dig up. Sound good?"

Jon stared at the pair of pigtails bouncing against the waitress's shoulders as she made her way back to their table. "You looked like you wanted two." She put a set of shot glasses on the table, the coconut decal nearly faded from one and brand-new on the other. "If you didn't, well then the second one's on the house." She smiled.

Well, fuck slowing down.

He downed the first shot. "Are you kidding me? I feel like saying 'I love you.'" Jon flashed the waitress the same magic smile that had won him box office dollars and more than his share of critical praise. "In fact, why don't you bring me the bottle?"

"Sure thing." Then she disappeared.

"Might want to watch it there, cowboy," Houser said when she left.

"Thanks, Mommy." Jon poured the second shot down his throat.

"You can drink the whole bottle, asshole. I don't give a shit. At least I'm at the same table tonight, so I know I won't get a phone call at 3-A-FUCKING-M that will send me driving from Orillas to the top of OC."

"Here ya go, gentleman." The waitress stepped awkwardly into their exchange, smiling as she set the bottle on the table, then slipped off toward the back of the bar.

Jon's head started to swim. He burst into laughter at the matching set of blurry Housers, both trying to make him feel bad. Then a thought occurred to him. "I think these onion rings are the only things I've eaten all day."

Houser was right, and the logical side of Jon knew it. But most of him was drunk and getting drunker.

Jon had grown reasonably skilled at staying on the shallow side of the drunk pool, and while he wasn't quite trashed yet, he'd already decided to dive and was now just seconds from hitting the water. He tried to remember the last time he'd been so drunk, then couldn't help but feel a soured smile spreading his face at the memory — a seemingly endless night of bacchanalia at the infamous Chateau Marmont.

The Chateau rose above the Sunset Strip like a leviathan of gothic glamour and was one of the more famous places in the world where writers, actors, musicians, and the affluent elite had been known to squirrel away in its paparazzi-free palatial environment.

Harry Cohn, founder of Columbia Pictures, said, "If you're gonna get in trouble, do it at Chateau Marmont." And Harry was right. Generations thought so. James Dean jumped through a window, Led Zeppelin rode their hogs into the lobby, and Jon had beat a few demons into the dirt himself. But getting into trouble at the Chateau was reasonably safe. Unlike Hamilton Island, where Jon was terrified of what he might say or even do.

He was glad Houser was there. Jon felt safe beside him, knowing Houser wouldn't let things get too far out of hand no matter what sorta shit fell from his mouth. Houser usually had the words, even when he said nothing.

Two shots of Jack later, and the first tear fell from Jon's eye. Jon didn't bother to wipe. "I'm such a fucking asshole."

"I've known an Army base worth of assholes, Hollywood. And you wouldn't have even cleared boot camp. A rich prick, sure, but only on accident. And yeah, you're a little bitch about your weight," Houser smiled. "But you're not an asshole."

Jon choked through his laughter, then said, "No, man. I am." He sipped his Jack, the first time he hadn't gulped, then added. "I think I knew Emma was my daughter, deep down. Just didn't want to admit it."

"Bullshit. You're just feeling guilty because that's what you do."

"No," Jon shook his head. "I had a hard time believing Sarah was with another guy so quick. I was her first, after all." His voice cracked. "And she was mine. But believing she had moved on made it easier for me to move on, too. Even if part of me wondered. I'm an asshole for letting it go. If I hadn't, everything would be different. Sarah never would've been on the island, and she never would've been in the classroom when that bullet tore through the wall."

"Okay, you're done," Houser scooped Jon's glass to the other side of the table. "You can't rewrite history. And who's to say Sarah wouldn't have been hit by a bus walking the Strip?"

Jon rubbed his temples. "Losing Sarah the first time was what made me want to step into the middle of the street without looking both ways, come home to my empty apartment and watch shit TV, and coat the acid and ache in the pit of my stomach with whatever I could pour from a bottle. Even after I moved on, a part of me always believed our story wasn't over. But now it is, and I can't live with it."

Jon started to quietly sob. Houser looked around the bar, then scooted his chair closer to Jon, softly patting the back of his shoulder.

"Sarah's different, there's no one like her," Jon kept shaking his head like it had a fresh set of batteries. "She loved me before I was on the cover of *Entertainment Weekly*. Before I was damaged. Back when I was still innocent, and before I'd ever been a punchline. I'll never be able to trust another woman the way I trusted her, because I'll never know another woman before the fame."

"You always had the money, Jon."

"Yeah," he said, "but I knew Sarah before she knew what it was, or at least why it mattered."

Houser's phone started buzzing on his belt. Jon barked out a laugh and pointed at Houser's waist. "You should keep that in a fanny pack." He laughed through his tears. "And you call *me* a bitch."

Houser looked at the screen. "It's local." He turned to Jon, then tapped the green button on his black phone. "Houser."

His eyes narrowed, then after a few seconds of silence, Houser said. "Yes, ma'am." Another few seconds later, he added, "How can I help you?"

Houser listened for around thirty seconds, then turned the phone from his ear, palmed the speaker, and whispered to Jon. "It's Heller's wife."

The wife of the man who murdered Sarah — and Jon's dreams.

Chapter 9 - Brock Houser

8:28 p.m.

"IS this the same Brock Houser who found the missing girl today?"

"Yes, ma'am" he said. "How can I help you?"

"I don't know who else I can turn to." She sounded less sad than upset. "My son is missing. And I'm afraid something bad has happened to him. Is there any chance I could hire you to find him? I don't have much money, and I'm not even sure what you guys charge, but I need help."

"Did you contact the police?" Houser asked.

"Yes, but I'm not sure how much help they can be. His father, Roger Heller, shot six people at the school. And I'm afraid that someone might have hurt Alex in retaliation."

"Why do you think that?"

Jon leaned close, listening to the conversation.

Liz told him about the shooting, then about how one of the victim's parents came to the house and assaulted her son. She also told Houser about MURDERER spray-painted in blood-red across her windshield. After Alex got in a fight with two kids at school — a fight that left one of the kids in a coma — and he and his girlfriend, Katie, ran into the woods. No one had seen them since.

Houser asked if it was possible that he and his girlfriend ran away together, as young lovers sometimes do.

"He wouldn't do that to us," Liz said. "He wouldn't leave me and his little sister behind. I know this is gonna sound ridiculous, but I know something has happened. I can feel it."

Houser looked at Jon, who shrugged on his way to another sip of whiskey.

"Hold on a second," Houser said and muted the phone.

"What do you think? It's probably nothing, but I could probably swing by and give her some peace of mind."

"You're gonna help the wife of the man who murdered Sarah?" Jon asked.

"She didn't murder Sarah. She's just as much a victim in this as the people her husband shot," Houser said, afraid Jon was too drunk to see things clearly.

"And if he *is* missing?" Jon said. "You wanna sink into the quicksand of another search?"

Houser sighed. "Worse comes to worst, if he really *is* missing, I can call one of my detectives in to help out, so I'll still be free to look into your shit."

Jon slurred, "Hey, don't worry about me. I'm not in a rush. Do what you gotta do, man."

"You sure?"

"Hell, I don't even know what I wanna do yet."

Houser un-muted the phone and said, "Mrs. Heller? Give me your address, and I'll be right over."

A few seconds later, he ended the call. Then he thanked Jon and asked, "You wanna go with me?"

"No, thanks," Jon said. "I'm thinking Pigtails is waiting for you to leave."

Houser looked over to see the waitress smiling at them.

"Okay, Just promise me you'll call a cab or a driver from your brother's house, eh?"

"Sure thing." Jon looked past Houser and flirted with the waitress.

"Call me if you need anything. Otherwise, I'll call you when I'm done meeting Mrs. Heller."

~

HOUSER ARRIVED at Mrs. Heller's house, immediately spotting the black SUV parked in front — a Paladin security truck keeping guard, just like Mrs. Heller said there would be.

Houser drove past the SUV, then pulled into the driveway. The moment Houser killed the engine and was out his vehicle, the security guard was approaching him. Houser already had his ID in hand and held it up for the guard.

"I'm a PI. Mrs. Heller is expecting me."

The guard stood there, hand on his gun, a flashlight swatting a beam between Houser's face then his ID.

Mrs. Heller called from the porch, "It's okay. I called him here."

"Okay, ma'am," the guard said, then clicked off his light and nodded to Houser before returning to his SUV.

Houser went to the porch and shook Mrs. Heller's hand. Her eyes and nose were red, and she looked exhausted.

"Thank you for coming," she said.

Houser said, "Thank you for calling," even though he wasn't actively seeking clients.

Mrs. Heller welcomed him into her home. He took a seat in the living room.

"Can I get you a drink?"

"Water, please?" He wasn't thirsty, but he wanted a minute to look around her living room without her eyes on him.

While she was in the kitchen, he absorbed the vibe beating between the walls of the house. It was a typical upper-middle-class home — slightly posh, but comfortable furniture, children's toys in plastic toy box next to a playpen, and a 64" LiquidTV set into the wall. Family photos from when Liz's son was younger and separate studio shots of her young daughter decorated the walls. No time for family photos these days, Houser figured. The living room was warm, nothing like what he expected to feel from the house of a man who snapped.

She handed him a purple plastic tumbler with ice water. He took a sip, then started to gulp, surprising himself at his genuine thirst.

Mrs. Heller sat and went over some of the same things she'd said on the phone, adding a few more details when Houser asked. She was afraid for her son, feared someone had hurt him for what his father had done.

"Did your husband have any enemies on the island before all this began?"

"No. Everybody loved Roger. Though he'd never admit it, he was a pushover when it came to his students, and I can't think of anytime he'd ever had any problems."

"Was your husband having, or had he ever had, an affair?"

"What? Why would you ask that?"

"It's a routine question in cases like this. I need to know everyone who might have a motive to hurt Alex."

"No. He barely had time for me, let alone another woman."

Houser scribbled notes in his spiral as he asked a few more general questions, then purposely took a bit of time after she stopped speaking to give her a minute to stew in her silence. Finally, he came out with the question she probably least wanted to answer. "Why did your husband shoot six people?"

Mrs. Heller seemed surprised by the question, or perhaps the point at the end of it. "I … don … don't know. How on Earth could I know something like that?"

Houser saw something squirreling inside her eyes. She was holding back. Sure, there was guilt, likely mixed with shame, and a fat handful of other ugly emotions. But she was also hiding something else. Something she'd been keeping to herself. Houser could feel it like it was standing in the middle of the room, an invisible guest waiting to be spoken to life.

"If you want me to find your son, I need to know *everything*, Mrs. Heller. Even things you might not think I need to know. Perhaps there's something you didn't tell the police."

There. That was it.

Houser saw the shift of her eyes, the momentary hitch in her breath. The way her hands started to fidget. She wanted to tell him but was afraid. *Afraid of what, though?* He considered saying something, but instead, let silence massage her.

"He had a list." She closed her eyes and swallowed as if she'd just confessed to the crime herself.

"A list?" Houser said.

"After Roger died, I found a list he'd hidden. He'd written the names of the students he shot. As if he'd planned to shoot them specifically."

Interesting.

"Was Mrs. Hughes on the list?"

"No. Just the students. And there was something else I found."

"What else did you find, Mrs. Heller?"

The front door swung open.

Mrs. Heller leapt to her feet and burst into tears. "Alex!" She ran to her son and hugged him, squeezing him as he dropped the backpack he'd been holding.

Alex shivered into his mother's hug. His black hoodie and jeans were filthy, his hair a mess, and his skin clammy. His eyes were exhausted, but also terrified, as if something had happened to him, or he'd seen something that spooked him. As their gazes met, the kid didn't wear the look of someone wondering who the big, black guy in his living room was. Empty eyes didn't wonder.

Just like Emma's had been when he found her.

The *This Shit Ain't Right* part of Houser's brain started to tingle.

"Are you okay?" his mother asked, pulling away and looking her son up and down. "What happened?"

"I got in a fight." his voice sounded off, filled with a gravel of fright or fear or something Houser couldn't place. "Then Katie and I were coming home through the woods, and it started to rain, so we hid in a cave."

The way Alex looked down when he said they'd hid in a cave made Houser wonder what else they'd done in the cave.

Alex went on, "We were waiting for the rain to die down, and we fell asleep waiting."

"Fell asleep?" Mrs. Heller asked, confounded. Apparently, she hadn't made the same connection Houser had.

"And then I woke up, and ... Katie was gone."

"Gone?"

"Yeah. I don't know where she went. I tried calling her. I tried calling you, but my phone's battery is dead. I have to call her house."

The life had returned to Alex's eyes, though he'd still not yet asked who the hell the black guy in their living room was. Maybe Houser had that look of cop or something. Alex went to the phone and was about to call Katie when the phone rang. He picked it up.

"Katie!" Alex said, excited, life returning to his eyes. "Where are you? ... What? What do you mean *I* was gone. No, I woke up and you were gone!" He ran his hand through his hair. "I ... I dunno. It doesn't matter. Are you okay?"

Houser watched Mrs. Heller watch her son, tears of happiness streaming down her face. The desperation and mourning on her face just moments ago had been replaced by joy and relief.

She turned and smiled at Houser, wiping the tears from her face. "Thank you."

"Easiest job I ever did." Houser grinned.

"How much do I owe you?" She looked around the living room for something, probably her purse.

"Don't worry about it. I'm just glad your son is back."

Alex looked at his mom and held up a finger. "I'll be right back, okay?" Then he disappeared up the stairs, continuing the conversation with his girlfriend.

"Nice to see you, too," Mrs. Heller said, laughing to hide the hurt that Alex was more concerned with how his girlfriend was than his mother who had been worried sick. She began to lead Houser toward the door. "Well, I don't wanna keep you."

He wasn't sure if he should ask, but he couldn't ignore the itch in the back of his brain. "Mrs. Heller? You were saying something about a list and something?"

She shook her head. "Can we forget I mentioned that? I really don't want to drag my husband's name through the mud any more than it has been already."

"I understand, Mrs. Heller, and I don't want to, either. But I can't help but feel there's something else you want to tell me."

She looked away for a second. Exactly long enough to confirm his suspicion.

He considered letting the silence do the heavy lifting again, but decided to talk instead. "Mrs. Heller, I can tell something has you scared. Something more than worrying about someone seeking vengeance on your family. I do more than just find missing kids, you know. I also help people."

She looked back at the stairs where her son might come down any second. Or in twenty minutes.

"I dunno." She turned back to Houser and rubbed her hands nervously together.

"Mrs. Heller, let me help you. I promise, whatever you tell me is confidential. I don't want to make the hard time your family is going through even harder."

She studied Houser, like she was searching for trust. Then she took a deep breath. "I found something else besides the list

— a flash drive my husband had hidden. I brought it to the library because the police, Paladin, and the feds took all our computers. All the files on the flash drive were locked, except one."

Houser could see the fear surfacing in Mrs. Heller's eyes, hear it in her voice.

"Roger said in the video that he had proof of something. But I didn't see what it was before I had to turn off the computer and leave the library."

"Proof?"

Alex began to descend the stairs, saying goodbye to his girlfriend.

"Can you open the files if I give the flash drive to you?"

"Yes," Houser said, though he couldn't truly be certain until he saw the security used with the flash drive.

Mrs. Heller reached into her pocket and pulled the flash drive from inside, then slipped it into his hand and whispered, "Don't show anybody." She then spoke in a loud, clear voice. "Thank you again, Mr. Houser. I appreciate your help."

"Yes, ma'am." Houser shook her hand and whispered, "Call me." Then he turned to Alex, who was still on the phone. "You take care."

"Thank you." He waved, though he probably had no clue what he was thanking Houser for.

As Houser left their house and climbed inside his rental, he felt the eyes of the Paladin guard on him, watching his every move.

Chapter 10 - Milo Anderson

Friday evening ...

MILO THOUGHT himself lonely two days earlier, but lying alone in his hospital room, soaking in the aftermath of Manny's death, Cody's call, and Beatrice's kamikaze run into Jordy's Foods, made the previous two days feel like a laugh riot.

The surgeon had already met with Milo, as did a pair of Paladin guards, who stayed twice as long as the surgeon and seemed to ask three times the number of questions.

Everyone seemed especially interested in what would possibly make Beatrice floor her way through the front of the store. As if Milo had any idea. He wished he knew. Milo had called Bea a crazy bitch plenty of times, but he had only meant the second part.

He felt sick to his stomach and had to reach for the barf bowl sitting by the bedside when the taller of the two Paladin officers informed him there were two fatalities in the accident — an elderly couple named the Marshalls whom Milo had known since forever. There were a few other injuries as well, but nobody else in critical condition. Milo and Beatrice got it the worst. But she shouldn't still be breathing, not if her breath had stopped the Marshalls from getting theirs.

Milo remembered the first time he saw Mrs. Marshall, in the produce section of Jordy's ironically enough, though back then the store had been called Lucky's.

Milo was in the middle of a temper tantrum, one of his worst ever. He wasn't sure if it was the severity of that particular tantrum, or Mrs. Marshall coming up to him that made him remember the incident, but the memory was clear as a perfect spring sky on the island.

Mrs. Marshall came up to Milo, mid-scream and kneeled on the linoleum. "How old are you, honey? You must be four!"

Something about her voice must have stopped Milo from crying. He sputtered to a stop, then turned to the old woman. "I turned three last birthday." Milo remembered holding three proud fingers to the sky.

"My goodness," Mrs. Marshall said, turning toward his mom. "He's quite tall for his age."

Milo's mom agreed. Mrs. Marshall then leaned closer to his mother and whispered, just loud enough for Milo to hear, "Don't worry, honey, it gets better. The only time I really hated being a mother was when my children were three. Well, three and thirteen. Those were the two years when I just didn't want to do it anymore. But I promise," she winked, "it does get a whole lot better."

The pills mostly numbed the pain in his body, but the pain inside Milo's mind was far worse. The thought of Mrs. Marshall flooded Milo with fresh memories of his mother and twisted the pain in his body closer to torment.

He could be dead.

Like the Marshalls. Or his mother. Or Jessica. Or Manny.

Home promised plenty more misery, but it would still be

better than lying alone in the hospital, where everyone seemed to agree Milo would be spending his next few days.

The nurse had removed his catheter. He was still tethered to an IV bag, a cuff on his arm, and a monitor on his finger. He wished he could just get up and flee. He didn't know where he'd go, but anywhere seemed better than his hospital room.

Milo had many wretched memories docked in a harbor of too little time. The memories were a festering wound, and the isolation an acid drop on it. Milo didn't believe misery loved company, but he was smart enough to know sharing was a salve on any wound.

Which made Milo wonder again where in the hell his father was.

Milo grunted as he swung his legs from bed. He detached the cuff and the finger device that measured the oxygen in his blood, then rolled into the bathroom with his IV drip bag.

He sat on the toilet, body aching, pissing for what felt like forever. At first, it hurt to piss. But then the pain ceded. And then Milo continued to sit there, crying, feeling sad, scared, and alone, missing his mother, maybe more than ever. He was terrified his father would fall into the same abyss that claimed him when Milo's mom vanished.

Milo's dad was mostly a ghost — an apparition of the man who once curled his fingers into the chain link at every baseball game, held the glue steady so it poured in thin lines, and made sure all Milo's A's and B's were displayed on the fridge with his homemade smiley face magnets.

Milo lost his father once. The wound, still raw, was bleeding again. He couldn't bear to do it a second time.

After a while, he flushed the toilet, washed his hands, then opened the bathroom door to find his father standing there.

"Dad!" Milo hobbled toward his dad and hugged him.

"Milo! I'm so glad you're okay."

Milo sat back on the bed and put the oxygen monitoring clip back on his finger. He looked up at his father.

Before he could say a word, his dad leaned onto the bed. "I'm sorry, Milo. I should've been here."

Dad looked like he was one shudder from sobbing, which sloshed the acid in Milo's stomach. His father never cried, or at least *almost* never. He always cried when he watched *Field of Dreams* and some baseball games, but almost never otherwise.

"It's okay, Dad." And he meant it. "I'm glad you're home, though." He smiled, though sent a spark of pain to his abdomen. "How's Beatrice?"

Milo's dad looked down, then shook his head. "Not great. Doctor says they'll know more later, but so far, the news isn't good."

"Sorry."

His dad tried to hold Milo's gaze as the edges of his mouth started to twitch, an expression more angry than sad.

"You okay, Dad?"

He smiled, the older smile that made him look more like a ghost. "Yeah, I'm fine, considering. It's just ..." His face flooded with apology. "Bea and I have been fighting lately, a lot actually, and that's part of the reason I've been out of the house more than usual. But that's not fair to you. Or to her, either. Now she's ..." He collapsed into tears. "Well, I dunno if she's gonna make it, and I can't get our last conversation outta my head."

"I'm sorry."

"It's okay." Dad wiped his eyes before pulling Milo's hands into his. "Everything for a reason. Everything will be okay. This is the wake-up call I needed. Now, tell me what happened." He patted his son on his hand.

Milo filled him in on everything — except for the Cody guy calling him, because he didn't want his dad to think he was crazy — until the nurse came in with medication that made Milo feel groggy.

He was barely aware of his father getting up to leave the room. He might not have even noticed had his dad not leaned in, kissed him on the head, then said, "I'm sorry this all happened. I love you."

His dad left the room, leaving Milo alone, but feeling more loved than he had since his mother turned to memory.

Chapter 11 - Stephen Anderson

Stephen Anderson closed the door to his son's room, then relaxed into the slight limp he'd kept well-hidden while inside, quickly putting distance between his son's room and his still-bleeding conscience.

Fifty feet from trading the bright white of the hospital for the dim gray outside, *Fur Elise* rang in his pocket. Stephen froze as a thin sheet of icy fear frosted the top of his boiling rage.

He held the phone, stared into his palm, and tried to keep his face calmer than his voice. "You have a lot of goddamned nerve calling me. My son was nearly killed! You said nobody else would be around. You said no collateral damage."

The grayed image on the other side of the call said, "You might want to remember who you're speaking to, Mr. Anderson. I don't do well with a lack of manners."

The best Stephen could do to mind his manners was stare and say nothing at all. The voice without a face said, "What does Milo know?"

"Nothing," Stephen lied.

"Are you certain? Because Paladin has shared a different

story, and you know how I like my stories to look one another in the eye."

"Don't worry," Stephen swallowed his lump. "I'll make sure he can't connect the dots."

"You'd better, Mr. Anderson. Or we'll activate his chip."

"Wait," Stephen huddled against the wall, the phone now inches from his face. "You put a fucking chip in him? When? How?!"

The grayed face crackled into a black screen.

The when and how was answered by the smiling surgeon, Dr. Edward Stone, nodding at Stephen as he stepped through a swinging set of double doors.

They now had him exactly where they wanted him.

Episode 5

Chapter 1 - Jon Conway (Age 13)

Jon stormed home from school, through the house, and into the kitchen, where he dropped the cardboard box on the floor with a resounding thud. He then tore open the refrigerator and grabbed an IBC root beer from the front of a neat column, leaving another eleven behind.

Mrs. Rasmussen entered the room and smiled. "I can't believe you didn't take a jacket with you." She shook her head. "And why do you look like something that's about to start shooting steam from its ears? Was it the ferry ride that has you all bothered or the science fair?"

Jon twisted the cap from the top of his bottle, then pitched it into the trashcan. "I suck."

Mrs. Rasmussen crossed the kitchen to the fridge where Jon was still standing. She knelt, crossed her legs, then pulled Jon to the floor beside her.

Though he was plenty used to Mrs. Rasmussen's unique brand of conflict resolution, the gesture still caught him slightly off guard. He had to balance his bottle on his way to the floor, tipping a sip's worth of liquid over the lip of the bottle, where it splashed onto the Pietra Firma tile below.

Jon looked up at Mrs. Rasmussen, horrified.

"Like you're going to clean it up?" She laughed.

Jon laughed, too, but looked down, embarrassed by the truth.

"So, what happened?" she said. "Your homemade plastic didn't go over so well? Is that what has you looking like you've been sucking on a jumbo bag of Sour Patch Kids all afternoon?"

"I'm not sucking on Sour Patch Kids."

"Well, you're thirteen now, young Mr. Conway, and pouting is for children. So, let's start all over and tell me what's in that head of yours."

"I suck."

"Say that again and see what happens." Her crimped, blonde hair draped between her breasts. Like always, it made Jon think of a mermaid. Mrs. Rasmussen was pretty, especially for being so much older than him, and Jon imagined she had been quite attractive, maybe even beautiful, when she was young.

She had on her dangerous face, even though her, "Say that again and see what happens" had never led to any sort of cruel or unusual punishment, or really anything at all. After years, Jon was curious. But not curious enough to push her. Not today.

He had gone to the science expo in Seattle with his class. His project was his own brand of homemade plastic. Jon hadn't known much about plastic, much less that you could make your own, until he started his research. Even though Jon couldn't see caring much beyond his presentation, he did find the research interesting. Though most plastics had to be made in factories, he used a recipe that allowed him to use milk, vinegar, and a concoction of other stuff from the kitchen and laundry room, which made the plastic not only stronger than the kind which used just milk and vinegar, but which seemed to provide for more uses.

Jon thought his idea was original, or at least an original

twist on a common project, but there were four other projects at the expo that used homemade plastics, just like his, but better. Only volcanoes were less original.

"I got one of those 'Nice Job' ribbons," Jon said. "It may as well say, 'Thanks for being total crap.'"

"Your work is not crap. You've never shown much of an interest in science before the Expo, so why do you even care what type of ribbon you earned? You entered the fair, did your best, and tried something you've never tried before. And that's exactly what you were acknowledged for. Nothing more, nothing less. I would count this one as a success."

Jon shook his head. "Warren got First Place when he did the expo. First out of everyone. And I mean like, the entire state. Every year he entered!"

Mrs. Rasmussen said, "I know, he wouldn't shut up about it for months each time."

Jon smiled.

"Ah, so that's what's bugging you — Warren." She broke into a wide grin and patted his shoulder.

He lost his smile, almost immediately. "He does everything better than me."

She shook her head. "No. He does *some* things better than you."

"Yeah, all the stuff that matters."

"Hot sauce and crackers," she said. "You are colorful and articulate, friendly and funny. You, Jon Conway, are a gentleman, and if you don't mind me saying so," she leaned in, just close enough to turn their conversation conspiratorial, "delightful. But total pain in the cactus patch."

Jon fueled his smile with another long swig of root beer. When he looked up, he saw his father, Blake Conway, enter the kitchen.

"Mind if I take it from here?" Jon's father turned to him, smiled, winked, then opened the fridge and grabbed an IBC from the front.

He twisted his cap and pitched it in the can.

"You're home!" Jon cried.

"Of course," his dad said. "Today was the science expo, right? Big day."

Jon looked puzzled. "But you weren't there?"

Like Jon, Mrs. Rasmussen was now standing. His father put his hand gently on her shoulder and said, "Thank you."

Mrs. Rasmussen nodded. "Of course, Mr. Conway." Then she left the kitchen.

Jon's dad hefted himself onto the countertop, then patted the granite and waited for Jon to join him. Jon boosted himself up beside his father.

His father said, "No, I wasn't there. I'll give you three guesses why. And please, no need to spare my feelings. I hate it when you pull that crap. If you can't learn to shoot straight, you'll never learn to shoot shit."

Jon said, "I don't know."

"I Don't Know lives on I Don't Give a Shit Street." His father took a sip of root bear. "Do you live on I Don't Give a Shit Street, or do you live in the beautiful, unblinking eye of Cedar Park?"

"I live in Cedar Park," Jon said. "Was it because you had a meeting at the same time, and it couldn't be rescheduled?"

"BZZZZZZZZ."

"Because Hillary messed up your schedule, like she always does, and it's a goddamned question of your sanity why you keep her on your payroll, especially with all the bonuses you throw her measured against the number of times she fucks shit up?"

"BZZZZZZZZ." His father grinned. "And don't be a smart ass."

Jon laughed. "Because I suck?"

"Just because I've never smacked you before, doesn't mean I won't start. I figure I have at least another few years before you get enough meat on your bones to kick my ass back. Now stop saying you suck. It pisses me off." His father wrapped his arm around Jon's shoulder. "None of those is the reason why, and no, I didn't forget. I saw your giant pile of homemade plastic sitting on the table this morning. I didn't need to go to Seattle and see it there, too. Not when I could arrange my day around being here when you came home instead. Know what I mean?"

"Sure," Jon said. "It means you pretty much figured I'd suck."

"Nope." His father shook his head. "I didn't figure anything of the sort, but I also didn't think your homemade plastic stood a chance against science geeks who've been working on their projects all year. If you had won, then you would have only won because you're Blake Conway's son. And that would've been bullshit. Right?"

"Right," Jon grumbled.

"Don't whine or pout. Listen. You entered the science fair to prove a point. I hope you feel you proved it. If not, better luck next time. I love you, son, but if you thought you were gonna waltz in and win that science fair because you decided to throw your dart at the board up around two weeks ago, well that's just downright disappointing to me, since I figured I raised a smarter boy than that. In general, shit in life is not that easy."

"It is for Warren."

His father smiled. "And *that's* why I'm here."

Jon took a swig of root beer then looked up at his father, suspicious.

His father said, "Warren is one of those science geeks who worked on his projects all year each time he entered. Unlike your homemade plastic, his projects *deserved* to win. His projects were groundbreaking. He built robots and grew artificial flesh, stuff that has applications at his job now! And hell, if Warren had the edge because he's Blake Conway's son, well that's an edge, son, not a conspiracy."

He clapped his hand hard on Jon's back. "Did Warren get the lead in that play your class put on last year?"

"No."

"And was I as sparkly as a firecracker when you did, even though I thought that shit was sorta gay?" Dad said with a laugh.

"Yes."

"What about art? What about when you wanted to play the guitar? What about everything you ever say you're going to do? Don't you always have my support, one hundred percent, even if you never finish a tenth of what you set out to do?"

"Yes, but …"

"But Warren is smarter, and you like talking to him more because he always talks about business." Dad finished Jon's sentence, nearly word for word, though in a whinier voice than Jon would have actually used.

His cheeks flushed. "I don't like it when you do that."

"I don't like it when you're predictable." His father set his bottle on the counter then turned his attention to Jon. "Warren is Warren. Stop trying to be so much like him that you're not enough of *you*."

"I don't *want* to be like Warren." Jon set his bottle beside his father's, then crossed his arms.

"Well, you could have fooled me . For the millionth time, I don't love Warren better than you, and I never will."

"If I was more like Warren, you'd want to spend more time with me."

"Oh, great," his father sighed. "Looks like today's gonna be a highlight reel displaying all of my favorites. Listen, Jon, I work with Warren. He's got twelve years on you. That means we're going to have plenty to talk about, naturally. Plus, more time to talk about all the stuff we have in common. You need to get over that. Our relationship is different. I admire you for who you are *and* for who you aren't. And I'm getting goddamned exhausted feeling like I have to renew our vows every few months."

"Sorry."

"It's fine, but I'd like you to stop it. You are you, and I will never stand in your way. I support your choices."

"You don't like Sarah," Jon said, not wanting to bring her up but unable not to in the moment.

"I never said anything about her one way or another."

"Warren hates her."

"Warren hates everybody, at least anyone he doesn't think is as smart as he is. But as you well know, he didn't get that shit from me. Warren may have been born with a license to drive life like an asshole, and that might be my fault, but he's the one who gets behind the wheel each day."

"Warren says that Sarah's not good enough for me, and that I'm making the family look bad."

"That's bullshit," his father said. "He *thinks* he's looking out for you. He probably thinks you're taking this relationship stuff a bit too serious at your age. You've got your whole future and the world ahead of you, so you don't want to settle with the first girl who lets you feel her tits."

Jon flushed with embarrassment, finished his root beer so he wouldn't have to acknowledge that comment, and got up from the counter to grab another drink from the fridge, plus one more for his dad.

They sipped their bottles to empty, while talking movies and books and plenty of other stuff Warren would never want to talk about, then they left the kitchen and the fridge with just six IBCs as they headed outside, the both of them laughing, with a book of matches, Jon's science project, and a bottle of bourbon.

Then Blake Conway showed Jon how easy and fun it was to burn shit that no longer mattered.

Chapter 2 - Brock Houser

Friday
Sept. 8
Nighttime …

BROCK HOUSER DROVE BACK to the Sands of Time, where he was staying in one of Jon's rooms on the rented floor. All he could think about was the flash drive and what might be on it.

The part of him that loved a good mystery believed maybe there was something explosive on the flash drive — something that would rock the island and give Roger Heller motive to mow down his classroom. But the more realistic, and experienced, part of Houser's brain said he was far more likely to find nothing but the ramblings of a tin-foil-hat-wearing conspiracy theorist.

In either case, he was curious to know why a seemingly happily married teacher — and by all accounts, helluva nice guy — would kill his students. Even if the *why* was batshit crazy, at least batshit crazy was a reason.

Houser considered himself an excellent judge of character. That made him an excellent judge of motivation. While

Houser hadn't known Heller, the picture painted by his wife didn't make him seem like your typical nut job. Of course, there was always the chance Liz didn't really know her husband as well as she thought she did. Maybe Roger Heller was so good at hiding his crazy or dark side that *nobody* could have seen what was coming. Which was all the more reason Houser couldn't wait to see what Heller put on the flash drive.

Martin Graves, Houser's longtime friend, had created a program that blended a brute force attack along with some new algorithmic shit beyond Houser's depth that could open and decrypt most files within a few hours. Most, but not all. Depending on what Heller was using to encrypt his files, there was a chance Houser might have to wait until he returned to California to discover the treasure buried on the drive.

Houser parked at the hotel, crossed the lobby, then went into the elevator. As he passed the front desk, the cute girl behind the counter smiled. He smiled back, resisting the urge to flirt. If Jonny Hollywood was behaving himself, Houser was obligated to do the same. Jon had left a message on Houser's phone saying he and his brother had a big blow up and he was gonna go to Cassidy's house to chill out and he'd call if he needed a ride to the hotel.

So Houser went to his room, removed his shoulder holster, laid it on the table beside his computer, then went in the bathroom and splashed cool water on his face. He grabbed a Diet Coke from the mini-fridge, popped it open, and took a drink as he opened the lid to his laptop and pressed the startup button.

As the computer chimed and booted, Houser stepped onto the balcony and looked out at the night sky. The moon hanging fat and low, hovering just inches above the island as the sound of waves crashing a block away rolled into the room. He loved the sound of the ocean. It reminded him of home. Below the balcony, a beautifully lit swimming pool beckoned. Late-night swims were always nice. Maybe once he was done for the night he'd take a dip, but only if the pool was heated. Houser didn't care much for hotels, even when Jon rented an entire floor, but he always enjoyed having a pool to relax in.

Houser left the doors open to the salty, cool breeze while he sat at the desk, logged into the computer, and slipped the flash drive into a USB port.

He waited for the computer to recognize the device, clicked to open the folder, then promptly received a corrupted data message.

"Fucking Shit."

Houser searched the Web for how to repair corrupted files but wasn't sure if the instructions applied to encrypted files as well. He certainly didn't want to lose anything, assuming the files could be recovered.

Even though it was likely too late, he called Graves. Got his voicemail.

"Hey, it's Houser. I'm in Washington, working a case. A client gave me a flash drive that I think is encrypted. When I put it in the port, I got a corrupted data error. I need your genius skills to walk me through a simple fix, if there is one. Call me back when you get this. If it's after one in the morning, hit me tomorrow. Thanks."

Houser ejected the device, closed his laptop, then placed the flash drive on top of his computer, annoyed that he'd have to wait even longer to see what secrets it held. He took another swig of Diet Coke, figuring all the trouble and anticipation would likely lead to nothing. It was pretty hard to imagine Heller's "secrets" were anything more than Grade-A loony bin material.

He clicked on the TV for some background noise as he sorted through his thoughts and tried to figure out what he wanted to do. He should get to bed, but he wasn't particularly tired. A brief thought of the girl working the desk downstairs flitted into his mind and right back out. He pictured himself hitting the hotel bar. Those couple of drinks he had with Jon didn't get him close to feeling inebriated.

Houser went into the bathroom to take a piss. He was in midstream when he heard the sound of his electronic door lock click.

What the fuck? Housekeeping? Jon?

He tried to stop pissing, but couldn't.

The door slowly opened, and he heard another sound, something bouncing into the room, before the door swung closed.

Shit.

Houser raised his zipper, wetting the front of his pants, as he ran back into the room to grab his gun from the table.

A small grenade was lying on the ground, breathing gray smoke like a dragon.

Houser held his breath, put his shirt over his nose and mouth to block the harsh smoke, then grabbed the gun and flash drive from the table and ran back outside onto the balcony.

Houser slid the door shut and saw two men in full-black gear with masks storm into his room. One had an AR-15. The other wielded a pistol equipped with a silencer. Both were looking for him.

They saw him and fired.

The glass doors shattered. Houser spun around and leaped over the balcony railing, pushing himself out as far out as he could. He plummeted into the pool, five stories below, holding the flash drive and gun as tightly as he could.

Icy water screamed on his skin. The pool was not heated.

Fuck, fuck, fuck.

Houser surfaced, coughing chlorinated water from his lungs, and glanced back up toward the balcony from where he had just jumped. He wouldn't have long until his attackers were taking aim.

He put the flash drive in his mouth, then swam as fast as

he could toward the closest ledge. He pulled himself up and then out of the pool, his soaking clothes adding what seemed to be fifty pounds to his already bulky frame. Houser slipped the flash drive into his wet pants pocket and then took a quick glance around.

He cringed, fully expecting to get shot as he ran from the pool, then toward the hotel, getting as close to the wall as he could until he was out of the gunmen's range.

Who the hell are these people?

And are there more?

Houser ran forward toward the parking lot, scanning the night for any more men in black. Whoever his attackers were, they meant business, and he had little doubt he'd find more of them lurking.

Houser grabbed his keys from his wet pocket and made his way toward his rental car.

A gunman appeared between him and the vehicle, aiming an AR-15 at him.

Houser squeezed two shots, one hitting the man in the chest, knocking him back about a foot and a half. The other landed in his head, sending him to the ground, firing wildly as he died.

The gunshots had murdered the night's silence. Eyes would be on the parking lot in seconds.

Fuck, fuck!

If there were others lurking nearby, Houser didn't yet see them.

He opened the car door and threw the AR-15 in, then held the pistol in his left hand as he started the car with the key in his right. He threw the car into reverse and gunned the engine, tearing from the lot with a rubber-on-asphalt shriek.

More gunfire erupted behind him, and his back windshield shattered.

Houser took a hard left, racing onto the street.

The two-lane road leading from the hotel was long and

narrow, and he hoped no traffic was on it. He had to put as much distance between himself and his pursuers as he could. He had to get away, then call Jon.

Fuck, I left the phone in my room!

He could circle back if he had to. He could take these fuckers out. But the phone wasn't worth going back for.

A red Toyota appeared in the right lane ahead of him, going a hundred miles under the speed limit.

Shit! Shit! Shit!

He wanted to weave around the bastard, but there were too many cars in the oncoming traffic lane. Houser spotted a fast-moving pair of headlights about a block behind him. It had to be his pursuers.

Shit! Shit! Shit!

"Come on!" Houser screamed, slapping the steering wheel and waiting for a break in the other lane, as he was stuck behind a battery-operated shit wagon.

At a gap in the traffic, he took a hard left and gunned the engine, racing up the street into the path of oncoming cars before swerving back into the right lane. He drove a block, and then took the first right along another small road in the tourist district. The boulevard was crowded, as patrons from the bars and restaurants spilled into the street.

Shit, fuck, shit!

Houser looked back in the rearview to see if he could back up, but two fast-moving headlights appeared in the mirror, gaining inches by the second.

Fuck, shit, fuck!

"Come on, you stupid fucks!" he shouted.

Houser honked his horn and gunned the engine, racing toward a cluster of people just standing in the road, drinking and not realizing enough to give a shit that they were seconds from roadkill.

They scattered all at once, their eyes wide and mouths cursing him as he flew past. A beer bottle hit the side of his car and shattered. Houser kept going, taking his first left, then turning again, until he found himself on the main road — four lanes along the coast.

Not knowing which was the best way to go, he headed north, figuring he'd probably have to navigate through less traffic on the north end of the island. He kept his eyes on the rearview, half surprised and the rest of him relieved, not to see any sign of pursuit.

Houser didn't think he was clever enough to have lost them so quickly. Particularly if they had any familiarity with the island, which he had barely at all. He drove until he found a left turn that looked like it wouldn't lead to a dead-end or back to a road that might put him face to face with the men in black.

He took a few more turns until he found himself at the end of a cul de sac in a residential neighborhood. He killed his lights, then backed up to a vacant-looking house. Many of the homes on the island were used as island getaways, the sort of homes you'd visit often when the ink was still fresh on the mortgage, but less and less as years passed, until you eventually decided to rent the place or sell it.

After parking in the driveway, he killed the engine, then rolled his window down, listening for any sound of a threat. He wished like hell he'd thought to take his phone now. He could call Jon to tell him what was going on. Maybe he'd call the cops, too.

Who the hell are these people? What do they want?

Houser saw three possibilities.

One, it was a kidnapping gone bad, in which case Jon Conway was the most likely target. That meant Houser had to get a hold of Jon as soon as possible so he could make sure he was safe and didn't go back to the hotel.

Option two was that Houser had made an enemy, but that seemed unlikely, especially given the weapons and number of people. He'd pissed off a lot of people in his lifetime, scumbags each and every one, but none with that kind of firepower or organization.

And then there was option three — the flash drive.

As weird and unlikely as option three appeared, it made the most sense. If it *had* been a botched kidnapping, they wouldn't have chased Houser from the hotel or drawn so much attention to themselves.

Houser dug into his wet pocket and found the flash drive. He shook the water from it then wiped it off with a napkin he had in his console, hoping the impromptu swim hadn't damaged the flash drive's contents further. He held it between his fingers and narrowed his eyes, wondering what in the hell could possibly be on it.

What had Roger Heller stumbled onto? What enemies had Roger made? And how did they know Houser had the flash drive? Had they already gone to the Heller house and extracted the information from Liz? Had they harmed her family?

Houser felt a stew of sick stirring in his gut.

He had to check on Liz. But first, he had to find Jon and make sure he was safe. Houser glanced down at Ted E. Bear. "I bet you weren't expecting this kinda action, eh, buddy?"

He was about to key the engine back on when he saw a black sedan cruising along the connecting road with its headlights dimmed.

The car turned onto the cul de sac.

"Shit," Houser said, leaving the key in the ignition and reaching over to the AR-15. His left hand wrapped around the mag well, and his right finger slipped in front of the trigger as he raised the rifle.

He watched as the car slowly rolled toward his end of the block. The windows were jet black, so he couldn't see who was inside, but as the car drew closer, Houser grew certain it was the men looking for him.

He was parked far enough back a deep driveway, under a

thicket of shadows from the surrounding trees. That they might not notice him if he stayed perfectly still. He considered ducking, but wanted to keep his eyes on the sedan, in case he had to fire.

The car was three houses away, closing in.

Houser's heart pounded. He could taste metal on his tongue as his nerves worked triple time.

He adjusted his grip on the AR-15, ready to use it, but hoping he wouldn't have to.

The car was now one house away, cruising just faster than a crawl. It rolled silently by him, its black windows looking like black robot eyes scanning for life.

The car passed him and though he couldn't see it past the trees to his left, he imagined it would soon start its turn at the end of the cul de sac and head back up the street on its way toward Houser. This time, the passenger side occupant would have a much better view of Houser.

If shit's gonna happen, it's gonna happen now.

The car, still out of Houser's line of sight, seemed to be taking forever to crawl back up the street.

Had it stopped?

Had the driver noticed something worth investigating at another house?

Did the car simply belong to someone who lived in one of the houses at the end of the street?

Houser waited for the car to appear again, holding his breath the entire time.

The car finally came into view, now just one house away. Houser raised the rifle, bringing it level with the dashboard. He inhaled, exhaled, inhaled again, then held his breath.

Come on, you fuckers. Keep driving.

The car pulled even with the house, and Houser glared into its black windows, wondering if the person on the other side could see him. He watched as the car slowed even more, as he stared into the abyss of those black windows. Houser waited for the red of brake lights. The second he saw them, he would launch into action.

Come on, come on, come on.

The brake lights stayed dim, and the car kept crawling.

Houser exhaled a sigh of relief.

He stared at the car as it went back up the street, then counted the seconds until it turned back onto the arterial road.

Once the car was out of sight, Houser keyed the ignition. As he did, he heard something just above the sound of night. Something out of place.

Something *mechanical.*

Then he saw it in his rearview. A bird. But not a bird.

The thing was shaped like a bird, but was obviously robotic. It had no wings. It just hovered in place, breathing with the slightest of mechanical hums, as though spying on him.

Houser started to reach for his pistol when blue sparks shot from the robo-bird and sent Houser into a painful seizure.

He screamed. Or tried to, but nothing came from his mouth as his entire body was seized by the robotic thing and its electric leash, which burst from its chest and shot its electricity into Houser's skull.

Though the world was little more than a painful, violent blur, Houser was still aware enough to see the robo-bird zip to the right and then back into view, before slowly floating toward him.

Houser stared helplessly as it made its way toward his face, looking even more like a bird, if nature had a workshop where it added black sensors to dead eyes. The electric arc shut off, but the pain, and immobility, remained. Houser watched as the robo-bird hovered inches from his face, as if inspecting him.

He caught movement in the rearview — one of the men in black coming around to his side of the car.

Oh, fuck me.

Movement began returning to his limbs. Not slow, but all at once. He reached up, grabbed the robotic bird, hot in his hands, and threw it back and through where the rear window had shattered, outside toward the man behind him.

Houser's right hand found the gear shift, threw the car into drive, slammed his foot down all the way on the gas, then lurched forward, peeling out onto the street.

Gunshots erupted behind him, a few slapping into the metal on his car. The others missed him entirely.

The car quickly accelerated, roaring forward faster than Houser had ever driven on a residential road. He nearly lost control as he turned onto the main road, his heart hammering in his chest.

What the fuck was that thing?

Who are these people?!

Ahead, Houser saw the car that had been looking for him. It was in the opposite lane headed back toward the street where he'd just been.

He jerked his car into the oncoming lane and aimed straight for his enemy.

The other car swerved at the last minute, then plowed through someone's yard and hit a tree.

Houser considered stopping, getting his rifle, and taking care of business right there, but his body was still buzzing from whatever the bird had done to him, and he couldn't be sure he'd be able to accurately hit his targets.

So he kept going, as fast as he could.

He raced back to the main road and had the car nudging one-twenty as he raced north to find somewhere to call Jon and put as much distance between himself and the men as possible. The road narrowed from four lanes to two, and it twisted and turned as it went up a steep incline. Thick forest buried the night on either side, obscuring him from anyone who might be following.

Houser was so distracted, staring into the rearview, that he didn't see the car without its lights in the middle of the street until it was too late.

He slammed on the brakes and swerved right off the road. His car tumbled down the steep incline and into the forest below. The car kept flipping, turning over and over as the airbags on the sides and steering wheel exploded open and Houser felt as if he were being pummeled by darkness.

The car finally came to a stop.

For a minute, there was nothing but silence and pain, followed by darkness.

Chapter 3 - Jon Conway

Jon flew his Porsche past the Chamber of Commerce and Visitors Bureau, then up and along the snaking coast to Greenwood, counting the myriad ways he hated Warren throughout the short, zippy drive up and into the mansion-peppered Cedar Park.

Fuck. Him.

Jon planned to use his thumbs to give that pile of shit brother of his a brand new set of eye sockets.

He yelled as his Porsche fishtailed across the center lines of the road, having to swerve his car across the dividing line to avoid a deer that may or may not have been standing in the middle of the road. He barely missed the metal guardrail, which was the only thing that might prevent him from going off the road and down a two-hundred-foot or so drop.

The car evened out, and Jon floored the accelerator, wondering how many times he'd imagined crashing through those same barriers, metal crinkling as he flew from one side, hovering in the air for a moment before gravity sent him plunging to the depths of the Pacific and certain death under her surface.

And while Jon could easily see himself dying in a fiery car

crash, he didn't see it happening any time soon. He had been driving these roads since before he was legally allowed. It didn't matter how much he'd had to drink, he wasn't too drunk to drive.

He was, however, just drunk enough to tell Warren exactly what he thought.

Jon pulled the Porsche to the gate of Conway Gardens.

"Good evening, Mr. Conway," Xavier said over the intercom.

"Good evening to you, Xavier," Jon said, trying not to scowl. "I won't be long tonight."

"Take your time, Mr. Conway. And welcome home."

The gate opened, and Jon pulled into the circular drive, killed his engine, and got out of the car. He rang the doorbell, then went to knock, but the door swung open before his knuckles hit the wood. "Good evening, Madge." Jon did everything in his mortal power to keep his words from slurring.

"Well, good evening, Mr. Conway. Seems like you've been at yours for a while." She winked, then smiled and held the door open.

Jon smiled. "I won't be long, I promise. Just wanna talk to my brother for a minute."

"Anything you want to talk about with me first?" She looked nervous.

He shook his head. "Not this time, Madge."

"Jon!" Warren appeared on the other side of the foyer. He folded his tablet, set it on a long table against the wall, then started walking toward Jon.

Asshole.

Warren's tablet was slicker than snail snot — so paper-thin and remarkably pliable, Jon could see it from across the foyer. It looked at least two years ahead of anything Jon had seen.

Fucking showoff.

Jon wondered if Warren had actually had the tablet in his hands, or if he went to get it when he heard the bell.

"What brings you here at, oh, whatever time it might be?" Warren said. "Unless it's the promise of our bottomless wine cellar?" He laughed.

Jon turned to Madge, put his hand gently on her shoulder. "Thank you."

"Of course." Then she left the foyer.

Warren allowed a half minute for Madge's footsteps to fade to nothing, then turned to Jon. "You look, and smell, like you're here to have one of those long chats where you do all of the talking, except for the few moments when you pause and wait for me to say, 'I'm *so* sorry, Jon! Whatever I've done to offend the everyman inside you, please forgive my trespasses.' Not gonna happen." He didn't wait for Jon to respond. "Follow me." Then he disappeared down the hallway, expecting Jon to follow.

Jon did, but it took everything inside him to keep his hands at his side instead of pounding his knuckles into the back of his brother's skull.

When they reached the end of the corridor, Warren gestured toward the bookcase against the wall. It slid to the left with an almost elegant-sounding whoosh to reveal Warren's office.

Impressive. Last time Jon had been inside his brother's office, the sliding bookcase had worked with an old-fashioned remote, and it took nearly five seconds to fully open.

The room's interior was more impressive than the entrance, with exercise equipment, three wide workbenches, and a long, circular desk with two dozen gleaming monitors making a mosaic on the wall behind it, all of them off.

The bookshelf slid closed behind them, giving them privacy. Warren then turned to Jon. "What?"

Jon wondered if he should start the conversation by making Warren eat a knuckle sandwich but opted to impale him on the sharp end of a question instead. He took a step closer to Warren and staring him in the eye. "What happened with Sarah nine years ago? And don't give me any of that 'I don't know' shit. I want to know why I never knew about my baby. And I want to know exactly what you did to make Sarah push me away!"

His eye started to twitch — the cost of keeping his rage at a boil and fists at his side.

Warren laughed. "That? My God, Hamlet, you act like we're in the third act of some great tragedy. *That* was nothing. She already hated you for fucking some model, so it didn't take much to convince her she was better off without you."

Jon inhaled then exhaled, his labored breath falling from his mouth with the speed and rhythm of a rabid dying dog. He wondered if Warren realized how far he was pushing it.

"Tell me what happened. Now."

"Simple," he said. "Sarah and Cassidy." Warren's face twisted in mock confusion. "Cassidy is the trashy one, right? Sorry, I mean trashier." Warren looked at Jon, waiting to see if he was going to strike.

But Jon didn't. Wouldn't. Not yet, anyway.

"Anyway," Warren went on. "It turns out Cassidy was quite the pill popper. And like most pill poppers, she had a run-in with Johnny Law. The old Johnny, not the new one." Warren winked. "As you well know, charges at a police station are like charges on your credit card. If you pay them immediately, they go right away." Warren shrugged his shoulders. "We made a fair trade. Sarah kept her mouth shut about the baby, the junkie got all of her charges dropped, and we sent her to one of those nice dry-out places you Hollywood types love so much. A good, or even great, deal for her, considering. If memory serves, we spent around a grand a day to flush her out. As you can imagine, she was there for quite a while." He shook his head. "And really, Jon. You should've seen the mile of charges." Warren dropped his voice to a whisper. "Some of the charges might surprise you. You sure you want to hear this?"

Jon's fingernails were deep enough into his palm to dig blood, but he wasn't sure whether the slick on his skin was blood or sweat. "My life is not a piece on a board for you to move around." He stepped toward Warren, teeth clenched.

Warren's eyes widened, broadcasting fear for the first time. He retreated a step.

Jon took one more forward. "What are you afraid of, Warren?"

"Calm down." He held his palms out in front of his body. "Just calm down."

Jon spoke, slightly above a whisper. "You have no idea how calm I am. If I wasn't calm, I would have already delivered your head to Madge on my way out the front door, apologizing a final time for a mess I was leaving her to clean."

"Okay, killer, I get it. You're mad." Warren chuckled and took another step back. "Let's talk about this. I'm sorry for being a dick. Of course, you have questions."

Jon smiled. He'd have to do the smoldering volcano bit with Warren again. This shit was working. Maybe next time he'd even bring Houser. He continued to whisper through his rage. "Why would you do something like that, Warren? Why are you so intent on making my life miserable? Why wouldn't you want me to be happy?"

"You got it wrong, little brother." Warren shook his head, then leaned his palms behind him on the top of his desk. "Sometimes, you don't really have a clue what's gonna make you happy. When that happens, it's my job to step in and fiddle the dials. And believe me, some trailer park chippie living over on the far side of Seabreeze isn't gonna cut it. I stepped in because you were born for bigger and better things. And fine, you weren't going to work the family biz, but you'd finally done something with yourself. You made it in Hollywood! And as much as I may make fun of you for it, you know what you've done this last decade is amazing. Sarah was holding you back. And she refused to get an abortion. So, as fate would have it, the stars aligned, and you fucked some model and pissed her off. Tell me that Hollywood pussy isn't so much better than the homegrown variety, brother."

Jon said nothing, glaring at his brother.

"I know you, Jon. You were all ready to come back here to grovel and apologize to Sarah. You would've thrown your whole career away, and for what? For her? For some brat? Please. I fucking saved you from a life of utter boredom and misery."

Jon swallowed. "Who are you to say what I would or wouldn't have done with Sarah? Or where we would have, or could have, taken our lives together? You think I didn't deserve to know I was a father?" Jon clenched his fist tighter. "How would you feel if someone did this to you?"

"To me?" Warren pointed at his chest. "To me?" He shook his head. "No, Jon, that would never happen. I draw the plans of my life with straight lines and use pencil in case I have to erase. You don't. And never have. You refuse to use rulers because you wrongly believe that everything can be eyeballed, and you prefer using pen because you think you're above making mistakes."

Like an asshole, Warren pushed himself from his desk, ambled to the bar, and poured himself a drink, assuming in his arrogance his brother would stand, heaving, while waiting for his next crumb.

It chapped Jon's ass that he did just that.

He replaced the lid on the decanter and lifted the tumbler to his lips. "Sorry, Jon. I'd offer you something, but I think you're best cut off." He took a sip.

"You had no right to interfere with my life. My mistakes are mine to make. I've done amazing things on my own. Is it so hard for you to believe I could have done them all, maybe even more, without your interference?"

Warren laughed. "Oh, kid, you've never done anything on your own. Not once. Business is business, and we Conways are our best assets. Your life must be managed like anything else in the portfolio. You think you got 'discovered' in Hollywood? That you made it on your talents, alone? Please, brother. Dad made calls and got you in the right doors. Hell, I made calls to clean up your many little messes each time you pissed someone off over the years. The Conways are the only thing that stood between you and your self-destruction, so don't come in here all high and mighty like you've been wronged. We made you. We saved you from yourself."

Jon was seconds from unleashing a bottomless fury on his brother.

Warren would be lucky if Jon didn't leave the Gardens with him bleeding out from a shard of shattered decanter. He shook so violently, and from places he'd never shaken before. Warren's next words would determine whether he ended the evening with breath in his lungs. Jon growled, "Dad would never stand for this."

Warren looked surprised. He blinked, then took a step back. "Stand for what?"

"Any of this. What you pulled with Cassidy and Sarah, treating me like a pawn on a chessboard. None of it."

Warren had the nerve to start laughing, first soft and quickly loud. His broken cackle might have been enough to end his life all on its own, but then he caught his breath and spoke. "Jon, who the hell do you think told me to make your little Sarah problem go away?"

Chapter 4 - Cassidy Hughes

Friday night

CASSIDY SAT in the hospital room doing something she never, ever did — she sang Vivian's praises in the back of her head.

Cassidy was eighteen miles past exhausted. When Vivian called, offering to spend the night in the room with Emma so Cassidy could have the evening off, she didn't know what to say.

At first, she said no, arguing with Viv like she always did. But when her mom insisted on staying, saying it was the least she could do after being MIA for the search, Cassidy finally relented and instantly started dreaming about being back in her place, back in her own bed, if only for a night, by herself.

As she waited for her mom to arrive, Cassidy sat at Emma's bedside, wrapped snug in the comfort of knowing her niece was safe. She had seen her safe return, and even if Jon were to take her away, at least she didn't have to feel the wretched horror of not knowing where Emma was.

When Emma was missing, Cassidy was a failure, not just as a temporary mother to Emma, but with everything in her life. Like always. Sarah was gone, and her sister's absence served to reinforce a lifelong law — Sarah was good at everything, Cassidy at nothing.

Sarah had died so suddenly that it was difficult, if not altogether impossible, to properly mourn her passing. Cassidy had gone from the "fun aunt" who refused to grow up to full-time guardian in the ringing silence that sits between one second and the next. Cassidy didn't have so much as a minute to process or reflect. She felt like she'd done the right thing, stepping in to care for Emma. But had she really?

Was it fair to her or Emma? Perhaps Emma was better off with Viv. Crazy as she was, she did raise two girls on her own. Or now that Jon knew the truth, perhaps Emma was better off with her father. That seemed like the option which made the most sense to Cassidy.

But was it the right thing for Emma?

Emma had been asleep in her hospital bed for a while. Yet, as much as Cassidy was looking forward to an empty house and cool sheets, she wasn't quite ready to leave. She slouched in a surprisingly comfortable chair next to Emma's hospital bed, stroking her niece's hair as she quietly snored.

Cassidy's mind began sifting through an impossible number of what-ifs — from her own life, along with the many whos, whats, wheres, and whys that came from living life with Sarah.

Cassidy had never known life without her sister. At one time, they'd been tighter than the threads of a rope. Even when they didn't get along, they still had a bond that went deeper than temporary mood swings, rivalries, or any of the other shit that you go through with your siblings. They were, in some ways, like halves of a whole.

Now, one half of Cassidy's was gone forever.

She'd never felt more alone and was tangled in the thickest self-doubt of her life.

Life was never easy when you were Sarah's sister. Sarah

was always so smart and happy and warm. She was easy to love and even easier to be around. Sarah was a giver — of both her time and love. Whereas Cassidy always felt like a taker. And no matter how brightly Cassidy managed to shine, she was only a shadow beside her sister's brilliance.

Cassidy had spent her life comparing herself to her other, better half. She sometimes let the pain pool deep enough to wallow in, especially when her addict was around and happy to help. Cassidy wished she believed in a God so she could pray for help to get her through this.

That was one other thing that Sarah had over her — faith.

Lack of faith might have been the number one divider between Cassidy and her sister. Cassidy saw believing in God as only slightly less stupid than believing in Santa. The only difference was, you grew out of the Santa lie.

In her weakest moments, Cassidy often wondered if Sarah's unwavering faith was one of the things that made her light shine through Cassidy's shadows.

That last thought sent a sharp and sudden stabbing into the depths of her chest. She wondered how she would get through the night.

Her addict reminded her.

What are you waiting for, Cass? The bottle is full.

FUCK.

She looked at Emma, resting so peacefully, and wondered how on Earth she could possibly take care of the child. Once an addict, always an addict. And addicts couldn't be trusted.

That's right. Why bloody your knuckles beating down a wall with an open door? Jon can take care of her.

You should take care of yourself.

Cassidy's ears started to ring.

FUCK.

The engine of her self-loathing was starting to purr.

Cassidy already knew exactly what she was going to do.

After Viv arrived, she leaned across the hospital bed,

kissed Emma on the forehead, then neatly readjusted her body, softly against the pillows. She thanked her mom for coming and then left the hospital, thinking about everything from Jon to her waiting pills.

Even if Jon came to claim Emma tomorrow, no one could take their nine years together away. Cassidy would have their history forever. She knew her niece up and down and inside out. It would take Jon years to understand a fraction of her, let alone know how much she liked spaghetti tacos.

Cassidy hit the bottom of the hill and turned left.

Maybe Jon wouldn't want to take her. A child isn't exactly an easy accessory for someone wearing Jon's particular brand of lifestyle. She asked herself for the millionth time what Sarah would have wanted, then reminded herself that her sister's preference didn't really matter at all. Not when there was reality to deal with.

What does Emma want or need?

The question filled her with an aching nausea.

Cassidy wanted to pull over, roll down the window, and throw up — evacuate the rising bile inside her.

There are better ways to beat the pain.

Six more minutes.

Cassidy didn't want to think about what Sarah would have wanted and hated that she had to. *Fuck Sarah. I did my part. I've been the good aunt. It's time for me to live my life!* She thought back to all the Fridays she'd come over to spend movie night with Emma and Sarah — pretty much any Friday when she wasn't scheduled at The Shipwreck — then imagined how many of those times the girl had fallen asleep on her chest.

She would scoop Emma into her arms, then carry her to the bedroom, each time wondering how much longer she'd be able to manage before her niece finally grew too heavy. She had carried her twice in the last week and didn't think her arms would make it another year.

Cassidy imagined Jon scooping Emma in his strong arms

like she was nothing. Her imagination lingered longer as she pictured Jon slipping Emma under her sheets, then pulling the covers up to her chin in her brand-new bed — a big, white four-poster, with princess pinks and wintery whites. Hell, there was probably a stable of horses and ponies on the back of his property.

Jon would cover Emma, kiss her on the cheek, then turn to Cassidy and smile.

Ha! You and Jon Conway? That's ripe with hilarity. Even I can't help you there.

Her addict was an asshole.

But tonight belonged to the addict.

Cassidy pulled into the driveway of Viv's house, opened the door, then ran up the stairs and into the bedroom, tapping two pills from bottle to palm just thirty seconds after killing the engine. She decided she didn't feel like driving home.

She looked at the ceiling, dropped the pair of pills into her mouth, then swallowed. It used to be one pill. Now it was two. Soon, she'd need three, four, and more to achieve the same feeling. That's when things could get ugly.

She told herself she'd stop before she needed three pills. If she could manage to do that, she'd be fine, thank you very much.

Cassidy crawled into the bed, closed her eyes, and waited for the pills to work their magic.

Her anxiety melted like snow under sun.

The air in her lungs turned cotton candy-warm beneath the blanket.

Pain turned to pleasure — rolling waves in the wake of nirvana.

See, I told you.

The ringing that had started in the hospital was still in her ears just a few minutes before but was quickly fading to a soft, relaxing hum.

She wanted nothing.

Her escape was nearly complete.

This was exactly what she had been waiting for.

Cassidy swam through ripples of silence.

Her hands curled into fists, slowly but happily clapping beneath her chin as she lay in a closed apostrophe, diagonally across on the bed.

She was deep in her nothing, seconds from drifting deeper, and then quickly into sleep when her ringing phone killed the thundering quiet.

FUCK!

The screen said *Jon Conway*.

Of course.

"Hello?"

"Hey, Cass," he said or slurred. "You home?"

"You're calling me, aren't ya?"

A second of silence, then, "Yeah, but this is your cell, right?" Jon sounded genuinely confused.

Cassidy laughed. "Oh, yeah, well, yeah." Wow. Embarrassing. "Guess I wasn't thinking. Yes, I'm home. I mean, I'm at Viv's house. Not my place. Why? What's up?"

"Just wanted to talk." Jon sounded off. "I'm outside right now. Mind if I come in?"

"Give me a minute," Cassidy said, not sure if she loved or hated the idea. "I'll be right down."

Cassidy tossed the phone on her desktop, then went to the bathroom and stared at herself in the mirror. She had no idea whether she looked amazing or terrible since her brain seemed to be sending her both lies at once.

She ran downstairs, hoping the entire way down that Jon wouldn't be able to tell she was fucked up. Not just because he could one day use it against her in court, but because she genuinely didn't want him to know what a triple-A loser she was.

Cassidy saw she had nothing to worry about the second she opened the door.

Jon wasn't just shitfaced. He was downright fuckered.

"Hey, Cass," he slurred.

"You drove here?"

He shook his head, then used his Jack Nicholson face to loudly, say, "Nope, I raced!"

"Sssshhhh." Cassidy pulled him into the house. She looked behind him and saw his car parked diagonally on the lawn. "You're going to have to lower your volume like eight notches unless you want to wake five of the six neighbors who can still hear."

She took another look at him and shook her head. "You're definitely not driving anywhere else tonight. You can sleep in my room. I'll sleep in my mom's."

Jon stepped through the threshold and into the house, making it three long strides before collapsing on the couch and knocking over a tall water glass, which made more noise rolling across the table than it did landing and spilling onto the ancient carpet below.

Jon looked down, embarrassed. "Sorry."

"It's fine. Let's go."

Cassidy held out her hand, pulled Jon to his feet, then led him up the stairs. When they got to her room, Cassidy started peeling the blankets from her mattress and making Jon a small but cozy bed at the foot. "You get the soft blankets and pillows, and I get the mattress, cool?"

Jon said, "Sure, if that's what's best for you. I'm the drunk guest. But I thought I was sleeping in here and you were going to sleep in Viv's?"

Cassidy's head was swimming. She was ninety-five percent sure this was real and not a dream, but the five percent kept slapping her across the face with a dull thud.

She shrugged. "I figured you wanted to talk otherwise you wouldn't be here. I'm inches from sleep and was fading in and out when you called. I figure this way we can talk until one of us is out. Cool?"

Jon nodded, his eyes half-open, and mouth in a half-smile.

"So," she said, "to what *do* I owe the pleasure of your company then, Popcorn?"

"Wasn't sure where else to go, but I sure as shit didn't want to head back to the Sands of Time."

"Room service too slow?"

He laughed. "No. It's perfect. Just like every other hotel. But I'll have a million more hours in empty hotel rooms. I wasn't in a hurry to spend any more tonight."

"Good news, then," Cassidy said.

"What?"

"You made it. No hotel room, at least not tonight. And you can count this as two days since it's almost tomorrow if it isn't already."

Jon laughed.

Cassidy dropped to her knees and started fluffing the pillows at the top of his makeshift bed. He crashed beside her.

"I went to Warren's."

"Ah," Cassidy nodded. "That explains things a bit or a lot. Were you shitfaced before you got there, or was your liquid adventure after you left?"

"I was diarrhea faced."

Cassidy lightly laughed, stopped fluffing, then dropped her pillow to the pillow. "Everything okay?"

Jon shook his head but didn't make words.

"I'm so sorry," Cassidy said. "Do you want to talk about it at all?"

Jon kept shaking his head.

"Okay," Her voice went suddenly perky. She felt stoned out of her fucking mind. "What do you want to talk about, then?"

Jon pulled her back down to the floor, then said, "Nothing," and swallowed her lips.

Cassidy pulled back, but only for a second so that she

could later swear that she did, then shoved Jon against the floor and met his tongue, dart for dart.

She started grinding her body against him. Jon finished mashing his mouth against hers, then quickly drifted to Cassidy's neck, then her shoulders, then up and along the length of her arms.

Cassidy moaned, letting her mind wander to her sister.

What would she think?

Sarah's dead, she'd be happy for you.

Cassidy ignored the screaming inside her and kissed Jon harder, her hands drifting down toward his belt buckle. But he wasn't wearing a belt, so Cassidy started unfastening the buttons on his fly instead.

His hand slipped up the front of her shirt. His thumb hooked into the front of Cassidy's bra, then followed the natural slope to the middle of her left breast. He cruised around the edge of her nipple as she moaned louder, then squealed.

Cassidy unwound herself from Jon, then climbed onto the mattress. She reached for his hand and pulled him up behind her.

She peeled the tee from her body, then unclasped her bra and tossed it on the floor. Jon had her right nipple, the one he'd missed earlier, warming beneath the heat of his hot mouth as Cassidy's body made rainbows on the bed, rising and falling as Jon crossed her body with his lips, kissing every inch, like the million times he never had before.

Cassidy let him kiss her and enjoying every inch of her body. She was surprised at how long he was able to draw out the foreplay, especially considering the alcohol soaking his blood.

She slid her hand around his hard cock, and he moaned, "Oh, Sarah."

Cassidy cringed, but only for a moment. And then there was a second where she thought *he* might realize what he'd said. But then she felt his animal side take over, and she knew they were seconds from changing things between them forever.

She nibbled on his ear and whispered permission. "It's okay to think of Sarah when you fuck me."

Chapter 5 - Liz Heller

Friday night …

LIZ LAY in the darkness with the low whoosh of Aubrey's fan on the baby monitor the only thing sparing her room from total silence.

While she was glad to have Alex home safe and sound, she couldn't help but worry what tomorrow would bring. She would be calling Chief Brady in the morning to let him know her son had returned home. Brady had insisted on speaking with Alex. But Liz had to wonder if "talking" was just a precursor to an arrest.

In many ways, her son's fate seemed tied to the fate of the boy Alex put into a coma. And given that Manny Ortega — the boy her *husband* had put into a coma — just died, Liz couldn't help but worry.

How many deaths would her family be held responsible for? And how could they ever stay on Hamilton Island? Where could they even go? It wasn't like she was going to get an insurance payout from her husband's suicide that she could use to pay off her mortgage and move far away. And they had maybe four months savings, at most, before she'd need to go back to work — assuming she *could* go back to the school. Even if they would take her back, she wasn't sure she could go back without constantly worrying that someone would target her, or eventually her daughter, once she was in kindergarten.

Liz closed her eyes and prayed God would make everything okay.

She also prayed the private investigator, Brock Houser, would find something on Roger's flash drive that would help her make sense of the senseless. Beneath the still in the room and the whoosh from the baby monitor, Liz slowly drifted to sleep.

LIZ WOKE to the sound of Aubrey giggling, a sound which carried the same creepy feeling it had earlier in the week when she thought she'd heard a voice in her daughter's room.

Aubrey giggled again, but it was a wide awake-sounding giggle, not something that made her laugh in her sleep.

Liz opened her eyes and saw the time — 1:11 a.m. — for one second before the clock blinked on and off, along with the monitor.

The power went off again, and then on.

The clock blinked 12:00 a.m.

Something in the back of Liz's brain was drawn to the time, 1:11, but she was still too thick in her sleep to effectively connect the dots.

"Da-da," Aubrey said over the monitor.

"Shh," a voice whispered.

It was as if someone poured ice water over her entire body.

Liz leaped from her bed, threw her door open, then ran into the hallway. She wrenched Aubrey's doorknob and flung the door open.

And there, standing in front of Aubrey's crib, was Roger.

Except, it wasn't completely Roger. It was as if she were watching a ghosted image on a TV station that wasn't really coming in, like something bleeding from one TV channel to another. She could see through him, to the window beyond, as if he were maybe twenty percent there — just enough to see.

Roger was nude, his body pale, and his hair messy, as if he'd been awake for days. He turned to her, tilting his head sideways, as though surprised to see her there.

"You can see me?" he said, his voice barely there, from behind a wall of what sounded like static.

"Roger?" she whispered back and began to approach him, the hairs on her arm all standing on end.

As she inched closer, Roger's body flickered on and off like a bad TV signal.

On-off. On-off. On-off. Then he was gone.

Liz stared at the empty space where her husband had occupied the impossible. She waved her hand through as if she'd feel something. And she did feel something — a chill, which started at her hand and spread over her entire body.

"Da-da?" Aubrey cried.

Liz could do nothing but stare at the still-empty space and swore she was losing her mind.

Then she remembered Roger's last message. Eleven.

1:11 a.m.?

~

SATURDAY MORNING …

KEVIN BRADY WAS SITTING at the dining room table eating Corn Flakes with his six-year-old son, Aidan, when he saw the black Paladin van idling on the street outside.

What the hell are they doing here?

Paladin usually called when they needed something. If they were showing up at his house, something big must've gone down.

He took a sip of orange juice, then wiped his mouth. "Be right back, buddy. Daddy's got some work stuff to take care of outside."

"Okay." Aidan shoved another spoonful of Corn Flakes into his mouth.

Brady's sneakers sat beside the front door. He slipped them on then went outside.

The black window of the SUV purred as it lowered, revealing the jagged scar of Carl Kaiser, the second in charge at Paladin, a forty-five-year-old, six-foot-five bald man with a wicked scar creeping over his left eyebrow then fleeing his face down to the bottom of his left cheek. The crown jewel in Kaiser's blemish was the bleeding edge in artificial eyes, one of several Conway Industries state-of-the-art prosthetics. It was unnerving because the eye wasn't designed to look, or even work, like normal. It was an augmented eye, glowing bright-blue, and providing the wearer certain visual abilities. It worked a lot like the sight of a rifle, with zoom, infrared, and God knows what else. Kaiser was one of the first civilian subjects to test the eye. The company had already signed a big, fat contract to provide the artificial tech-augmented eyes to injured soldiers.

Something about the eye, in combination with the ugly mug of its former Marine host, gave Brady the absolute creeps. He was not happy to see him at his house.

"Nice house you have here," Kaiser said. The way he looked past Brady and at the red of his front door was a veiled threat, though not particularly subtle.

"What are you doing here? You lose my phone number?" Brady asked.

"No, I was in the neighborhood and wanted to update you on the status of the Heller boy incident."

"Hmm, that's odd. I don't remember this involving Paladin."

Kaiser smiled his snake-like smile and ignored Brady. "Jake Brewster has made a full recovery. His parents would like to apologize to Mrs. Heller and wish for the whole situation to go away."

"Full recovery? He was in a coma yesterday, with all kinds of injuries."

"Miracles of modern medicine, eh?" Kaiser's smile broadened. "That's all she wrote. Case closed. Understand?"

"Well, we've still got two missing kids, so the case is not 'over.'"

"The kids both returned home last night. Safe and sound, everything is all right in the world again."

"How the hell do you know that?" Brady asked, immediately wishing he hadn't asked.

"The question is, how the hell do you *not know* that, *Chief?*"

Kaiser was so fat with condescension, Brady wanted to punch him in the center of his stupid fucking eye. Hell, the eye was probably reading Brady's biometrics and shit right now, telling Kaiser how much he wanted to fucking punch him. Brady forced himself to calm down before he said, or did, something he regretted.

"I'll call the parents, and if everything checks out, the case is closed."

"Everything will check out." Kaiser rolled up the window and drove away.

Brady went back inside the house to find his wife, Molly, standing on the other side of the door in her pajamas, worry haunting her face.

Oh, God. Why couldn't she have just stayed in bed until noon like she usually does?

"What was that all about?"

"Just work stuff." Brady closed the door and locked the bolt.

"What's going on?" Her voice was still calm, but a blush of hysteria brewed just under the surface.

"Nothing you need to worry about, dear," Brady said as if his words could detour the inevitable.

"Why aren't you telling me? Is it something about Aidan?" Molly's voice rose five octaves. Her eyes were wild.

"Why would it be about Aidan?" Brady asked as if logic would unlatch the crazy in her head.

"I dunno." She gazed at her son with the expression of a mother with a terminally ill child. "Then what's wrong?"

Brady kept his voice calm, like always, and put his hands on her shoulders, gently trying to talk her down, "Some kids ran off yesterday, but Mr. Kaiser just told me they were found, safe and sound."

"What do you mean *ran away*? They were missing?"

Oh, God, not this. Not now. Don't bring up Christina. Not now.

"Nobody was *missing*. It was a couple of kids, a boyfriend and girlfriend, just sneaking off for some quick nookie somewhere. That's all."

"Are you sure?" Her eyes were as wide as they were worried, but seemingly open to his offer of good news.

"Yes, I'm sure."

"And everything is okay?"

"Yes, I swear. Want some breakfast? We're having Corn Flakes, but I can make you eggs and turkey bacon if you like."

"I'd like that very much." She hugged him as if he had just given her the news that their son was safe.

And that Christina had been found.

~

SATURDAY MORNING …

LIZ WOKE to the hostile bray of the telephone ringing.

She wasn't sure what time it was, but it felt late.

What about Aubrey?

Liz ignored the phone, then ran into the hallway and down the stairs to find Alex and Aubrey sitting on the couch watching Nick Jr.

The time on the TV read 9:28 a.m.

"You're up." Alex looked rather exhausted. He held the phone and looked at the Caller ID as the call went to voicemail.

"Yeah, I woke up with her last night, and couldn't get back to sleep." Liz didn't dare mention the impossible sighting of his father, which, in the cloud of her headache, seemed like it must've been a dream.

She played the message. "Hello, Mrs. Heller. It's Chief Brady ..."

It was now or never. He was probably calling to find out if she'd found Alex yet, and if so, how soon could she get him to the station? Maybe he'd already heard from Katie's mom.

Liz swallowed, went to the kitchen and dialed.

"Hi, Chief."

"Hello, Mrs. Heller. I heard Alex came home last night."

"Yes, I was going to call you this morning. I figured we could all use the sleep." Had the chief had been up all night looking? Guilt flooded her for not telling him sooner so he could call off the search ... if officers, were in fact, out looking for the kids.

"It's okay, Mrs. Heller. I was actually calling you with some good news."

Tears started to swell in her eyes. Good news would be warm sun in December.

"Jake Brewster came out of his coma. He's got a few bumps, but other than that, he's in great shape. His parents aren't pressing charges. They feel enough has happened and just want to let bygones be bygones."

Liz was speechless.

Just like that, everything is okay?

Did she dare believe her prayers had been not only heard, but answered?

"Mrs. Heller, are you there?"

Her tears answered for her for a half minute or so before she said, "Yes, I'm sorry. I'm just so happy." She sniffed. "So, that's it? Everything's over? We don't need to come in?"

"Not unless you want to press charges for the kids attacking your son. But I've gotta be honest, Mrs. Heller. It might be best to just move on."

"Of course," she said.

Before Alex had gone missing, she never would have dropped the matter. Two boys had jumped her son. They might have killed him had his girlfriend not been there. But as she looked at him sitting on the couch beside Aubrey, together like one almost happy family, she said, "I'll talk to Alex. But I would like to put this behind us, too. Thank you, Chief Brady. Thank you for everything."

"Take care, Mrs. Heller."

She felt something else in his voice … something he'd wanted to say or ask. But she was overly emotional and probably imagining things. It was probably best to just hang up.

So, she did.

As she stood there, overwhelmed by joy, Alex stared from the couch, waiting to hear the news.

"They're not pressing charges. Jake is okay, and his parents said they want to put this whole thing behind them."

She wasn't sure how Alex would respond, maybe he was still holding his anger, maybe he was ready to move on. A sudden creeping sadness swallowed his face.

"I saw on the news this morning about Manny. He died. And Milo's in the hospital now. His stepmom tried to kill herself, they think. She drove into Jordy's."

"I know, honey, I'm so sorry."

Alex collapsed into tears.

She was at his side in a second, pulling him into a hug.

"Why did Dad do this?" Alex wept, his voice shredded by tears. "Why?"

"I don't know," Liz said, crying herself.

Aubrey stared at them, her face puzzled. She looked from her mom to her brother, then back to her mom. Her lip trembled, and she started to cry.

Liz picked her baby up and held her, tears now filling her eyes. Tears of joy to have Alex back. Tears of pain for all that they'd lost. And tears for all they had yet to endure.

As she looked at Alex, safely back home, she thanked God for returning her son.

And maybe soon, she'd have answers as well, once Mr. Houser found out what was on the flash drive. Or, if she wasn't losing her mind and her husband had somehow returned from the beyond, perhaps she could ask him directly, and maybe heal her wounds.

After they had a good, long cry, the phone rang, bouncing the fear of more bad news against the walls.

She dreaded the dull ache of more bad news.

It was the funeral home. They'd *finally* gotten Roger's body from the coroner and were ready to provide a funeral. Just one problem — they accidentally cremated him.

Chapter 6 - Jon Conway

Saturday morning …

JON'S HEAD was a grinding transmission.

Even with practice, that was a helluva lot of alcohol. Man was not made to consume so much.

He felt the sun outside but wasn't ready to open his eyes to the ocean. He turned, pulling the pillow closer to his body, hugging it tighter and trying to piece together the previous evening.

His pillow felt weird. When did he get home?

Warren was the first tangible thought to crystallize in his mind.

Jon had been ready to tear that fucker in two, but Warren managed to beat the holy heaping shit from inside him with a sentence. He left Conway Gardens without another goddamned word.

Jon had left the house so angry, he was actually laughing. And had laughed himself silly, all the way to … Cassidy's.

Jon opened his eyes, then turned over. He was in Cassidy's room, but her bed was empty.

Jon's feet hit the carpet. He crossed the room and grabbed his jeans from the floor. His right foot was dipping into his pants leg when Cassidy entered the room with two cups of steaming coffee.

"Well, good morning. Would you like some coffee? It's probably not good enough for the Duke of Fancy Pants like all the ritzy shit, picked by a free-range Brazilian migrant worker, like you're used to. But I'm sure it will do for now."

Jon took the cup and looked inside, an eyebrow raised in mock suspicion. "This coffee looks lighter than my white ass," he said. "How much milk is in here? Good coffee shouldn't need more than a splash."

"It is just a splash," Cassidy said, smiling.

Jon brought the mug to his lips and sipped, then soured his face as though his throat was suddenly soaked in cat piss.

Cassidy's face flooded with hurt.

Jon started to laugh. "Just kidding. It's perfect. Just a little too hot. Could probably use some more milk," he said with a wink. "I'm going to set it on the nightstand to cool while you remind me what in the hell happened last night."

Jon smiled, set the coffee on the nightstand, then found her gaze and held it. He patted the mattress beside him. Cassidy stepped tentatively toward the edge of the bed, then sat beside him. A few minutes of silence stretched all the way from awkward to uncertain.

Cassidy finally cracked the quiet between them, skipping the part about what they'd done the night before and settling on, "How did you sleep?"

"Like a rock," he said. "I'm shocked I don't have a hang-over, though, considering I swallowed a bar last night."

Cassidy laughed.

"Will you take it personally if I admit to not remembering shit about last night, at least not much after I left my brother's?"

"Actually," Cassidy laughed, "I'm not sure anything would

make me happier." She covered her face with her hand, but Jon could still see the flush of her cheeks bleeding from behind the splay of her fingers.

The awkward air thinned between them, until the warmth on Cassidy's bed was catching up with the warmth through her window. Jon reached to the nightstand, picked up his cup of coffee, blew across the top, then took another small sip. "Perfect, Cass. And thanks."

She set her palm on his knee and started lightly brushing her hand back and forth. She seemed determined but uncertain. "So, what happened at your brother's? Did he finally admit to being the world's biggest dick?"

Jon laughed. "Yeah, he sure did. Though he didn't use those exact words."

"It's cool if you don't want to talk about it."

Jon shook his head, eased himself up on the bed, accidentally pulling his knee from the brush of Cassidy's palm. Her hand dropped to the covers, and Jon took another sip of coffee. "No, it might feel good to hear the truth out loud, get it out of my head and into the air."

He took one more sip then set his mug back on the nightstand. "I was drunk when I got there, drunker than drunk actually. Downright polluted. And madder than I've probably ever been. I felt like I could kill the fucker. Especially after he called me Hamlet."

"He called you Hamlet?" She covered a sputtered chuckle by taking a sip of coffee.

"Yeah," Jon admitted, cracking his own smile. He looked down, then back up at Cassidy. "Warren told me everything. He told me all about *the deal*."

"You mean about the rehab center, Promises Kept?"

Jon nodded. "He didn't say the place by name, but yeah, he told me all about it. And about your charges, and about Sarah. He told me everything."

Cassidy swallowed. It looked like a question hovered on her lips.

Her voice cracked when she started to speak, then she started over. "I'm sorry. We never should've done that. It was a mistake."

Jon tried not to cry and measured his words, knowing he was just one wrong sentence away. "It hurts so much, Cass. More than I thought possible."

Cassidy put her hand on his shoulder. "I know. Sarah regretted it every day. I don't know how many times she said she would've given anything to take it all back. If that makes you feel any better."

Jon shook his head. Of course, it didn't.

He could barely get the words out. "Why didn't she ever tell me? Even after you were clean and sober and the charges long since dropped and forgotten?"

"I actually asked her once. But I'm not sure you're gonna like what she said."

Jon swallowed past the lump in his throat. "Tell me."

"She said too much had changed between you both. I think she would have forgiven the model, though I doubt she ever would've forgotten. Sarah was the sweetest person ever, but stuff like that, she never completely got over. Anyway, after Emma was born, you were making the rounds on the news. A lot."

Jon looked down, embarrassed.

"No, I mean a *lot*. Wow, some of the shit you did." Cassidy laughed, obviously trying to inject some humor to lighten the pain of what she was saying.

"Thanks," he said. "I get it. We've all got our demons."

"Yes," she said. "Yes, we do. Anyway, she thought you were living it up and having the time of your life. She didn't want to be a burden. She didn't want to mess up your life."

"What? Damn it! I would have loved to have known I was a

father. I would have loved to have had a chance to start a family with her! Hell, it's all I thought about when I wasn't getting drunk. But I thought she was happy without me. With her kid from some guy I didn't know. Jesus, this could have all been so different."

"You're right," Cassidy said. "Of course, I would've gone to jail if Sarah hadn't taken the deal. But hell, maybe if I'd done my time, I would've gotten my shit together sooner."

"He used you to drive a wedge between me and Sarah. Between me and my child."

"I'm surprised you didn't kill him."

Jon almost laughed. "I wanted to. For a minute, I thought I might. I don't think I've ever been angrier. He was taunting me, too."

"Why didn't you?" Cassidy said, her voice suddenly teasing. "You didn't want to be another Hollywood bad boy who had to buy his way out of a murder charge?"

Jon laughed, finding odd comfort in the womb of Cassidy's barb. "I don't know if I ever would have had the balls to do it, but when I was seconds from doing … something, the asshole gutted me to nothing."

"What do you mean?"

"Warren said Dad was the one who orchestrated it all, made everything happen." Jon's voice cracked. "He said Dad was behind it all."

Between chewing his lip and imagining Houser making fun of him, Jon managed to keep the tears from falling. And for a second, he actually managed to smile, thinking it was easier to lose it for a scene than hold it together in real life.

"What's the surprise?" Cassidy said. "You didn't know your dad was capable of that? Do you not know your own father?"

Jon admired how Cassidy could stare into the center of his pain and twist the knife anyway. He nodded his head. "Sure, I knew he was capable. But that didn't mean I thought he would be so ruthless and calculating when it came to *me.*"

If Cassidy wanted to say anything, she kept her mouth shut.

Jon looked into her eyes. "Why would *you* do it? Why would you make a deal with my family if you hate us all so much?"

It looked like she was fighting to stave off tears of her own. "I didn't know all the details until I came back from rehab. Warren went straight to Sarah with the deal. God only knows what he said to convince her. She wouldn't ever tell me. I guess she didn't want me to feel any guiltier than I already did, but I'm guessing he bullied her, told her all sorts of shit about you."

"Why do you think that?"

"Just things she said, indirectly, but never fully." Then Cassidy lost her battle against tears. "Sarah wanted so much for me to be off the pills. Hell, she wanted it for me, more than I did — more than she wanted you for Emma Ryan."

"Emma Ryan?"

Cassidy wiped her eye. "Yeah, Emma Ryan. That's what Sarah called the baby until she knew for sure it was a girl. If it had been a boy, he would've been named Ryan."

He shook his head. "I don't know what to say. I wish I'd known."

"Don't say anything." She nuzzled into Jon and lay her head on his chest. "I'll be sorry enough for the both of us."

Jon started stroking her hair, so much like Sarah's. Within two minutes, his lips were again on hers as his hands rubbed her breasts through her shirt.

"No," she moaned, squirming against him.

"Do you want me to stop?"

"No," she whispered, rubbing her body against him.

Cassidy pulled herself from him, tore the boxers from his body, then rubbed her half-naked self against him.

Fourteen minutes later, Jon was ready to start snoring again. Cassidy lay breathing beside him, her inner thighs, now sticky, braided in between his as she grazed her nails along the length of his chest.

He drifted off, thinking of the life that could have been with Sarah, a life all the more painfully evident as he lay entwined with her doppelgänger.

Chapter 7 - Milo Anderson

MILO WAS READING *Imajica* on his tablet, trying to ignore the itching beneath the bandages on his arms, when the nurse came into his room.

"You have a visitor."

Milo looked up, smiling, hoping his dad had returned.

It was Alex, not his father.

Alex had a backpack slung across his shoulder, and his face was bruised like he'd been in a fight. The nurse left the room and closed the door behind her, leaving Milo to face Alex alone.

"Hey," Alex said awkwardly. "I heard about the accident. Sorry to hear about Beatrice."

Milo said nothing, keeping his eyes on his tablet, pretending to read the words on the screen.

"Are you okay?"

Milo said nothing, unable to release the anger and rage he felt for what Alex's dad had done.

Alex stayed rooted between the foot of the bed and the door, as though afraid to come closer uninvited.

"I just want to say I'm sorry about what my dad did. I know no amount of words will ever make up for it. And I know you must hate me. But I don't want to lose you as a friend. You've been my best friend forever, man."

Tears stung Milo's eyes, but he refused to let them flow in front of Alex.

Alex continued, sniffling back his own tears, "I'm sorry he killed Manny. I'm sorry he killed Jessica. I wish it would have been me instead of either of them. If I could go back in time, I would take the bullets. I'd take all of them!"

Milo looked up, finally moved to speak. "Yeah? How about Katie? Would you let Katie take one of those bullets instead of Jessica?"

Alex looked at him, confused.

"What? Why would you even ask that?"

"Real convenient that your dad killed the girl *I* liked, but not *your* girlfriend!"

"What the hell are you saying? That I'm *glad* he killed Jessica? That he killed her for me like he was trying to help me out or something?!"

The accusation fell from Milo's mouth without logic or sense. Yet, there was something that felt right about this path. Felt right in attacking Katie's fate versus Jessica's. Milo suddenly saw the center of his anger. Sure, some of it was directed at Alex for what Mr. Heller had done. But there was something else, something ugly, and surprising, for Milo to see in himself — jealousy.

Jealousy that Alex — once again — got the girl, while Milo's first true shot at love was dead and buried. And before he could stop the rest of the words from coming, they spewed forth like black bile in a stew of vomit.

"It should've been Katie! Then you'd know how this feels!

To lose someone you love!" Milo screamed, anger and tears mixing into an embarrassingly volatile concoction.

Alex's face turned an angry shade of crimson and he stepped forward. "*I* don't know how it feels to lose someone I love? *I* don't know? I lost my *dad*! Yeah, he went nuts or something and shot up the class, but before that, he was my fucking dad! And now he's gone, and I'm burying him this week. So don't fucking tell me I don't know how it feels to lose someone *I* love. I'd say on the scale of deaths, dad is a bit higher up there than a girl you had a crush on!"

Alex unzipped his backpack, reached in and grabbed a thick black spiral, then threw it at Milo.

"I brought this so maybe we could finish it together, but fuck it. You've already decided our friendship is finished."

Alex turned toward the door and stormed from the room, leaving Milo alone and crying, their last unfinished screenplay setting in his lap.

Chapter 8 - Brock Houser

Saturday morning ...

HOUSER WOKE up from the blackness feeling like he'd been hit by a truck.

Light slowly bled through his blurred and sleep-crusted eyes as he tried to turn his heavy head and make sense of his surroundings.

He couldn't move.

Houser's arms were bound by straps.

A machine was beeping behind him.

"He's waking up," a woman's voice said.

What the hell?

"Where am I?" he asked. Or tried to ask. A tube in his throat kept the words in his mouth.

An overwhelming feeling of being trapped seeped through his brain. Houser struggled, trying to get up, craning his neck to see what the hell was happening.

Several hands held his body down.

What's happening to me?

"Please don't move, sir. You've been in an accident and we're operating on you."

Operating?

What happened?

That's when he saw the surgeon sawing his right leg off below the knee.

Houser fell back into the blackness.

Chapter 9 - Warren Conway

The Conway house
  Saturday afternoon …

THE PHONE RANG.

The screen said *Jones,* but that wasn't the man's real name. He answered, barking his name into the phone. "Warren."

"Hello, sir. I just wanted to report the operation was successful."

"Good. And the flash drive? Did we recover it?"

"Yes, sir."

"And? What was on it?"

"We're not sure. It was damaged by the water. I've got my guys trying to recover it now. What should we do about the mother?"

"Do you think she saw what was on it?"

"No. If she did, she wouldn't have given it to Houser. And if she did, well, who's gonna believe her?"

"Very well.   And what about Mr. Houser? What's the situation there?"

"Mr. Houser has been taken care of."

"Good," Warren said. "Stay by your phone. I might have another job for you soon."

Episode 6

Chapter 1 - Sarah Hughes

Hamilton Island, Washington
> *Friday*
> *Sept. 1 (11 days ago: the day of the shooting)*
> *Morning*

SARAH WOKE up with the same hollow feeling that had haunted her every time she dreamed of Jon.

Mourning the unspooled fantasy of a life spent with him and their daughter, Emma. One big happy family, together. *The way it was always supposed to be.*

It had been nearly a decade since she'd seen Jon, and yet, after the dreams, it still felt as though he had only been gone for days. His wide smile, his gentle touch, his voice whispering in her ear. Even the undeniable sexiness of his scent were still so strong in her memory — fixtures in her mind as comforting and familiar as home.

I have to stop watching his damned movies.

It was always worse after the dreams. Months could go by and she'd be fine, going on, content — hell, even happy — with her life. But then something would happen to remind her of him. She'd see him on the news, run into his family, or Emma would make a face just like him, and the next thing she knew, she found herself in front of the TV watching one of his movies and taking trips down memory lane.

But the trips did little more than rip the wounds of his betrayal and her decision fresh open. And 'what-if's' served as salt.

What if she had taken Jon back?

What if she had told Warren to go to hell?

What if she had just let Cassidy do the time she'd rightfully earned?

Had her wrong choice been right? And even it was, did right mean worth it?

No matter how many times Sarah played *what-if*, she always ended up feeling like the loser, filled with resentment, and mourning the best life she never had a chance to live.

Sarah hated feeling bitter or like a loser. She had done just fine on her own, great even, raising Emma as a single mom. Besides, it wasn't as if there were any guarantees of a golden life, even if she had managed to stay with Jon. It wasn't like he hadn't cheated on her fifteen minutes into his first flicker of fame. Who was to say he wouldn't have done it again? Probably on repeat. Sarah had read the tabloids covering his many drunken exploits — indulging in women from co-stars to runway models. And then there were the drunken, violent encounters with the paparazzi. How many cameras had he grabbed? How many photographers had he beaten up? How many lawsuits had he been involved in? Too many to count.

That Jon was barely a shadow of the man she once knew. This fixture in *People* and *Entertainment Weekly* and on *TMZ* was miles apart from the Jon of her dreams.

She had made the best possible choice.

So, why the hell do I always feel so bad?

Sarah squeezed her eyes shut and pulled the covers over her head, gifting herself with a few more minutes of self-pity before crawling from bed to begin her day, determined to return to her regular happy self before the first bell rang.

Her door creaked open. Seconds later, Emma plopped on her bed. "Wake up, Mom," she said in her usual song. "Time to go to school."

Sarah wiped her eyes as Emma ripped the covers from her head, smiling her giant *I'm up way too early, with way too much energy* smile.

"Why are you crying, Mom?"

Sarah was immediately embarrassed like she always was when caught thinking of Jon. She never cared if Emma saw her cry, except when the tears were caused by the girl's father — the father Emma might never know the truth about. "I had a sad dream, that's all."

Emma stared at her mom as if she didn't quite believe her. "About what?"

"Nothing for you to worry about, sweetie. Just a dream, baby. All ready for school?"

Emma stood up and twirled, showing Sarah her blue and pink striped shirt and flared blue jeans with the embroidered bottoms. "Readier than you! Just need to put my shoes on."

"Okay, I'll be out in a few minutes. Can you make me a bagel with butter?"

"Regular or everything?"

"Surprise me," Sarah said.

Emma's right eyebrow arched with the weight of a sudden, great idea. "Okay!" Then she hopped from the bed and ran from the room.

Sarah forced her feet onto the carpet, and then her body into the shower, thanking God it was finally Friday.

SARAH HIT THE BOTTOM STAIR, then rounded the corner into the kitchen to find a dinner plate decorated with a bagel and a sliced orange, and a Snoopy mug brimmed with coffee, all of it arranged and displayed like it was waiting for a tip when finished.

"Do you like your surprise?" Emma surfaced from the other side of the kitchen bar.

Sarah looked down to see that her bagel was two different halves — one regular and one everything. She smiled, mustering as much enthusiasm as she could before the caffeine. "It looks amazing."

Emma pranced to the living room and looked out the window. "We should bring our umbrellas. It looks like rain, today."

A chill ran down Sarah's spine. Not at the thought of rain. It *always* seemed like it *might* rain. This chill had nothing to do with the cold. It was an odd feeling — sudden and unmistakable and without a molecule of sense. Though the feeling might have been impossible to define, if Sarah were forced to give it breath, she would have an immediate answer.

It felt like today was the day she was going to die.

SARAH LEANED over and kissed Emma on the forehead as she dropped her off in front of her classroom. "I love you."

Emma stared over her mother's head at a row of lockers, her face reddening as Hudson Ralston walked by into their classroom, stealing a smiling glance at Emma.

"Who's that?" Sarah asked, as though she didn't know Wendy Ralston's rascally son.

"Nobody." She shifted her feet, obviously wanting to get to class.

Oh, my God, she has a crush! Too cute.

"Okay, then. See you later." Sarah smiled. "But I wanna know everything tonight."

"Stop, Mom." Emma made her eyes big. She turned,

waved goodbye, then disappeared into her classroom. She sat beside Hudson. When she looked up and saw her mother in the doorway, she waved a hand anxiously to shoo her away.

Sarah smiled and turned toward her class, tears welling in her eyes.

My baby is growing up WAY too fast.

I didn't like boys until … oh, wait. Yeah, about the same age.

Sarah went to her classroom, then sat at her desk, waiting for her students to start shuffling in. As she graded quizzes from the day before, her thoughts kept circling back to Emma's rather adorable crush.

When Sarah was Emma's age, she had a thing for Jon, even though she hid it fairly well so as not to upset the obvious crush Cassidy was carrying. If Cassidy had known how she felt, she would've made Sarah's life miserable. It wasn't that her sister was a bully — though some people saw her that way — but she was super-competitive with Sarah for reasons Sarah couldn't understand at the time.

It was only after Cassidy started dating Tommy Decker that Sarah finally began entertaining the thought of liking Jon. When they started dating in middle school, Sarah was terrified Cassidy would get upset. Things were great between them, better than ever, and she didn't want to upset the harmony. But her sister had taken the news surprisingly well. She was happy with her steady stream of guys, or at least it seemed so at the time. Cassidy said she would be bored to tears going out with one guy, especially a "rich prick" like Jon.

"Hey, Ms. Hughes."

A girl's voice cut through the chaos in her head, pulling Sarah from her train of thought. Her gaze moved from Ben Johnson's quiz to Melody Quinn, one of her best students. Early, as usual.

"Hi, Melody," Sarah said." How are you this morning?"

"Great!" Melody beamed, chipper as always. Sarah

suspected that beneath Melody's happy exterior lurked the restless soul of a very sad girl.

Or maybe you're just projecting, Sarah.

Yeah, maybe.

Melody sat in the front row and was quickly followed by a steady stream of incoming students until the first bell brayed against the soft sea of morning chatters. Of course, not all her students were there. But Sarah was lax. As long as everyone was sitting within a minute or two of the bell, she paid no mind to a few tardies. Some kids had to defy authority a bit, bend the rules to thicken their teenage blood — just like Cassidy. As long as it didn't distract them from their best work, Sarah pretended not to notice.

She took attendance as the final few students took their seats. Two kids either absent or especially tardy.

Sarah moved her gaze from the roll sheet to her students. "Today class, we will be writing to a prompt. I want you to choose one of the ten prompts on this sheet." Sarah held a stack of papers in the air as she stood.

"I'd like to see at least five hundred words from everyone. And please," she turned to Frank, "no more than a thousand, okay?"

Frank, along with a handful of other students, laughed. Frank was the class's resident future scribe, who often turned essays into novellas that soared past boring into "impossible to care." He loved the spotlight, reading his lengthy prose, and even his nickname, "tree murderer."

"Okay, Miss Hughes ... *I'll try.*"

"That's all we can ask, Frank." Sarah smiled as she handed a stack of papers to the student sitting in the first desk of each row. "Please, take one and pass the rest back."

Sarah returned to her desk, sneaking a sip of Diet Pepsi as the class fell silent, rolling pens across papers. The morning was ten minutes old when Frank was already turning his paper to the other side.

Sarah's classroom door burst open.

Half the room looked up in unison as Mr. Heller, the teacher next door, ambled into class, clutching his briefcase close to his chest and gazing around the room as though he was stepping from a bus in an unfamiliar city.

Something was off, and that was putting it mildly.

Heller's hair was a mess, his shirt wrinkled and untucked. His eyes were bloodshot as if he'd been up all night working, crying, or as unlikely as it might be, getting plastered. More than anything, he looked confused, like he didn't know which classroom he'd stumbled into.

"Hello, Mr. Heller." Sarah's earlier unease made a return visit.

Heller looked up, as if suddenly realizing his error. An uneasy smile claimed his mouth. He cleared his throat, said, "Oh, I'm sorry," then left, leaving the door ajar behind him.

Well, that was bizarre.

"Want me to close the door, Miss Hughes?" Jeremy Whitburn asked.

"Yes, please."

Sarah wondered if she should go and check on Mr. Heller, or maybe call the office and have someone else check on him. He was likely sick and up all night, maybe with his baby. There was a bug going around, which explained the sudden abundance of absences, both students and teachers.

Mr. Heller was one of the most devoted teachers Sarah knew — he *never* missed a day of school. It definitely fit his character, coming to school even when he should have been in bed with a bucket of soup. Just as she was ready to dismiss Mr. Heller's odd entry into her classroom as nothing more than sickness, the odd feeling sloshed again in her stomach, adding acid to its insistence.

Something wasn't right.

You're going to die, today.

Sarah was rarely superstitious, yet she couldn't shake the

growing certainty that there was meat on the bones of her feeling.

She had to do something, since doing nothing felt altogether wrong.

Sarah stood and walked to the corner. She picked up the phone and called Nancy in the dean's office.

"It's Miss Hughes," Sarah whispered into the phone, low enough so her students would hear nothing, even if they strained. "I think someone should check on Mr. Heller."

"What's wrong?" Nancy asked, her voice concerned.

"I don't …"

The unmistakable — and unforgettable — the thunder of gunshots crashed through the walls.

What the . . .?

"Oh, God, someone is shooting!" Sarah said into the phone, loud enough for every ear in class to hear it. Then, even louder, "I think Mr. Heller has a gun!"

"What?" Nancy asked.

Sarah's students started to scream, scatter, and run toward the door.

More shots, then a sharp pain split through the center of Sarah's chest as her body slammed against the wall.

She looked down, stunned to see the small sea of crimson quickly spreading into ocean across the front of her aqua blue blouse.

Oh, God.

I'm going to die, today.

As Sarah's world blurred at its edges, she thought of Emma sitting in her classroom.

Emma and her little crush.

Oh, God, please keep her safe …

Her eyelids closed.

Everything went black.

Chapter 2 - Brock Houser

Hamilton Island, Washington
  Tuesday
  Sept. 12
  Afternoon

BROCK'S BRAIN was mostly fog as he blinked his eyes and tried to gain his bearings.

He had no idea where he was, but there was a small girl smiling at him.

She looked immediately familiar, though it took Brock a full minute to realize it was the same girl he had found in the woods. Her name escaped him.

Belle? Bella? Ella?

"He's awake!" the girl shouted, running to his bedside.

Where am I?

What happened?

The girl returned moments later, carrying with her the welcome sight of his good friend Jon.

"Jesus, you look like hell." Jon smiled.

Houser was about to jokingly tell Jon to fuck off but

remembered the little girl — *Emma, that's her name!* — standing at Jon's side. "Nice to see you, too. What happened? Where am I?"

His upper body — his ribs, his head, his left shoulder — all ached as if he'd taken a roll in a giant dryer with bags of rocks.

"You're at Conway Medical Center." Jon's mouth twitched. "And you've been in a car accident."

"A car accident? I don't remember …" Houser trailed off, losing his train of thought for a moment as he tried to think back to the last thing he *could* remember. Everything was a confusing haze.

"Yeah," Jon nodded. "A couple out hiking found you in your car. You apparently drove off the road and down a steep incline before crashing into a tree, hard. The couple called for help."

"Jesus, I don't remember any of that." Houser rubbed his temples, frustrated.

"What *do* you remember?"

Houser had to think for a moment, sorting through flashes of memory.

"I remember us talking at the bar. And you drinking enough to knock most men out cold for a week. Fu … freaking irony that *I'm* the one who crashed into a tree." He half-smiled at Jon, then said, "I remember going to see Mrs. … um … Mrs. Heller."

Houser wanted to continue, but that's when things got fuzzy again. He couldn't even be certain if he'd made it to Heller's house or not. "How long have I been here?"

"Three days. It's Tuesday night. You were in bad shape, a fair bit of internal bleeding. And …"

"What?" Houser asked, hating the look on Hollywood's face.

Jon turned to Cassidy, who had just entered the room and

was standing close behind him. "Can you and Emma get me something to eat?"

"Sure thing," she said. "Come on, Emma. Let's go see if we can find something yummy."

Emma pulled Cassidy from the room, leaving Houser alone with Jon.

"What is it, man?" Houser said, searching Jon's face for some sign of good news. There wasn't any.

Jon said, "They couldn't save your leg."

"What?" Houser asked, confused. He tried to sit but his body was stiff, aching, and entirely uncooperative.

Jon helped him, pushing him up against the pillows then peeling the sheet and blanket back from to reveal a bandaged stump, ending at Houser's right knee.

Houser stared down in disbelief.

Oh, Jesus. My leg.

He reached down and touched the bandaged stump.

"I can't feel anything," he said.

Jon's eyes were heavy. "I'm sure that's just temporary, man."

"How . . . how did this happen?"

"Like I said, you were hurt pretty badly. They weren't even sure you were gonna make it."

The door opened, then a young man in a blue shirt and yellow tie entered the room. He was tall and handsome, with the trademark swagger Houser immediately identified as belonging to a surgeon.

"This is Dr. Mark Thompson," Jon said.

"Hello, Mr. Houser." Thompson smiled and extended his hand.

Houser shook it.

"I'm the surgeon who operated on you, and I'm here to answer any questions you have. First off, how are you feeling?"

"Groggy. And I can't remember a thing about what happened."

"That's normal." Thompson looked at his clipboard, then back at Houser. "How about your pain? On a level of one to ten, with ten being the worst pain of your life. How are you feeling?"

"I dunno, a five?"

"Okay." Thompson nodded. "We have a morphine drip going into you every hour. If you need more, don't be shy. Just press the button on the side of your bed, and it will be given to you. If the button's not working, press this one here to call for a nurse." Thompson gestured toward a second button on a console on the bed rail to his left.

"What happened to me, Doc?"

Thompson went over the details, much as Jon had, now sprinkled with a handful of medical terms, many Houser recognized from his years working insurance cases.

"You're kind of lucky you lost your leg here," Thompson said.

"Lucky?" Houser asked. "Funny, I was just thinking the same thing. Oh, wait. No, I wasn't."

Thompson smiled. "What I mean to say is that Conway Medical is the best place you could have wound up because of our limb replacement technology. We'll have you up and running within a month."

"A month?"

"Maybe less, if your rehab goes as well as we expect," Thompson said. "You're in the best hands possible, I assure you."

They talked more specifically about his injury, how he might feel phantom limb sensations, and how his amputation allowed for the best possible fit with a prosthetic limb — another 'lucky break,' no pun intended.

The information was flying too fast for the mud in Houser's mind. It was a bit much for him to swallow all at once.

He nearly died. He lost his leg and was going to get a prosthetic.

Houser had never been one for self-pity. Never one to dwell on his situation for too long, no matter how negative it might be. He lived life always willing to roll with the punches and leap to his feet for a fresh fight and a brand new day.

This was a setback, sure, but he was alive. He'd get through this.

Once Dr. Thompson left the room, Houser sat still, considering what might be coming next down this unexpected turn in his life. A nurse brought him a plastic container with ice water, poured Houser a cup, then sat the foam-insulated cooler on the bedside table.

Houser took a long sip of the best tasting water of his life.

He wanted, oddly enough, to go back to sleep. But at the same time, he wanted to know everything he needed to know. Wanted to know what was next.

"You okay?" Jon asked.

"Yeah," Houser said. "I hope to hell my insurance covers this shit."

"Relax, it's covered," Jon said.

"What? No. I can't have you paying for this. It's gonna be crazy expensive."

"No, not really." Jon shook his head. "One of the only good things I can say about my family is that they take care of the people on the island extremely well."

"What do you mean?"

"Conway Industries not only owns the hospital they also pay for most, if not all, of the residents' health care costs."

"That's crazy. How the hell do they do that?"

"By making a shit ton of money. They have a lot of employees here. And those who don't work for them, work for someone who services their employees, so it's in their interest to keep the island healthy. They've been doing it for decades. Wellness programs, free medical treatment, and free and reduced medicine. I'm surprised you never saw anything on the news. Conway Industries was being used by proponents for and opponents of socialized medicine in the last election."

"For *and* against?"

"Yeah, you know how politics can twist anything to serve any side. Anyway, I talked to Warren, and he offered to cover all of the costs related to your surgery and rehab. I'm not sure if he did it to be nice, to try to smooth things over between him and me after our fight, which I'll tell you about later, or for some positive press, since you're the investigator who found Emma. I'd guess a blend of the last two, but in any event, you're set."

"Set," Houser said, settling into his new reality. He finished his cup of water then set it on the bedside table.

"I'm so sorry," Jon said. "This never would've happened if you hadn't come here to help me out."

"You're right," Houser said, in mock sincerity. "So, I'd better get a co-starring role in your next movie. And not one of those shitty *artistic* movies, either. I want to be in a fucking blockbuster, with points and everything."

"Points? Well, look who's dropping Hollywood lingo like some kind of player."

"Believe it or not, I actually listen when you're drunk and rambling."

The door opened, and Cassidy's face surfaced through the slit, with Emma's a foot and a half or so beneath. "Is it okay to come in?"

"Yeah," Houser nodded.

Cassidy handed Jon a bag of pretzels as Emma approached Houser's bed, her hands behind her back and a huge smile on her face.

"Guess what I've got," Emma said.

"I dunno," he said, playing along. "A giraffe?"

Emma laughed, scrunching her nose and squinting her eyes. "Noooo."

"Um, if it's not a giraffe, I don't know. Can I have a hint?"

"He's a friend of yours," she said, her smile giant.

Houser saw a glimpse of his teddy bear as the girl twisted back and forth, waiting for him to guess.

"Um, is it Billy Wagner?"

"Who's Billy Wagner?"

The confusion on her face pushed Brock into a laugh. The laughter hurt his ribs. He winced and pressed the button on the arm of his bed to get more drugs. "Billy's a friend of mine back home. Though I'm not sure how he'd fit behind you since he's seven-foot-nine."

"Seven-foot-nine? No, he's not!"

"Okay, maybe he's *a bit* shorter than that. But he's still a lot taller than you. So, if it's not Billy, and it's not Jon, I'm all out of friends."

"You only have two friends?" Emma asked, surprised again.

Houser smiled, "Two friends I can count on, anyway. Well, there's one other."

"Yeah? Who is it?" she asked, her smile growing bigger.

"Well, he's short. Like super-short. Even shorter than you."

Emma stuck out her bottom lip at the short crack.

"And, let's see … He's brown and furry, and he eats my cookies all the time."

"Ta-da!" Her hand thrust forward to display Ted E. Bear.

Houser took his bear, still wearing both his furry legs, despite being in a car accident with him. "How did you find him?"

Jon answered, "The cops on the scene collected your stuff. I asked them if I could get the bear to bring you in the hospital. I'd hate for the big man to be without his teddy."

"Hey," Houser warned, "you watch it. Or you're gonna fall to number two, behind Ted on my best friend list."

Jon laughed, and they all made small talk while Houser

couldn't help but notice the shift between Cassidy and Jon. Like animals, they circled one another differently, almost like they'd changed their scent. They seemed much closer than they had the other day. As if they'd …

Oh, Jon, you slept with her? What the hell are you doing?

Houser set the topic on his mind's back burner so he could discuss it with Jon the next time they were alone. And when his head wasn't throbbing. He wasn't sure how much longer he could keep his eyes open.

"Thank you for my bear," he said to Emma. "I appreciate it."

Houser tucked the bear next to the bed rail and then said, "I hope you all don't mind, but I'm tired."

"No problem, buddy," Jon said. "We've gotta get something to eat, anyway. These pretzels only made me hungrier."

He thanked everyone for coming, then waited for their collective goodbyes and promises to return soon.

Before they left, Jon reached into his pocket and said, "One more thing. I grabbed your phone from the hotel room. I couldn't find your laptop, though. Maybe it's in the car, which is at the tow yard."

Jon handed the phone to Houser.

He glanced at the screen — twenty-five messages and a nearly dead battery. "Can you get my charger when you think about it? It's back at the hotel."

"I already thought about it. One step ahead of you." Jon pulled the charger from his pocket. "Though, if I were two steps ahead, I would have charged it. Hold up a second." He found an outlet behind Houser's bed, then plugged in the cell and set it on his bedside table. "There you go. Need anything else before I leave?"

He was trying to think of something clever to say but nodded off mid-thought.

As Houser slept, he dreamed of Liz Heller.

She had given him something before he left her house.

Something important. Something she seemed almost afraid to give him. Something small. Something which he could not lose. Something that …

And though she'd not said it, a voice in his mind filled in the blank … something worth killing for.

Chapter 3 - Liz Heller

Wednesday
12:57 a.m.

LIZ COULDN'T SLEEP.

Tomorrow, she was burying her husband's ashes. Ashes because someone at the funeral home screwed up and cremated her husband, despite her specifically ticking the box marked "burial" on the forms she was forced to fill out, and double-checking her work like everything else she did.

She was livid at the screw-up and had cried for an hour straight after slamming the phone in its cradle.

While Roger had consistently said, in more conversations than she could count, that he didn't care what happened to him after he died, Liz wanted him buried beside her — bodies, not ashes. She couldn't help but feel that even though Roger was dead, some part of him suffered during the cremation process.

The cremation also meant that she never got the closure she was seeking in seeing his body.

She never had the chance to make an identification, since

the medical examiner's office determined that her husband's head was too destroyed to make a positive visual ID. She wasn't sure how they verified that it was her husband who shot up the school and then himself, but positive identification had definitely been made.

It wasn't that Liz doubted her husband was dead. Too many people had seen what happened for her to believe otherwise. The act was probably caught on video, given the number of cameras in the school, even though she'd not heard anything from anyone about a video of the event. She was sure it was just a matter of time before someone would leak it, and her husband's final acts would be streaming from any number of disgusting websites that reveled in showing the latest disturbing video so anonymous cowards could make stupid jokes and condemn him for years to come.

Still, some part of her needed to see and touch him, to find that sense of closure.

Until then, Liz couldn't help but believe that there was a chance he might walk through the door any day, as irrational as the thought so obviously was.

As 1:11 a.m. drew closer on the clock, Liz found herself tuned into the baby monitor, listening carefully.

It had been a few nights since she'd seen Roger ... or thought she had. She found herself waiting up each night to see if he'd return. Each time he didn't, the more likely it seemed that Liz was only imagining things the other night. She wouldn't be the least bit surprised if the combination of stress and exhaustion was finally taking its toll on her sanity.

She wasn't sure which would be more of a relief — losing her mind or having seen Roger's ghost. She was worried not only for herself but her daughter's safety. If Liz lost touch with reality, who would take care of Aubrey? And if Roger was a ghost, was he dangerous?

What the hell? I'm seriously contemplating the existence of ghosts?! I should just go to bed. Right now. The more I stay up, the more likely I am to see things.

1:08 a.m.

She turned up the baby monitor's volume, listening to the whir of Aubrey's fan whispering through the speaker. No sign of Aubrey waking yet.

No other voices.

Liz thought about getting up and going into Aubrey's room, which was what she'd done the night before but thought better of it. Perhaps if Roger's ghost saw her, he couldn't, or wouldn't, show. Liz debated the rules of ghost travel in her head, waiting for the clock to bleed another minute.

1:09 a.m.

Her heart pounded with anticipation. Liz picked up the monitor and set it beside her pillow, watching the row of unlit lights, indicating noise, and the green light glowing at the top to prove it was on.

1:10 a.m.

Something banged in Aubrey's room and the row of lights lit from the bottom blue to the top orange, then back to dead as the room fell silent of every sound except for the fan.

What was that?

Liz forced herself to relax. She often heard noises just like that, at times that weren't around 1:11; sounds of the house settling or something falling in another room. Surely the din was somehow amplified by the monitor in Aubrey's room.

Liz sat in bed, one foot on the floor, waiting to burst from the room.

The clock's digits changed.

1:11 a.m.

Liz heard a faint whisper — something she couldn't quite make out.

Then two words, this time clear and audible over the speaker.

Roger's voice: "Hi, sweetie."

A chill iced her entire body.

I am not imagining this.

I heard it!

Liz leapt from her bed, ran to her door, threw it open, then burst into Aubrey's room. As the door swung open, Liz saw Roger standing in the center of the room, holding his daughter, lightly swaying back and forth humming, "Itsy Bitsy Spider."

Only now he wasn't a ghost. Roger wasn't half there. He was all there — in the flesh, looking exactly like he had the last time Liz had kissed him goodbye.

Her mouth hung open. A loud gasp fell from her and into the room, teetering at the edge of a scream.

Roger shook his head, turning to Liz as he whispered, "Shhh, you'll wake her."

"H-h-how?"

Roger held his daughter close, stroking the wispy hair at the back of her head.

"I wasn't done," he said. "I had to come back."

She stared at Roger, unable to believe what she was seeing.

How can he be here?

How is this possible?

Wasn't done with what?

Liz inched closer, trying to get a closer look at her dead husband, clearly breathing on the other side of the room. He looked perfectly healthy, no sign of injury. Yet, there was something off in his eyes, and looking more wrong with every inch.

His gaze narrowed. His face turned angry as he took a step back. He growled, "Stay away."

"It's me, Roger. It's Liz," she cried, not sure why he was turning her away.

A miracle meant he had somehow survived. Why was he

rejecting her? He seemed almost afraid of her. She inched closer, despite his warning.

Pressing Aubrey against his left shoulder with his left hand, Roger reached behind him with his right, pulling a pistol from nowhere and aiming it at Liz.

"I said, stay the fuck back!" he snapped, backing his body toward the window.

"What are you doing?" Liz cried, confused, suddenly terrified for her baby. "Please, Roger, put Aubrey down. Let's talk."

"You'd like that, wouldn't you? *Talk.* So you can trick me. What then? You gonna turn me over to them? Are you one of them, Liz?"

"One of what?" she cried.

"One of them!" he screamed.

Aubrey woke and started crying.

"Don't you fucking lie!" Roger screamed, the barrel of his gun shaking between her eyes.

Liz was paralyzed with fear. If she said the wrong thing, he would kill her.

God knew what he'd do with Aubrey.

"Please," she cried. "Please, Roger, I love you."

Aubrey screamed, turning to Liz, eyes wide and wanting her mommy.

"Shut up!" Roger screamed not at Liz, but at Aubrey. "Shut the fuck up!"

How can he scream at a baby?!

Roger turned the gun from Liz, then put it to the back of Aubrey's head, his face twisted in rage as he screamed, "Shut the fuck up, you little cunt!"

Liz screamed, reaching out to stop Roger.

But she was too late.

He pulled the trigger.

She screamed as her heart shattered.

〜

LIZ WOKE UP SCREAMING, "NO!" and wailing, "Oh God!"

"Mom, are you okay?" Alex said, shaking her awake. "Mom?"

Liz opened her eyes to the stark daylight soaking her room. Alex was sitting on the bed beside her, holding Aubrey, who was very much alive and drooling.

Liz broke down sobbing, hugging both her children close to her body, thanking God that she'd only been dreaming.

<h1 style="text-align:center">Chapter 4 - Milo Anderson</h1>

Wednesday morning …

MILO AIMED the remote in front of him, trying to give a shit about anything on any one of the nine billion fucking channels on the TV.

His dad was upstairs, probably trying to decide between the red tie with the black stripes, or the black tie with the red stripes. He had to look good for work. He could dress for his son's misery in sweats, but that would have to wait until sometime at night when he got home — assuming Milo was still awake.

Milo wasn't bitter, though his credit in the Bullshit He Had a Right to be Pissed About department was damned high.

Someone at work was riding his dad. His father's stupid phone had rung three times just that morning. Not the phone from AT&T. It was the new one, the one that looked like a glass credit card. The one his dad always had to answer, no matter what.

Milo wasn't pissed his dad had to go into work. Wasn't even pissed that he'd taken every crooked road around an actual conversation since first visiting him in the hospital. Milo was pissed, however, that no matter how many times he stared into the mirror, the kid staring back was living a life that had been shattered by a half-clip's worth of bullets and a Big Bang's worth of downright impossible.

Beatrice was still in the hospital. She would make it, sort of. All of her was working, except for most of her brain. That part didn't seem to be working right at all.

Conway Medical had an amazing psych ward. As good as anything in Seattle, at least according to his dad. Milo wondered what came first, the chicken or the egg. From Mrs. Lindley to Mr. Carney, and all the island oddballs in between, Hamilton had more than its share of folks who not only *seemed* slightly off, but were.

Were there more weirdoes because there were so many doctors, or so many doctors because of the excess of weirdoes?

Milo's mother had been treated for her mental problems at Conway Medical years earlier, and maybe even by the same doctors working on Beatrice. Maybe that was just coincidence, but the part of Milo that wrote stories with Alex didn't like the coincidence a bit. It smelled like the dumpsters at The Fish Tail.

He didn't wonder *if* his father knew more than he was saying, he only wondered *how much* more he knew. Dad was the obvious common denominator between Milo's mom and Beatrice. And he knew his dad well enough to know when he was keeping shit to himself, being evasive, or hiding his eyes to bury truth.

The psych ward. Prison for your brain.

Would his mother have eventually found herself in Conway Medical's psych ward if she hadn't disappeared?

Dad cleared his throat and stepped in front of the TV, obscuring the face of a man talking about how Bible stories could easily be interpreted as descriptions of ancient aliens. It was the first thing that actually grabbed Milo's interest, so of course, his father would pick that moment to step in front of the TV.

"I have to go to work. I'm sorry."

Milo shrugged. "No big deal, Dad. I get it." Milo looked past his dad and toward the TV. "I think he's gonna start talking about Peru next. Do you mind?"

Stephen frowned, faced the TV, then flipped it off. He turned back to Milo. "I really am sorry, Milo. This has nothing to do with you, and everything to do with me and bullshit at work."

"So, you're allowed to swear?" Milo almost smiled.

"When appropriate." Stephen's lips quirked. "I'm asking Dani to come by and stay with you."

"What? Why?" Milo said. "I don't need anything. Or anyone."

"She has to clean anyway. I promise, it's not just because of you. There's plenty for her to do, especially with Bea gone. Dani can stock the fridge, or handle anything we need her to do. So don't be proud. It's not one of your best qualities. I swear, you must get it from your father."

Stephen smiled awkwardly, then squeezed Milo's shoulder and said, "I'll be home when I can, okay, Milo? Let Dani know what you want for dinner. It can be anything. If she can cook it, great. If not, have her find a place that will. I love you." He kissed Milo on the forehead, said, "I'll be home a little after five," then walked toward the front door, pulling the glass card-sized phone from his pocket and checking for messages on the way.

He turned back toward Milo, gave him one last half-smile, then stepped from the house, closing the door behind him.

Milo didn't feel alone, even though he thought he probably should. He wondered how long it would take for the loneliness to creep in but didn't get a chance to find out since his phone buzzed showing Katie's face smiling from her side of the glass.

"Hey." Milo looked into the phone, absentmindedly scratching his left arm through the gauze wrap that covered the stitched lacerations. Both arms were cut, but his left one was particularly itchy.

"Hey. How are you doing?" Katie's face didn't look nearly as pretty once set to motion. Her eyes were red and cheeks thin. And not the beginning of summer thin. Sad thin.

"Okay. Just a few bumps and bruises."

"I'm glad you're okay. And sorry to hear about Bea."

"Yeah," Milo said, not having much to say about Other Mother.

Katie paused for a moment and then said, "You know Alex's dad is being buried at one."

"Good."

"I know, Milo. I get it. I do." She swallowed, then said, "But you might regret it if you don't go."

"I doubt it."

Katie waited a few seconds, then said, "You're smarter than that, Milo. And yeah, you can hate Alex right now. I understand that. But I know you, and you won't hate Alex forever. And when you're not hating him anymore, and some of your hurt has settled down, you're going to wish you went and were there for your best friend."

"Wished I went to a murderer's funeral? Sorry, Katie, not sure I can ever see living to regret that."

Katie shook her head. "Milo, I can't even say that's not fair because it is. What Mr. Heller did was horrible. The most horrible thing that's ever happened, to me or to anyone I know. And we'll probably never understand why he did what he did. But that doesn't change the Mr. Heller you knew before the shooting. It doesn't change him being a totally dorky but pretty awesome history teacher, or the fact that he was Alex's dad, and was always cool to all of us every time we saw him. Obviously, something happened to him. He snapped or something. You should get it more than anyone."

"What the hell does that mean?" Milo asked, pissed. "My mom didn't try to kill people!"

Katie sighed. "I'm not saying she did. But sometimes things happen to people we love and we're left picking up the pieces. Just like Alex is right now. I'm not sure what else to say, Milo. Bean snapped and killed two people. She almost killed you. I think you should come."

Milo said nothing.

"Please?" Her eyes were wide and wet. "Just say that you'll think about it?"

"I'll think about it."

"Promise and mean it?"

Milo thought about it, then nodded. "I promise and mean it. But I want to hang up now."

Katie smiled. "Thanks, Milo. Really. And I'm sorry about all of this. Things will settle down, get back to normal. I'm sure of it."

Milo said, "I'm sure we'll all be friends someday, Katie. But I don't think there's such a thing as 'normal' after this. See ya' when I see ya'." He severed the line, then slowly turned the phone in his hand, waiting.

Milo could have easily traded miseries with Katie for another hour, but he didn't want to be on the other line if Cody called. The call that wouldn't come, even though Milo had been waiting for it since Jordy's booked their unexpected remodel.

From the second Cody informed him that Manny was dead, Milo had developed an itch in his brain that hadn't gone anywhere near fading. How could Cody have known about Manny as fast as he had? And who in the hell were his *sources*?

Milo wasn't sure what bothered him more, the mystery behind Cody's sources, or the way he said, "They got him." Though even that might have been better than, "They have their ways."

Cody had warned Milo to get out of town, and that he'd be in touch later that night. Of course, Milo had boarded Bea's train to Crazy Town, so he never had the opportunity to ignore Cody's advice.

He hadn't heard from Cody since.

Milo was starting to think Cody — or whatever his name really was — was full of shit. Just some asshole messing with him simply because he could. Milo didn't think it was Jesus, couldn't even imagine Manny's brother would do something like that. But it could have been anyone of Jesus' asshole friends. There were certainly plenty. And while Milo couldn't see anyone thinking that sort of prank was even remotely funny, he had been surprised by Jesus' asshole friends before.

It didn't have to be one of Jesus' asshole friends, though. People were mean, and the Internet practically granted superpowers to assholes through the radioactive spider of anonymity. Maybe Milo had run into an especially well-sourced cyber asshole.

Weirder things had happened.

Milo shifted his position on the foldout couch, pulled the blanket up under his chin, then pointed the remote back at the TV so he could hear what the alternative archeologists had to say about the pyramids.

A dull ache persisted in his head, so he went to the kitchen to take one of the pain pills prescribed to him. He wished the doc had given him something for the itching, though, which was now in his other arm.

He scratched the itch as he returned to the TV, enjoying the moments alone until Dani arrived. Even though she was in her early twenties, blonde, and one of the hotter girls he'd known, he wasn't in the mood to be around anyone.

As Milo watched the show, he flashed back to Bea in her trance, watching snow on the TV.

A chill ran through Milo, and he clicked the TV off.

Chapter 5 - Cassidy Hughes

Wednesday morning …

"REALLY?" Cassidy said. "You had *no idea* I had a crush on you? You're not half as smart as you pretend to be in interviews." Cassidy moved her sandals, switching them from her sweaty right hand to the crook of her arm.

She and Jon were walking the beach on a morning stroll, trading honest exchange with the sound and scent of the salted Pacific to their right. Cassidy was carrying her $4.99 sandals. She had no idea how much Jon had spent on the shoes he left sitting at the foot of the stairs winding down to the boardwalk.

He smiled, then shrugged. "Really, I had no idea. I don't ever remember a time when you weren't punching me, by fist or by mouth."

Cassidy laughed. "It was huge until it wasn't. But I was crushing on you way before Sarah. Which is why I guess I was so jealous of you both back in the day. Like many things with Sarah, your relationship was a giant, neon sign glowing over all the stupid relationships I had."

Cassidy didn't think she sounded bitter but hoped Jon didn't think so either.

"I was totally clueless," he said. "Not just about you, but Sarah, too. I had no clue she liked me when I first asked her out."

"Idiot. Anyone could see she was gaga over you. She tried to hide it from me, but you'd have to be blind not to have seen it."

A gallon of sand slipped through their toes before another word was whispered. The words, barely-there above the crash of the foam, were hers.

"Why not me?" Cassidy couldn't look at him. Maybe even hated him right there in this lonely moment of hers. "Why did you ask Sarah out instead of me?"

Sand kept slipping between their toes as Jon pulled Cassidy's fingers into his hand. "Because," he said, "you seemed eternally disinterested. And while I like the unicorns and rainbows in your version of our history, the one I clearly remember had you playing Wicked Witch of the Jerk to me — especially as we grew older. Yeah, you were a ton of fun when we were in fifth grade, but I don't remember too many times from middle school on when you weren't trying to make me feel like shit for having money."

Her cheeks burned against the ocean's cool salty mist.

Cassidy wanted to justify her behavior, say it was all sorta-kinda his fault anyway. But the truth was, right there in the rotten core of that lonely moment, Cassidy couldn't think of a single mean thing Jon had ever done just because he had money, or to somehow prove he was better than her.

The salty air was a sudden rock in her throat. Cassidy swallowed hard, her eyes stinging. Another gallon of sand slipped between their toes. "I'm sorry. I wasn't always nice to you, and you didn't deserve that." Then, because she couldn't help it, Cassidy added, "You've gotta admit, though, you did run with a couple of total assholes."

"Most guys are assholes," Jon said. "It's impossible not to run with a couple."

"I'm really sorry," Cassidy shook her head and kept her eyes toward the sea. "For real, I mean it." Her last five words crashed together as though they were only three.

Jon nodded toward the boardwalk. "That place any good?"

"That place" was a trendy, barely three-year-old Swedish bakery and cafe called Powdered Sugar.

Cassidy turned her gaze from ocean to boardwalk, then smiled at a memory. "Great waffles. Everything else is meh. But if you like waffles, the place is fucking killer."

Jon turned toward the boardwalk.

Cassidy followed. "The Breakfast Nook has killer waffles, too. Probably even better. When they're good, they're explode-in-your-mouth good. Problem is, Pauly started staring off into space — a lot. Half the time he needed a smoking iron to tell him the waffle's done. The other half Pauly spends not paying attention to the same exact batter he's made a million times before." Cassidy made a face, remembering her last order of slightly sour waffles. "When they're good, they're the best on the island. But the last two times were awful. Powdered Sugar kicks ass every time."

They hit the boardwalk. Jon climbed to the other side, then held his hand out for Cassidy. She clambered across, then hopped to the wood landing with her eyes at Jon's naked feet.

Cassidy slipped her sandals on and looked up at him. "Are we okay?"

His eyes sparkled. "I'm okay if you're okay."

Jon's smile would have made her angry a week earlier. Now it made Cassidy tingle, right down to her sloppy center.

The hostess seemed too young, like she should have been in class, rather than sorting menus from behind the counter of Powdered Sugar. "Good morning, Mr. Conway." Then she turned to Cassidy and offered a smile. "Miss." She nodded to them both. "Will you be joining us for breakfast this morning?"

Jon said, "Definitely."

The hostess glanced at Jon's feet, then quickly away. She gestured toward the back of the restaurant and led them to a quiet table in the corner.

"Thanks," Jon said.

The hostess nodded again. "Ryan will be right with you." She practically curtsied, then left.

Cassidy laughed, then in a low voice, said, "You've gotta be fucking kidding me."

Jon shrugged. "I'd say you get used to it because you sort of do, but then again, you never really can."

Cassidy said, "I guess you'd be an asshole if you could."

He grinned. "Yeah, I've known a few of them."

"I bet." She hurried to merge back into the conversation they were having when sand was still slipping between their toes. "How did you know Sarah was *The One?*"

Jon sniffed and blinked twice before rearranging his face. "I don't know. I've never really thought about it."

"Think about it now," Cassidy said. "If Sarah was The One That Got Away, like you said, then you must know when she became The One."

Jon bit his bottom lip and nodded slowly. "That's a damn good question."

"Do you have a moment in mind?"

Jon nodded. "I do."

"So?"

"So, you're gonna have to wait." He turned to Ryan, standing at their table, notepad in hand. He seemed surprised to see Ryan was an attractive woman in her late twenties, rather than the pimply-faced teenage boy he probably expected. "Good morning, Ryan."

"Good morning." She smiled, looking surprised by the greeting.

Cassidy tried her best not to roll her eyes.

"Welcome to Powdered Sugar. I see your menus are closed. Does that mean you already know what you want, or maybe you'd like me to come back, or I could give you a suggestion?"

Jon smiled. "Yes, and no thank you twice."

Ryan smiled back.

Cassidy opened her menu, waiting to see what Jon would order before she decided what she'd get. "One second. You order first, Jon."

Jon said, "Okay, I'll have an order of waffles. And a glass of ice water."

Ryan scribbled on her notepad, then said, "That it? Anything special on the waffles?"

"How would you eat it?" Jon asked. "What do you think makes the perfect waffle?"

Ryan's face flooded with red, as though blushing at the reality of Jon Conway asking for her honest opinion. She said, "Well, I'm really not sure. I like my waffles all sorts of ways. They're all really great, every one on the menu."

Jon said, "You think about it. Whatever waffle you think is the best waffle, that's the one I want. If there's a better way to make it that you guys aren't telling anyone about, then I want it that way."

She laughed. "Okay."

Cassidy said, "I'll have waffles with butter, maple syrup, and some whipped cream, please. And a glass of milk."

Ryan left the table, and Cassidy whispered to Jon, "What if she likes waffles buttered with shit?"

Jon laughed. "I've had worse."

"Ha, I doubt that," Cassidy scoffed. She rolled her silverware from its napkin nest, then sat the napkin on her lap and said, "So, after all the suspense, your story better be good."

"All my stories are good," Jon said. "That's why they pay me to tell them."

Cassidy shook her head. "Nope. They pay writers to tell them. They pay you to be pretty and show people who are too lazy to read what the stories look and sound like."

Jon laughed.

Ryan returned to the table with a glass of water for Jon and milk for Cassidy. "I forgot to ask if you wanted coffee."

"That'd be great," Jon said. "I'll take mine black, please."

"No, thanks," Cassidy said.

Ryan left the table.

Jon took a sip of water, then turned back to Cassidy. "Do you remember the junior trip to D.C.?"

"Of course. The optional trip that cost a million dollars and only fuckers from Cedar Park could afford to go?"

Jon said, "Most of the class came, Cassidy. More than two-thirds. And half of the trip was paid for by the school."

Cassidy sipped her water, ignoring Jon's facts.

"Look, it sucks that you guys couldn't go. But being away from Sarah for that long, well, that's when I knew. Sure, we left the island all the time for family vacations and stuff like that, but I'd never been away from Sarah for so long in a place where she should have been, too. And seriously, I ached." Jon laughed. "I couldn't get her off my mind the entire time we were gone. Remember when we came back, the picnic we had that weekend?"

Cassidy nodded.

"The second I saw Sarah step onto the grass, I wanted to drop to one knee and ask her if she'd marry me. Totally ridiculous. I barely had my driver's license." He shook his head, laughing. "So, I guess that's when I knew."

Cassidy let Jon's story sit for a moment, and then said, "So, what's next?"

"What do you mean?"

"For you, for everything … for Emma." She left out the other part of the question she was also wondering — what was next for them? Had this been a fling? Or was there something real between them worth exploring? Given that she hated him just a week ago, a relationship with Jon Conway seemed unlikely, if not impossible. But she couldn't stop thinking about their encounter.

She didn't think she was alone in feeling *something*.

"Oh," Jon said.

"I know it's not exactly pleasant," Cassidy said, "but this shit needs to be hashed. Are you planning to tell Emma you're her father? Do you want to take her with you back to California? Are you going to stay here on the island?"

Some part of her wished he would stay, and they could live together like one big, weird family. She felt foolish for even allowing the thought to enter her mind.

She felt more foolish when Jon shook his head, exactly like she expected.

"I've no idea what's next. I haven't read this script yet." He managed half an anemic laugh. "I'm not sure what the right thing to do is. Whatever it is, it has to be right for Emma. I have no right to abandon her needs in pursuit of my own." He took a sip of water. "On the other hand, I can't ignore my responsibility, and I'm surprised to say I'm looking forward to carrying it."

Jon sipped at his water, then sucked on an ice cube, as though he were considering every syllable inside his next sentence. Finally, he set his glass on the table, pushed it toward the center and said, "I don't want to tear Emma away from the only family she's ever known. But I also think she has every right to know who her father is." Then, measuring his words, Jon leaned toward Cassidy. "What did Sarah tell Emma? About her father, about me?"

Cassidy shrugged. "Not much. Though I guess you could say she never really lied, either. She told Emma her daddy was the sort of daddy who could probably never be able to stay in one place. And that just because he was never around and that Emma had never met him didn't mean he was a bad person. She said he had important things to do in the world."

Cassidy wiped at her eyes. "Emma asked her mom a million times if she'd ever get to meet her daddy. Sarah never changed her answer, no matter how many times Emma changed the way she asked."

"What was her answer?"

"Yes, probably." Cassidy shrugged. "I guess she figured it was only a matter of time until you came back to the island and she'd work up the courage to tell you."

Cassidy couldn't tell if Jon looked hurt or angry or a little of both.

He said, "I'm going to tell her the truth. She deserves to know."

"No argument from me." Cassidy lifted her milk as if in a *cheers*, then took a sip.

Inside, she was terrified.

Emma was Cassidy's best, and perhaps final, connection to Sarah. That connection was quickly slipping.

Dark was about to get darker, which meant sleeping with Jon was more than a maybe of a mistake.

The enemy hadn't just pitched a tent in her bed, she'd let his sleeping soldier play. She never should have listened to her lust.

Except it wasn't lust. There was a kindness in Jon she could only ignore by lying to herself.

Who was she kidding? Jon would never share a Happily Ever After with her. Not in Hollywood or anywhere else.

Cassidy pushed her chair from the table.

"Where are you going?"

She said, "You know how your food always comes to the table when you go to the restroom?"

Jon laughed. "Yeah, I guess."

"I'm going to make that happen."

Cassidy left the table, went into the restroom, pulled two pills from her pocket, then swallowed.

Chapter 6 - Alex Heller

Wednesday afternoon …

AS PASTOR AVERY delivered his sermon, Alex couldn't help but remember the dozens of people huddled outside the funeral home when they arrived — the victims' families, local and national news reporters, and a few demonstrators waving signs with blood-red ink that read, *Murderer.*

Fortunately, Paladin guards were standing at the gates along with some of the island's police, doing all they could to hold the people back.

But they couldn't keep the people from screaming obscenities at Alex and his family. Twenty-five steps from car to funeral home was twenty-three more than Alex needed to taste the hate bleeding from the eyes of people he'd known nearly all of his life.

Alex had never hated people more than he did at that moment.

Give him a gun and he could see himself following in his father's legacy.

Alex understood their anger. Hell, he even shared their fury toward his father. But they had to recognize that his family was not responsible for the sins of his father. The shooting certainly wasn't the execution of some sinister plot set in motion by the Heller family including, baby Aubrey, the ringleader.

The tragedy hadn't just affected them, it had robbed Alex of a father, his mom of a husband, and his sister of ever knowing her dad.

It was a suck sandwich all around, and no amount of anger would make it any easier to swallow.

As they had entered the funeral home, Alex glanced back and saw the video cameras targeting his family. Struck with an aching sadness for his mother and sister, he mouthed the words, "I'm sorry" to whoever might be watching them on TV, on the off chance his message might be well received, might soften the pain or dull the wrath of a raging mob.

As he sat, listening to Pastor Avery speechify forgiveness for thy neighbor, even as he acts against you, Alex had to stifle a laugh.

Avery should be giving his speech to the people out there, not in here.

He wondered if God really forgave murderers. Hell, Alex wasn't even sure if his dad believed in God.

If hell existed, then his father was surely burning in it.

Alex's mother wiping her tears with a tissue as her gaze was locked on the pastor. Aubrey sat in her lap, sipping from a bottle, oblivious to her dead father sitting in the bottom of a canister, front and center of the room.

Despite his countless questions of faith, Alex closed his eyes and prayed to a God, who may or not have been up in heaven, to forgive his father for any sins he'd committed on Earth.

Please, God. If you're up there, please forgive my dad. He was one of the kindest people in the world. He was always helping anyone who needed a hand, always setting the needs of his family and students ahead of his own.

He's not the monster people think he is.

He's good. I swear.

Alex wondered if the people outside were praying that Roger Heller went straight to hell without passing Go or collecting $200.

He closed his eyes to quell his anger.

The door opened behind them. Katie and her mother, both dressed in black, made their way into the room, bringing the total to five mourners at Roger Heller's service, except the pastor and an old man Alex didn't know.

So, that's what? Five people who still care about Roger Heller.

Not a single friend, neighbor, or co-worker could find the same forgiveness that Pastor Avery swore was inside all men and women.

Katie and her mom approached their row. Alex's mom leaned over and whispered, "Thank you for coming."

Katie's mom turned to Liz, smiled, then sat two seats from Alex.

Katie sat beside him and linked their fingers. He held her warm hand in his lap, fighting his rising tide of tears.

The pastor asked if anyone wished to speak on Roger Heller's behalf.

Alex turned to his mom, who couldn't dam her flood of tears. Seeing her shaking, almost violently, while quietly sobbing, was the cold of a knife slipping into the raw, red meat of his heart.

"Come here, sweetie." Katie reached for Aubrey and took her from Liz.

Aubrey turned to her mom, her confused expression flickering at the edge of tears.

Katie distracted her, offering her the bottle. Aubrey took it, then started sucking on the nipple. Pastor Avery asked again if anyone wanted to come to the front and speak on behalf of the departed.

Alex looked over at Liz, face buried in her palms. He knew she'd been planning to say something and had even talked a little bit about it on the ride over, trying to gather her courage.

She could never speak if she couldn't stop crying.

Alex stood, then went to the front of the chapel. His father's urn, an ornate gold-colored container, sat on a pedestal surrounded by wreaths and flowers. Alex wondered if those were the flowers his mother paid for as part of the service or if someone had sent them.

He met Pastor Avery at the podium. The pastor hugged him, then gave Alex his space, sitting several feet away in the front row of pews.

Alex's leg was shaking. He had no idea what to say. Alex had torn pages from his notebook until well past midnight the night before, scribbling ideas for stuff that he might like to say, just in case. In the end, he hated every drop of ink he'd spilled. It all seemed so trite. Yet, as Alex stared out at the eyes of the pastor, his mother, sister, Katie, her mom, and of course, the old stranger, he would have happily settled for trite.

Alex ignored the upset in his stomach, swallowed the lump in his throat, then opened his mouth to wing it.

"My dad was my hero growing up. I suppose most kids, or most boys, anyway, probably would say the same thing about their own dads. Your father can do no wrong. He's Superman, hero, and mentor, rolled into one. When I was seven, I borrowed a toy from my best friend, Milo. It was this super-expensive robot. I can't imagine why Milo even let me borrow it, except that he always had cool expensive toys that we couldn't afford. I think he felt bad I didn't have anything as cool as that robot. So Milo let me take it home over the weekend. I took that robot everywhere with me on Saturday. I even woke up with him and watched cartoons with him sitting beside me on the couch. I brought him to lunch at McDonald's and napped with him when my mom said I had to take a rest. When I woke up, I took him to my treehouse to play. Sunday morning, I couldn't find the robot anywhere. Turns out, I left him in the treehouse, and he got ruined by the rain. I was so scared to tell anyone what happened. I felt horrible. I wanted to lie to Milo, to swear that the robot had simply stopped working. I wanted to tell him that I had no idea what happened. Anything would be better than my best friend being mad at me."

Alex wiped the tears from his eyes and continued, "The night before I was going to bring the broken robot back to school and lie to Milo, Dad asked me how I would feel if Milo had broken my robot. I told him I'd probably be mad for a little while, anyway. Then Dad asked me how I would feel if Milo lied to me. I said I'd feel sad. Dad asked if I'd be sadder over the lie or a broken toy? Of course," Alex shook his head, "a toy is nothing compared to the truth, even when you're seven. Dad told me I owed my friend the truth, even if it looked uglier than the lie."

Alex looked past the small handful of people breathing in his broadcast and saw Milo standing in the doorway, watching.

Alex quickly turned, not wanting to make eye contact with Milo, or lose his train of thought.

"My dad taught me many things over the years. How to play ball, how to write, even how to fish — though we were both horrible at fishing. But what I remember most, is how he taught me the importance of being a friend, and always treating the people you love with kindness and respect."

Alex swallowed, struggling to avoid his mother's eyes. The wrong look would send him into a matching torrent of tears.

"I don't know why my dad did what he did, and I guess I never will. But the man I know, the same man who taught me to treat the people I love with kindness and respect, would never harm anyone, especially his students." Alex hung his head. "And I'm so, so sorry for what he did to the families."

Alex wanted to say something else to wrap it up. Something profound that would summarize his father in the most beautiful, meaningful way possible.

He drew a blank and allowed fresh tears to fall down his face instead.

"I'm sorry," Alex said again, then stepped down from the podium. He pretended not to see Milo standing in the doorway as he returned to his seat beside his mom.

She wrapped her arms tightly around him and whispered. "That was perfect. Thank you, honey. He would be so proud of you."

They sat in silence as Pastor Avery finished the services. Katie squeezed his hand. Tears welled up in her eyes and she whispered, "I love you."

"I love you, too," he whispered back.

AFTER THE SERVICE, the mourners filed out towards the center doors. Alex's mom held his father's urn while Katie held Aubrey, asleep in her arms.

Milo sat alone in the back row.

Alex felt uneasy. Was he there to shout at them, just like the people outside were waiting to do?

He'd better not cause a scene, or I'll kick his ass.

Milo slowly approached.

Alex felt his jaw clench, prepping for attack. Hell, he almost wanted a reason to punch someone, though not in front of his mother or sister. Or Katie and her mom.

Milo cleared his throat. "Hi, Alex."

"I'll meet you all outside." Alex met Katie's gaze.

She nodded, then ushered his family into the family room.

Alex and Milo were suddenly alone.

At first, Milo could hardly look at him, let alone speak. He finally stuttered, then said, "I just want to say, I'm sorry for being such a dick."

Alex was surprised and dropped his guard immediately. He wasn't sure what to say, but ended up with, "I'm sorry, too … for everything."

"I know," Milo said. "I heard your speech. And you're right. I've been thinking about what happened a lot. What your dad did and what Beatrice did aren't really all that different. Something happened to her. I don't know how much you know or what's been on the news since I didn't see anyone saying what really happened."

"What are you talking about?" Alex asked.

Milo said, "Beatrice didn't lose control of the car. She was *aiming* for the front of Jordy's."

Alex stared at his best friend, who was finally meeting his eyes for the first time since the unimaginable. In those eyes, Alex saw the unmistakable shadow of fear. "Are you sure?"

"Well, I don't know that Beatrice was *trying* to hurt us, but she was all weird looking, sort of all pod people and not really there." Milo shook his head. "And it wasn't the first time she was like that. The day before, I came home, and she was just standing in front of the TV, watching nothing but snow, just staring like she was in a trance or something. When she finally started blinking like a minute later, she went straight to the fridge and started shoving meat into a handbag that cost twice as much as my bike. She left the house like a minute later. Weirdest thing ever."

Alex stared at Milo, feeling slightly dazed. "What the hell? That *is* weird."

Milo nodded, "I know, and I swear man something weird is going on. I think whatever happened with Beatrice might have been similar to whatever happened to your dad. He had that weird *not himself* look when he …"

Alex wasn't sure where Milo was going, or if this was a

natural reaction of trying to make sense of tragedy. Under normal circumstances, Alex would have been happy to debate Milo on the merits of his suggestion. For the moment, though, Alex was just glad Milo was speaking to him.

While Alex hadn't seen weird signs from his father, like cold cuts in a purse or standing in a trance, the two of them had spent practically zero meaningful minutes together in recent weeks, if not months. His dad could have been zoning in front of a snowy TV screen every night for months, while slipping deli cut slices of salami into his wallet. Alex would have been clueless.

Alex wondered if Milo was onto something, or if his friend was thinking Hitchcock like he sometimes did. "What do you think might be happening?"

"I dunno, but some guy named Cody contacted me, swearing I was in danger. Right before Other Mother drove us through the front of Jordy's, actually. He also said Manny was in danger, right before he died."

"Who the hell is Cody?"

"No idea. And I haven't heard from him since the accident. He was on LiveLyfe, claiming to be in the classroom when your dad started shooting. I called bullshit. A minute later, he private messaged me, telling me weird shit was going on. But every time I ask for more, Cody pulls a vanishing act."

"Sounds like he's trolling you, don't you think?"

"Could be. I've thought that a few times, but ..." Milo shrugged. "To be honest, I'm not sure what to think. I do know I'll think better when you and I put the worst of this behind us."

Milo's hand was in Alex's in a second. He pulled his best friend into a hug. "There's nowhere I want it more." Alex managed to hold his tears inside. Barely.

It was one thing to cry while holding your girlfriend, another while hugging your best dude.

As they hugged, Katie peeked inside the chapel. He gave

her a thumbs-up then pulled away from Milo. "Thank you for coming."

"Well, I couldn't let you finish that script on your own. Man, it was shit."

Alex laughed, not taking the feeling's beauty for granted. Maybe for the first time ever.

Chapter 7 - Milo Anderson

Milo headed home from the funeral, finally free from the fat emotional splinter that had been stuck in his psyche. While he'd been resistant to forgiving Alex, he felt infinitely better after having gone to the funeral.

He went straight upstairs, collapsed into bed, and closed his eyes. He was out in seconds. When he woke up, it took Milo a good ten minutes to pull himself from the warm blanket of sleep. He could have slept until morning. It felt later than five, so his dad would be home soon. Though he shouldn't give a half-shit or otherwise, Milo didn't want his dad to think he'd moped the day to nothing.

He went to his bathroom, turned on the faucet, then waited for it to get warm since he hated splashing cold water on his face. He soaked his cheeks in the basin of his palms, rubbing his eyes bright before flipping off the light and heading downstairs.

Milo hit the bottom step then rounded the banister. A slip of blue paper, half wedged beneath the doorframe, caught his attention on his way by.

He bent over, heart beating fast, wondering if it were some

message from Cody. The sheet was face down, blank on the back. On the front, it read:

SURVIVOR'S MEETING — *WEDNESDAY* 6 *p.m.* *at HAMILTON K-12 AUDITORIUM. CONNECT, DISCUSS, HEAL — TOGETHER.*

MILO CRUMPLED THE PAPER. Then he opened his fist, flattened it out, folded it in fourths, and slipped it inside his back pocket instead.

He went into the kitchen. The red light was blinking. He touched the answering machine and heard his father's voice:

"Hey, Milo. I'm really, really sorry man. I'm caught up at work. Just go ahead and order a pizza or whatever you want, assuming Dani's lunch is already gone. Get started without me. Be home soon. Sorry."

The message ended.

Figures.

Milo pulled the flyer from his back pocket and unfolded it.

I should go.

Milo was happy to be mending things with Alex, but he was still angry, fat with feelings he couldn't even find a place for. A group of survivors would give him an intersection of pain and honesty, and the crossroads to see clearly.

But that wasn't why he felt he should go.

He had to go to the meeting because the hush inside him was screaming.

Something weird was happening on the island, and the survivors' group might be a great place to see more of the pieces, maybe even fit a few of them together.

Milo scribbled a note to his dad, then went to the garage, grabbed his bike, and pedaled furiously toward the meeting, racing the dark clouds gathering overhead.

MILO LOCKED his bike on the rack just outside the school auditorium, then zipped up his hoodie, climbed the stairs, and entered the dimly lit auditorium. There was still seating available for around four hundred sixty or so of the five hundred people the room could hold.

A few chairs were scattered randomly across the stage. Most of the attendees were sitting in the first few front rows, though there were others dotted across the theater, as well. Milo took a seat in the second to last row and pulled his hood over his head as if it would make him invisible in the dark room.

He listened as survivors took the stage and considered the difference between the general anonymity of LiveLyfe and the world in front of him, filled with red eyes and sad faces.

Milo wasn't exactly sure what he expected a survivors' group to be like, but he did think he'd see some of the students from the recent shooting. But none of these survivors were telling tales about Mr. Heller, or Hamilton K-12, despite the location.

The last thing Milo thought was that he'd be the youngest person in the room by at least a decade.

The moderator, a rail-thin woman with a fat braid of silvery-white hair, thanked Jenna — the tiny blonde mom with the missing husband — for sharing. She reminded the room that the group was "a place to share and connect with others going through similar struggles," then told her story, like Milo was sure she must have done to open each meeting.

Silver Braid's name was Connie Fawcett. Connie never had children when she was younger and thought she couldn't. She was even more surprised than her husband Tom when the blue line lit the white plastic just three weeks after her forty-second birthday. She about had a heart attack. Tom did, though it took him another four years to have it. He died at fifty-nine, just a few months shy of retirement from Lab E at Conway, where he worked most of the past three decades.

Connie raised her son, Nathan, as if the moon would dim if he wasn't smiling. At least for the first seventeen years, until Nathan vanished into thin air.

Others were vanishing, too. So, Connie went to the police. But they didn't care. No one did.

The police said they were runaways. All of them.

Words from the stage echoed the pamphlet in his hand. Milo slowly turned the narrow, glossy pages, moving his eyes from the type to the stage and back.

Connie lost her son five years ago, then started the survivors group three years into her grief because she recognized the need for a single harbor to dock the island's collective sorrow.

She cleared her throat. "We've extended the meeting to survivors and family members of the Hamilton K-12 Shooting. Everyone deserves a place to connect and bond with others suffering through a similar loss."

Her expression saddened, probably remembering her Nathan, then she invited Suzanne Hawthorne up onto the stage.

As Suzanne curled her hands around the front of the podium, slowly breathing her way into an introduction, a short man with thinning hair slipped into Milo's row and sat six seats away.

Like the place isn't big enough?

Suzanne Hawthorne, the ninth grade algebra teacher at Hamilton, told the room about how she saw Mr. Heller a few days before the shooting and *knew* something was wrong. She blamed herself, since she knew deep inside, right at that moment, that something was off. Really off. Instead of doing something, she simply ignored it. The format was AA, not Q&A, so it took Mrs. Hawthorne a while to say why. When she did, Milo felt a frost inside his veins.

She went into Heller's room to ask if he happened to know if the Williams brothers were sick since both boys seemed to have been sporadically absent throughout the week. Heller's head never budged. He just stared at the TV, the screen full of snow, his eyes wide and jaw swinging low, like he was watching live footage of the end of the world.

She called three times. "Mr. Heller. Mr. Heller. *Roger!*"

But it was as if he was in a trance.

In a trance!

Mrs. Hawthorne shook it off and figured he must be exhausted. Since the theory matched the red in his eyes, she left. He probably just wanted to be alone, anyway. Ignoring the stir in her gut, she went back to algebra and didn't think about Mr. Heller's red eyes or swinging jaw again, at least until she heard the first gunshot and found Jimmy Marlowe running through the hallway a half-minute later yelling, "Mr. Heller has a gun!"

Milo kept hearing her words, "he was in a trance." Each time, he pictured Beatrice, dazed and staring ahead without blinking, then shoving cold cuts into her handbag a minute later.

The guy six seats from Milo seemed to be studying his reaction to every story. Milo kept his face straight, his expression fixed. He barely moved except for the occasional itch he had to scratch beneath his bandages.

The man was in his late thirties to early forties, slight and with glasses. Hardly threatening, and certainly not scary. Still, Milo couldn't ignore the scrutiny, or the creep in his glare.

Mrs. Hawthorne's confession about Mr. Heller gave Mrs. Dalquist the confidence to say she saw almost the same exact thing. Except her words rang with a hollow thud. Milo could tell from the room's expression — she was a regular leech and no one believed a word that she said.

Milo didn't think that was true about Sam, a man who had lost his brother three years before. He saw something similar, though different. His brother was playing the same playlist on his iPod repeatedly, over and over and over. His brother was usually a monkey, always swinging from tree to tree, repetition his foe. That was why he'd been married four times, after all.

He didn't listen to playlists, especially when they were two songs long.

The thing that bothered Sam most, he confessed with a shake of his head, was that he couldn't for the life of him remember what either of the two songs were.

Milo wanted to stand up, walk to the front, and tell the room about Beatrice, but he was having a hard time working up the courage. He was about to raise his hand when the guy six seats down whispered, "Don't say a word."

Milo bristled.

The man stood, crossed four chairs, then sat two seats from Milo.

"It's Cody," he whispered. "Don't say a word right now, not to these people. We'll talk when this is over."

And here he is, without his tinfoil hat.

The rest of the sharing took a million years, with no new revelations and the stories mostly sad. Cody slipped from the auditorium as the last speaker stepped to the stage.

Milo went outside and saw Cody standing by the bike rack.

He looked up at the sky, hating the island for its dark clouds, chilly breeze, and the distant thunder forever rumbling the distance.

"So, you always look for grieving kids to talk to in chat rooms?" Milo said. "You some kinda pervert?"

Cody ignored him, looking into the shadows as though hunting the dark, and rubbing his arms like they were covered in ants.

"I'm sorry about that," he said. "But I had to talk to you,

or someone like you, and I couldn't exactly use my real name."

"Why not?" Milo said.

"Because I like breathing." He leaned into Milo. "Look, I meant what I said the other day, before your accident with Other Mother."

Milo's eyes widened at the words other and mother, used together and with an implied capital. "How did you know I called her that?"

"I know a lot," Cody said. "A shit ton more than I want to." He swallowed. "More than you want to."

"I want to go home. So unless you're about to enlighten me with something concrete, I'd rather you leave me alone."

"Understood." Then he said, "My name's not Cody. It's Don Bellows. Like a lot of the folks in there," he jerked his thumb toward the auditorium, "my loved ones disappeared under mysterious circumstances."

"What happened?" Milo said.

"Most of the disappearances are a person at a time. My entire family disappeared. Gone, overnight. My wife, Lucinda, and our twins, Mark and Ryan."

"Fraternal or identical?" Milo asked as if it mattered.

Don looked up from his sleeve. "Identical." He cleared his throat. "Anyway, they all went missing three years ago, and nothing made sense. No bodies, no ferry rides — they have a camera twenty-four hours, you know — nothing. So I started investigating all the weird shit on the island. And there's plenty." He shook his head. "I still can't believe all of the layers in this onion."

Milo was willing to buy into conspiracy, but his patience was paper-thin, and the guy was giving off some weird stalker vibes. Milo glanced around, suddenly aware nobody else had left the auditorium yet. If Don wanted, he could easily pull a knife or gun on Milo.

Don was too busy scratching at his arm beneath his jacket, however, to make Milo too concerned.

He looked at Don's arm. "You okay?"

Don stopped scratching, then looked at Milo and said, "Sorry, one of the symptoms."

"Symptoms of what?"

"Well," he shook his head. "It's something like Morgellons, I imagine, though I don't know that for sure. And if it is, it's only like Morgellons in *some* ways. It's also altogether different." Don went back to scratching, like he couldn't help it. "These … things in my skin. It's the stuff they put in us."

Something about the way Don was speaking reminded Milo of Beatrice staring at the snowy TV, and all the many weird ripened stories he'd just heard in the Hamilton Auditorium.

Milo wasn't strong enough to stand up to the power of suggestion, so he started dragging his nails across his own arms, too. "What are you talking about? What's Morgellons?" he said.

"You've got it, too? The itching?"

Milo shook his head. "It's nothing. Probably just itching from the healing wounds."

Don lifted his shirt and jacket, displaying a long line of red welts dotting the length of his arm, armies of scars where his torn skin had healed over.

Milo's stomach flopped like a fish.

Above them, clouds parted and returned their wet to the ocean floor.

"*They're* doing this to us," Don said. "Everything is connected." He looked up as the first of the exiting survivors opened the door to the auditorium and began to flow out.

Milo was done. "You're not saying anything. And I'm not willing to stick around to get drenched and jerked around."

"Research for yourself." Don handed Milo a flash drive. "There's some docs on here to get you started. And some advice on how to do research undetected. Well, relatively undetected. And whatever you do, don't tell anyone what you find."

"Do you think I'm still in danger?" Milo asked, not really sure he was buying what Don was selling just yet, but too curious not to ask.

"Not at the moment. If they wanted you gone, you wouldn't have come out of the hospital."

People began to walk past them on the way to the parking lot.

"I should go, I'll be in touch." Don walked toward the parking lot.

Milo unlocked his bike and watched the people filing out, but not making eye contact with anyone who might recognize him. As Milo began to ride home, he noticed Don had kept walking, through the parking lot, and into the woods beyond.

Where the hell is he going?

Milo wasn't about to follow. Instead, he biked home — scared, alone, and itching like crazy as the sky began to open up.

Chapter 8 - Jon Conway

Wednesday night …

THE FOUR OF them sat around the small, circular table in Cassidy's kitchen, while Cassidy tried not to look embarrassed about the size or shape of her miniature house. Jon could see her stealing glances at the peeling paint, probably thinking that her square footage was probably less than Jon's smallest guest bathroom in his L.A. villa.

Jon's smallest guest bathroom was about the size of a small closet, and he couldn't have given a giant squishy shit about the size of Cassidy's house. He was happy to be sharing a meal with the Hughes family, even if it was forever missing a vital member.

Truth was, the Hughes and Conway families were now forever linked.

Jon and Emma sat across from Cassidy and Viv. Dinner started with nothing but scowls from Vivian, but once Jon managed to keep her laughing for fifteen straight minutes, she lost the flare in her nostrils and settled somewhere between her granddaughter's glee and her daughter's cautious affection.

"I don't remember the last time you made anything this delicious for me," Vivian said, smiling at Cassidy.

"That's not fair," Cassidy said. "I make you dinner all the time."

"I never said you didn't make me dinner. I said it was a long time since you made something this good. Most of the time it's microwave or nothing, and you know it."

"That's not true." Cassidy's face started to flush.

"Yes, it is!" Vivian howled. "Even on Mother's Day last year, when it was your turn to take me out somewhere, you said, 'Sorry Ma, I'm broke. It's Lean Cuisine or nothing.' Your sister made pork chops."

Cassidy stared at her placemat. Jon couldn't tell if she was smiling or scowling, but he figured it was an even blend of each.

"I remember that," Emma said. "They were good." She laughed and said, "The other white meat." Then she laughed to herself again, as though recalling something funny.

Jon exchanged a glance with Cassidy and felt a sinking in his stomach. He was minutes from telling Emma that he was her father. A million butterflies fluttered in anticipation.

Presenting the award for Best Supporting Actor at the Oscars.

His first red carpet.

His first acceptance of Best Actor — Golden Globes, not Oscar.

Telling Sarah he'd cheated on her while in California.

None of it compared to the sort of anxiety stirring in his gut as he glanced at his daughter.

Daughter! Me, of all people! I still can't believe it.

"Who wants ice cream?" Cassidy asked everyone, though her eyes were aimed at Emma.

"Me!" Emma yelled.

Vivian said, "As long as it's not that Moose Tracks crap. Stuff is way too sweet."

Emma said, "Mom said you shouldn't say crap."

"You're right." Vivian smiled. "Sorry, dear, I meant to say *shit.*"

Emma burst out laughing, and the others followed suit until everyone was cracking up.

Cassidy returned with Breyers chocolate chip — Jon's choice. He preferred ice cream with ingredients you could count on one hand.

They all shoved ice cream into their smiles and let it melt in their mouths as they laughed and shared their favorite and funniest Sarah stories.

"Mom," Cassidy said, "would you mind helping me with the dishes? Jon wants to show Emma a magic trick." Just as they'd planned, nearly word-for-word.

"A magic trick?" She looked up at Cassidy. "What makes you think I don't want to see the trick?"

Cassidy narrowed her eyes in her best *don't challenge me, Mom* look.

"Sure thing." Vivian cackled as she turned to Emma. "Watch his hands. The tricks are always in the hands."

"Thanks, ladies." Jon stood and held his hand out to Emma.

She took it, smiling as he led her from the kitchen and into the tiny living room.

He knew some basic magic, taught to him by Jimmy Stardust, an FX guy Jon had worked with on the *Eternal* films. He'd already prepped a simpler trick since his aim wasn't to impress Emma so much as let her figure the trick out for herself.

He pulled a deck of cards from his pocket, presorted with red and black. Jon had gently bent all the red cards so their faces were slightly concave, and all the blacks so they were slightly convex. He shuffled the deck as Emma kept her eyes on his hands.

He set the pack face down on the table, then looked at Emma and said, "Is the top card going to be red or black?"

She stared at the deck for several seconds. "Red."

Jon smiled. "Wrong." He turned over the nine of clubs. "How about now?"

"Red."

"Wrong." Jon showed her the two of spades.

She smiled.

"How about now?"

"Red."

"Ooh, I like that," he said, "sticking to your guns and playing the odds. That worked. This one is red for sure." He smiled, then flipped over the seven of hearts.

Jon wasn't sure how long the trick would hold Emma's attention, but he was hoping it would be at least long enough for her to feel the victory of figuring it out before he shifted her world with a sentence or two.

They were halfway through the cards when Emma pointed at the deck and said, "They're all bendy. That's how you know, right? Hearts and Diamonds one way, spades and clubs another?"

Jon nodded, smiling. "You're good at figuring stuff out. That's a great quality to have."

He leaned in closer, making sure Emma was looking into his eyes. "If you can do that, you can figure out most of life."

"My mom used to say stuff like that."

"Your mom was a smart woman," Jon said. "I'm not always so good at figuring stuff out, myself. That's why I loved being with her so much." He pulled Emma's right hand into his. She seemed slightly uncomfortable, and like she was going to pull it away, but it was only a moment before she let her five fingers settle into the nest of his palm.

"Do you know I loved your mother?" Jon said.

Emma shrugged, then shook her head. "Not really. Though I figured you *might* have, and you had to know her pretty well."

"Why did you figure that?"

She shrugged again. "I guess because you're here. You would have to care a lot since you came to the island. You're a famous actor and everything, right? Plus, I know she used to cry sometimes after she watched your movies, even though she didn't know I knew."

"You're better at figuring stuff out than I am." Jon winked, then squeezed her hand tighter. "I just figured something out myself a couple of days ago. And it's something I have to tell you."

Emma's eyes looked up to Jon, waiting.

Jon sighed into a long, lingering, and nearly endless silence. Finally, he ripped off the Band-Aid.

"I'm your father."

Emma said nothing, only nodded.

After a minute of silence, Jon said, "Do you understand?"

Of course, she understands. Asshole.

Emma nodded. "How come you didn't know before?"

The last thing Jon wanted to do was condemn Sarah for never telling her daughter, but he was staring at a truth he'd never shaded before. "I just didn't. I left the island before I found out and didn't know until I came back."

"How come you know now?"

Jon leaned against the cushion and sighed. "Well, I guess I first knew when I saw the way you wrinkled your nose while you were stashing your cookies. But that was just a guess. I knew for sure once I started asking questions."

Emma's face changed. She looked like she might cry. "Did Cassidy know?"

Jon nodded.

"How about Nana?"

Jon nodded again, then said, "But they weren't doing

anything wrong by not telling you. It wasn't like I was here and they were keeping it from you. I didn't know, and I'm sure your mom would have told you the truth when the time was right."

Awkward silence buttered the air. Dishes clattering in the kitchen were practically thunder.

"I'm sorry," Jon said. "Not that I'm your dad, I'm *thrilled* about that." The thin smile felt foreign on his face. "But I'm sorry you didn't know, and that you had to find out this way, so soon after everything that's happened."

He squeezed her hand.

Emma squeezed back. "So, what happens now? Am I still going to stay with Aunt Cassidy?"

Jon shrugged. "I'm not sure. This is all new to me. I think we should do what's best, and what's best for all of us is what's best for you."

Goddammit, Jon. Don't do it. Give the girl time to process.

He ignored the voice inside him. "Do you know what you might want?"

"Could I live with you if I wanted?"

Jon nodded. "Yes."

"Would I have to leave the island?" A tear painted her right cheek.

"Yes."

"Would Cassidy stay here?"

"Probably."

"How about Nana."

"Yes, I'm sure of it."

"Why can't you and Cassidy and me live together? You already like each other, don't you? Can't you just do that?"

Jon bit his lip to keep from losing it completely. "That's not up to me, Emma. It's complicated. That might not be what's best for me *or* for your Aunt Cassidy. And if it isn't best for us, it won't be best for you."

Emma's face held its expression for several seconds before

it began twitching, hanging at the lip of collapse for a full minute before finally spilling into a sea of sudden tears.

Emma sobbed into her father's chest, trying to push words from her throat that Jon couldn't understand. When she was finally breathing regularly enough to get her words out in a clear and unbroken string, Jon was chilled by their clarity.

"Why did my mother have to die?" Emma sobbed.

Jon pulled her tighter and whispered, "I don't know, sweetie, I don't know."

He stroked her hair, staring at a small living room table and the well-lit photo of Sarah and Emma together, probably the Easter before, with Emma wearing bunny ears and hugging a big basket of brightly-colored eggs.

Jon closed his eyes, aching at the everything he would never have.

That they would never have.

Epilogue

Hamilton Island, Washington
   Friday
   Sept. 1 (the day of the shooting)
   Morning

THE UNMISTAKABLE — and unforgettable — the thunder of gunshots crashed through the walls.

What the . . . ?

"Oh, God, someone has a gun!" Sarah said into the phone, loud enough for every ear in class to hear it. Then, even louder, "I think Mr. Heller has a gun!"

"What?" Nancy said.

Sarah's students started to scream, scatter, and run toward the door.

More shots, then a sharp pain split through the center of Sarah's chest as her body slammed against the wall.

She looked down, stunned to see the small sea of crimson quickly spreading to an ocean across the front of her aqua blue blouse.

Oh, God.

I'm going to die today.

As Sarah's world blurred at its edges, she thought of Emma sitting in her classroom.

Emma and her little crush.

Oh, God, please keep her safe …

Sarah's lids fell closed.

Everything went black.

She woke in darkness, in an unfamiliar bed, in an unfamiliar room.

The room was cold and hummed with the sound of circulated air.

A soft-blue light above and behind her bed killed just enough of the surrounding black for Sarah to see the raw outline of a few blurry shapes — the bed, a chair, and small table, and curtains. Two doors, one that presumably led to a bathroom. The other likely led to a hallway.

How did I get in a hotel room?

Where's Emma?

Her head was foggy as if she'd been sleeping forever. She felt like she'd been drugged or something.

Oh, God, did someone drug and rape me?

Sarah sat up in the bed, searching the room for a sign of whoever the hell had brought her there. But she was alone. She didn't feel like she'd had sex, willing or otherwise. Nor did she feel any pain, other than a dull ache in her bones.

It was then that Sarah remembered Roger Heller and the bullet that pierced her chest.

She looked down. The shirt she was wearing wasn't hers. It was silky and long like a gown, all one piece, ending at her knees. Sarah pulled the neck of the gown down enough to see that the flesh of her chest was perfectly pale and smooth, no wounds. Not even a scar.

Am I in a hospital?

Sarah stood, wobbled, and braced herself against the bed to find her balance. She wanted to call out but didn't. Almost *couldn't.* Something in the back of her mind warned her to stay silent.

She made her way toward the door, which seemed to lead out of the room. Inches from the door, Sarah saw there was no doorknob.

What the hell?

She looked along the side of the door for a button or something, *anything,* that could open the door, but found nothing.

She turned back and went to the other door.

It slid open in a whisper upon her approach, the thin alloy frame of the door sliding into a recess in the wall. A soft blue light illuminated a bathroom on the other side.

Sarah stepped into the bathroom and looked in the mirror, then closer at her gown. It reminded her of a hospital gown, except it didn't tie in back. She hiked it up, sat on the toilet, and peed. When she stood, the toilet flushed automatically.

Nice bathroom.

Where the hell am I?

It had been a while since Sarah had been to Conway Medical Center, but she wouldn't doubt if the hospital had this kind of cutting edge fancy stuff. Weird, though, that the doors didn't have knobs. Perhaps it was a way to keep patients from wandering off at nighttime.

Sarah wondered if it was, in fact, nighttime. The room was dark, but the lights were off, and the curtains drawn. Any room would be dark under such circumstances. Sarah walked from the bathroom toward the curtain, figuring she'd look out to determine the time of day. Or perhaps she could figure out where she was by looking for landmarks.

She parted the curtains and gasped at the impossibility.

Sarah was staring at nothing but ink-black sky, a billion stars, and the big, blue marble of the planet Earth below.

A Note from the Author

Thanks for reading *WhiteSpace Season One.*

If you liked this book, please leave a review on your favorite bookselling site so others can enjoy it too. Just a couple of sentences would be great.

Thanks!

Sean & Dave

About the Authors

Sean Platt is an entrepreneur and founder of Sterling & Stone, where he makes stories with his partners, Johnny B. Truant, and David W. Wright, and a family of storytellers.

Sean is the bestselling author of over 10 million words' worth of books, including the Yesterday's Gone and Invasion series. Sean is also co-author of the indie publishing cornerstone, Write. Publish. Repeat. and co-host of the Story Studio Podcast.

Originally from Long Beach, California, Sean now lives in Austin, Texas with his wife and two children. He has more than his share of nose.

~

David W. Wright is the co-author of edge-of-your seat thrillers including the best-selling post-apocalyptic series *Yesterday's Gone*, the paranoid sci-fi *WhiteSpace* series, and the vigilante series, *No Justice*, as well as standalone thrillers *12*, and *Crash* which was recently optioned for a movie.

David is an accomplished, though intermittent, cartoonist who lives in [LOCATION REDACTED] with his wife and son [NAMES REDACTED.]

He is not at all paranoid.

He is "the grumpy one" on the *The Story Studio Podcast* with fellow Sterling and Stone founders, Sean Platt and Johnny B. Truant.

You can email him at <u>david@sterlingandstone.net</u>

We swear, he almost never bites. Unless you feed him after midnight.

Karma Police Series

Jumper

Karma Police

The Collectors

Deviant

The Fall

Homecoming

Yesterday's Gone

October's Gone

Yesterday's Gone Season One

Yesterday's Gone Season Two

Yesterday's Gone Season Three

Yesterday's Gone Season Four

Yesterday's Gone Season Five

Yesterday's Gone Season Six

Tomorrow's Gone

Tomorrow's Gone Season One

Tomorrow's Gone Season Two

Tomorrow's Gone Season Three

Available Darkness

Darkness Itself

Available Darkness Book One

Available Darkness Book Two

Available Darkness Book Three

WhiteSpace

WhiteSpace Season One

WhiteSpace Season Two

WhiteSpace Season Three

Stand Alone Novels

Burnout

The Island

Crash

Emily's List

Pattern Black

Devil May Care

The Secret Within

Also By David W. Wright

Cold Justice

Cold Justice

Cold Reckoning

Hidden Justice

Hidden Justice

Hidden Honor

Hidden Shame

Hidden Virtue

No Justice

No Justice

No Escape

No Hope

No Return

No Stopping

No Fear

Karma Police

Jumper

Karma Police

The Collectors

Deviant

The Fall

Homecoming

Yesterday's Gone

October's Gone

Yesterday's Gone Season One

Yesterday's Gone Season Two

Yesterday's Gone Season Three

Yesterday's Gone Season Four

Yesterday's Gone Season Five

Yesterday's Gone Season Six

Tomorrow's Gone

Tomorrow's Gone Season One

Tomorrow's Gone Season Two

Tomorrow's Gone Season Three

Available Darkness

Darkness Itself

Available Darkness Book One

Available Darkness Book Two

Available Darkness Book Three

WhiteSpace

WhiteSpace Season One

WhiteSpace Season Two

WhiteSpace Season Three

Stand Alone Novels

12

Crash

Emily's List

Threshold

The Secret Within